THE VERY
PRINCIPLED
MAGGIE MAYFIELD

ALSO BY KATHY COOPERMAN

Crimes Against a Book Club

THE VERY
PRINCIPLED
MAGGIE MAYFIELD

Kathy Cooperman

LAKE UNION
PUBLISHING

Text copyright © 2018 by Kathy Chen
All rights reserved.

No part of this book may be reproduced, or stored in a retrieval system, or transmitted in any form or by any means, electronic, mechanical, photocopying, recording, or otherwise, without express written permission of the publisher.

Published by Lake Union Publishing, Seattle

www.apub.com

Amazon, the Amazon logo, and Lake Union Publishing are trademarks of Amazon.com, Inc., or its affiliates.

ISBN-13: 9781503903357
ISBN-10: 1503903354

Cover design and illustration by Liz Casal

Interior worm illustrations by Jacob Chen

Printed in the United States of America

To my children—Jacob, Lily, Daisy, and Oliver.
I love you equally and endlessly.

A Note to the Reader—
That's You!

Please don't judge Maggie Mayfield too harshly. I'm not telling you to *never* judge people. Hell no! Judging people is big fun. Nothing livens up a wait at the supermarket like those "Worst Dressed" lists or grainy snapshots of some actress who chubbed up by eating a whole sandwich.

But I digress. I tend to do that. Maggie says I should be kind to myself about it. She says it's the ADD—that's attention deficit disorder—that makes me run off into the weeds. Maggie always tells me, "Diane, you're very insightful." Maggie throws around words like "insightful" a lot, kind words that make people sit up straighter. Maggie's a kind woman. She's smart and strong too. Just not all the time.

And her crimes—if you have to call them that—were stuff that happened when she wasn't being her usual smart self. She was trying too hard was all, trying to take care of the kids in her school. She lives for those kids. And I guess she got tempted to do something sorta shady to make sure they got what they needed.

Education costs money, dammit. Without art class, that dyslexic kid Rachel—I love that gal—would have had nowhere to shine. Without PE, hyper little Connor would have ended up on meds. And without science lab, that whiz kid Lucy Wong would have been bored out of her mind.

Maggie was looking out for those misfits and hundreds like them. So don't believe what they say about Maggie on the internet: the fraud, the secret love nest, the sex show. It's 100 percent lies—mostly.

Respectfully yours,
Diane Porter
Administrative Assistant
Carmel Knolls Elementary

1

How It Started

Sometimes, life hands you a cupcake with a rock inside it. And that's what happened to Principal Maggie Mayfield—fate sent her a curse disguised as a blessing.

Maggie and her administrative assistant, Diane Porter, were in the school's front office when they got the "good" news. It was early August, so the rest of Carmel Knolls Elementary was empty—think tumbleweeds. Diane was fiddling with the school's website while Maggie tried to make headway on her paperwork. But it was hopeless. Maggie was a wreck—bags under her eyes, her desktop littered with Hershey's Kisses wrappers.

The silence grew oppressive, so Diane goosed the elephant in the room with characteristic tact. "Well, Fearless Leader, have you decided whose life you're gonna ruin?"

Maggie gave Diane one of her trademark behave-yourself glares. That look could drop a misbehaving child at fifty yards, but—after a decade working together—Diane had built up an immunity. Maggie said pointedly, "I don't want to *ruin* anyone's life, Diane."

Diane persisted, "Arlene hasn't called yet, has she?" Arlene was Maggie's boss, the district superintendent. For days, Arlene had been in secret talks with Silicon Valley bigwigs, wizards who could solve the district's problems with a wave of their financial wands.

Maggie groused, "No, dammit. No word yet."

"Don't worry, she'll get the funding," said Diane.

Maggie eyed her. "You don't really believe that."

Diane threw up her hands. "Well, no. But I always think the world's going in the shitter. Earthquakes, A-bombs, zombies. Civilization could go down any second."

Maggie frowned. "You sound like the world's most depressing greeting card."

"Thank you." Diane batted her eyelashes as if Maggie had just complimented her cotillion gown. Then she serioused up. "My point is, I always think the world's gonna end. But up to now, I've been wrong. So maybe I'll be wrong again. Maybe Arlene will come through, and you won't have to fire anybody."

Maggie forced a smile. She knew Diane was doing her pathetic best.

Diane prodded, "If Arlene doesn't come through, who do you want to cut?"

"I don't *want* to cut anybody," said Maggie.

"I don't see much choice if Arlene fails. We only got money for two STEAM teachers, not five. Way I see it, either you're firing somebody or we'll just have to throw the teachers in a pit and have them duke it out *Hunger Games*–style."

Maggie blew her bangs out of her eyes. "I don't know who to cut. I can't get rid of Mr. Baran. The kids would mutiny."

Diane nodded. Carmel Knolls students *loved* Mr. Baran. He oozed third-world dictator levels of charisma, but he used his powers for good as a humble PE teacher. Without PE, it'd be impossible to teach Maggie's antsier kids. They'd be as unfocused as tabloid photos of UFOs.

Maggie went on, "And Mr. Carlsen's off the table. So's Ms. Seborne." Mr. Carlsen was the school's science guy. Ms. Seborne taught tech.

Diane pointed out the obvious. "Art's got to go." Maggie put her face in her hands and groaned. Diane told her, "Now, don't you go beating up on yourself. You were straight with Miss Pearl from the get-go." Sadie Pearl was the school's new art teacher. Diane added, "You warned her she was a provisional hire. If there's layoffs, it'll be last in, first out."

Maggie cringed. "Don't play bureaucratic tough guy. I know you feel bad for her too."

"I *do* feel bad for her," admitted Diane. "But she's not my jurisdiction. You are. I don't want you to torture yourself over her."

Maggie answered, "I'm not torturing myself over her. It's not about just her."

Diane cocked her head in puzzlement. Then comprehension dawned. She asked, "It's the mansion, isn't it?" Maggie nodded. Like a kid asking for a much-loved bedtime story, Diane said, "Tell me about the mansion, Maggie."

Maggie leaned back in her chair and gazed at the corkboard ceiling. She spoke softly. "A child's mind is like a mansion with dozens of rooms: one room for art, one for math, one for literature, and so on. The child can make each room as elaborate as she wants it to be—but only if she spends time there. To do that, she needs someone—a teacher—to unlock the room for her, to show her how to move around in it, to show her what's possible. The younger you are, the easier it is to enter a new room, to explore. So not letting a child explore, that's worse than a sin. It's like a little death.

"If Arlene can't cut this deal with the Silicon Valley people, we'll have to chop art and music. Then next year, it'll be tech. And after that, science and probably PE will go. Our kids' minds will become narrower each year till they're down to just math and English."

Diane nodded. Both women knew the California legislature wouldn't cut funding for math and English because those subjects were the guts of the state's standardized tests. California loved to brag about its test results. Being ignorant was fine, but looking ignorant was a big no-no.

Maggie went on, "Some kids can make do. Their parents are smart or rich enough to supplement with lessons and tutors. But a lot of kids can't. With no PE, the restless ones won't get their wiggles out. No art or music means the artsy kids will have nowhere to shine. And no science means budding nerds won't have anyone to show them what's out there, what to dream about. Intellectually, the kids'll be squatting in two rooms, while their mansions sit vacant, rotting away like . . ."

"Like a kiddie Detroit," said Diane.

And then it happened—a miracle. The phone rang. Arlene Horvath called to report that she'd made a deal. Silicon Valley's hottest for-profit education company—Edutek—had come to the rescue. They'd give the district just enough cash to pay for one year of science, tech, PE, art, maybe even music. And all the district had to do in exchange was let Edutek beta test some dopey tech program at one of its schools. What a deal!

Maggie thanked Arlene profusely, then asked, "But what about next year? I thought Edutek was planning on a five-year STEAM grant?" STEAM was the clumsy acronym the district used for subjects the state didn't fund: science, technology, engineering, arts, and mathematics— no mention of gym, and math was actually already funded, but still, an imprecise moniker was better than having to itemize everything on the district's wish list.

Arlene said, "No, we get only enough cash to pay for *this* year."

Maggie winced. She had hoped Edutek's money would free her from tedious, nerve-racking fund-raising forever, or at least for the next five years—the timeline Edutek had bandied about. But Edutek was only offering a short reprieve, not a full pardon.

Arlene crowed, "For the other four years, we get something else, something *better*."

"What's better than cash?" asked Maggie. She feared Arlene would start babbling about magic beans.

But instead, Arlene said, "Stock. Edutek stock. Just imagine it. If Edutek's software is a hit, their stock will go through the roof. We'll have enough cash to fund STEAM programs for the next ten, maybe twenty, years. It'll be like having an endowment." Arlene savored the word "endowment," giving it an almost erotic charge.

Maggie frowned. She didn't share Arlene's faith in Edutek's bright, shiny destiny, but there was nothing to be gained in harshing Arlene's buzz at this point. So Maggie gushed, "Wow, I guess it doesn't get any better than that."

"No, Maggie dear, it doesn't."

Maggie thanked Arlene some more until the great bureaucrat was sated. Then Maggie got off the phone and high-fived Diane until both women's palms hurt. And just like that, Maggie set out on a course that would screw up her life forever.

2

The First Day of School

The four children stood like tiny mourners at a pet-hamster funeral, their heads bent as they stared silently at something on the ground. Maggie couldn't see what that something was, but her school-principal senses were tingling. Not wanting to sneak up on them, she put two fingers in her mouth and wolf-whistled like a lusty construction worker.

The children knew that sound. Only one person in their world whistled like that: the *principal*. They whipped around, watching Maggie as she made her way toward them. She was not a physically intimidating figure. Just five feet tall, she had to crane her neck when meeting most parents. And even though she was in her late thirties, her face remained stubbornly girlish: pert nose and Cupid's-bow lips set in a heart-shaped pale face. In a bid for urbanity, Maggie wore her thick dark-brown hair in a bob with a shock of bangs that ended just above her lively green eyes.

And for the first day of school only, she sported high heels. Maggie's height worked fine for her with the kids, but the parents were another story. If she didn't wear heels, other adults towered over her. It was hard for her to feel authoritative when talking to a couple who could easily take her by the hands and swing-walk her down the street. So the heels. As she drew closer, Maggie said, "Hey, kids. Whatcha got there?"

Third grader Lucy Wong announced: "A rattlesnake! And I saw it first!" Lucy held her pigtailed head high, her face aglow with self-importance. She pointed at her discovery.

Maggie's eyes widened. But she forced a smile as she came up alongside the children. She saw that, yes sirree, it was indeed a rattler: a three-foot-long diamondback. Very poisonous. Maggie, a New Englander born and bred, would never get used to rattlers. Even after fifteen years in San Diego, coming across a rattler on the playground felt surreal to her, like running into a lion at the bank. But Maggie was grateful the snake had shown up so early. With thirty minutes to go before the first bell, only a handful of kids were on the playground. Still, there were enough of them, enough to delude themselves into feeling safe so they'd do something cataclysmically stupid.

Maggie needed to get them out of there, but she'd have to do it slowly. Rattlers tend to get bitey in a stampede. A few yards from the children, the rattler coiled itself and turned to look at them. A boy with a surfer's shag haircut said, "Dude, it's huge." He pronounced "dude" with its California-mandated five beats ("duuuuuuuuude").

The snake punctuated dude-man's point by rattling its tail, and the kids stepped back—all but a freckly, brown-haired first grader named Connor. He crouched down, murmuring, "It's legendary." Connor's word choice confirmed he'd spent half his summer playing *Pokémon Go*.

Rachel, a chubby, tall girl who towered over the other children like an awkward skyscraper, warned, "It's poisonous. See those brown patches? That's a Southern Pacific rattler." Like most San Diego kids, Rachel had done her time at the city's famous zoo. She was ready to host her own show on Animal Planet.

But Connor wasn't listening. His blue eyes took on a dreamy cast. Maggie had seen that look before. Connor was zoning. In his mind, he wasn't even on the playground anymore. He probably thought he was in a *Ninjago* episode, facing off against the Great Devourer, a gigantic serpent who wanted to take over the world. Maggie was careful to stay current on her students' interests, so she'd force-fed herself a few hours of Lego's *Ninjago* cartoons. It was about as much fun as force-feeding herself actual Legos.

Maggie decided to tug Connor's mental leash. As loudly as she dared, she commanded: "One, two, three. Eyes on me." The kids' programming, long dormant for the summer months, suddenly kicked in. All eyes, Connor's too, snapped to Maggie's. In her best this-is-your-mission-should-you-choose-to-accept-it voice, Maggie said, "I've got a job for all of you. You've seen a guy walk across a tightrope, right?"

The children nodded yes. Maggie continued, "Good. Now tell me, how fast does a tightrope walker move?"

"Not fast at all," said Lucy.

Maggie nodded. "That's right." Lucy puffed out her tiny chest. "And that's what we're going to do. We're going to tightrope-walk backwards together. And we'll do it on the count of three, slow and quiet. Okay?"

The children nodded, their faces earnest with a sense of mission. Maggie said, "Okay. One, two, three." Maggie took one slow, giant step back, and the children copied her. Then another and another. As the children moved across the playground, Maggie murmured encouragement: "Nice and slow . . . that's it."

When the kids were at a safe distance, she said, "Okay, now stop." The children froze. Maggie beamed at them. "You guys did great. Best tightrope walkers I've ever seen."

She leaned down toward them. "Now, I've got another big job for you. The other students are going to arrive soon, and we need to keep them off this playground. We don't want any of them running into that rattler, do we?" The kids shook their heads, proud to be consulted on a matter of such importance. "So, I need you guys to run over to the office and tell Mrs. Porter there's a snake on the playground. Can you do that?"

The children nodded again, pleased that their role in the Great Snake Drama had not yet come to an end—and also pleased that their next job was to *tell* people. Telling had become an urgent, almost physical need. Maggie squinted at them, pretending to size them up. "Good. Now go tell Mrs. Porter about the snake while I shut the gate."

The children turned and ran for the office, big kids in front and little Connor behind, struggling under the weight of his ridiculously oversize backpack. Once they were out of earshot, Maggie removed her walkie-talkie from her side pocket and clicked through to Diane. "Diane, you there?"

Diane answered, "Yes, Fearless Leader, I'm here."

"Tell the teachers up front to send kids straight to class, no playground. There's a rattler out here. And call Animal Control." As she spoke, Maggie closed the playground's chain-link gate.

Diane sighed. "A rattler on the first day of school. That's like starting a pool party with somebody taking a dump in the deep end."

"I sent the kids who found it over to you to break the news. So act surprised when they tell you."

Diane said tartly, "I'm never surprised by bad news." This was true. Diane lived on a diet of disaster movies, apocalyptic zombie novels, and cable news.

"Do me a favor and fake it, Diane. And keep those kids with you as long as you can so they don't go off and scare the others. I want to break the news about the snake to the rest of the school in my own calm, boring way."

"Time for Monotone Maggie." Diane imitated the "mwah-mwah-mwah" trombone patter adults used in the old *Charlie Brown* TV specials.

Maggie smiled and clicked off her walkie-talkie. Just then, a prop plane flew noisily overhead, sending the snake slithering off the sun-baked dirt onto a patch of grass. Maggie glared up at the plane. It flew low, trailing out an ad banner behind it. The banner read: "BIRACHI'S

TOYS—EVERY KID NEEDS ONE!" Maggie hated those ad planes. The kids always read them and then begged their parents accordingly. Parents then whined to Maggie about it, as if she were an air traffic controller.

Careful not to lose sight of the snake, Maggie checked where it was and then walked along the playground's perimeter fence till she found what she was looking for—the holes. Back when the school district had been flush with cash, it had installed low, wire-mesh fencing to keep out the rattlers. That had been eons ago, when the district could afford luxuries like infrastructure upgrades, teacher aides, and Spanish classes. Now, after years of neglect, the wire mesh had sprouted more holes than a doily. And like a doily, it served no real purpose, just decoration.

Maggie had complained about the fencing to Arlene, but Arlene had ignored her. Maggie'd have to drag the parents in on this one. Sighing, she removed a chocolate Hershey's Kiss from her skirt pocket, unwrapped it, and popped it into her mouth. Not even 8:00 a.m., and she had already cheated on her diet. Oh well, she would be perfect tomorrow. She would commit herself to Paleo or Atkins or some other grim slog, and this time, she'd stick to it. Through sheer force of will, she would transform herself into a thin, buff, proudly sexual woman—the sort of creature who could dance seductively in a nightclub or saunter down the beach in a bikini, a woman who would not experience Nike's "Just Do It" slogan as a personal rebuke. As Maggie envisioned her future, perfect self, pride swelled within her, so she celebrated with another chocolate.

The chocolates quickly worked their magic, and a tiny surge of well-being suffused her. Then Maggie looked back down at the dilapidated snake fence and braced herself for another battle.

3

THE PEOPLE IN YOUR NEIGHBORHOOD

After checking the snake fence, Maggie raced over to the front office. Sure enough, the kids from the playground were telling Diane about the rattler. As always, Diane was a gratifying audience. She nodded eagerly at this, widened her gray eyes at that. Diane had earned her status as a favorite with the students. A tall, slightly weathered thirty-seven-year-old with a stringy figure, Diane kept her desk stuffed with snacks she shared freely with all comers. She laughed loudly and often at the kids' jokes. And though she always wore her light-blond hair in a long braid down her back, its color changed more often than a mood ring. This week, it was dyed a vibrant Smurf blue.

Keeping her gaze on the kids, Diane pulled a traffic vest from its hook on the wall and handed it off to Maggie—a smooth baton pass in the morning relay race. Maggie murmured her thanks and pivoted back toward the door, hearing Diane say squeamishly, "Ewwww. Did it really hiss at you?" This from a woman who feeds live mice to her five-foot-long Burmese python, Snookums.

Maggie pulled on the battered fluorescent yellow vest as she rushed over to the school parking lot. Wearing the vest made her feel like a Walmart greeter, but the sight of it slowed down the parents. And that was a minor miracle. Maggie would never understand why, but Californians' "hey dude" mellowness dissolved as soon as they got behind the wheel.

Most of the students' families lived within a two-mile radius of the school, but just a few dozen moms bothered to make the morning trek on foot. This merry band included alpha, fortysomething moms sporting skintight lululemon yoga pants, sculpted upper arms, and sanctimonious "I'm saving the planet *and* getting in shape!" smirks. Then came the slightly younger, slovenly moms pushing strollers. The stroller moms were invariably slowed down by exhaustion and dawdling kindergartners who stopped to fuss over every dandelion "wish" spared by the neighborhood's gardening crews. At the end of the procession came the caramel-colored Chicana nannies holding hands with their lily-white charges.

The rest of the parents, the majority, drove their kids up alongside the school's front gate. These car parents formed a half-mile-long, colorfully mismatched motorcade. There were the usual suspects you'd find in any American suburb: the harried soccer moms, the power-suited working moms, and the rare dad auditioning for sainthood by actually taking his kids to school himself.

But affluent, suburban Carmel Valley had a few added touches of its own. Firstly, all the cars were immaculate—from the outside at least, and in California, the outside was what mattered most. The dent-free, newly washed cars glittered in the morning sunlight. In Carmel Valley, the slightest film of dust would invite teenagers to scrawl "WASH ME" across the rear windshield, a badge of shame. The cars were also dizzyingly expensive: Mercedes GLSs, Lexus SUVs, Cadillac Escalades, BMWs, Porsches, Teslas, and so on. The occasional Toyota Camry stuck out like Bernie Sanders in a *Vanity Fair* spread.

People from Carmel Valley describe themselves as middle class. They are, in fact, comfortably *upper* middle class. But who's counting? The place is packed with earnest, hardworking professionals, recently arrived Asian engineers, and other strivers. The fathers drive on the expressway to middle-management jobs and check their iPhones constantly. The mothers either work in offices or stay home, depending on their inclinations and finances. And the kids attend public school and spend their afternoons darting between soccer, piano, ballet, and other ambitious activities. Carmel Valley people live in row upon row of cookie-cutter, stucco houses. Each house comes with a small rectangle of carefully tended lawn and a million-dollar mortgage. That million-dollar debt does not get you an ocean view. Carmel Valley is too far inland for that, but people flock here because it offers big, new houses, a quick commute to downtown San Diego, and—for the time being—decent schools. Everything the rich in utero need to keep "movin' on up," *Jeffersons'* style.

With so much wealth on display, finding signs of money trouble required a practiced eye. And—after more than a decade in Carmel Valley—Maggie was a reluctant maestro at the *Where's Waldo?* of financial misery. Over the summer, San Diego's biggest employer, tech behemoth Gallcomm, had laid off nine thousand people: engineers, researchers, project managers on down. Some of the fallen rebounded quickly, picking up new jobs with the grace of a figure skater retrieving fans' flowers from the ice. Others faltered. They kept up appearances as long as possible. They fired the maid, not the gardeners. Little Isabelle quit piano lessons. Young Bryce dropped tennis. The country club membership was used to the hilt until it suddenly lapsed. Mom gave up her pricey Brazilian blowout and started hiding her now-frizzy hair under a cap. Dad sported a bandage on his right hand, a souvenir from botched home repairs that had looked deceptively easy on YouTube. Slowly but relentlessly, the thin topsoil of gentility eroded.

Standing before the school's front gate, Maggie greeted the returning students and their parents by name. She had studied the names over the summer from a yearbook on her nightstand. Knowing the kids' names helped build trust. It's hard for a weepy, bruised kid to ID his bully if the principal starts the conversation asking, "And your name is?" Knowing the kids' names made them feel seen and valued. And Maggie did value the kids, *her* kids. She wanted things for them—more than she could ever actually deliver.

This morning, though, she'd settle for a snake-proof fence, so she put on a big smile and headed over to greet the school's unofficial minister of disaster and finance: PTA president Felicia Manis. A former model turned part-time Pilates instructor, Felicia was a tall, lithe blonde with a breathy voice. She was also the lucky owner of softball-size, fake boobs that had been installed and periodically upgraded—like an iPhone—by her plastic surgeon husband. A full-on MILF-asaurus, Felicia guest starred in the masturbatory fantasies of every teenage boy in her zip code. Maggie—a vertically challenged (sounds kinder than "stunted"), zaftig brunette trapped in an endless battle with her bathroom scale—should have disliked Felicia, but she couldn't. No one could. Felicia was unrelentingly friendly and anxious, a golden retriever in need of Xanax.

Felicia had spearheaded the informal, but effective, whispering campaigns that had produced the school's wrought-iron fence (to keep out gun-wielding maniacs!), freestanding Purell dispensers on the playground (germs were everywhere!), and a total ban on peanuts (allergies!). A yelly lunatic on a street corner would never have been able to push such an agenda through, but Felicia's breathy voice and chummy manner made her exclamation-point fearfulness credible, even fun. Plus, she had an uncanny knack for fund-raising.

As Maggie approached, Felicia beamed down at her. "So, how's my favorite principal?"

Maggie grumbled, "I'm your *only* principal."

"Love the one you're with. That's what the song says, right?"

Maggie said ominously, "Not if the one you're with is a snake."

Felicia frowned. "Ohmigod, are you talking about Russell? Did you hear something? What have you heard?" Russell was Felicia's husband. His tomcatting was yet another source of worry to her.

Maggie shook her head. "No, not Russell. I was talking about the snake we found on the playground this morning."

Relief flickered across Felicia's face only to be shoved aside by fresh worry. "A snake? Was it poisonous?"

Maggie nodded. "Yep. A rattler. A third grader found it."

"A third grader? We're lucky no one got killed!" Felicia put her hand on Maggie's arm and leaned in, her breathy voice even breathier than usual with alarm. "Rattlers kill at least one child a week in Southern California. I saw something about it on the news." Felicia firmly believed in statistics, especially the ones she made up.

"That sounds a little high to me," said Maggie.

"Maybe, but even one child's death is too much." Felicia held Maggie's gaze, as if waiting for Maggie to argue the point.

Maggie pursed her lips, as if Felicia had said something profound. "You're *so* right."

Felicia nodded. "So what do we do? Is the snake still out there? Is that why the kids had to go straight to class?"

"Yes, but I think we'll be okay on this one. Animal Control is on the way. They'll bag the snake and take it off somewhere. But . . ." Maggie trailed off.

Like a Baryshnikov of Panic, Felicia made the next leap on cue. "But what about the *next* snake? Where there's one, there's got to be dozens. Maybe hundreds." One snake and, to Felicia, the playground was now the tomb from *Raiders of the Lost Ark*.

Maggie sighed. "Well, it'd be great if we could fix up the snake fence. That's the low wire mesh along the school's perimeter. It's sprouted a few holes. I put in a work order, but the district's been dragging its feet." Maggie shrugged. "Ah well, there's nothing we can do." Maggie's resignation was false, the administrative equivalent of a damsel in distress batting her eyes at Superman, asking, "But who can save us now?"

Felicia jutted out her pretty chin. "Hmm, we'll just see about that."

Maggie grinned up at her. "You look fierce."

This seemed to please Felicia. "I *am* fierce."

"Good, but save most of that ferocity for fund-raising. We're going to need it."

Felicia wrinkled her nose in distaste. "I can't believe it. After all Edutek's big talk about five-year plans, they're only funding STEAM for a year. It's like someone gives you a kidney and then tells you it's just a loaner."

Maggie said nothing. She would have loved to vent about Edutek's stingy generosity, but she had to stay positive. As principal, she had to play cheerleader while staff and parents engaged in yet another year of Sisyphean fund-raising. Feigning optimism, Maggie said, "But, hey, I'm excited. I have some great ideas up my sleeve for this year."

"Like what?" asked Felicia.

Maggie flailed her arms. "Oh, lots of ideas, really terrific stuff. I'll need to hone them, check out some of the logistics. But you're gonna love them." Maggie winced at her own vagueness. She sounded like a forgetful boyfriend promising big things to come on Valentine's Day.

"I can't wait," said Felicia. There was no sarcasm in her tone. Felicia—like most of the parents at Carmel Knolls Elementary—*believed* in Maggie. Maggie would set everything right. That was her job, after all.

4

The Spider and the Fly

After the third bell, the kids were all snug in their classrooms, and Maggie made the morning announcements over the school's antiquated PA system. She warmed up with the Pledge and then moved on to the snake incident, downplaying it as best she could. Yes, Animal Control had taken the snake away. But don't worry: they won't kill it. They'll set it free in some faraway canyon where it can play with its snake brothers. Probably bullshit, but that was Maggie's story, and she was sticking to it.

Then Maggie moved on to more serious business. "I want you to take a good look at the kids sitting in your classroom. Go ahead, give each other the once-over." All over the school, children eyed each other, giggling shyly.

"Some of you are tall. Some are short. Some spent the summer at camp. Some stayed here. But you all have one thing in common: you're nervous. You're nervous about whether you'll get to keep your old friends or have to make new ones. You're nervous about whether your teacher will turn out to be a sweetheart or a dragon lady." This prompted many children to eye their teachers speculatively.

Maggie went on, "Some of you are nervous about schoolwork. Others are nervous about what the hot lunch will be and how it'll smell. I can't make your nervousness go away. But I can give you some advice to make it easier on everyone. Be kind. If you see a kid eating by himself, invite him to sit with you. If you see someone wandering alone at recess, ask her to play ball. And if someone asks a dumb question during class, don't laugh or roll your eyes. People have to ask a lot of dumb questions on the way to getting smart. Just let your teacher do her job, and you do yours. Let's start this year off right. Principal out."

Maggie switched off the PA and leaned back in her desk chair. She enjoyed a millisecond of self-satisfaction and then lurched toward self-doubt. She probably shouldn't have said that stuff about dumb questions. "Dumb" was a loaded word, a verbal stink bomb. "Dumb" implied the existence of dummies. A big no-no. Maggie pulled a Hershey's Kiss from the top drawer of her desk, unwrapped it, and popped it in her mouth. As the chocolate coated her tongue, she grinned—the dopey, relieved grin of a gal whose pee has just hit the water. The grin fell away when Maggie looked up to see her boss standing in the doorway of her office. Maggie blushed furiously, as if she'd been caught playing with herself.

She stammered, "Arlene. Uh, hello."

Superintendent Arlene Horvath simpered, "I hope I didn't startle you." This was a lie. Arlene loved to sneak up on people. Maggie wished she could hang a bell around the woman's neck.

Maggie said, "No, of course not." Maggie could lie too. "Please have a seat." Maggie gestured to one of the two padded chairs opposite her desk.

Sitting down in one chair and resting her voluminous handbag on the other, Arlene said, "That was a lovely speech, Maggie. But I'd lay off the jokes about smelly hot lunches. The Choosy Chow people are doing the best they can." Arlene had a low, throaty voice. Diane could mimic it perfectly.

Maggie winced. "My bad." Arlene had hired Choosy Chow to prepare the district's school lunches. Ergo, their slop was above reproach.

"No matter." Arlene literally waved the remark away, causing her clunky bracelets to jangle on her wrist. Arlene Horvath, Maggie's personal overlord, was somewhere in her early fifties. She was a thickset brunette with a permanently pinched expression. The skin around her heavily lipsticked mouth puckered in, making it look like a bright-red anus. A fashion refugee from the 1980s, she used fistfuls of mousse to secure her feathered hairdo, and she sported oversize, plastic-framed purple eyeglasses. Arlene completed her look with pastel pantsuits. In one of her precalculated I'm-officially-bonding-with-you moments, she'd confided to Maggie that pastels make the wearer look more approachable. Maggie's mind had flashed to the nursery rhyme: "'Will you walk into my parlor?' said the spider to the fly."

Maggie's dislike for Arlene did not stem from any sense of sartorial superiority. Maggie hadn't bothered to revise her own "meh" fashion statement until after her painful divorce, so she could sympathize. No, Maggie clashed with Arlene on the big stuff: the *why*. One imperative drove Maggie: to provide the best education she could for her kids. She wasn't a saint. She didn't aim to educate all humanity, or even all the kids in San Diego. No, Maggie was as tribal as any Bantu. Her circle of concern encompassed only *her* kids, the kids at *her* school. Oh sure, she played nicely with other principals whenever possible, whenever there was nothing to lose. But when resources were scarce—as they almost always were these days—Maggie would ruthlessly elbow the other principals out of the way in the desperate Black Friday scramble for the district's best teachers, the top programs, and the newest equipment. The other principals in the district didn't resent this. They respected it.

What they—or at least Maggie—didn't respect was empty careerism: the me-me-me, résumé-building ethos of district administrators like Arlene. Maggie kept her focus on the students and teachers under her, the ones she was responsible to and for. But Arlene didn't look down. An ambitious creature, Arlene was always looking up, and all she saw was the rump of the person ahead of her on the ladder. That was the person to beat. To ascend quickly, competence wasn't enough. Hell, competence wasn't even necessary. The day-to-day fallout of this or that education program often did not become evident until years had passed. No, what counted—what made people rocket to the top—were flashy *new* programs.

Arlene began, "I couldn't resist a little visit with you today, Maggie." Arlene loved making surprise inspections on all the principals in the district. Arlene called them her "little visits." Like every dictator, Arlene loved her euphemisms. Rubbing her hands together, she said, "It's an exciting day. Isn't it?"

Maggie agreed, "The first day of school is always exciting. It's—"

Arlene cut her off. "Not the first day of school. We've both seen plenty of those. No, I was talking about the start of our grand, new venture with Edutek." Arlene looked expectantly at Maggie.

Maggie forced a smile, saying lamely, "Uh, yes." Then, deciding this wasn't fulsome enough, she echoed Arlene. "Very exciting."

Arlene eyed Maggie. "Now, Maggie, I told you. You've got nothing to worry about. You're not going to lose an inch of your precious curriculum."

Maggie nodded. "I know."

Arlene continued, "The MathPal is only going to take up a tiny fraction of the students' time."

Maggie kept nodding. "True." Long experience had taught Maggie that Arlene liked a responsive audience. She needed Maggie to nod and "uh-huh"—little verbal pats to ease out Arlene's oratory burps.

"Just twenty minutes a day. It's—"

Maggie interrupted, "Wait, I thought we agreed to ten minutes."

Arlene blinked, as if Maggie's disruption had thrown off her programming. "Yes, but no."

"What does that mean?"

"Yes, it's true that—in the beginning—Edutek indicated that ten minutes a day would suffice. But over the summer, I spoke with Danny a few times." Daniel Zelinsky—or Danny Z as he obnoxiously called himself—was Edutek's smooth-talking, high-profile CEO. Arlene seemed to savor the implied intimacy of using his first name. She purred, "Danny says his team went back over the numbers and realized they actually needed twenty minutes a day. I'm sure you understand."

"No, I don't understand," said Maggie. "We agreed to ten minutes. That's what I told my teachers. That's what they planned for. We can't just double that."

Arlene said placidly, "I'm sure the teachers can make a few minor snips to their lesson plans to make room for this. It's just twenty minutes a day."

Maggie shot back, "It's not *just* twenty minutes. It's more like thirty when you take into account all the time handing out those special MathPal tablets, getting all the kids started on the software, getting them *off* the software. Making a kid turn off a computer isn't easy. It's like yanking a bone away from a big dog. You have to do it gently. It's—"

Arlene cut in, "It's part of a well-rounded, modern education, Maggie. Surely, you're not against computers in the classroom."

Maggie's cheeks reddened. In education circles, being labeled "anti-tech" was career kryptonite. Maggie righteously pointed out, "We already have computers in the classroom. We had Chromebooks as soon as they came out, and our tech lab—"

Arlene nodded. "No need to tell me. I've done three webcasts about the Chromebook program. Terrific stuff, if I say so myself." Arlene ran a weekly webcast on the district website, implicitly taking credit for anything interesting that happened anywhere in Carmel Valley. She ran her videos under a multicolored (suggestive of diversity) "K-A-P-O-W!" logo. KAPOW! stood for knowledge, aptitude, persistence, opportunity—wow! It was an awkward name, but far better than Arlene's first, short-lived title: *Superintendent Horvath's Initial Take*. No one had ever designed an S-H-I-T logo.

Maggie lied, "Yes, the webcasts were wonderful. And since we already have such a strong tech program at the school, I don't see why we need more than ten minutes a day with Edutek software."

Arlene smirked, "Well, I'm afraid that's what Edutek is demanding. And even if we don't need Edutek's software—and I disagree with you on that one, Maggie dear—we *do* need their money."

"True." Maggie blew her bangs out of her eyes, literally and emotionally deflating.

Arlene chided her, "Stop looking like that. Trust me, this is a win-win. Edutek gets to work out the kinks in the MathPal, and your students get access to the most advanced educational software in the country."

"But we don't know anything about this software. They haven't even let us see it yet." Maggie's voice squeaked a bit as she said this, betraying her anxiety.

Arlene said, "No worries. Danny promised me he'd have a MathPal tablet on your desk first thing tomorrow morning."

"So I get it just one day before my students do? Doesn't that strike you as odd? I mean, why has Edutek been so cagey with us?"

Arlene leaned forward in her chair, lowering her voice to a conspiratorial whisper. "Edutek has to be careful, Maggie. They don't want their trade secrets leaking out."

"We're not going to leak anything. We signed confidentiality agreements."

"This is cutting-edge stuff, Maggie."

Maggie sighed. "I guess so."

Arlene returned to full volume. "I *know* so. And just think of it. Your students will be the very first to benefit from this technology. I've spoken with the Edutek people. And trust me, their teaching methods are revolutionary. We are talking some very out-of-the-box thinking."

Arlene loved anything outside the box. Maggie didn't understand it. Like most teachers and principals, Maggie loved it inside the box. It was warm and cozy in there. Maggie had gone into education and stayed on its front line because she loved the beauty and tradition of it: the way that hard work and solid technique produced amazing, albeit gradual, results. Most principals and teachers were secretly traditional, borderline Amish about shaking up their curriculum and methods. They'd seen too many new programs go bust: the educational equivalent of those as-seen-on-TV inventions that ended up on the back shelves at CVS, except way more expensive. Maggie knew better than to voice any of this, so instead she nodded, murmuring, "Sounds wonderful."

"It *is* wonderful, Maggie. And even if it isn't, even if it's schlock, think of what you'll get out of it. Your precious art, music, and science programs will be fully funded for a whole year. Not to mention the children's beloved Mr. Barone."

Maggie corrected gently, "Baran."

Arlene blathered on, "Yes, the PE teacher, whatever. The children will get another year of his relays and whatnot. And all for just twenty minutes a day. I think we can spare that. Don't you?"

Eager to end the conversation, Maggie faked a smile and said her line. "Yes, Arlene. It's a win-win."

5

LUCY'S BIG PLAN

Lucy Wong held it in all morning. Every time Mrs. Canfield asked her third-grade class a question, Lucy forced herself to say nothing. Thanks to the many hours of outside academic coaching Lucy'd received, regular school held no surprises for her. It was like sitting through a poorly produced reality show contest she'd already seen. Calling out answers—showing off—was the only fun part.

Still, Lucy would have to clam up if she wanted to make any friends. She started playing the *Teen Titans Go!* theme song in her head. Everybody loved *Teen Titans Go!*, and Lucy wanted to be part of the everybody this year.

As always, she had done her homework. Over the summer, she had sat through three seasons of *Teen Titans Go!* It wasn't easy. As usual, Lucy's parents had overloaded her schedule with lessons and violin practice. Still, Lucy had made the time. She'd also filled her notebook—the one with the purple unicorns on the cover—with lists of social dos and don'ts. *Do* talk about *Teen Titans Go!* and YouTube videos. *Do not* raise your hand in class! Also, *do not* talk about anything that fascinates Chinese parents: test scores, the best colleges, who the smart kids are (act like them!), who the dumb kids are (stay away!), or live-in grandparents. White kids think it's creepy to have your grandparents living with you, unless your grandma is wacky fun like the ones in *Mulan* and *Moana*. Lucy's grandmother was not wacky fun.

Do wear T-shirts and multicolored sneakers. *Do not* wear anything that looks like it could be part of a school uniform. White people hate uniforms. They want to be unique, but in the same way. So no uniforms.

Lucy was not aiming to become popular. She knew popularity was impossible for her, like bending nails with her mind (she'd tried). No, Lucy just wanted to make friends. She was tired of reading by herself at recess or hiding out during lunchtime in the school library.

True, she had some sort-of friends already, the other kids from Chinese school. She rode with them after regular school in a white van with big golden letters on the side saying: "GOLDEN TIGERS." Golden Tigers did three hours of lessons every afternoon: Mandarin, mathematics, violin, and Ping-Pong, or sometimes kung fu.

Lucy knew what to say at Golden Tigers. It was "opposite world," so raising her hand was a good thing there. But Lucy felt lonely there too. The students at Chinese school could never fully relax around each other. They knew their parents were constantly gossiping and comparing their children's accomplishments. One child's shining moment became a whip for other parents to use on their kids, and no third grader shined as brightly as little Lucy Wong.

Lucy's mom told Lucy she was lonely now because she was the best. Mrs. Wong promised Lucy she would not be lonely forever. Someday, Lucy would make friends with other people who were the best. They could all be best together and tell the not-best people what to do. When Lucy talked about fitting in at regular school, her mom told her not to act white. Don't be a banana or a Twinkie—yellow on the outside, but white on the inside. Lucy said she didn't want to be all yellow or all white, inside or out. She wanted to be a blend. American mixed with Chinese. White mixed with yellow. Mrs. Wong countered, "That's just snow with pee in it. Nobody wants that."

27

Now, looking out over the sea of crowded lunch tables, Lucy was determined to prove her mother wrong. She would blend in; she would *make* herself fit. She noticed a few seats open next to that big, dumb girl who was repeating third grade, Rachel Klemper. No thanks on that one. Then she spotted an empty seat next to Isabelle Lowry. Isabelle was a small-boned, brown-haired girl who wore sparkly headbands. She was quiet most of the time, but Lucy liked her because she had a big, warm laugh that made her whole body shake. Isabelle sat next to another third-grade girl Lucy barely knew: Sophia something-or-other.

Lucy steeled herself and approached the girls' table with her lunch box in hand. "Hey there, Isabelle, can I sit with you guys?"

Isabelle smiled. "Sure. Suit yourself."

Lucy sat. This was good. Contact had been established. She listened for a few minutes as the girls chatted about characters from a TV show she had never seen. Lucy waited for some pause so she could jump in like in double Dutch. When the pause came, she said—a bit too loudly—"Do you guys like *Teen Titans Go!*?"

Isabelle answered, "I used to watch that show . . . back in second grade." Isabelle looked wistfully off into the distance, as if second grade—just four months ago!—existed in some nether-past of horse-drawn carriages and pocket watches.

Lucy would not be deterred. She turned to Sophia. "What about you? Do you like *Teen Titans*?"

Sophia—her mouth full of turkey sandwich—widened her eyes and pointed to her chewing mouth. When she'd swallowed, she said, "It's okay, I guess. I'm more into *The Magicians of*—"

Lucy flailed. Without *Teen Titans*, she had no idea what to talk about with these girls. Like a lawyer leading a hostile witness, she pressed Sophia. "Yes, but you have seen *Teen Titans*, haven't you?"

Sophia nodded. "Yes, but . . ."

Lucy smiled with relief. It would all be okay. "So, who's your favorite character on *Teen Titans*? Raven or Beast Boy?"

Sophia said, "I dunno. I haven't seen it in a while. Um, maybe Starfire? She's the pink one, right?"

Lucy brightened. They were finally getting somewhere. "Yes. Starfire is pink. She has cool powers, but I don't like her too much 'cause she's weak in her mind. She's always believing everything people tell her. She doesn't have her own plan. You *have* to have your own plan." Lucy looked expectantly at the other girls. They looked back at her with vacant stares, obviously not big planners. Lucy rummaged around in her brain for more words to throw at them. Something had to work. "Oooh, and Starfire doesn't wear enough clothes. Her belly is always showing."

Sophia frowned. She didn't care about *Teen Titans*, but now that she'd stated her preference for Starfire, she felt slighted by Lucy's attack on the character. "There's nothing wrong with showing your belly. I wear a bikini all summer. Lots of girls do."

Isabelle echoed, "Yeah, lots of girls do."

Lucy sensed a disturbance in the force. She tried to reingratiate herself. "That's different. That's at the beach. Bikinis make sense at the beach. I have a bikini too." This was true, although her mother would never let Lucy wear it. Mrs. Wong said too much sunshine makes people leathery, like handbags.

Sophia wasn't placated. "You can show your belly on places not the beach. It's called crop tops. Cool girls—*teenager* girls—wear them all the time. My big sister has a blue one, a purple one, a—"

Lucy cut in, "Okay, but—"

Sophia went on relentlessly—convinced that the many colors of her sister's crop top inventory constituted a coup de grâce in this tense, intellectual argument. "An orange one with spangles, a green one, and a red one with the American flag on it, for, like, America." Sophia jutted out her chin, daring Lucy to say something unpatriotic about crop tops.

Lucy countered, "Okay, but nobody wears crop tops all the time. You don't wear them to school."

Sophia countered, "Only 'cause Mrs. Mayfield won't let us. I hate the stupid dress code."

Lucy pressed, "Yes, but there's a reason why it's part of the dress code. We don't want everyone walking around with their bellies sticking out." Lucy pooched out her stomach to demonstrate.

Sophia balked. "Are you saying I'm fat?"

Isabelle told Sophia, "You are *not fat*." She placed a soothing hand on Sophia's forearm. "There is no way you could be fat. You are one of my best friends."

Lucy fumed, telling Sophia, "I didn't say you were fat. I was just saying that the school doesn't want people walking around with their bellies out all the time. It's . . . inappropriate." "Inappropriate" was the word adults used for all the rules that they could not explain. Lucy was not sure what it meant. But she respected the word's power. The other girls did too. Silence fell over the table for a moment.

Sophia rallied. "Jasmine showed her belly in *Aladdin*. And she was a big hero."

Lucy was tempted to inform Sophia that girl heroes are called "heroines." Lucy's mom always loved it when Lucy corrected someone else's grammar. Mrs. Wong would taunt the befuddled person in her thick Shanghai accent, "You're in America now. You need to speak English." But Lucy stepped on her impulse's foot. She said, "Yes. But nobody in the Middle East dresses like Jasmine anymore. They all wear black shower curtains now." Lucy didn't know the word for "burka."

Sophia countered, "You can't wear a shower curtain."

Lucy said, "It's not really a curtain, more like a big black sheet."

Isabelle stretched languidly and said—almost through a yawn—"I don't like the Middle East. My dad made me and my mom go to a wedding in Idaho, and it was so boring."

Lucy corrected her. "That's the Midwest. That's part of America. The Middle East is on the other side of the world, like Egypt and stuff."

Isabelle shot back, "Well, if it's on the other side of the world, it can't be that important."

Lucy didn't know a lot about the Middle East, but she knew adults used it as the example of everything important and depressingly complicated. She said, "It is so important. America throws all our wars there."

Isabelle frowned, irritation dawning on her face. "We don't have any wars going on."

Lucy's eyes widened. Forget *Teen Titans Go!* This girl didn't know anything. "Are you kidding? We have lots of wars."

Isabelle answered, "Nuh-uh, we don't."

Lucy's cheeks reddened. She knew these girls would not like her if she corrected them. But still, Lucy felt pulled along—caught in some emotional riptide she didn't understand—to point out the truth. In later years, she'd recognize that pulling as a sort of integrity. But for now, it was just an inconvenient urge. She said, "We have two big wars—one in Afghanistan and one in Iraq. Plus, we dropped bombs on Syria."

Isabelle blinked in confusion, as if she'd just been roused from a cozy nap. "Okay, but no big wars. Big wars are like when all the men get dressed up in uniforms and go off to France or something. I don't see anybody going to France, do you?"

Lucy retorted, "No, but these wars aren't *in* France."

Isabelle rolled her eyes, bored with Lucy's tedious details. She clearly regretted letting Lucy sit with her.

From then on, she and Sophia excluded Lucy from their conversation. And when the bell rang, they ran ahead together to their classroom while Lucy trudged behind.

That afternoon, Lucy raised her hand seven times, easily fielding the teacher's questions. Flipping the old aphorism on its head, she thought bitterly, *If you can't join them, beat them.*

6

RAGING RACHEL

Halfway through recess, the school hit a milestone: the first fight of the year. Rachel Klemper had charged like a bull at her twin brother, Alec. Alec—a tall, fair-haired soccer prodigy—had suffered a bruise and a few scratches, but was otherwise unharmed. Still, like most playground victims, he wanted his attacker prosecuted to the full extent of the law—sister or not.

By the time Maggie got back to the front office, the perp—Rachel— was planted in a seat across from Diane's desk. Maggie's heart sank when she saw the girl. As a principal, Maggie wasn't supposed to pick favorites, but as a human being, she had no choice. And Rachel was one of her secret favorites. Rachel was tall like her brother, but she looked like she came from a different wolf pack. Dark-haired and chubby, she wore her long, bushy hair in a low ponytail. She kept her arms crossed defensively against her chest most of the time, like a live-action poster for low self-esteem.

Up until a year ago, it had looked like Rachel had come up snake eyes at the genetic craps table: her brilliant lawyer father's bad looks, and her gorgeous blond mother's (lack of) brains. Rachel had been a triple threat: lousy at math, reading, and writing. Her teacher had sensed something amiss, so Maggie had the girl tested. The child's intellectual colonoscopy uncovered big news. Rachel was dyslexic, but her IQ was sky-high. Maggie set her up with a special reading tutor to get her up to speed over the summer. Rachel worked hard and made up lost ground quickly. But she still had to repeat third grade.

Now Maggie led Rachel into her private office. She started off stern. Maggie had to do that whenever things got violent. Warnings had to be given. Parents had to be called, due process and all that. But she cut short her usual "no hitting" spiel when Rachel started crying. Rachel began with a whimper and then moved into full-on sobbing territory. Maggie got up from her chair and came round her desk to comfort the child. Elementary school principals do a lot of comforting. Funeral director amounts.

When Rachel got her breathing under control, Maggie asked what had happened. Sniffling, Rachel answered, "Alec called me a name."

"What name, sweetheart?"

"Pickles."

It took a long time—and more than a few Kleenex—but Maggie managed to coax out the pickles story. Evidently, Rachel's mother, Andrea Klemper, had arranged for the family's bathrooms to be renovated over the summer. The Klempers lived in a posh McMansion, and Andrea got it in her head that each of her bathrooms needed a bidet. Rachel explained, "A bidet's a fancy fountain that shoots water up your butt."

Maggie nodded. She knew what a bidet was, and more importantly, she knew what Andrea Klemper was. Andrea was one of the school's alpha moms. An attractive blonde with a slightly upturned nose, Andrea pranced her tight, overaerobicized tush all over the place, showily volunteering for everything.

While the bidets were being installed, all but one of the house's bathrooms were off-limits, and toilet access became a problem. Alec took to secretly peeing on a houseplant near the grand piano. Rachel explained, "So, one day, Mom was off cheering Alec at some soccer game, and I'm home with Gramma. And I had to go. So I ran for the bathroom, but Gramma was in there. And Gramma likes to, um, take her time. So I didn't know what to do."

Maggie nodded. "It's a tough call."

"So I ran back to the kitchen, and I grabbed this pickle jar from the recycling bin, and I . . ." Rachel faltered, her cheeks reddening.

Maggie prodded, "You used it?"

Rachel blushed furiously. "It was number two."

Maggie repressed her impulse to say "yick." Instead, she patted Rachel's arm. "I think you were very resourceful."

Rachel looked up in surprise at Maggie. The girl had obviously never thought of herself as resourceful. "I didn't want to stink up the house. So I put the lid back on the jar and closed it real tight. But then, I couldn't just stick the jar back in the recycling bin. Someone would see it. You know?"

Maggie nodded.

Rachel went on, "So I started getting all nervous and stupid." She pantomimed panic for Maggie: waving her hands, widening her eyes, and saying, "Ohmigod. Ohmigod." Maggie struggled not to smile. "So I hid the jar in the garage behind some of Alec's soccer stuff. I figured I'd take it out later on—when Gramma got out of the bathroom—and, uh, get rid of it."

"Ohhhkay. So then?"

"But then, I forgot." Rachel hastened to add, "I know it's weird I forgot, but I did. Honest."

Maggie believed her. It was classic kid: out of sight, out of mind. Kids' distractibility made them lousy criminals. Maggie prodded her again. "Then what?"

"So, a week ago, my mom had people over for dinner. My mom is going on and on about how great Alec is, how he won all his soccer games. Whatever. And it got me mad. So I said he's not perfect. And Alec says, 'Better than you, twerp.' And I say, 'Oh yeah?' And he's like, 'Yeah.' And then, I just lose it, and I go, 'At least I don't pee on Mom's plant!'"

Maggie winced. "How'd that go over?"

Rachel bit down on her lower lip. "Bad. My mom got real angry. She's like, 'Alexander'—my mom calls him that when she's mad—'I can't believe you peed on my plant.'

"So then, he runs out of the room. My mom says something about how Alec needs to cool off. She and the guests start talking about boring adult stuff: calories and real estate. And I'm sitting there, feeling guilty but sorta happy, 'cause Alec can be such a . . ." Rachel stopped herself.

"So, after a while, Alec comes back in. He has this serious look on his face, like a superhero about to make a big move. And everybody's looking at him, and he says—real loud—'Hey, Mom, *look what your daughter did!*' And he pulls out the pickle jar and holds it up so everybody can see. Only it didn't look like poop anymore. It'd been in the garage for weeks, so it just looked like nasty soup. But then Alec opened the jar, and everybody knew what it was 'cause the smell was . . ." Rachel stuck out her tongue and gagged. "The guests ran out of the house. And my mom ran after them, yelling, 'Sorry! Alec didn't mean it. He's lactose intolerant' or something."

The aftershocks of the poop incident were still rocking Rachel's home life. Rachel overheard her mom telling her dad Rachel "wasn't normal." She took Rachel to a shrink named Miss Madeline, and Rachel had to sit through fifty minutes of prodding: Why did Rachel poop in the jar? How did it *feel* to poop in the jar? Did she get pleasure out of pooping in jars? Because if so, there's nothing wrong with that. That's something Rachel could "explore" when she got older. But for now, pooping in the toilet would be best.

Rachel went on, "It wasn't fair. Alec didn't have to talk to a shrink about peeing on Mom's plant. Mom just made the plant disappear. She kept right on taking him to soccer games. Every time he scores, my mom jumps up and yells, 'Bull's-eye!'"

The envy and longing in Rachel's face as she said this was unmistakable. And Maggie felt a surge of rage at Andrea Klemper. Maggie hated it when parents were stingy with their love. "So that's where Pickles comes from?"

Rachel nodded. "Alec calls me that when our parents aren't around. Only, I didn't think he'd say it at school. I . . ." Her chin trembled with the threat of tears again. "I hate coming back to school. I suck at everything here."

Maggie countered, "You *don't* suck. Your tutor says she's never seen anyone work as hard as you did over the summer. You'll be caught up in no time."

"Okay, I don't suck. But I'm not *good* at anything. Not like Alec. He's got soccer and all those friends. And I've got . . ." She trailed off to nothing.

Maggie said, "That's not how I see it. You've got a spark. It's like there's this energy coming off you, this raw potential."

"Potential?" Rachel raised an eyebrow.

"Yes. It's like with dragons." Maggie had been binge-watching *Game of Thrones*, hardly a model for sibling harmony. She continued, "There's this story where a princess has nothing. No castle, no family, no money. But then she finds some baby dragons. Other people avoid the dragons, but not the princess. She loves them. She sees what they can become, how strong and beautiful they can be. So she feeds them and protects them until they get to be big and strong. And then . . ."

"They smite her enemies?" Rachel brightened.

"Uh, well, yes. That, but other things too. They carry packages through the air. They give people rides in the clouds." By now, Maggie had totally Disneyfied the khaleesi's dragons.

"The point is, your potential is huge," Maggie said. "And a lot of people can't see that yet. They don't know what you'll be able to do when you grow up, and you don't either. So for now, your job is to be like that princess. Hope for the best, and care for your talents. Make them grow. And one day, you and your talents will soar."

Rachel said happily, "And I'll smite my enemies?"

"Hopefully, there won't be much need for smiting."

7

MAGGIE'S WORSE HALF

By four o'clock, Maggie was exhausted. Her facial muscles were sore from smiling so much, and her feet ached from her high heels.

And the day wasn't done yet. She'd have to sit through Edutek's "Community Listening Session" later that night. For now, all she wanted to do was sink into a bath, like the star of her own private Calgon commercial. But her bubble burst as soon as she rounded the street corner near her house. There, on her front porch, stood her ex-husband, Richard.

Though their marriage had ended two years ago, Richard still occupied prime real estate in Maggie's psyche. He had not just broken her heart. He had diced and pureed it. She had fallen hard for him. He had been an everything-she-wanted buffet: a sweet-natured midwestern boy with brains, a wry sense of humor, a solid job as a software engineer, and a dazzling, aw-shucks-ma'am smile. His face was almost too pretty: blond hair, high cheekbones, strong jaw, and blue eyes framed by long lashes. What saved him from girlishness was his physique. A triathlete in his spare time, Richard was just six inches taller than Maggie, but every inch of his body was as firm as whipcord. He was, to be blunt, sexy as hell. Just the sight of his well-muscled calf could cause a stir in Maggie's groin.

Early on in their courtship, Maggie had worried that some woman would steal him away. But Richard's over-the-top, borderline compulsive honesty made her relax her guard. He was so unrelentingly decent that any suspicion of him seemed not just stupid, but pathological—like Gollum clutching at "the precious" as a Boy Scout walks past.

And Maggie had been right. There wasn't a single woman alive who could have lured Richard away. No, it took legions of women to do that, legions of pixelated porn stars to be more exact.

The trouble began three years into the marriage when hyperathletic Richard got benched by a biking accident. The doctor ordered him off his bike for six months, and Maggie foolishly hoped he'd lavish his newfound free time on her. Instead, he began pouring all his time into his "work." He still tromped through the front door every night by six—he had a hitherto almost sleepy job in corporate compliance at a big company. But now, he always headed straight for his study, mumbling about projects and deadlines. When Maggie pressed him for details, he'd turn a fire hose of mind-numbingly dull financial information on her, boring her inquisitiveness away. When his six-month recovery milestone came, Richard did not even try to return to his bike.

Blissfully ignorant of her hard—but not hardworking—husband's new secret life as a porn addict, Maggie tried to be supportive. When Richard started having trouble performing in the bedroom, he blamed stress, and Maggie nodded in sympathy. Later, much later, she'd learn all about porn-induced erectile dysfunction (PIED). Whacking off for hours a day to an online harem made it impossible for heavy porn users to be aroused by an actual flesh-and-blood woman.

On the increasingly rare occasions when they did have sex, Maggie made heroic efforts to seem turned on by her husband's growingly elaborate stage directions. One time, he told her to strip, bend over, and then slowly rise up and look back at him over her right shoulder.

She complied but was tempted to ask what scores the judge from the Czech Republic would give her for this. She also feigned delight at the sleazy lingerie he started bringing her, though she'd drawn the line at a full-body fishnet suit because it made her feel like a butterball turkey in plastic netting.

Eventually, their sex life flatlined. When Maggie complained about it, delicately at first and more bluntly later on, Richard told her she was "oversexed" and that sex was "not that important" to him. His ascetic posturing shamed and enraged her. A more sexually confident woman would have challenged him outright, demanding explanations for his celibacy.

But Maggie was not confident that way. True, she had her va-va-voom, I-feel-pretty moments. And she knew her coloring was beautiful: green eyes against milky white skin, framed by dark hair. But Maggie's faith in her own desirability, like that of many women, was far from unshakable. In fact, it was highly shakable. She hated her body's proportions: oversize boobs (okay, no man had ever complained to her about those), long torso, and short legs. It was as if God had used too much modeling clay on the top part of her and had skimped on the rest. And worst of all, thanks to her short stature, Maggie could never discreetly hide extra weight. Every pound she gained announced itself—with trumpets.

Lacking the confidence to have it out with Richard, Maggie threw herself into work and food, approaching despair with a planner in one hand and a doughnut in the other. Already a workaholic, she pulled longer hours than ever before. And when she did come home, while Richard "slaved away" in his secret porn cave, Maggie stress-ate, and the pounds poured on. Eventually, Richard started using her girth as an excuse for his sexual disinterest, which only prompted more stress eating. As she grew more disgusted with herself and ever more desperate to save her marriage, she began compulsively exercising and even flirted with bulimia. She wasn't big on vomiting, but she developed a taste for chocolate laxatives, the bulimic's after-dinner mint of choice.

She finally discovered her husband's porn habit while he was away on a business trip. He usually kept his study door closed, and Maggie rarely went in there. She intended to surprise him by tidying, maybe even sprucing up the room with some flowers. But as soon as she entered the study, she knew something was very wrong. She did not find a psycho-killer-style wall of hard-core porn photos à la *Criminal Minds* or *SVU.* And inept as she was with computers, she was not capable of any Lisbeth Salander–esque hacking to uncover her husband's tracks. No, it was Richard's wastebasket that tipped her off. It was overflowing with used, wadded Kleenex and an empty Costco-sized bottle of Jergens. Plus, the telltale odor of semen made the room smell saltier than Lot's wife.

Maggie immediately lost all interest in her cleaning spree. She walked out of the study, sobbed on the living room couch for a long time, and called the one person she always called: Diane. Diane came right away. She made Maggie lie down on her couch, put a damp washcloth across her temples, and tucked a blanket around her—as if Maggie were a child who'd had a bad scare. Diane then asked if she could go into the study and "sort this out." Maggie nodded, and then—amazingly—fell into a deep sleep.

When she woke up, Diane was sitting in an armchair next to the couch, a stack of papers in her lap. She fetched Maggie a glass of water, and then treated her to an Agatha Christie–style drawing room recounting of Richard's crimes. Computer-savvy Diane had crawled through Richard's browser history. He had been so confident of Maggie's misplaced trust that he had not bothered to conceal anything.

Diane found that Richard—the same man who'd taunted Maggie as "oversexed"—visited dozens of hard-core porn sites every day. His favorites sounded like a perverse Parade of Nations: Russian prostitutes, British blow jobs, Finnish fisting, Swedish S&M. The list went on and on. He'd paid for access to all this, using untraceable, store-bought hundred-dollar credit cards. Diane found $5,000 worth of them in his top drawer alone. She also considerately cleaned out his wastebasket, a feat that should have required a hazmat suit.

The news devastated Maggie. To lose her husband to a flesh-and-blood woman would have been hard enough, but to lose him to a computer screen was particularly galling. And creepy. A little porn would not have unnerved her. And she was all for a bit of self-love. But she squirmed at the thought of Richard locked up in his study for hours every night—a thirtysomething man whacking off to dozens of videos of surgically enhanced, sticky-looking women. Maggie wished she could Purell her brain.

Before and after confronting Richard, she researched porn addiction on her own, experiencing bitter pangs with each fresh explanation of her husband's bizarre behavior. She sobbed when she read about the Coolidge effect, a man's biological hardwiring to endlessly seek sexual novelty whenever possible. When only one female was sexually available, a man had incentive to court and care for her, even after she'd grown familiar to him. But the male libido—forged millions of years ago—did not differentiate between live women and the naked ones prancing across a computer screen. Confronted with the infinite array of beautiful, oh-so-willing women doing *everything* all the time on the internet, a man's libido went wild, like a kid with a bottomless bag of tokens at the world's largest Chuck E. Cheese's. In one session, a man could "have" more beautiful women than Elvis did in a lifetime, without swiveling his hips once.

Maggie read about how porn addicts withdrew from their real-life partners. After marathon-porn sessions with a bevy of gorgeous naked women engaging in ever-more-exotic behavior, sex with one's wife felt like going from a wide-screen, 3-D blockbuster to circle time at the local library. Sexual withdrawal led to emotional withdrawal. The wife's complaints went from a concern to an annoyance and—finally—an irrelevance. Some divorced porn users became so hostile to their "porn widows" that they hired online vixens to troll them. Maggie winced as she read of one freshly divorced porn widow who'd opened her desktop at work to find emails from a naked blonde splayed across a Ferrari, taunting her in giant type: "SORRY YOU COULDN'T PLEASE HIM."

When Maggie confronted Richard, he went through the predictable stages of an addict: denial, contrition, vows to change, sincere attempts at change, followed by complete relapse. Meanwhile, Maggie trudged back toward her old self. She found herself a therapist, regained her figure, and started the brutal business of disentangling herself from her marriage.

Even as she rebuilt her life, Maggie scolded herself for having been so trusting, so stupid. She cringed when she thought of all the crap she'd tolerated. Only later would she realize that her marriage had been trench warfare. Day after day, she had given up a little ground, then a little more. And—bam!—one morning she woke up to find the enemy had taken Paris.

Now, as she pulled into her driveway, her divorce was two years old, a legal toddler. And here was Richard messing up her life again. Ruthlessly handsome in a button-down oxford and khaki shorts, he smiled down at her as she mounted the porch steps. He held up a bouquet of pink roses, saying, "For you."

Maggie accepted the flowers. "They're beautiful." And they were.

Richard grinned. "Only the best for my wife."

"Ex-wife."

He nodded. "Ex-wife."

Maggie smelled the flowers for a moment, then eyed Richard warily. "So what's the big occasion?"

"It's the first day of school. I always bring you flowers on the first day." Maggie raised an eyebrow. Richard hastened to add, "Almost always, um, when I remember."

Maggie countered, "You haven't brought me flowers in years."

Richard looked surprised for a moment. "Really? In my mind, I'm always giving you flowers."

"As we both know, your complex inner life doesn't help me much." Maggie handed the flowers back to him while she unlocked her front door. They walked into the foyer, and she peeled off her high heels as unsexily as she could. She padded across the living room and into the kitchen, then retrieved a vase from the cupboard while Richard surveyed the room.

He said, "You've changed the place. It looks great."

"Yes, I got rid of all the things I didn't like." She looked meaningfully at Richard as she said this. He clutched a hand to his chest as if he'd been struck by gunshot, and Maggie forced back a smile. Careful to sound disinterested, she asked, "So, what do you call home these days? Still at Plaza Luna?" Richard had moved into a seedy apartment at Plaza Luna after the divorce.

Richard sighed. "Yes, Mag. And it's still a dump. There was an armed robbery at the pool there yesterday. It was all over the local news. The idiot robber didn't realize people don't carry loads of cash and jewelry with them in a hot tub."

Arranging the flowers, Maggie said, "Sounds lovely." She felt no need to tell Richard how she'd panicked when she'd heard about the robbery on the radio. She'd read everything she could about it until she'd confirmed his safety.

"How've you been, Mag?" Richard arranged his features into a soulful look.

Maggie's defenses went on high alert. "Busy. The first day of school is always exhausting, and it's not over yet. I've got a big meeting tonight. So, if you don't mind . . ." Maggie tapped her watch with her index finger.

Richard cleared his throat. "I have some news I wanted to share with you."

"Couldn't you have just called?" asked Maggie.

"I wanted to tell you in person." Maggie braced herself. She didn't know what else Richard could do to hurt her, but the man had proven himself inventive. "I wanted you to know that I've gotten help."

"A therapist?" Maggie was genuinely surprised. She'd begged Richard to go to therapy during the death throes of their marriage, but he'd always resisted.

Richard answered, "No, not a therapist."

Maggie caught the glint in Richard's eye, that it's-my-birthday vibe she always sensed around the newly devout. "Please don't tell me you found Jesus. Jesus already has far too much on his plate."

"No, not Jesus. I've joined a support group, a secular support group."

Maggie said, "That sounds promising, I guess. Do you go to meetings?" Despite all he'd done to her, Maggie still loved Richard, a begrudging, wounded love fraught with mistrust, but love all the same.

"No, at least no face-to-face meetings."

Maggie's brow furrowed. "So, how do you . . . ?"

"The group operates completely online."

Maggie smirked. "You've joined an online group to kick your online porn habit? Isn't that a bit like going to AA meetings at a bar?"

"No, it's great. It's just a bunch of guys, and some women, trying to recover from porn addiction. You get all that you-guys-understand-me sense-of-community stuff without ever having to embarrass yourself in person. It's easier to confide in each other when you don't have to actually face anyone."

Maggie raised an eyebrow. "So you feel you can be intimate with these strangers online?" History was repeating itself.

Richard caught her implication. He shook his head. "No, no. Not 'intimate' like that. The group is more . . . Jeez, Mag, you're such a technophobe."

Maggie threw up her hands. "I wonder why!"

Unfazed, Richard said, "Point taken. Look, I don't know why the group works for me, but it does. It's been months since I went onto a porn site."

Maggie was skeptical. "Months?"

"Ninety-two days to be exact."

"Wonderful. I'd offer to send you a card on your first anniversary, but I doubt Hallmark covers this one." Maggie folded her arms across her chest.

Richard smiled. "You never know." He gazed down at her, allowing the silence to stretch out between them. And Maggie felt herself thawing. The heat rose to her cheeks.

She regrouped. "So, uh, have you returned to biking yet?" She knew the answer was yes. Richard's indoor "sports" had made him pasty-white, but now, his biker's tan was back. He was his old unnervingly attractive self.

Richard nodded. "Yes, in fact, I'll be racing next weekend up in Carlsbad." Richard looked at her hopefully, as if expecting a pat on the head.

Maggie obliged. "Good for you. That sounds . . . wholesome."

"Yes, ma'am. A G-rated event, suitable for all ages. If you'd like to come watch . . ." He leaned in just a bit closer, and Maggie caught a whiff of his cologne.

Striving to sound brisk and efficient, she said, "No, thanks. But I hope you have a lovely time out there."

Richard shrugged. "No problem. I just thought you might want to watch me struggle against the younger guys."

Maggie said, "Time catches up with all of us."

"Not you, Mag. You look beautiful." His smile faded now.

For Maggie, like most women, this line immobilized most comebacks like a Taser. Picking a piece of imaginary lint off her blouse—anything to break eye contact—she said, "Uh, thank you. You look very nice as well."

"I miss you."

Maggie's head whipped up; she must have misheard. "What?"

He repeated, "I miss you."

"You miss me?" A hardness crept into Maggie's tone.

"Look, I know I hurt you. But I want you to know . . ."

Maggie folded her arms across her chest. "Know what? That you've managed to take a three-month break from playing yourself like a trombone?"

Richard countered, "Hey, that's a long time for me."

Maggie exhaled, blowing her bangs out of her eyes. "Great. But what do you want me to say?"

Richard flailed. "I thought, maybe with time . . ."

"With time, what?"

"We had so many great years together. I'd hate to throw all that away. You know, the group has a saying for situations like this—"

Maggie cut in, "Yes, regular human beings have a saying too: fuck off. But wait, I guess you'd enjoy doing that."

Richard remained maddeningly calm. "I get it. It's too soon. You're still miffed at me."

Maggie laughed. "Miffed? No, I am waaaay past miffed. Try furious. Try cutting your face out of the family photos and stabbing your voodoo doll. That's where I am, Richard."

Richard nodded. "Okay, I can see we've got a lot of work to do, a lot of trust to rebuild."

"No, Richard, there's no *we* anymore. You killed we when you left me for your right hand."

Richard raised his arms in surrender. "I got it. It's too soon."

Maggie balked. "No, it's not too soon. It's too late. We're divorced now. We're over. Got it?"

Richard shook his head. "No, Maggie. We're just getting started."

She answered him with a withering glare, then watched as he let himself out the front door. Before leaving, he winked at her.

8

Diane's Low-Budget Menagerie

Meanwhile, a dozen miles up the freeway . . .

When Diane opened the front door to her run-down ranch house, Murray screamed. This didn't startle Diane. Like most parrots, Murray screamed a lot. He screamed when the sun rose in the morning, when he was bored, when he was happy, and—of course—when Diane came home. Diane shut off the scream by calling out, "Hi, pretty bird."

This cue set off a round of Murray chanting more quietly, "Pretty bird, pretty bird." He said this as if agreeing with her assessment. She strode over to his cage and unlatched it. Murray kicked the door open and climbed up Diane's arm to perch on her shoulder. Next, she bent to pet her ancient basset hound, Bob Barker ("Barker" for short). He nuzzled her hand and then collapsed gracelessly back onto the carpet. Barker would soon be going to that great game show in the sky.

She dumped the day's mail on a table, calling out, "Hey, Dad, I'm home!" When her dad didn't answer right away, Diane paused, feeling a stab of panic. Like Bob Barker, Diane's father was close to shuffling off his mortal coil. She exhaled in relief when he called back, "Hey, darlin' girl!"

Diane then walked to the back of the house, passing more than a dozen terrariums as she went. The glass boxes held turtles, the Burmese python named Snookums, a Goliath birdeater tarantula, an African bullfrog, two ferrets, four hamsters, and a hedgehog. These animals—like Murray—were souvenirs of Diane's happy, but ill-fated, third marriage to Chaz Porter.

Diane had been thirty-one when she met Chaz. Burnt by two sleazy husbands, her customer satisfaction level with the opposite sex was at an all-time low. She'd been helping at a neighbor kid's birthday party, and Chaz had been the entertainment. A bear of a man with a loud, contagious laugh, Chaz dazzled the kids with his animals and his patter. Diane's neighbor invited him to stay around after his show, and he spent the rest of the party trailing after Diane with hearts in his eyes. Later on, he'd tell her that he fell for her on sight because she looked like Linda Hamilton in *Terminator 2*, only Diane was even better because she "wasn't all gloomy." After five months of dating, he persuaded her to "do the legal" and marry him.

Diane moved into Chaz's cramped ranch-style house on the edge of a not-so-scenic canyon in San Diego's parched far North County. Despite the coating of feathers and animal hair in the house, she was goofily happy. If she'd had to write a Yelp post on her marriage, she would have given it five stars: "Good conversation, great sex, and complete trust—I come early and often!"

Her domestic bliss came to an abrupt end when one of Chaz's snakes, a cottonmouth named Shirley, bit through his protective glove. The bite didn't kill him, but the antivenom did. The big man had an allergic reaction to the stuff, and his heart gave out minutes after he injected it. The doctor—an old guy with bushy gray eyebrows—told Diane that Chaz's reaction was a one-in-ten-million fluke. He said this as if she'd feel some sense of accomplishment at the sheer rarity of her husband's crappy luck. Diane nodded, tears coursing down her cheeks. She wept through the funeral too, a huge affair organized by Maggie.

Maggie'd gotten hold of Chaz's iPhone contacts, so she invited animal trainers from all over the Southwest, and they brought their exotic pets along. The subsequent wake looked like a sad, boozy boarding area for Noah's ark.

Afterward, and again with Maggie's help—that woman could haggle—Diane sold off the bulk of Chaz's menagerie. What remained were the dregs. Waking up every morning in Chaz's dilapidated ranch house to the sounds of her animal companions hooting and hissing, Diane felt like a white-trash Cinderella. In an uncharacteristic bout of self-pity, she had a T-shirt printed: "MY HUSBAND DIED, AND ALL I GOT WAS A LOUSY ZOO." But she didn't wear it often. She was grateful for every second she'd had with Chaz. Plus, the place perked up a bit when her dad moved in with her.

She found him sitting in his recliner, watching television at top volume. Thankfully, Lars's doctor had made him abandon cable news. Politics had caused Lars to stroke out twice while ranting at the TV set. So now, a much mellower Lars binge-watched Netflix all day. His tastes were all over the map: World War II documentaries, *Buffy the Vampire Slayer*, *Friday Night Lights*, and so on. *Downton Abbey* had been the worst. It was surreal listening to a seventy-four-year-old Minnesotan with emphysema waste his breath, fretting over which suitor Lady Mary should choose ("Jeezum Crow, she'll never learn!").

Diane kissed the top of his head, and Lars said, "So, how's Miss America doing today?"

"I dunno. Ask her." Diane deposited Murray on his perch by the window, then settled down on the couch.

Lars craned round to smile at her, his oxygen line just under his nose like a thin, clear plastic mustache. "Seriously, Lady Di, how was it?"

Diane shrugged. "Same as usual. Kids and teachers and parents, oh my." Diane knew her dad would catch this *Wizard of Oz* reference. Like most families, they spoke the same dialect of movie-ese.

"Any single dads?"

"Just one. He rode in on a white horse and handed me a red rose, but I think he does that with everybody."

Lars pressed on, "Sounds promising. Any new male teachers on staff?"

Diane shut him down. "It's not a singles bar, Dad."

"Yeah. But ya never know where you'll meet a fella." After a silence, Lars added brightly, "Or a gal. You could try being a lesbian. Lesbians are big nowadays."

"What do you mean 'big'?" Diane had a mental picture of a giant lesbian, a Godzilla-sized woman in a plaid shirt and work boots, ripping off the roof of a Home Depot.

"Ya know, they're real popular. They got Ellen, Melissa Etheridge, that frizzy-haired girl from *Roseanne*. They're everywhere. It's the new thing."

Diane answered, "Lesbians aren't new, Dad. They were born that way. They're just coming out now because it's safe."

"Sure, whatever. But I'm saying, it's okay to be that way nowadays. So if ya . . ."

Diane rolled her eyes. "I'm not gay."

"I'm just saying I've noticed you've got whatchamacallit, um, chemistry with Maggie. A real simpatico."

"For the last time, *I'm not gay*. And neither's Maggie." Hoping to quiet her father, Diane grabbed her laptop off the coffee table and switched it on. As her father turned back to watching *House of Cards*, Diane went straight to her blog DOB.com, *Doomsday on a Budget*. DOB.com was dedicated to helping people survive the apocalypse as inexpensively as possible. It catered to blue-collar "preppers." Preppers were what sane people preparing for Armageddon started calling themselves after kooks like the Unabomber disgraced the "survivalist" label. Most prepper websites shouted relentlessly at their readers about the forms their impending doom could take. Standard posts were: "5

Reasons Nuclear War Is Just Around the Corner!" and "10 Ways the World Will End, Number 6 Will Shock You!"

Diane, however, carved out a niche for herself by writing folksy posts about the best deals on canned goods, cheap-and-easy wind generators, and do-it-yourself hazmat suit repair. She made surviving the apocalypse seem almost cozy, like the long winters Laura Ingalls Wilder shared with Pa and Ma in the *Little House on the Prairie* books. Except there'd be cannibals.

Diane went through her readers' questions, answering each as thoroughly as she could. After half an hour, her father pestered her. "So, hey, any men write to you on that there website today?"

"No, Dad. I guess I'll just have to ride out the apocalypse on my own." This was a lie. Several fanboys had already propositioned Diane, using the routine prepper come-on: "Your bunker or mine?"

Lars huffed, "Well, that's no fun."

"The apocalypse isn't supposed to be fun."

"Oh, frig the apocalypse." He brought his fist down on his armrest, and the air hissed in his breathing tube.

Diane put aside her laptop. "Dad, we've gone through this. Don't get yourself worked up."

Lars laid his hand on hers. "I just don't want to see you end up all alone."

This triggered Murray. The bird squawked, "All alone! All alone! Pretty bird, all alone!" Diane rose, grabbed a Brazil nut from a dish, and shoved it into the bird's maw. Then, sitting down again, she said, "Relax, Dad. I'll never be alone. I've got you to keep me company."

"But what about after I'm gone?"

Diane said airily, "You've got a lot of good years left in you, Dad. Doc says if you'd try that new therapy, you could—"

Lars batted at the air dismissively. "Therapy, shmerapy. My body's more beat up than a piñata on Cinco de Mayo."

"Dad, you don't need to worry about me. I—"

Lars cut her off, saying softly, "Oh, I know you're strong enough to get by on your own. But I want you to do more than just get by. I want you to be happy, and happiness is hard when you're alone." Lars looked at her with his gray eyes—eyes that matched her own—and Diane was absurdly touched. Once a hale, hearty man—a force—Lars Hansen was now a thin, stooped figure who sucked air through a hose four hours a day, and *she* was the one he worried about.

Diane smiled. "I'll never be alone. I have Murray. Parrots can live up to seventy years, more sometimes."

She laid her wrist on her father's armrest, and he gave her hand a gentle squeeze. "No offense, darlin'. But you can do better."

9

DANNY Z'S INFOMERCIAL

At seven o'clock that night, the school auditorium was packed. Everyone wanted to get a glimpse of the great man. Daniel Zelinsky's public relations people had smoothed the way for him. The *Del Mar Times*, the *Carmel Valley News*, even the *San Diego Union Tribune* had published fawning pieces about the Edutek CEO over the past month. They used cheeky headlines like "Danny Z Hacks Education" and "Innovation Is Elementary (School)." And, oh yes, they ran color photos of their suave, dishy subject: a tall fortyish redhead with dark-brown eyes, perfect skin, and a generous mouth. Here he is being handsome as he talks to rapt school children; here he is being handsome and leadery at some ersatz staff meeting, his sleeves rolled up to convey seriousness and virility.

And now, for one night only, he would be handsome in person. His lackeys had set up a large screen and a high-tech sound system. The school's Flintstone-era one would not do for Danny Z. When he took the stage, the crowd murmured excitedly. He waved his hands to quiet them, but the whispering continued unabated. Exasperated, Maggie rose to her feet, put her fingers to her mouth, and gave her trademark wolf whistle. The room immediately fell silent, and Danny Z's eyebrows shot up. She gave him a perfunctory smile and gestured for him to get on with it.

Danny Z started, "Thanks for coming out on a school night. It's encouraging to see parents taking full charge of their children's education. My name is Daniel Zelinsky. Zelinsky's a mouthful, so my friends shorten it to Danny Z. We're all friends here, so I hope I'll be Danny Z to all of you." He smiled, radiating warmth down at his three hundred new buddies.

"I can't tell you how pleased I am that Edutek has been able to partner with Carmel Valley on its new software system. Carmel Valley's public schools are the gold standard for academic performance in Southern California." This was not exactly true, but close enough.

"That said, we can always make a good thing even better. As the late Steve Jobs once said"—Danny Z paused here to genuflect to Silicon Valley's lord and savior—"'There is always one thing left to learn.'"

Maggie thought rebelliously, *Just one?*

Danny Z continued, "Now, before I get started, I wanted to thank the two people who were instrumental in making all this possible. First, Superintendent Arlene Horvath." Danny Z gestured toward Arlene in the front row. "When Edutek announced that we were looking for students to test the MathPal, Arlene reached out to us. And let me tell you, she was a powerful advocate for Carmel Valley. Please, Arlene, stand up and take a bow." Arlene rose, a radiant smile on her lips. If the woman's ego had been any more inflated, she would have floated away.

When Arlene sat back down, Danny Z went on, "And, of course, Principal Maggie Mayfield. When we partnered with the district, we had to make the tough choice of which school to use as our test site. We knew we'd need strong leadership to implement our testing program, and Maggie fit the bill. Maggie *is* Carmel Knolls Elementary. C'mon, Maggie, stand up. After that whistle, we know you're not shy." Maggie stood, a fake smile plastered across her face. She understood full well that if Edutek's grand experiment failed, this little applause break would mark her as a target for blame. It was Danny Z's way of ensuring Maggie's full commitment to the project's success—or as he'd call it in his Silicon Valley–ese, her "buy-in." As she sat back down, her smile dissolved.

Danny Z had one of his minions dim the lights, and he began his PowerPoint presentation. Using a handheld control, he began with a slide with the words "CARMEL VALLEY" emblazoned over a gorgeous beach sunset—conveniently ignoring Carmel Valley's inland status. Next came a slide of three strategically diverse, attractive children laughing wholesomely on a playground. Danny Z said, "Carmel Valley is home to a highly educated population, world-class engineering firms, and—I don't need to tell you this—ever-rising property values." The audience chuckled obediently.

Next came a slide of a colorful graph showing test scores for Southern California's various school districts. "And as state test scores have proven time after time, Carmel Valley has some of the best public schools in Southern California." Maggie noted that Danny Z's graph included lower-performing districts, while judiciously omitting the few districts that outshone Carmel Valley. It was the statistical equivalent of a bride highlighting her beauty by choosing less attractive friends as bridesmaids.

Danny Z paused here, and Maggie—a veteran of countless "education in crisis" presentations—felt her stomach tighten. She knew what that pause meant. Danny Z was allowing the congratulatory appetizers he'd served to be cleared so he could get to his main dish: fear. "Now, all this would be great if our students just had to compete against kids down the block, or even kids in this state, but that's not the case. No, today's students will someday have to compete against students from other states, and other countries too."

Danny Z now clicked over to a slide proclaiming: "A CHANGING WORLD." Below that were three bullet points: "GLOBALIZATION,"

"MECHANIZATION," and "INCREASING COMPETITION FOR JOBS."

Maggie whispered to Diane, "Horror movies playing now in a white American male's brain near you."

Danny Z said, "Now more than ever, we face a changing world. Globalization has made capital and labor fully mobile. A company here in Carmel Valley can use capital from Saudi Arabia to hire new workers in Thailand." Danny Z clicked to a world map with green arrows to show money flowing into San Diego and blue arrows to show jobs flowing out. Maggie felt a palpable stillness in the room. The wounds inflicted by Gallcomm's layoffs were still fresh, and Danny Z was poking at them.

"We are also losing ever more jobs to mechanization." Danny Z clicked to a warehouse where robots were shown placing crates on shelves, no human being in sight.

Diane whispered, "It's like *Terminator*, but boring."

Danny Z continued, "And as communication becomes easier, companies are outsourcing highly skilled jobs too." He clicked to a split-screen photo. On the left side, a Caucasian male in blue hospital scrubs ran an X-ray through a scanner. On the right side, an Indian female doctor examined the same X-ray while talking into a phone. Danny Z explained, "Here, we see a radiation tech in South Carolina, scanning a fresh X-ray into a computer. Moments later, a radiologist in New Delhi examines that X-ray and calls the South Carolina hospital with her diagnosis. The American radiologist is no longer necessary." Maggie heard several parents murmuring. If a doctor could be replaced, no one was safe.

Danny Z went on, "In this hypercompetitive world, education is key." He clicked to another slide. This one showed a cartoon: a white-clad Princess Leia looking up at a building marked "COLLEGE." Underneath was the caption: "Help me, Education, you're my only hope."

Danny Z said, "So, how does California—and, by extension, Carmel Valley—stack up against the competition?" He clicked to yet another graph. "This slide shows the relative ranking of the fifty states' public school systems. As you can see, the top ten school systems are concentrated on the East Coast. Appropriately enough, towards the middle of the graph, we find midwestern states. And further over— much further over—we have California coming in fortieth, after Arkansas and just ahead of Alabama." Danny Z shook his head, repeating, "Alabama." The subtext was plain: *Yes, that's right, folks, your kids are just a teensy bit sharper than the state that gave us Forrest Gump.*

Maggie felt her face redden. She knew these statistics. She also knew Danny Z wouldn't bother with what lay behind them: *money.* The East Coast didn't have any special sauce. It simply spent more on education. Maggie felt a mutinous desire to shout: "You get what you pay for, cheapskates!" Instead, she reached into her purse only to find that her emergency chocolate was gone.

Danny Z clicked to a slide showing planet Earth. "Sadly, California isn't just losing the race against other states. It's also losing the global education race."

Danny Z pointed to a list marked "TOP TEN EDUCATION SYSTEMS IN THE WORLD." "Now, as you can see, the United States is nowhere on this list. Instead, the top four spots all go to East Asian countries: South Korea, Japan, Singapore, and Hong Kong. And it's not hard to see why."

Danny Z clicked to a slide showing white-coated Asian high school students working in a well-equipped, pristine laboratory. He said ominously, "East Asian countries invest heavily in education and research."

In a faux southern accent, Diane whispered in Maggie's ear, "Run for the hills, folks. Those China people are taking all the science." Maggie smiled bitterly.

Danny Z went on, "East Asian governments are also highly organized and disciplined." He pointed to a panoramic photo showing thousands of Chinese drummers lined up in neat rows at the Beijing Olympics. Maggie frowned, whispering, "No fair. China didn't make the top four."

Diane answered, "Nah, but China scares the shit out of everybody."

A hand flew up, and a parent blurted, "What about Finland? I thought Finland was the best in the world." Other parents in the audience nodded at this. There was something vaguely reassuring about quaint, snowy Finland being number one. They're white. They'll be nice to us!

Danny Z answered, "Finland is ranked fifth. It hasn't been able to keep up with East Asia." He clicked to a slide titled: "TOP TWENTY EDUCATION SYSTEMS RANKED." "As you can see, the United States does not even crack the top ten. Those spaces go to the United Kingdom, Canada, the Netherlands, Ireland, and Poland. Yes, that's right, Poland is way ahead of us." Danny Z teased, "So who's stupid now?" This provoked slightly embarrassed titters from the audience. Danny Z quickly added, "Relax. I'm a Polack myself. So you don't have to feel guilty laughing at that one." This triggered a second, louder round of laughter.

Danny Z continued, "The United States comes in fourteenth, right behind Russia."

Diane whispered to Maggie, "Dang. Russia's scary too." Maggie grimaced. Danny Z's scare tactics were blunt but effective.

In a more hopeful tone, Danny Z asked rhetorically, "So, what do we do? We do what Americans have always done. We innovate." He clicked, and the screen showed the word "INNOVATION" writ large.

"Old teaching methods may have worked in the past, but the past must give way to the future." Danny Z clicked to a split screen. One side featured a black-and-white still of a pioneer woman using a butter churn. On the other side, a gigantic gleaming steel machine poured out tons of butter into a vat. "And in the field of education, the future belongs to Edutek."

Danny Z motioned toward the Edutek logo with the company motto: "Hacking Education." To Maggie, this slogan conjured images of a stooped, wizened schoolmarm hacking up phlegm. "Edutek's new software aims to customize the learning experience. Each student will have a different learning experience each day, an experience tailored to that particular child's academic strengths and weaknesses."

Danny Z clicked over to a color photo of a delighted child pointing at some bit of wisdom displayed on the screen of an Edutek tablet.

"Edutek's MathPal software uses a three-step process." Danny Z's next slide showed a group of children tinkering industriously with Edutek tablets under "STEP ONE: ASSESSMENT." "It begins by creating an in-depth profile of each user. In just two twenty-minute sessions, the MathPal assesses the user's math skills and deficiencies. And just as importantly, it gains valuable information about that user's preferences, her tastes.

"This assessment enables Edutek to personalize its lessons." Danny Z clicked to another slide saying: "STEP TWO: INDIVIDUATION." Below that header was a photo of a female tailor hemming a little girl's pink dress. "Each child receives a personalized lesson plan that varies each day in accordance with her ever-changing skill set."

"What's more, the lesson plan uses information about the child's preferences to design stimulating questions. This turns bored, distracted users into fully engaged learners." Danny Z clicked to another split screen. On the left side, a bleary-eyed child looked down at a stack of dull worksheets. On the right side, a computer-animated child dressed as a pirate was pointing his scythe at a group of six red parrots over a math question: "How many parrots if you add three?" Danny Z said smugly, "I know which lesson I'd rather sit through." The audience murmured excited approval. Indulgent parents did not just like fun. They *believed* in it.

Danny Z clicked again, this time to a slide marked "STEP THREE: CONSTANT GROWTH." The slide showed a young, pretty teacher in a yellow twinset, sitting across a table from a small boy and his two parents. The teacher held forth while the parents and child listened in fascination. "Once we assess your child and tailor a perfect lesson plan for him, we will constantly grow his skill set. To do this effectively, we will need help from this school's most valuable resource: its teachers. We will work with your school's dedicated educators to constantly refine and remold our software to maximize results."

Danny Z clicked to another screen showing dozens of smiling schoolchildren. "Your children's education is Edutek's mission. And we will not fail you." The lights came on, and the room burst into applause. Danny Z smiled down at the crowd, letting his gaze linger a beat too long on Maggie. Unsure of what to do, she gave him a tight smile and a thumbs-up, but she vowed Danny Z would never have her "buy-in."

10

THE FUTURE HAS ARRIVED

The next morning, Maggie found a brand-new MathPal tablet atop her desk. Attached to its screen was a yellow Post-it Note saying, *"The Future has arrived. —Danny Z."* Maggie groaned. Danny Z was turning out to be the Mount Everest of male pomposity. She balled up the note and tossed it in her wastebasket.

After the morning announcements, she fired up the MathPal and took it for a spin. As promised, it was a gaming system. The MathPal icon—Buzzy Bear—was a cuddly bear in a hip-hop outfit. Buzzy asked Maggie all about herself. Name and grade were just foreplay. Buzzy wanted to know where her family vacationed, how often they went to the movies, and what cereals they ate. Maggie guessed this invasive vetting was part of the "individuation" that Danny Z had promised. Irritated, she posed as a third grader named Smelly Donut.

Once Smelly had shared her information, Buzzy Bear helped her set up her avatar. Again, the MathPal wanted details: gender, age, race, face shape, hairstyle, outfit, musical tastes, and on and on. Maggie was bracing herself to provide the date for her avatar's most recent Pap smear when the MathPal pronounced the avatar complete and then—finally—turned to the subject of math.

The MathPal offered five different, beautifully animated "worlds" to enter: Wild West, Superheroes, Dance Team, Summer Camp, and Lifeboat. Maggie clicked on Lifeboat out of sheer curiosity, and the MathPal deposited her on a skiff in the middle of the Atlantic. The *Titanic* was sinking in the background, but—this being a sanitized reality—Maggie saw no passengers flailing in the waves and heard no cries for help. Instead, there were frolicking dolphins, sun-dappled bright-blue water, and puffy white clouds. Maggie's lifeboat had ten passengers, counting her avatar. The game introduced each passenger, complete with backstories and sassy catchphrases. As Maggie progressed through the story, the game rewarded her every move with "flare points"—each flare point buying a chance to shoot a flare gun in hopes of rescue. And every time the flare gun went off, the characters held a (pointless) two-minute dance party.

Maggie couldn't help noticing how little math she was asked to do. Over thirty minutes, she did just two fraction problems: If the ten survivors agreed to equally divide two loaves of bread, how much bread would each person get? One-fifth of a loaf. What if two of the survivors can't eat gluten, how much would the remaining eight get then? One-fourth.

Maggie tried the other worlds, and her worries blossomed. The MathPal did not teach math concepts. It name-dropped them. It introduced principles without discipline, key points getting lost in a frenetic rush of noise, jokes, and color. Learning from the MathPal was like trying to understand art by sprinting through the Louvre in search of a bathroom—you might glimpse a painting or two, but you wouldn't have actually absorbed anything.

After an hour, Maggie pushed back from her desk and called out for Diane.

Diane sauntered over. "So how's the *future*?" Diane had obviously read Danny Z's note.

Maggie grumped, "I'm older there."

"And saggier," said Diane.

"Thanks. Have you got a minute?" Maggie gestured to one of the chairs opposite her desk.

"Yes, ma'am." Diane shut the door carefully behind her and sat. She studied Maggie's dark expression. "So it's bad, huh?"

Maggie nodded. She described her test-drive of the mathless MathPal. "I can't believe I committed the kids to sixty hours on that thing."

Diane raised an eyebrow. "Whoa. Sixty hours? I thought it was twenty minutes a day."

"Twenty minutes a day for 180 days. That's sixty hours of instruction time."

Diane grinned. "Wow, look at the math skills on you. At least we know the MathPal doesn't make people *more* stupid."

Maggie shot back miserably, "I *am* stupid."

"No, you're not, honey," cooed Diane.

"I am. I committed my kids to spending sixty hours on a glorified video game."

"Oh, c'mon. It can't be that bad. There's gotta be something educational on there."

Maggie fumed, "It's about as educational as having someone shout the word 'educational' in your face. It's . . . it's bullshit."

Diane winced. She'd never before heard Maggie curse on school grounds. Maggie usually acted like there was a G-rated force field around the place. Diane suggested, "Maybe they're still building it."

"Huh?"

Diane explained, "You said the MathPal was superdetailed at the start with the avatar and whatnot, but then it got real sloppy on the actual game. Maybe they just ran out of gas. It's like when I was little, I'd tell my kid sister about the three bears. I'd fill in Goldilocks real well— her wandering ways, her reputation as a troublemaker, her burglar's tools. I wore myself out talking. By the time I got to the bears finding her, I'd just say some bad shit went down."

"And your point is?" asked Maggie.

"My point is, maybe Edutek's still building this thing. Maybe they'll beef up the math part this year while our kids are working on it. Would that be so terrible?"

Maggie shot back, "Yes. It would be. Our kids should not have to sit through sixty hours of schlock just because—maybe, someday—the schlock *might* achieve an acceptable level of mediocrity."

Diane grinned. "Acceptable mediocrity—that sounds like the world's worst tattoo."

Maggie put her head in her hands. "I can't believe I agreed to this."

"*You* didn't agree to anything. Arlene got us into this deal."

"With me cheering from the sidelines." Maggie held tight to her guilt—as if it were her handbag, and she was passing through a bad neighborhood.

"Fine. You're a monster. Someday, they'll make a grainy documentary about your sins. But let's not forget there's a damn good reason you did this. Those kids need STEAM teachers. Sixty hours sounds like a lot, but it's worth it if it buys us science and PE and whatnot."

"But this deal only buys us a year."

"You don't know that. If the MathPal's a hit, that stock Edutek gave us could pay for years of goodies."

"That's not going to happen," said Maggie. "Once the world gets hold of this dud program, Edutek's stock price is going to tank."

Diane frowned for a moment, mentally regrouping. "Well, if you're right, we don't have time to sit around feeling sorry for ourselves. Do we?"

Maggie took a deep breath, then blew it out slowly. "You're right. When the MathPal tanks, we have to be ready to pay for STEAM by ourselves. We need to start raising cash right away."

The two women looked at each other, and something passed between them—an agreement cemented by steely resolve. With the solemnity of an ensign asking whether she should launch the torpedoes, Diane asked, "Shall I bring out the worm?"

Maggie straightened in her chair and said, "Yes. It is time."

11

THE WORM

Maggie didn't choose a worm as her school mascot. No, that sin belonged to one of her predecessors.

Back in the 1980s, other local principals had embraced aquatic mascots in a nod to Carmel Valley's almost-but-not-quite seaside status. Their students were the Dolphins, the Rays, the Marlins, and so on. One *Jaws*-loving principal went with the Great Whites, until he heard his students' cheer: "Who's the best? The Whites!" They became the Sharks after that.

But Maggie's predecessor, Lynn Tarvey, had gone in a different direction. A fervent environmentalist, Mrs. Tarvey chose Willy Worm as Carmel Knolls' mascot to raise public awareness about composting. She'd proposed a school logo showing a worm atop a pile of rotting food scraps, but parents had not let her go that far. Still, they let her paint worm murals on two school walls, put out a line of Willy Worm school T-shirts, and have a local sculptor build a giant, smiling worm statue in the courtyard.

Thanks to the statue's brown color, Maggie thought it looked like the world's largest, longest turd. She yearned to get rid of Willy Worm, but she couldn't. Repainting the murals and redesigning the spirit wear would have cost too much money (these days, any money was "too much" money). What's more, the kids had grown attached to the playground statue. They draped holiday-themed outfits on it as the year progressed, and they touched the worm's side for good luck when they passed it. They got perverse pleasure out of chanting, "We've got worms!"

So every year, Maggie marked the beginning of the school's pledge drive by hanging a huge Willy Worm banner on the school's front gates. It showed a grinning, big-eyed cartoon worm with a word bubble shouting: "SUPPORT OUR STEAM TEACHERS!" Beside it, a thermometer showed the amount raised thus far relative to the district's goal. The banner worm's smile never faltered, but Diane—depending on how the fund-raising actually was going—periodically redrew the worm mock-up she kept tucked away in her desk. Thanks to last year's meager haul, by June, Diane had redrawn her office worm as a bitter drunk, with an empty begging bowl in one anatomically incorrect hand and a bottle of tequila in the other.

This year, as Maggie and Diane hung the worm banner on the school's front gate, Maggie prayed Diane's office worm would smile all year long. She had no stomach for firing her popular, oh-so-necessary STEAM teachers. Every year, when it became apparent that she might have to lay off talented teachers, Maggie would feel nauseated. Diane called it "mourning sickness."

Maggie had daymares about playing the heavy: the back-seat Mafia hit man who left the gun and took the cannoli, the Monty Burns with a trapdoor wired to a button on her desk, the TV host who pulled up the cloche to reveal which contestant would be chopped. She hated being the pawn of a stingy, reckless system.

But no, not this year. This year, Maggie would raise all the money she needed. She and Diane just had to come up with a plan.

As if reading Maggie's thoughts, Diane mused, "Bake sales and galas won't cut it."

"But we'll still do them," said Maggie.

"Oh yeah. We'll do 'em," said Diane. "And we'll make money off them. But it won't be enough. It never is."

Maggie sighed. "I don't think we can up the direct appeals." This was fund-raising-speak for abject begging.

Diane nodded. "Too true. I think we wore out the parents last year. It's like those NPR pledge drives. If you give something in the first few days, you feel virtuous. Your halo lights up every time Terry Gross says how great it'd be if everybody else would be like you and give. And the everybody elses out there feel all guilty. Some of them cough up dough to make their consciences quit yapping, but others—and Ira Glass says there's lotsa others out there—they start getting ornery. It's like they missed the Cooperation Turnaround, so they head straight on to 'Not Doing Shit for You' Boulevard."

Maggie whispered, "Language, please."

Diane winced and looked around to make sure she hadn't inadvertently corrupted any young minds. She hadn't. "So anyways, we can't just rely on begging and bake sales. We need to think big. Halloween's more than a month away. That's plenty of time to—"

Maggie cut in, "No. We're not doing that."

Diane balked. "You don't know what I'm going to say."

Maggie replied, "For the last time, we are *not* turning our campus into a *Walking Dead* theme park."

"Hear me out," Diane protested. Like most preppers, she was a *Walking Dead* fan.

"I *did* hear you out. Every year, it's the same thing: 'Let's put the teachers in zombie makeup and have them chase the kids around the campus.' It's insane."

"It's a moneymaker. Do you have any idea how much teenagers pay to go to that Scream Zone out at the fairgrounds?"

"How much?" asked Maggie.

Diane blustered, "Well, I don't know. But it must be something 'cause they bring in actors from LA, special effects, the works. They wouldn't lay out that kinda money unless they're getting a big-ass return."

Maggie answered, "That's for teenagers. Parents *like* it when you scare the bejeezus out of their teens. It's the only thing that humbles them. Scaring elementary school kids is different. Half the kids at this school can't make it through a Harry Potter movie without soiling themselves."

Diane conceded. "Those Dementors *are* scary."

"Not as scary as a blood-soaked zombie teacher cornering you against the jungle gym," said Maggie.

Diane explained, "No, but I told you. The kids *won't* be cornered. They'll be empowered. We can give them paintball guns to shoot at—"

"Guns?!"

Diane flailed. "Okay, not guns. How about those retractable stage knives? They can stabby-stabby all they want with those things. It'll be fun."

Maggie put a hand to her temple. "Yes. I'm sure parents will be delighted at the specificity of their children's nightmares."

Diane persisted, "Okay, so we don't have zombie teachers. I can see how that might be . . . fraught. How about we use animals? Dress them up as zombies? We can call it Zombie Zoo. I'm still in touch with Chaz's buddies. They can hook us up with plenty of critters—goats, cows, sheep, dogs. It'll be . . ."

Maggie shook her head. "Enough. I am not turning this school into Old MacDonald's slaughterhouse."

Diane sniffed. "Okay, we'll stick a pin in that idea, come up with something else."

Maggie nodded, mumbling, "Something else." But what?

12

A WELL-OILED MACHINE

Maggie didn't see Danny Z for the first few weeks of school. But she felt Edutek's invisible hand jerking her this way and that. First, it forced her to knock her disgruntled teachers into line. Danny Z's well-publicized digs against "outdated" teaching methods—*their* teaching methods—stung. It was like seeing your face painted on Cinderella's ugly stepsister. And Danny Z's "community meeting" only intensified the faculty's disdain. They were not distracted by Danny Z's charms or his blather about them as "dedicated educators." Instead, they focused on the way he'd compared their "traditional" pedagogy—and them themselves!—to butter churns.

Their wounds still fresh, the teachers were galled when Maggie broke the news—at the first staff meeting of the year—that Edutek had upped its daily testing quota from ten to twenty minutes. Like Maggie, the teachers immediately recognized the magnitude of this time suck. California's bloated battery of tests—coupled with its ever-shrinking education budget—had already required amputations of healthy educational tissue over the past decade. So Edutek's new demands cut to the bone.

Jeannie Pacer would have to give up her fabulous first-grade poetry unit and its poetry-slam finale. Mrs. Brandl would say goodbye to her fifth-grade unit on the spice trade, a brilliant project that combined geography, history, and economic theory. And poor Ms. MacPhail would have to compress her colonial history unit, cutting the faux-colonial newspapers the kids always loved creating. There'd be no more "Hear Ye, Hear Ye!" gossip sections speculating on whether the old lady down the lane had used black "magicke" to retain her teeth all the way into her forties.

As the teachers processed their grief, all Maggie could do was listen. She listened to them rant as a group at faculty meetings and later in one-on-one bull sessions. She nodded and murmured apposite condolences through it all, and then—over and over—she drew her trump card: the children's well-being. Yes, the cuts were painful. No, Maggie wasn't sure whether Edutek's software worked, but its money definitely did. And the school needed that money to keep its beloved STEAM specialist teachers for another year. And who knew, if the company's stock rose, its stock grant to the district could cover those teachers for years to come, years without the MathPal.

After so many cutbacks, Maggie's faculty could not bear to watch yet another talented colleague get shoved out of their professional life-boat. They knew how much the kids adored charismatic Mr. Carlsen, with his grand experiments and his lab full of lizards, snakes, and mice. They knew how quickly their students learned to code under the tutelage of Ms. Seborne, the intense, Diet Coke–swigging technology teacher. Or how about Mrs. Maugham, the flamboyant music teacher who'd somehow managed to trick kids into singing—and actually enjoying!—opera? And it was galactically stupid to even consider firing Mr. Baran, the physical education teacher who'd used his loud, gravelly voice to teach kids flag football one week and the cha-cha the next.

The only expendable specialist on staff was the new art teacher, Miss Pearl. Maggie liked her. Miss Pearl was that rarest of birds: sporting a gorgeous plumage of academic credentials (Art Institute of Chicago), boundless enthusiasm, creative energy, and—dream within a dream— humility. She was exactly what the school needed: new blood. But her sheer newness made her vulnerable. Despite rave performance reviews, the poor girl had already been dismissed twice from other schools; her lack of seniority made her vulnerable to budget cuts. She'd burn out if she was forced to wander much longer.

While Maggie helped the faculty adapt to their increasingly stingy circumstances, Edutek moved into its "on-site" headquarters. The company took over the school's only empty classroom, the classroom where—in another professional lifetime a decade earlier—Maggie used to teach Spanish as "Señora Marguerite."

Edutek sent a pale, lanky computer whiz named Shawn to man its "HQ." To Maggie's eye, Shawn appeared egregiously young, as if he'd only recently started to get hair "down there." She lectured him on the school's dress code when he'd first arrived on campus in baggy blue jeans and a *Doctor Who* T-shirt, reminding him that he was now working at an elementary school, not Comic-Con, so khakis and button-down shirts, please. Shawn had nodded and given her a snappy *Star Trek* salute. "I shall make it so, Captain." As Maggie watched him retreat, she felt a millisecond of remorse on behalf of principals everywhere for the many times Shawn must have been pantsed at recess.

But Maggie's sympathy for the young man dissolved when she saw what Edutek had done to her once-modest classroom. After clearing out the school's cheap furniture, Edutek kitted out the room with ultra-modern, ergonomic office furniture, soft lighting, and a large stainless-steel refrigerator stocked with eleven-dollar-a-bottle pressed juices and other pretentious fare. A massive bookshelf in one corner held hundreds of new Edutek computer tablets, to be used by students solely for Edutek's purposes. In another corner, Edutek had installed a freestanding, old-timey *Pac-Man* arcade game—consistent with the tech world's faux playful image. Expensively framed, kitschy *Deep Space Nine* and

Battlestar Galactica posters hung on the walls. And at the center of it all was Shawn's workstation, featuring a keyboard and six huge wall-mounted monitors, as if he'd won some contest at Best Buy.

Maggie couldn't decide what annoyed her more: the sheer opulence of the room's contents or its studied "ain't-we-cute" enfant terrible vibe. Both rankled in an underfunded school where teachers used their own money to buy many of their students' school supplies and infrastructure dated back to the Soviet Union.

So Maggie had to work hard to hold on to her smile when she ran across Danny Z just outside the doors of the school's noisy cafeteria. "Mr. Zelinsky, what a pleasant surprise."

He smiled down at her. "Please, call me Danny."

Maggie stiffened. "I'm sorry. I can't do that. 'Danny' sounds like one of my fourth graders. Oh wait, Danny *is* one of my fourth graders."

"Do you have any fourth graders named Maggie?" He pronounced the name "Maggie" in a singsong so as to accentuate its childishness.

Maggie countered, "Our situations are not comparable. You have no reason to tamper with your given name. Daniel is fine. Margaret sounds fat."

He looked her over appraisingly—not quite a full-body scan, but close enough. With mock indignation, he said, "You are not fat."

Maggie reddened. "I didn't say I was fat. I said Margaret *sounds* fat, like Bertha or Mabel."

Danny Z gasped. "Mabel was my mother's name."

Maggie sputtered, "I, uh, what I meant to say . . ."

"I'm just playing. My mom was a Wendy."

Maggie frowned at him. "That wasn't very nice, Mr. Zelinsky."

"Sorry, at least call me Daniel."

Maggie nodded. "All right, Daniel it is." She smoothed the pleats of her skirt and wished she'd worn her heels. In her flats, she had to crane her neck back to look up into Danny's eyes. The stance made her feel like a bird-watcher. "Um, so can we expect many visits from you this year?"

Danny said, "Yes. I would have been down here before, but I had to raise another round of financing for the launch."

"Ah yes, the launch." Maggie tried to sound like she knew what he was talking about. She pictured smoke billowing out from under a rocket. That couldn't be right.

Danny simpered, "The MathPal is going to be big, like *Titanic*."

"The *Titanic* sunk," said Maggie.

He grinned, unperturbed. "I mean the movie *Titanic*, not the ship."

"Ah," said Maggie. Based on what she'd seen of the MathPal, she was pretty sure the market's reaction to it would be iceberg-chilly.

Danny went on, "We'll need massive cash reserves so we can pivot quickly from the US market."

Maggie nodded and furrowed her brow to convey her sage-like understanding. She said, "Yes, pivoting can be difficult." She pictured a model whipping about on a runway. That couldn't be right either. "So, uh, did you manage to raise enough funds?"

"Yes." Danny heaved a satisfied breath of relief, and Maggie pretended not to notice what a pretty sight his well-muscled chest made during that process. "And now that we've got enough in the bank, I can focus on what really matters: product development. I'll be down here a lot."

"Oh really?" Maggie tried not to sound personally interested in this fact.

"Yes. I like to get into the trenches. I'm very hands-on." Danny winked as he said this.

Catching this bit of ham-fisted sexual innuendo, Maggie felt flustered. She was hopelessly rusty at flirting. She felt like squeaking, "Oilcan." Instead, she just managed, "Well, good for you."

"I hope you don't mind that I filled our HQ with so much of my own stuff. When I spend serious time somewhere, I like to make it homey."

Maggie said, "Ahh, so the fridge is yours? The *Pac-Man* game too?"

"Yup. I think work should be fun, don't you?"

Maggie said primly, "So long as fun doesn't get in the way." As she said this, she winced inwardly at her own prudishness.

"So tell me, what do you do for fun, Maggie?"

Maggie sensed the trap in this. The truth—reading books, binge-watching Netflix, eating chocolates—would seem lame and spinstery. So she went the other way: "Whoring and drinking, same as everyone else."

Danny's eyebrows shot up in surprise. "I'm glad to hear you're so well rounded."

"Thank you, sir." She said this stiffly, but felt an absurd pride bloom inside her. If she'd had a tail, it would have been wagging.

A fifth-grade teacher—Mrs. Brandl—ruined the moment. As she passed, she gave Maggie a warm hello, pointedly ignoring Danny. When Mrs. Brandl disappeared through the cafeteria doors, he commented, "Ouf, that was cold. She doesn't like me, does she?"

Maggie said, "Well, you did cost her the spice trade."

"What?"

"When you, I mean Edutek, upped the testing quota to twenty minutes a day, that took a huge bite out of class time. All the teachers had to make deep cuts to their lesson plans. And Mrs. Brandl lost her unit on the spice trade."

Danny asked, "Was it any good?"

"Not good, it was brilliant. A truly inventive lesson plan on the medieval spice trade—it taught kids about geography, history, and economic theory. One of the highlights of their year."

Danny shrugged. "Oh well. I'm sure the other teachers—"

Maggie cut him off. "The other teachers lost great stuff too. They can't cover all the material required by state testing, blow twenty minutes a day on Edutek's stuff, *and* do creative projects with the kids."

"Can't they just tweak their schedules? Move a few things around?" Danny grinned down at her smugly, no doubt assuming Edutek's sexy product research was far more important than the teachers' glamour-free classwork. He probably thought the school's curriculum was glutted with macaroni art and circle time.

Maddened by this bit of condescension, Maggie huffed, "No, I'm afraid they can't just move a few things around. Our teachers don't just 'wing it' in the classroom. Every day—every minute—has to be planned out so we can cover the state's curriculum. Don't let the sunny posters and warm smiles fool you, every classroom in this building is a well-oiled machine, a . . ." At that moment, Maggie felt a tap on her shoulder.

She turned to find an out-of-breath Diane, who said, "They need you in Room 12. Right away." Room 12 was Jeannie Pacer's first-grade classroom.

Maggie asked, "What's happened?"

"Jeannie put Connor Bellman in the corner for a time-out. He got hold of a cell phone and dialed 9-1-1."

"What?!"

Diane went on, "Connor said he was being tortured. The cops are on their way."

Maggie put a hand on her forehead for a moment. Christ, she needed a chocolate, a vat of chocolate. She turned to make her excuses to Danny. And plainly amused, he told her, "Sounds like one of your well-oiled machines broke down."

Maggie nodded with what she hoped was brisk efficiency. "Ah yes. Right." Then, she walk-ran down the corridor after Diane, fully aware of Danny's gaze on her every step of the way.

13

CONNOR

By the time Maggie made it to Room 12, chaos had descended. A stony-faced police officer stood by the doorway, listening as Jeannie Pacer explained how this was "just a big misunderstanding." As always, the sixtysomething Brooklyn refugee spoke eloquently, totally unaware of how her accent and appearance undermined her credibility. Her long, flowy skirt, Indian print top, and oversize dangling earrings made her look like a geriatric hippie. And her long gray hair—piled messily atop her head—only heightened this impression. Worst of all were the three dark-red scratches on her left cheek.

Credibility hinges on context, and this policeman did not realize that in Jeannie's context, her school, she was a great figure. He had no way of knowing that the scratches on her cheek, like dozens before them, had been inflicted by Jeannie's aging pet cat, *not* by her students. He didn't know that—despite Jeannie's loosey-goosey, flower child sartorial style—she was a strict disciplinarian, demanding hard work and excellent manners from her human charges. It was only Jeannie's cat that remained untamed.

Over the years, parents of Jeannie's students had giggled over the incongruity of a feline abuse victim urging them to "establish firm boundaries" with their children. But still, Jeannie had the parents' respect. In one year, she turned their cute six-year-olds into still-cute-but-fiercely-competent students. The kids went from scratching out their ABCs to writing poetry—odes to recess and screeds against bedtime. They went from counting on their fingers to doing sums in their heads. They had to or they couldn't bluff in Jeannie's many card games. Her classroom sometimes resembled the high-stakes room at the Bellagio. Jeannie wasn't all business. She gave kids "wiggle breaks" and wore costumes to get their imaginations going, but she planned every moment of her class's day—except for the moments created by Connor Bellman.

Now, as Jeannie spoke, she kept her liver-spotted hands planted on little Connor's freckly shoulders so as to restrain him and highlight his outlaw status. Meanwhile, the children—inspired by the cop's holstered weapon—ran about the classroom, firing imaginary guns.

Maggie introduced herself to the policeman, said a demure "excuse me," and then entered the classroom with Diane in tow. Maggie wolf-whistled, and the children froze. She growled, "To your desks, *now*." The children scrambled to their seats. They folded their hands on their desks and looked sweetly up at Maggie in a pantomime of innocence. She eyed them for a moment, long enough to allow any residual cheekiness to subside. "Children, I am going to step outside into the hallway with your teacher to speak with this policeman. While I am gone, Mrs. Porter will take charge of this classroom. And every single one of you will behave perfectly for her. Do you understand?"

The children chorused, "Yes, Mrs. Mayfield."

Maggie nodded. "Good."

As Maggie shut the door behind her, she heard Diane begin, "All right, time to show me what you got. Who here can tell me the five most dangerous sharks known to man?"

Maggie crossed over to the policeman, saying, "Officer, I am so sorry about all this."

Connor asked Jeannie, "Do I need a lawyer?"

Jeannie shook her head. "No, Connor." She hazarded a grin, telling the policeman, "We talked about civil rights last week."

Connor volunteered, "Mrs. Pacer says I have a right not to inseminate myself. It's in the Constipation."

Coloring, Jeannie corrected him. "The Constitution, Connor. And you have a right against incrimination, not . . . Oy, never mind."

The cop folded his brawny arms across his chest, still glowering. Connor was not striking the proper tone of contrition.

No doubt sensing the cop's displeasure, Jeannie took a knee so she could look Connor in the eye. She explained, "Connor, you owe Officer Nelson here an apology. Do you know why?"

Connor mumbled, "'Cause it's wrong to call 9-1-1?"

Jeannie nodded, "It *is* wrong to call 9-1-1 if it's not an emergency. It makes police waste time when they should be . . ."

"Fighting evildoers?!" Connor's eyes widened. He looked up at the policeman with unabashed awe, and the cop's stern expression softened a bit.

Jeannie went on, "Yes, and policemen can't put, um, evildoers in jail if they get distracted by . . ." Jeannie paused, asking, "Do you know what 'distracted' means?"

"You bet I do!" said Connor. "My mom calls me that all the time." This drew a flicker of a smile from the cop.

Jeannie said, "Yes, great. Anyways, if you call 9-1-1 when you don't actually need the police, they get distracted. They can't get their jobs done, and . . . uh . . ." Jeannie faltered.

Connor blurted, "Evildoers might go free?" The boy finally seemed to realize his error.

Jeannie nodded.

Connor looked up at Officer Nelson, asking, "Did any bad guys go free 'cause I called you?" The boy's lower lip started to tremble. "I didn't mean for . . ." A tear slid down his cheek.

Officer Nelson said quickly, "Just don't do it again. All right, kid?"

Connor nodded and sniffed back a tear. "Yes, sir."

Maggie thanked the cop, and he left. Jeannie gently wiped Connor's tears away with the end of her billowy shirtsleeve. "There, there, sweetie. No harm done. It was just a mistake, an oopsy, a little fall. And what does your *Batman* movie say about falling?"

"What?" asked Connor.

Jeannie took his face in her hands, so she could look straight into his eyes. "Batman says we fall so we can 'learn to pick ourselves up.' You see, even Batman falls sometimes, but he learns from it. Okay?"

Connor nodded solemnly. And Maggie was touched. She wondered how many times Jeannie'd rewatched superhero movies—mining them for nuggets like the one she'd just recited.

Now Jeannie rose from her crouch with some effort, her knees creaking indiscreetly. So it was Maggie's turn to kneel down next to the boy. "Why did you call the police, Connor?"

Connor wiped tears away with his sleeve. "I didn't mean to. It's just, I did some bad stuff and then . . ."

Maggie asked, "What bad stuff?"

He looked down, saying quietly, "I broke Melissa's diorama." Then his head whipped up, and he practically yelled, "I didn't mean to do it! It was a accident!" Like most kids, Connor confessed softly but made excuses in stereo.

Maggie blew her bangs out of her eyes. "Okay, so then what?"

Connor went on, "Mrs. Pacer stuck me in time-out. And I started thinking about Superman, how when he was captured once, he called for help. I needed help too. So I borrowed Mrs. Pacer's phone and . . ."

"I see," said Maggie. "Connor, I think it's best if you come back to the office with me. Go into the classroom now and—quietly—gather your things. All right?"

Connor nodded. "Yes, Mrs. Mayfield." The boy slipped into the classroom, leaving Maggie alone with Jeannie.

Jeannie folded her arms against her chest. "Maggie, you know what I'm going to say on this one."

Maggie guessed: "Medication?"

Jeannie nodded. Fashion sense was not the only hippie-ish thing about her—she believed in 'just saying yes' to drugs whenever possible. She'd crop-dust the school with Ritalin if she could. She told Maggie, "That boy's a peach. But he can't sit still. And I'm not talking about minor fidgeting. This is beyond." In Jeannie's Brooklyn accent, "beyond" had four syllables ("be-yaw-un-da"). "It's ADD, plain and simple."

Maggie winced. "C'mon, Jeannie. He's only six. It's early to make a diagnosis, don't you think?"

Jeannie bristled. "I'll tell you what I think. I think it's unfair to my other students for me to spend half my time racing after—"

Connor reemerged into the hallway, and Jeannie immediately fell silent. Her voice suddenly gentle, she asked, "Do you have everything you need, honey?"

Connor answered, "Yes, Mrs. Pacer, but . . ."

"But what?" asked Jeannie.

"Can you tell Melissa I'm sorry?"

Jeannie nodded. "Yes, Connor. I'll do that. But maybe you should make a card for her or something. Draw some daffodils. She likes daffodils."

Connor nodded eagerly—grateful to be given some tangible way to atone. As Jeannie returned to her classroom, Maggie extended her hand to the boy. "Come with me."

Connor put his small hand in hers, and Maggie began the long walk back to her office.

14

MAGGIE'S DAYMARE

The condemned man lies helpless as a doctor inserts an IV into his arm. The doctor works with care so as not to cause any unnecessary discomfort, oblivious to the incongruity of this small kindness. An elderly priest stands in the corner speed-reading the last rites. Once the doctor finishes, the warden asks the prisoner if he has any last words. Turning his head so that he can see the witnesses seated behind the glass, the freckly, blue-eyed prisoner says, "I'm sorry for the bad stuff I did today, and all the other days. So now, it's up, up, and away." Someone flicks a switch, and poison flows into the man's veins.

Maggie roused herself and blinked furiously to erase her awful daymare about little Connor Bellman. She pushed aside her paperwork and reached into her desk for a chocolate, but then decided that wouldn't suffice. She needed the harder stuff. She'd have to go to her dealer. Though four o'clock had come and gone, she found Diane hunched over her desk, working on a flyer for the school rummage sale. Diane looked up and eyed Maggie's weary face. Then, without a word, Diane reached down and opened her desk's deep right drawer, revealing a massive cache of candies and cookies.

Surveying the loot, Maggie asked, "You got an Oompa Loompa in there?"

Diane deadpanned, "He's off on Tuesdays."

"Got any Girl Scouts?"

Diane smirked. "Yes, ma'am. I got Samoas, Thin Mints, Trefoils, Tagalongs . . ."

"I'll take . . ."

Diane raised her hand. "I'm not done yet. I also got Do-si-dos and a whole box of Savannah Smiles."

Maggie frowned. "You have a serious cookie addiction."

Diane feigned indignation. "Don't judge me! I don't have any office to hide in. I'm a captive audience to hundreds of Girl Scouts. You can't imagine that kind of pressure."

Maggie nodded solemnly. "Everybody breaks in the end." Then, taking a seat alongside Diane's desk, she said, "I'll take two Thin Mints, please." Diane retrieved the cookies and handed them over. Maggie took a bite of one and mumbled "thank you" as she chewed. As the chocolate coated her tongue, she knew she'd made the right wrong choice, diet be damned.

Diane asked, "What's got you down today?"

Maggie told Diane about her daymare, featuring little Connor Bellman's execution. Diane inhaled sharply, then murmured, "It's a vision." She crossed herself.

Maggie bristled. "Why are you crossing yourself? You're not religious."

Diane answered primly, "No, but I always liked that gesture. It's got oomph. Besides, I figure Jesus wouldn't mind."

Maggie conceded, "He never struck me as a huffy type."

Returning to her theme, Diane said, "You have the gift, Maggie."

Maggie rolled her eyes. "Please don't get started on that Psychic Friends crap." She took another bite of her cookie.

Diane countered, "Remember when little Abby Cofner broke her arm? Two seconds before she fell, you told me to check the playground. Some part of your subconscious mind knew that girl was in danger."

"No, what I knew was that it had rained and Mrs. Ryerson was too flaky to warn the kids off the jungle gym. Nothing paranormal, just common sense."

Diane shook her head. "I could go on all day with examples like that, and we both know it. Face it, Maggie. You're psychic."

Her mouth crammed with cookie, Maggie said, "If I'm psychic, then why didn't I know about Richard's indoor sports?"

Diane shrugged. "I dunno. Maybe you're not psychic with everyone, maybe you just have psychic links with your students. Or maybe romantic feelings jam up your frequencies."

"If that's true, my frequencies must be crystal clear these days."

Diane wiggled her eyebrows. "I'm not so sure about that. You and Homeland looked pretty cozy to me back in that hallway." Diane called Danny "Homeland" because he was a gorgeous redhead, like the senator-turned-fundamentalist-spy on that TV show.

Maggie waved this off. "We were *not* cozy. Just the opposite. We were arguing."

In a sexy, throaty voice, Diane asked, "Was it a *heated* argument?"

Ignoring this, Maggie pointed to the unfinished drawing on Diane's desk. "How's our rummage sale flyer coming along?"

"Don't change the subject. Our Homeland boy has real potential."

Maggie stiffened. "It would be unprofessional for me to get into a romantic relationship with—"

Diane balked. "Whoa, honey. You been watching too many of those Zales commercials. Nobody said nothing 'bout a relationship." Diane wrinkled her nose in distaste at the dreaded R-word. "No, what you need is to get laid properly."

Maggie began, "My sex life is none of your . . ." She wavered. It was idiotic to huffily assert boundaries with Diane. For years, the woman had served as Maggie's living diary.

Diane said, "It's been too long, Maggie. If you don't get some action soon, you might as well donate your snatch to the rummage sale 'cause you ain't using it."

Maggie sighed. "I need another cookie." Diane handed her one, and Maggie took a bite. "Can I see the flyer now?"

Diane held it up proudly. "Another masterpiece. They could hang this thing in the Louvre." She pronounced "Louvre" as "lube."

Maggie studied the flyer. It showed a pigtailed schoolgirl rubbing her hands together greedily as a dump truck unloaded a massive pile of clothes, DVDs, skateboards, and other loot. Across the top, the flyer shouted: "DONATE TO THE RUMMAGE SALE!—YOUR TRASH IS OUR TREASURE." Toward the bottom, the flyer read: "SUPPORT OUR STEAM TEACHERS."

Maggie smiled at Diane. "Brilliant as usual. We're going to make a bundle this year."

Diane brightened. "You think so?"

Maggie nodded. "The rummage sale's always a hit. Parents love giving us their trash. They love buying stuff too. I just wish they'd give us their cash from the get-go so we could ditch all this fund-raising." This was a sore point for Maggie. The district could fund all its STEAM teachers' salaries if every student's family would just cough up a few hundred bucks every year. Most parents did, but many—far too many—refused. A few couldn't afford it, and so far as Maggie was concerned, those families could go with God. But the other holdouts' fancy cars, McMansions, and collagen-injected trout pouts meant they couldn't convincingly cry poor.

Diane sighed. "You know they'll never do that."

"Why not?" Maggie folded her arms, as petulant as any third grader. She hated it when people wouldn't do the obviously right thing she wanted them to do.

"It's like the plastic bags, Maggie darlin'. This summer, they finally did the green thing and said we couldn't hand out plastic bags for free." Diane worked summers at Ralphs. "So June first, we started charging ten cents a bag, paper or plastic. Ten measly cents! Most folks were fine with it. I guess they got the memo about the Little Mermaid and her buddies choking to death like they're stuck in some underwater Beijing. But some people couldn't resist making a stink. The grumblers came from all walks: soccer moms, geezers, frat boys, you name it. They'd buy bags, but not until after giving me major attitude. Those people sucked. But what really balled me over were the idiots who just wouldn't pay for the damn bags. One guy—an older dude in a toupee—he bought four bottles of superpricey cognac, must've run him $200 easy. When I told him he had to pay ten cents for a bag, he wouldn't do it. He starts ranting at me about freedom and the guv'ment and global warming being a hoax—like he's putting on a whole AM radio show just for me. Dude tries to carry those four fancy-ass weird-shaped bottles using just his hands. He gets halfway to the door, and two bottles go crash, splat."

Maggie nudged her to continue. "And your point is?"

Diane said, "My point is—Maggie darlin'—people get monumentally pissed if you make them pay for something they've been getting free all their lives. Parents at this school grew up in a world where public education was free, no qualifiers—none of this 'some restrictions may apply' crap. They got it all: gym, science, art, and music, right along with the three Rs. Now, suddenly, you're telling them they have to pay. And they're just not having it. They'd rather do without."

Maggie shuddered. She rubbed her temples. "I can't talk about this right now. It makes me too depressed." She pointed at the box of Thin Mints. "Hit me again."

Diane handed over two more cookies. Dutifully changing the subject, she asked, "So, how do you solve a problem like our Connor?" Diane singsonged this to match *The Sound of Music*'s "How do you solve a problem like Maria?"

Maggie sighed. "I don't know, but I better come up with a plan. His mom's coming in tomorrow at ten. And Jeannie's already told me she wants him on meds."

Diane frowned. "I like Jeannie, but she pushes those meds like a Pez dispenser."

Maggie shrugged. "Jeannie likes an orderly classroom."

"Orderly's fine. But sedated?"

"Those meds do a lot of good for some kids," said Maggie.

"Oh sure, they're helpful—*if* you need them. But if you don't, whew, those things'll mess you up. You get nausea, insomnia, tics. Dammit, it's worse than being in love."

"I know," said Maggie. "But if Connor needs—"

Diane cut in, "That boy does not need meds. He can focus just fine. He must've spent an hour reading that *Batman* comic." After the 9-1-1 fiasco, Connor had spent the rest of the school day in detention. "Detention" meant camping in the front office's small conference room while eating cookies and reading comics—courtesy of Diane. If detention was kiddie prison, Diane was the "guy who could get you things," only for free and with a smile.

Maggie was skeptical. "An entire hour on one comic?"

"Sat just as still as my sister does when the check comes," said Diane.

Maggie weighed this news. She was no therapist, but she'd seen plenty of kids with attention disorders. Only a tranquilizer gun could make them sit and focus on one thing for that long. But that didn't mean some shrink wouldn't whip out his prescription pad. Maggie had plenty of respect for shrinks as a tribe. They'd worked wonders for some of her students, but she'd met more than a few who handed out meds to every third patient, like they were playing a pharmaceutical game of Duck, Duck, Goose. And parents—terrified of being "in denial"—often went right along with it, especially if no other option presented itself.

Maggie's job was to find that other option. "Maybe we should sic Mr. Baran on this?"

Diane frowned. "I don't think push-ups are going to get us out of this, Kemosabe."

Maggie shook her head. "Not push-ups. But maybe Connor just needs to get some energy out, the way you'd run a hyper dog in the morning so it won't eat the couch while you're at work."

"You think Baran would be up for it?" asked Diane.

Maggie grinned. "Only if we ask him."

Diane nodded. "That just might work. Hell, we might turn that boy into a model student. We . . ." Diane suddenly gasped and put a hand to her chest. "Your prison vision."

"What about it?" asked Maggie.

"Maybe Connor wasn't the death-row prisoner. Maybe he was the doctor!"

"A doctor?" Maggie considered this, then simpered, "How about that, a prison doctor! He'll make us so proud."

15

SHOUTING FROM THE SAME PAGE

As soon as Diane left, Maggie called Mr. Baran, the school's beloved PE teacher. He was a gravelly voiced, shouty man with a stiff, bow-legged gait and a formal, almost militaristic, manner. His muscles had muscles. But despite his jock persona, Maggie—like everyone else at the school—adored the man. His boundless enthusiasm and energy were hard enough to resist. But for Maggie, the clincher was his slav-ish devotion to his first and only wife, "the Judge." He called her that because he loved to remind everyone in hollering distance that she sat on California's "esteemed" Superior Court. Diane speculated that he called her "Your Honor" during sex, when he "banged her with his gavel."

He answered gruffly on the first ring: "State your business." Maggie laid out the situation, and Mr. Baran immediately barked out his diag-nosis: "No drugs! That boy just needs to move!"

Maggie said, "I agree."

Baran went on, "'A strong body makes the mind strong.' Thomas Jefferson said that."

"He did?"

Baran hedged. "Um, somethin' like that."

Maggie came right out with it. Would Mr. Baran be willing to work with Connor before school a few mornings a week?

Mr. Baran asked, "You sure the budget can cover this? I don't want to get in trouble with the union again." Union rules demanded teachers get paid extra for any work done outside of regular school hours.

"I'm sure," said Maggie. But it would be a stretch. Even with the Edutek grant, she'd have to scrounge for change under some budgetary couch cushions.

"Early mornings are for the Judge. I'll have to check with her."

Maggie began, "Of course. You . . ." A clunk let her know that Mr. Baran had put the receiver down on a table. She guessed that he must have trudged over to talk with his wife because she heard voices, his loud and clear, hers a murmur.

A moment later, he returned, "Motion sustained. The Judge doesn't hold with tranq darts for minor offenders."

"Excellent. I'll meet with the boy's mother tomorrow at ten. Can you stop by?" Maggie wanted to feel out Mrs. Bellman before exposing her to the gale-force power of Mr. Baran's personality.

"Yes, ma'am." Baran sounded like he was saluting on the other end of the line.

So Maggie said the only thing she could: "Very good. Dismissed."

Often, parents turned out to be like the dinosaur babies in *Jurassic Park*—they imprinted on whichever caring professional got to them first. So the next morning, Maggie arranged some alone time with Connor's mother before Jeannie could get to her.

Susan Bellman was a pale, mousy creature with big, trusting blue eyes and a strong lisp so that "Susan" came out "Thoo-thin." She apologized frantically for her son, saying, "I've tried everything. I've read tho many parenting bookth: *I'm Not Kidding Thith Time!, Mommy*

Machiavelli. Nothing helpth. My huthband thayth I don't dithipline him enough. He thayth I have to remember I'm in charge." Susan squinted in determination. "I'm in charge. I *am* in charge. I am *in* charge." She shifted the emphasis around as she practiced this impotent mantra, like an actress hunting for the right line reading. She finished, saying, "I'll do it."

"Do what?" asked Maggie.

"Medication. I'm willing to do it," said Mrs. Bellman.

"No one's said anything about medication."

Mrs. Bellman reported cheerfully, "Mrth. Pather did. No, wait, thhe thaid 'therapy,' but I knew where thhe wath going. Thhe called me latht night."

"Did she now?" Maggie forced a smile while a "FUCK!" banner unfurled inside her brain.

"Yeth. Thhe thayth loth of boyth hith age have attenthion problemth. And there'th no need for him to thuffer. Thhe wath tho nithe about it."

Maggie's smile was beginning to hurt. "I bet she was."

"I thpoke to our pediatrithian thith morning."

"Did you?" Now the banner said: "FUCKETY FUCK FUCK."

"Yeth, and he'th going to refer uth to a therapitht."

"I see." In Maggie's experience, therapists tend to recommend— guess what—therapy. In therapy, Connor's twitchiness would become a "symptom." And symptoms demand medication. And meds would bring gnarly side effects. "Side effects" were Big Pharma's greatest semantic trick. The phrase implied that a drug's benefits were the entrée, while its drawbacks were mere side dishes that could somehow be skipped.

Maggie hedged. "Therapy is definitely an option, but we might want to gather more information before we go that route." Information gathering, like therapy, was presumptively benign and could potentially go on forever.

Mrs. Bellman's eyes widened. "What kind of informathion?"

Maggie said, "We could check to see if exercise helps. Exercise often improves focus for our more active children."

Susan weighed this. "Maybe we thould try both—therapy *and* extherthithe. Come at thith problem with everything we've got."

Maggie stalled. "That *is* one way to go, but, uh . . ." Maggie knew this evenhanded approach would lead inexorably to therapy and medication. The "two options" approach defied several Parental Laws of Physics. First, the Law of Exhaustion—that is, parents have limited time, energy, *and* money. Pursuing multiple options exhausts all three. More importantly, there's the Law of Bargain Discrimination. If one option costs money (therapy), and another costs zilch (exercise), parents will overvalue the option they pay for and undervalue the option they get for free, figuring that if they pay for something, it must be worth more. This is a corollary of the Market Is Never Wrong Theorem (see Milton Friedman et al.). And, finally, the Law of "My Poor Baby!"— parents are phenomenally uncomfortable with their children experiencing discomfort. Accordingly, the quickest relief (medication) is always the best. Follow both paths, then fast-forward a month or two, and Connor's "exercise regimen" would be gathering dust in the attic (like much of Maggie's gym equipment), but the pills would stay. Nobody puts pills in the attic.

But Maggie could say none of this. She ransacked her brain for an argument *against* therapy, but came up with nothing. Fortunately, Mr. Baran saved her.

He entered and took a seat. Maggie explained, "I've asked Mr. Baran— he's in charge of our PE program—to sit in with us this morning. He might be able to assist us with Connor." Even sitting, Mr. Baran dominated the room. Energy radiated off him in waves. He sat ramrod straight with his hands splayed on the table, his chin in a perpetual jut, his lips pursed.

Mr. Baran told Mrs. Bellman. "I've seen plenty of tough cases. Sometimes, it's a kid with a bad attitude, but that's not what we got here. I've met your boy. He's a good kid. You're raising him right."

Mrs. Bellman brightened at this. And Maggie wondered idly why male compliments carried so much more weight than female ones. *Probably because us ladies are starving for them,* she thought.

Mr. Baran went on, "The way I see it, we've got ourselves a physical problem. To get Connor to focus, we got to siphon off some of his energy, redirect it. Tell me, what's the boy's sport?"

Mrs. Bellman said, "He doethn't have a thport."

Mr. Baran blinked rapidly, his brain seemingly short-circuited by the notion of a boy without a sport. He recovered quickly. "Great! We're not stuck with one game. We can try them all: soccer, basketball, tennis. We'll find his thing. Everyone's got some beat he can dance to."

After more of Mr. Baran's mini-infomercial, Mrs. Bellman agreed to have Connor work with him before school three mornings each week.

And as for therapy? No worries. Maggie would "make a few calls" to "her contacts" to find a top-notch therapist. Maggie said piously, "It's so important to find the right fit." What Maggie didn't mention was that her few calls would be aimed at identifying which therapists had the longest waiting lists for new patients. Sometimes, the best defense is a slow, tedious surrender.

16

BACK TO LUCY

Lucy's mother made her read a kiddie biography of Hillary Clinton. Mrs. Wong said Hillary was the "best politics woman" in the world, but Hillary seemed lonely to Lucy. Supersmart, but still lonely. She lost the election because she was not popular enough to get into the electoral college. Lucy wondered if Hillary went into politics to make friends so she'd have an excuse to talk to people and shake hands.

Lucy knew all about loneliness. She made a few more half-hearted assaults on Friend Hill, but they all ended in retreat. So Lucy was soon back to reading alone at recess and raising her hand in class to ward off boredom.

The only bright spot was science class with Mr. Carlsen. He looked like the type of man Lucy had seen in her mom's romantic comedies—not the dreamy leading man, but one of the unkissable guys in a montage of the heroine's failed blind dates. Somewhere in his thirties, Mr. Carlsen was a tall, spindly man with thick glasses. He sported short-sleeve, button-down shirts, clip-on ties, and a thick mustache that fascinated Lucy. It looked like a giant, fuzzy brown caterpillar.

Mr. Carlsen began by talking about the scientific method. "It's how scientists figure out answers to their wacky questions." He made jazz hands as he said "wacky," and Lucy rolled her eyes. Adults use exclamation points and zany adjectives to trick kids into thinking dull things are fun. Lucy raised her hand when Mr. Carlsen asked what "hypothesis" meant, and he called on her right away—which is what teachers ought to do.

Lucy said, "Hypothesis. A theory designed to predict or explain something. Hypothesis." Lucy's mom had made her watch the national spelling bee too many times, and it had influenced her phrasing.

"That's right, Lucy." Mr. Carlsen smacked his hands together. "Can anyone tell me how you figure out if a hypothesis is right or wrong?" Again, Lucy was the only one to raise her hand. Mr. Carlsen waited a beat, then pointed to her, "All right, brave Lucy, let's have it."

Lucy felt her cheeks redden. No one had ever called her brave before. "You test it. You do an experiment."

"Yes, ma'am. And that's what we are going to do today. We are going to come up with a hypothesis, and we are going to test it." He reached into his pocket, pulled out two matchbox cars, and held them high. "Who can tell me what these are?"

Lucy decided to leave this low-hanging fruit to her classmates.

A boy called out, "Race cars."

Mr. Carlsen pointed to the boy. "Correctamundo. Now, there's only one visible difference between these two cars: color. One's red, and one's blue. Raise your hand if you think the red car is faster." Everybody in the class raised their hands, everybody but Lucy and big Rachel Klemper, that girl who'd gotten into a fight on the first day of school. "Raise your hand if you think the blue car is faster." The other kids lowered their hands, but Lucy and Rachel did not move.

Mr. Carlsen pointed to Rachel. "I notice that you did not vote for either car. Why's that?"

Rachel said, almost in a whisper, "The car's color doesn't matter in a race."

Mr. Carlsen asked Rachel for her name, then turned to Lucy. "How about you, brave Lucy? You agree with Rachel here?"

Lucy nodded. She didn't like being lumped in with Rachel, but logic had pushed her there.

Looking from Lucy to Rachel, Mr. Carlsen said, "I'm not sure you've thought this through." He laid the red car flat on his left palm and ran his right index finger along its sides—as if trying to sell it on the Home Shopping Network. "This isn't just any red vehicle. It's shiny and has flames on its sides. Do the flames change your minds, ladies?"

Lucy and Rachel glanced at each other, both repressing smiles. Then they shook their heads in unison.

Mr. Carlsen eyed them warily. "I see. What if I told you there was another difference between these two cars? What if I told you the blue car is heavier than the red car? Would that make a difference?"

Lucy frowned. She'd never studied this before. Mr. Carlsen took another poll of the classroom. "How many of you think the heavy blue car is faster?" Half the kids raised their hands—Lucy too. "And how many vote for the lighter red car?" The other kids raised their hands. This time, Rachel joined them—thus ending her two-minute alliance with Lucy.

Mr. Carlsen said, "All righty, so we've got two teams. The blue team thinks heavy blue cars are faster, and the red team thinks lighter red cars are faster." Mr. Carlsen rubbed his chin and looked at them thoughtfully. "You guys seem pretty sure. Well, let's find out. Let's experiment." He strode across the classroom to a large shape concealed under a dark-green tablecloth. He whipped the cloth off with a flourish like a low-rent magician to reveal a wooden ramp with a yellow line down its center.

"We are going to race the red and blue cars against each other down this ramp. I need two volunteers to help me." He chose two volunteers. They immediately positioned themselves at the top of the ramp. Mr. Carlsen handed them the cars, then drew back, shaking his head in dismay. "No. This won't do. Let's spice things up. Let's give the blue car a little head start, say one foot." He had the boy with the blue car move the car down the ramp, drawing grumbles from the red team. Lucy and her fellow blue teamers smirked. Then Mr. Carlsen demonstrated how the Lord taketh away by adding, "And let's give the red car an extrahard shove. That should even things up, give the red car a fighting chance." Now it was the blues' turn to whisper angrily, while the reds gloated.

Mr. Carlsen stood aside and gave the "ready-set-go." The red car flew down the ramp, easily beating the blue car. Mr. Carlsen turned to the class, holding the red car aloft. "We have a winner!" Two of the red team boys high-fived each other, and Lucy's hand darted up into the air. Mr. Carlsen called on her. "Yes, Lucy, what is it?"

Lucy said, "That's not fair!"

Mr. Carlsen's eyes widened. "Why not?"

"Because Joey gave the red car a big push. He practically threw it." Blue-team heads bobbed in agreement. By unanimous, telepathic vote, Lucy became their spokesman.

Mr. Carlsen frowned. "Hmm, perhaps Joey's shove did tip the scales." Mr. Carlsen turned and studied Joey for a moment. "He *does* look like an exceptionally strong boy." Joey beamed. Mr. Carlsen continued, "I guess we'll have to redesign the experiment."

And so they did. Joey was instructed to push the red car gently. So now, the blue team won, making the red team furious. So Mr. Carlsen ran the experiment over and over, altering it slightly each time. After every race, the winners high-fived while the losers scrounged for objections.

At the end of class, Mr. Carlsen put the green cover over the ramp and said to the students, "So, what did we learn?"

Lucy raised her hand. "We didn't learn anything. We can't tell whether cars go faster 'cause of weight or color or pushing or whatever. All that stuff, and don't know anything."

Mr. Carlsen beamed. "Yes! If you design an experiment with too many different factors—we call those variables—then you don't learn anything. So tell me, if you want to find out whether blue cars are faster than red cars, what's the best way to figure that out?"

Eugene what's-his-name—Lucy'd never heard him speak in class before—volunteered, "You make sure the cars are the same, the starting point the same, everything is the same *except* color."

Mr. Carlsen said, "*Yes!* Give that man a Kewpie doll. And how do you figure out whether heavier cars move faster than lighter ones?"

Rachel answered, "You run a test where everything's the same except the cars' weight."

Mr. Carlsen smacked his hands together. "Yes! Brilliant, Rachel!"

Rachel smiled.

Mr. Carlsen told the class, "This year, we are going to run lots of experiments. And I want every one of you to be a world-class referee. Whenever you see me running an experiment that's unfair—an experiment with too many variables—I want you to call me out. I want you to watch every move I make to see if I'm getting away with something I shouldn't." The bell rang, and Mr. Carlsen said, "Class dismissed."

As the students left the classroom, Lucy headed for the front. She needed to know she was right. She needed the truth. "Mr. Carlsen, I know the experiment had a lot going on, but heavy things fall faster, right?"

Mr. Carlsen answered, "Well, there's two schools of thought on that, Lucy. There's a law, one of Newton's laws, that says weight doesn't matter at all. If you drop a heavy thing and a light thing into a vacuum, then they'll fall at exactly the same speed."

Lucy tried again. "Well, maybe things get weird if you drop them into a vacuum cleaner, but in the real world . . ."

Mr. Carlsen smiled. "Not a vacuum cleaner, a vacuum. A vacuum is a special, sciency place where there's no air, like in outer space."

Lucy retrenched. "Okay, so in outer space, weight doesn't matter. But here on Earth, heavier things fall faster, right?"

"Not necessarily. It depends on something called friction."

Lucy raised an eyebrow. "Friction" sounded like a made-up word to her.

Mr. Carlsen added, "You don't have to believe me, Lucy. You shouldn't believe anyone without proof."

Lucy remembered her manners and nodded. "Thank you, Mr. Carlsen." As she ran to catch up with her classmates in the hallway, her brain began to hum as she worked on how to get her proof.

17

HAPPY HALLOWEEN

Californians need holidays more than other people do—at least that's what Maggie thought. Back east, people had seasons to punctuate the passage of time. But in relentlessly sunny San Diego, life was one long run-on sentence. Without holidays, every day in San Diego would have been just like the one before it, give or take five degrees. A New Englander, Maggie missed the seasons bitterly: the fall foliage, the snow, even the "wicked bastard" mud season. She never mentioned these longings to her relatives back east. To Vermonters who'd been pistol-whipped by blizzards for decades, her complaints would have been about as welcome as Snoop Dogg at a KKK rally.

To give form to her students' monotonously sun-drenched lives, Maggie marked the holidays with pomp and circumstance, starting with Halloween. Teachers festooned their classrooms with decorations while Maggie and Diane tackled the common areas. The staff did all this on their own dime. They also hung black-and-orange "HAPPY HALLOWEEN" banners on the school gates, along with Dollar Store cobwebs, dangling ghosts, and oversize spiders. Paper witches and monsters were drawn with cheerful smiles, a fact that irritated Diane—who grumbled that the place was about as menacing as a Care Bears convention.

On the great day itself, everyone—students, staff, and even some parents—came to school in full costume for the Halloween parade. Maggie and Diane usually teamed up, playing Diane's ample height off Maggie's stunted frame. Maggie had been Frodo to Diane's Gandalf, Mini-Me to Diane's Dr. Evil, and Mike Wazowski to Diane's Sully.

This Halloween morning, Maggie greeted the children at the school gates as Little Red Riding Hood while Diane was gussied up as her tasty, ill-fated grandmother. The children giggled as Diane hammed it up, hobbling along on her cane and saying in her creakiest voice, "I remember when college was a nickel!" and "You want to see my enormous wart?" Meanwhile, Maggie tossed out costume compliments like confetti. For kids, compliments from "the Principal" carried extra weight. If Maggie was the queen, her compliments were like a down-market version of knighthood. She beamed as the children marched past. There were the usual Disney recidivists (princesses), Marvel superheroes, and old-timey monsters, plus a few genuine originals—a jellyfish made of an umbrella with streamers flowing down from it, a Marie Antoinette carrying a tray of little cakes, and a human fidget spinner.

To Maggie, Halloween's only drawback was her role as censor in chief. Her few well-publicized costume rules boiled down to one commonsensical principle: "DON'T SCARE THE LIVING SHIT OUT OF THE KINDERGARTNERS!" But every year, she had to turn a few kids away. She had to explain that little Justin couldn't parade about as a blood-spattered murder victim with a meat cleaver lodged in his head. And so sorry, but precious Brianna can't be a machete-wielding evil clown with fangs.

What Maggie couldn't censor—much as she wanted to—were the moms' costumes. The lingerie show had gotten increasingly out of hand:

naughty nurses, sexy sailors, and frisky French maids. No doubt, the slutty Supreme Court judge was on its way, with Ruth Bader Ginsburg's large lacy collar reduced to a bondage-themed choker ("You've been a bad boy. I'm ruling against you"). Maggie didn't mind these costumes in an adult setting, but in an elementary school?! She knew these curvy fortysomething moms had worked hard to "get their bodies back" after whelping their young. But did they really want to star in some confused fifth-grade boy's first wet dream?

The leader of the MILF brigade—gorgeous, buxom Felicia Manis—squealed in delight when she caught sight of Maggie. In her breathy voice, Felicia exclaimed, "Little Red Riding Hood?! I love it. We're from the same story."

Maggie smiled uncertainly. Felicia was packed into some sort of costume, but Maggie had no idea what she was supposed to be. The statuesque blonde wore a gray fur-lined hood, a matching fur-covered bustier and miniskirt, and furry white Ugg boots. She looked like a slutty Iditarod racer. Maggie stammered, "You're the . . . um . . ."

Felicia blurted, "I'm the Big Bad Wolf!" Then she struck a decidedly unwolflike pose, hands on her hips with her leg cocked so as to highlight her enviable everything.

Maggie said, "Wow! Those three pigs better watch out."

Felicia tossed her head back and howled like a wolf: "A-rooo." The geekiness of this gesture reminded Maggie why she liked Felicia so much. Then Felicia immediately snapped back into her other mode: doomsayer, leaning down and telling Maggie, "But seriously, I do *not* eat pork anymore. It's way too dangerous."

"How so?" Maggie girded herself against another of Felicia's revelations. Maggie loved her bacon.

Felicia reported, "The *New York Times* says pork can give you avian flu."

"Really?"

"Yes. You see, we import tons of pork from China every year, and they have practically no health regulations. I mean, the chickens shit all over the meat."

Maggie nodded thoughtfully, straining to give this grave news the reception it deserved. She did not say what she knew—that the US exported pork *to* China every year, not vice versa. She also didn't say what she suspected—that Felicia had not picked up this factoid from the *New York Times*, but had instead "learned" it from the movie *Contagion* when Gwyneth Paltrow's character caught a fatal virus by eating tainted pork on a business trip. Felicia had probably seen the movie, decided it "felt" true, and then assumed the *Times* must have covered it. Over time, this suspicion must have hardened into fact the same way a dinosaur turd can fossilize into a boulder. Maggie had been down this road with Felicia many times.

Diverting Felicia's attention to a real threat, Maggie asked, "Any luck with the snake fence?" Since deputizing Felicia to start a whispering campaign, Maggie had heard nothing. Usually, Felicia was a much more effective town crier.

Felicia sighed. "I have gotten all the way to nowhere on that. People just don't realize how dangerous snakes are. Also, I dunno, people are tight this year. The radio says the economy's getting better, but it doesn't feel that way here . . . what with the Gallcomm layoffs."

Maggie blew her bangs out of her eyes, frustrated. "I know."

"How's the STEAM fund-raising going?" asked Felicia.

Maggie forced a smile and gestured to the Willy Worm sign. "All right." The STEAM fund thermometer level had risen quickly with the first gush of donations, but there was still a long way to go. Experience had taught Maggie that once Halloween ended and Christmas decorations went up, donations would dry up until January. She was due for another tough slog.

Felicia pressed, "The rummage sale brought in some real money. Didn't it?"

"Yes, oh yes."

"So what have you got planned next?"

Maggie scrounged around in her brain for something spectacular, yet came up with nothing but old candy wrappers and pocket lint. She bluffed. "Diane's been ginning up some ideas. She's going to present them to the board. Good stuff, good stuff." This was only partly true. Diane *had* come up with more ideas. But they were all flamboyantly terrible. The latest involved shaming all the parents who had not yet donated to the STEAM fund by putting their names up on giant, brightly colored billboards—an idea she'd pilfered from her favorite movie: *Three Billboards Outside Ebbing, Missouri.*

Felicia opened her mouth to respond, but fell silent as Danny arrived at Maggie's side. "Happy Halloween, ladies." He had not bothered with a costume.

The women said their hellos. As Maggie felt the weight of Danny's gaze, her heart sunk. Standing next to gorgeous, tall Felicia made her feel like a troll. An awkward silence fell, and Maggie roused herself. "Where are my manners? Daniel, this is—"

Danny cut in, "Felicia Manis."

Maggie said, "You've met?"

Danny said, "Yes. Felicia stopped by HQ to introduce herself."

Grinning hard, Maggie said, "She did?"

Danny went on, "Yes. We had a lively debate about the dangers of too much screen time. Felicia had me on the ropes."

Felicia put her hand on his forearm, cooing, "Oh, that's not true, and you know it." She laughed a bit too loud and looked slightly embarrassed, like a woman laughing to cover up the sound of her own fart. Frowning up at her, Maggie realized Felicia had a crush on Danny. The thought rankled.

Fortunately, Felicia's son intervened. He tugged at her hand, whining, "C'mon, Mom. I wanna see Brian."

Felicia made her excuses and bustled away on her long, shapely legs. Watching her disappear into the courtyard, Maggie resolved to get back to the gym—as soon as Halloween was over. Or maybe after the post-Halloween candy sales wound down. Maggie never could resist bargain chocolate. Watching Felicia, Danny asked Maggie, "What's she supposed to be?"

"The Big Bad Wolf," answered Maggie. She added tartly, "Some people need a costume for that."

Danny grinned at Maggie. "You're much prettier than she is, you know that?"

Embarrassed, Maggie blew her bangs out of her eyes, saying, "Yeah, I mean, Felicia's only good-looking if you're into that whole gorgeous-ness thing."

Danny held his hands up in defeat. "Have it your way, Maggie."

Maggie changed tack. "I'm surprised you didn't bother to dress up today." She gestured to Danny's costume-less form. As usual, he looked like he'd just stepped out of a J.Crew catalog. For today's runway, he wore an open-throated, button-down shirt and chinos.

"Are you disappointed that I didn't wear a costume?"

Maggie sputtered, "Pff, I don't . . ." These conversations always went so much more smoothly in her head.

"'Cause if you want to see me in a costume, Maggie, all you have to do is ask."

Maggie said evenly, "I'll restrain myself."

Danny shrugged. "Your loss."

They stood for a moment watching more kids shuffle by in their costumes. During a lull, Maggie turned to him. "So, tell me, what can I do for you on this fine morning?" Maggie was like her school's version of the Godfather. People always wanted things from her.

Danny leaned down, saying, "Actually, if I could just have a moment with you, in private."

This caused Maggie to suffer a flash of déjà vu. Danny had said this to her in several of her more salacious daydreams. Giving away nothing, Maggie harrumphed, "Of course." A few of the teachers—including Mr. Baran dressed as Elvis—had joined Diane as greeters, so Maggie could be spared. She gestured for Danny to follow her as she walked over to the closest empty classroom, Miss Pearl's art room. Closing the door behind her, Maggie asked, "What's on your mind?"

Danny started, "This is a little awkward. It's, um, it's about our sampling group. As you know, we've designed our pilot testing to measure exactly how well the MathPal works for typical students."

Maggie nodded. "Okay?" She was surprised to hear Danny using teaching jargon. In education circles, *her* circles, "typical" was code for kids without disabilities. Kids with learning disabilities were "atypicals."

Danny went on, "But so far, we've been testing everyone at the school, not just the typical students." Danny punched the word "typical."

"So?"

Danny struggled on, "So, since we've designed the MathPal for normal—I mean *typical*—learners, we were thinking it would make sense, uh, going forward, to exclude atypical learners from our test population."

Maggie suddenly understood what Danny was asking, and she didn't like it one bit. "Let me get this straight. After two months of having our special needs kids work on the MathPal every day alongside their typical peers, you want me to suddenly yank them—*but only them*—out of testing. Is that right?"

Danny flailed. "Yes, but not in a mean way."

Maggie snarked, "Oh yes. So I should exclude them in a nice way? How lovely."

Danny ran a hand distractedly through his red hair. "Look, the truth is we didn't design the MathPal for disabled students. And we don't intend to market it that way. So, when investors look at our testing results, our scores shouldn't be brought down by . . . um . . ."

"Kids with special needs?"

Danny looked relieved not to spell it out. "Yes."

Maggie asked, "Since when am I supposed to make teaching decisions based on your precious investors?"

Danny frowned. "You say 'investor' like it's a dirty word. Let me guess. You're one of those holier-than-thou academics who thinks raising money—for its own sake—is morally repulsive, aren't you?"

Maggie shot back, "Money 'for its own sake'? Money doesn't have a sake."

Danny inclined his head slightly, affecting an Irish accent, "Oh, Saint Margaret. I forgot what a noble lass you are. But let me remind you of a wee fact you seem to have forgotten." He gave up the Irish brogue now. "On top of the cash grant my company gave you oh-so-generously, we also gave you guys stock. If the market likes the MathPal's test results, the stock price will go through the roof, and that stock I gave you will be worth a lot. You'll be able to buy all the gym teachers and crappy Halloween decorations you want. So maybe show my investors a little respect."

Maggie sidled up as menacingly as she could to Danny. "When I signed on to your little experiment, I was given the impression that the MathPal was going to be sold as a learning tool for *all* children, not just the problem-free ones."

Danny held up his hands defensively, like a tired shopper warding off a petitioner outside Whole Foods. "Look. I don't know what Arlene told you about the MathPal. But we didn't engineer it for atypical learners. Those kids have totally different needs. For Chrissake, that's why we call them 'special needs' students—it's right there in the name."

Maggie planted her hands on her hips and glared up at Danny. "Let me tell you something. Our school believes in a little something called 'mainstreaming.' Mainstreaming means including disabled kids in regular classroom activities whenever we can. We don't give up on a kid just because she's got dyslexia or high-functioning autism. We don't make them spend all day off in some special ed classroom like . . . like Rudolph's Island of Screwed-Up Toys."

Danny corrected her. "Misfit Toys."

"What?"

"It was Rudolph's Island of Misfit Toys. Now *that* was a great Christmas special. Jeez, can you believe that weird elf wanted to be a dentist? That was code for 'gay,' wasn't it?"

Maggie put her hand to her temple.

Danny tried again. "Look, I feel for disabled kids. I really do."

"I'm sure you do." Maggie's voice dripped with sarcasm.

Danny said, "What if I were to tell you that I myself am dyslexic?"

Maggie pulled back. "You're dyslexic?"

"No. But I could tell you I was."

"What the . . ."

Danny grimaced. "Sorry, that's ridiculous. I just don't like being the bad guy in a conversation."

"Then don't *be* a bad guy."

"I know this whole mainstreaming thing is fraught territory for you people."

"You people?" What a smug bastard. She would fire him from the cast of her more salacious fantasies right away.

Danny smiled. "Yes, 'you people'—principals dressed as Lolita."

Maggie put her hand to her cloak's neckline. "I'm not Lolita. I'm Little Red Riding Hood."

"Whoa. I don't remember Little Red Riding Hood looking like that." He looked her up and down. "Maybe my storybook was drawn wrong."

Maggie said flatly, "That would explain a lot." Okay, so maybe she wouldn't recast her fantasies just yet. But Christ, it was sick to be turned on by a compliment like that, right?

Danny studied her for a moment, tapping his fingers against his chin. "What if I had something to trade?"

"Go on."

"What if I were to drop our daily testing time down to ten minutes?" asked Danny.

"You'd do that?"

"I might be able to swing it."

This sounded too good to be true. Maggie raised her eyebrow at him.

Danny said, "Don't look so surprised. This is what you asked for. So I've been quietly looking into whether we can whittle the time frame down, now that we already have so much data."

Maggie was stunned. "You mean you actually listened to me?"

"Yes, ma'am. So, tell me, if I dropped it down to ten minutes a day, that would take some of the sting out of exclusion, right?"

Maggie thought for a moment. If the testing dropped to ten minutes, that would be a godsend. Jeannie Pacer would get back her poetry slam. Mrs. Brandl could cover the spice trade again. All would be happy in the land. And Maggie could cover up the special ed pothole by having the younger special ed kids spend extra time in special ed with guru Mrs. Jensen. Maggie eyed Danny speculatively. "You would drop testing down to ten minutes—for the entire year?"

Danny nodded. "Yep, so long as the testing excludes all kids with learning disabilities." He extended his hand. "Do we have a deal?"

For a millisecond, Maggie almost asked why Danny didn't just toss out the disabled kids' results himself. Then she knew—he couldn't do that. It was better for him, cleaner, if she culled the outliers herself. She would be the one responsible for their exclusion. She would be on the hook. But still, she wanted that ten minutes back for her kids. She could taste it. Maggie took Danny's hand. "Deal."

Later on, when Maggie replayed this scene for Diane, she berated herself for caving so quickly. Would the special needs kids be upset? Could she have gotten them a better deal?

Diane responded, "Wait a sec. Don't forget, the MathPal's a dud. I don't care how much Homeland brags about all its bells and whistles. A pebble doesn't turn into a diamond just because you put it in a Tiffany box."

Maggie said, "True. But even if the MathPal doesn't work, think of the stigma. I don't want the special ed kids to feel like they're different or . . ."

"The horse has left the barn on that one. Those kids know they're different. That's why they go to Mrs. Jensen in the first place. And you've done great work training everybody—kids and all—to accept them. None of them's been bullied. Hell, the rest of the kids go out of their way to look after them. Extra time with Mrs. Jensen isn't going to change that."

Maggie nodded. And she managed to eat just five, okay six, chocolates that evening.

It wasn't until the next morning that she thought of the one kid she couldn't discreetly off-load onto Mrs. Jensen: Rachel Klemper. Rachel was too advanced, too "typical," for Mrs. Jensen's class. But thanks to Rachel's official dyslexia diagnosis, she was too "atypical" for the MathPal. Maggie needed to find this Goldilocks a spot that was just right.

18

THE ART TEACHER'S BLUE PERIOD

Teaching was not a steady job, not for twenty-seven-year-old Sadie Pearl. As the ink was still drying on her teacher credential, states began gutting their education budgets. The profession became a terrifying game of musical chairs. There were only two ways to avoid having your chair yanked away: seniority credentials, and a role in one of the "essential" fields. As a newly minted art teacher, Sadie had neither. Professionally speaking, she was whipped cream.

So she roamed from one school to the next—fired every spring when the budgets came out, and hired again in late August, whenever some school suddenly found itself with a few extra bucks. Everywhere Sadie went, students and parents gushed about her. But it never mattered.

For sustenance, Sadie turned to the thin gruel of self-help books. She was desperate for someone—anyone!—to point the way. But only one book resonated for her, a book called *Flow*. It was written by some eastern European guy with one of those consonant-heavy names that looked like a bad hand at Scrabble. The book argued that the key to happiness, to a meaningful life, was to spend big chunks of time doing something that completely absorbs you, something that makes you lose all sense of space and time. You'd become one with the universe or whatever. Sadie had experienced snatches of "flow" at her easel, riding horses, even doing yoga—but those moments had been as effervescent as soap bubbles.

Her only reliable, lasting experiences of "flow" came when she was teaching. She never grew bored, because each student was a new puzzle, a new collection of talents and stories for her to tease out. It was like finding buried treasure, but a treasure that she herself helped to create.

Teaching was her vocation, but she was tired of being a refugee, tired of moving every year to whichever town hired her, tired of her end-lessly changing gaggle of unsuitable roommates, and, most of all, tired of the constant hum of anxiety and its growing list of symptoms (stom-achaches, nail biting, picking bits of imaginary lint off her clothes).

She wanted Carmel Knolls Elementary to become her home. So when Principal Mayfield asked—*pretty please*—if Sadie could give up fifteen minutes of her free period each day to "work with" Rachel Klemper while Rachel's class fiddled with the MathPal, Sadie tripped over herself to oblige. Fifteen minutes was an awkwardly short time slot, but Sadie was determined to do something meaningful with it.

When Rachel arrived for her first "independent learning" session, Sadie would pull out all the stops. She would unlock Rachel's artis-tic potential, however meager that might be. As big, ungainly Rachel settled at a desk, Sadie told her how "over-the-moon happy" she was to have some "one-on-one time with a student," to "really delve" into the arts.

Rachel sat impassively—a great Easter Island statue of a girl—and said nothing. She did not seem excited to delve.

But Sadie wasn't worried. She would put on a show no nine-year-old could resist. The first day, a Tuesday, they tried clay. What kid doesn't love clay? Survey says: this kid. On Wednesday, it was painting, another flop. Sadie figured maybe Rachel was lousy at art; maybe she was self-conscious. So, on Thursday, Sadie tried something idiot-proof—collages. No drawing, no skill—just cutting and pasting stuff that interests you. That was strike three. Rachel wasn't rude. She did as she was instructed. But she did it in a joyless, workmanlike fashion. Sadie was tempted to ask Rachel if her dog had died, but she was afraid of the answer.

On Friday, Sadie tried papier-mâché—a giant gluey mess that no kid could resist. As Sadie bustled about quickly gathering her materials, Rachel sat doodling on the newspaper that Sadie'd put out as a tarp to catch the mess. Sadie said over her shoulder, "So, any big plans for your weekend?"

"No."

Sadie tried again. "Not SeaWorld or the zoo?"

"No."

Working hard to sound perky, Sadie said, "Well, you gotta be doing something. You're not going to sit perfectly still in your room, are you?"

"No."

"How about TV? Do you like TV?" Sadie was annoyed now. Talking to this kid was like trying to take the pulse of a rock.

"Yes."

Sadie brightened. "What shows do you like?"

Rachel shrugged. "I dunno."

Sadie smiled as she put the glue pan down on the table and came alongside Rachel, saying, "So, I've already cut the paper into strips. Now, we'll just have to . . ."

Sadie trailed off. She stared in shock at what Rachel had doodled on the newspaper covering the table. As Sadie studied the drawing, she felt Rachel's eyes on her. It was like turning to find some long-sought-after woodland creature staring right at you. Sadie somehow sensed that Rachel would be able to talk more freely if she didn't have to bear the weight of Sadie's gaze. So, still looking at the drawing, Sadie asked, "Who taught you to draw this?"

"Uh, nobody," said Rachel.

"Is it from TV or the movies?"

Rachel said nervously, "No, nothing like that."

"You didn't see it in a comic, did you?"

"No, I made it up myself," said Rachel.

Sadie tilted her head as she studied the drawing. "How long have you been drawing this character?"

"A few months. I started drawing her over the summer. What do you think of her, Miss Pearl?"

"Do you want my real opinion?" asked Sadie.

Rachel nodded. "Uh-huh."

Sadie looked Rachel straight in the eye. "It's brilliant." She was careful not to smile, not to do anything that might come across as treacly. Rachel's eyes widened, and she broke into a big, toothy grin. Pointing to the drawing, Sadie asked, "What's her name?"

"Cora Breaker. She's a superspy. That book she's carrying has keys to all the codes in the universe, but only she can understand it. It looks like gibberish to everyone else."

Sadie nodded. She knew Rachel was dyslexic—so it made sense she'd dream up a hero who could decipher things no one else could. But Sadie knew enough to leave that little insight on the cutting room floor. Instead, she asked, "Can I teach you a few tricks—you know, to make her even better?"

Rachel nodded eagerly.

The next fifteen minutes did not just fly by—they flowed.

19

CUPID'S PENNIES

Maggie heard Danny before she saw him. As she walked past the door to the stairwell, an adult male voice cried out, "Ow, dammit."

Maggie swung the door open to find Danny standing there, clutching the right side of his scalp. Maggie asked, "What happened?"

Through clenched teeth, he said, "I dunno. Something fell on me." Then he took his palm off his scalp, looked at it for a moment, and turned it so Maggie could see. His palm had blood on it, not much, but still . . . blood.

Maggie walked over and peered up the stairwell, but saw no one. Then she looked down and spotted what had bonked Danny on the head: a roll of pennies. Maggie picked the roll off the floor and showed it to him. Wincing, he said, "Someone dropped pennies on me? What the hell, Maggie? This school can afford drone strikes? I thought you people were broke."

"We *are* broke," said Maggie. Looking up the stairwell again, she called out, "Is anybody there?" She heard a faint whimper. In her best "come-out-with-your-hands-up" voice, she said, "This is Principal Mayfield. I know you're up there. So come out now and explain yourself." No answer. Maggie added, "If you do, I'll go easier on you."

Suddenly, Lucy Wong's little pigtailed face peered over the railing. "It was an accident, Mrs. Mayfield. He wasn't supposed to be there."

Danny grumbled, "I'll be more careful next time."

"Lucy Wong, come down here this instant," commanded Maggie.

Her face full of worry, Lucy asked, "What are you going to do with me?"

Maggie pointed at the ground beside her. "Now!" Lucy ran quickly down to them, the squeaks of her sneakers telegraphing her imminent arrival. When she got to the bottom of the stairs, she stopped dead. She stood at rigid attention, eyes fixed on Maggie and hands behind her back. Maggie demanded, "Do you realize that you hurt Mr. Zelinsky when you threw those pennies?"

Lucy's eyes flickered to Danny, then back to Maggie. She repeated, more meekly this time, "He wasn't supposed to be there."

Maggie wasn't sure Lucy understood the magnitude of what she'd done. She said, more sternly, "He's bleeding, Lucy."

Lucy's mouth began to tremble with the threat of tears. "Please don't dispel me, Mrs. Mayfield. My mom will kill me."

"It's expel, Lucy—not dispel. And your mom won't *kill* you."

Lucy answered, "No, she will! She says it all the time. When they show stories about criminals on the news, she says if I make a crime, she'll kill me . . . then *she'll. Kill. Herself.*"

Maggie repressed a smile. She had no trouble imagining Mrs. Wong saying this. She'd witnessed Mrs. Wong's formidable temper.

Danny said gallantly, "Oh, I'm all right." Then, with the self-gratified look of a tourist to Kidworld suddenly recalling a tidbit from his phrase book, he added, "It's just a 'boo-boo.' Nothing serious." Maggie pursed her lips in disgust. She didn't plan to crucify Lucy, but let the kid squirm for a millisecond.

Lucy's eyes filled with tears, and she furiously blinked them back as remorse and fear square-danced across her face. Having seen countless children sob or holler in unrighteous indignation at moments like these,

Maggie recognized that—for a third grader—Lucy was carrying herself with stoic dignity. Softening, Maggie kneeled down before Lucy so they were at eye level. "Why'd you throw the pennies, Lucy?"

Sniffling, Lucy said, "I didn't throw them. I dropped them. It was an experiment."

"An experiment?" Maggie had never heard that one before.

Lucy nodded. "I dropped the pennies and a feather to see which would hit the floor first."

Maggie scanned the floor of the stairwell and saw a long gray feather in the corner. "What were you—"

Lucy said eagerly, "I wanted to see if Mr. Carlsen was right, if a light thing would fall as fast as a heavy thing. I thought the pennies would hit the floor first, 'cause they're so heavy. Only Mr. Carlsen says some old Fig Newton guy says no. Fig Newton thinks heavy and light things fall the same in a vacuum."

Maggie nodded dully. "A vacuum?" She needed a chocolate for this one.

Danny said, a bit too cheerfully for Maggie's taste, "Isaac Newton's first law of motion. Objects of different masses will fall at the same rate. But it only works in a vacuum, thanks to friction." Maggie raised an eyebrow at Danny, and he straightened his collar, smirking, "I'm not just a pretty face."

Maggie turned back to Lucy. Gesturing at the stairwell, Maggie said, "This isn't a vacuum. It's . . ."

Emboldened by Danny's approving gaze, Lucy countered, "Yeah. I know. It's not like a *real* sciency vacuum, like in a lab. But it's close. It's a long skinny place without air blowing. I mean, there's air, but none of those indoor, um, drafts."

Danny asked, "So, tell me, which landed first? The pennies or the feather?" These two were getting on famously now.

Maggie put a hand to her temple. "I fail to see . . ."

Lucy said, "The pennies landed first 'cause—"

Maggie cut in, "Only they didn't land on the floor, did they? They landed on Mr. Zelinsky's head." Maggie felt Lucy and Danny were not striking the proper tone.

Chastened, Lucy told Danny, "I'm sorry, Mr. Zelinsky."

Danny shrugged. "No problem. Anything for science."

Maggie shot Danny a withering "what-the-hell-are-you-doing" look. Danny mimicked Lucy's contrite stance, putting his hands behind his back and looking somewhat sheepishly at the floor. He did not bother to hide his grin.

Maggie said to Lucy, "I appreciate that you were trying to learn, but you can't go around dropping things down stairwells. You could have hurt somebody, somebody a lot less forgiving than Mr. Zelinsky. Do you understand?"

Lucy said, "Yes, Mrs. Mayfield."

Maggie pressed, "Now, please promise me you won't do it again."

Staring at the floor, Lucy said solemnly, "I promise. I promise I won't drop things ever again . . . in the stairwell."

Maggie squinted at the child. She sensed a loophole being punched in the fabric of her authority. "Or off the jungle gym."

Lucy looked up sharply, disappointment writ large on her face. "Or off the jungle gym."

Laying a hand on Lucy's shoulder, Maggie said, "Now, scoot back to class. Lunch is almost over."

Lucy stammered, "But what about . . ."

"Your punishment?"

Lucy shook her head. "No, what about my pennies?"

Maggie frowned. "I think it's best that I hold on to them for now. I'll put them in the June Box." Everybody at Carmel Knolls Elementary knew about Maggie's June Box. All year long, she confiscated any items used in the commission of an offense and held on to them until the end of the school year in her June Box. School-yard legend had it that the June Box was the size of a steam trunk, overflowing with tools for making mischief. Diane called it "the devil's footlocker."

Lucy bit her lower lip. "Are you going to call my mom?"

Maggie folded her arms against her chest and gravely studied Lucy for a moment. Maggie liked and respected Mrs. Wong. But Maggie was not ready to unleash that woman's high-pitched fury on Lucy for what was, essentially, an accident. That would be too much—like swatting a fly with a sledgehammer. After a pause—unlike Danny, Maggie could be steely—she said, "No, not this time. But *if* I catch you at this again . . ." Sometimes, it was best to let children's feverish imaginations fill in the blanks.

Lucy nodded. "Thank you, Mrs. Mayfield."

"Now, scoot," said Maggie. Lucy turned and ran back up the stairs to class.

As the second-floor door slammed shut, Maggie turned back to Danny. "How's your head?"

Danny put his hand to his scalp and winced. "I'll have a helluva bump, but I'll live."

"I apologize. We've never had anything like this happen before."

"Really? You've never had an accident at this school?"

Maggie sensed the challenge in his tone. "Well, of course, we have accidents. Who doesn't? But we've never had a student hurt an adult." Maggie had to qualify this, "I mean, yes, staff members get hurt once in a great while. Parents too, and relatives and . . ."

"Random people within a ten-mile radius?" Danny snarked.

Maggie grimaced. "Anyway, I'm very sorry."

"Thank you. I'm sure my lawyer will take that into account."

"Your lawyer?" Maggie startled as if she'd been goosed. Lawsuits were a curse upon the land—or at least upon the school district. Even the frivolous cases siphoned thousands from the district's meager coffers.

Danny's expression was grave for a moment. Then he grinned. "Nah, I'm playing."

Maggie said icily, "I'm afraid I don't enjoy that game."

"Let me make it up to you."

"How?"

"By taking you out this weekend," said Danny.

The effort killed Maggie, but she managed to say the words: "I'm sorry. I can't go on a date with you. It wouldn't be appropriate."

"Who said anything about a date?"

"What?" Maggie was officially lost.

Danny said matter-of-factly, "This would not be a date. It'd be strictly business."

Maggie frowned. What did "strictly business" mean? Was he asking her to play *Pretty Woman* to his Richard Gere? Because she was not up for that—maybe in her fantasies, but never in real life. "What do you mean, Daniel?"

He sighed theatrically. "I love the way you say my name. It's like . . . like you're about to send me to the principal's office."

Maggie cut her eyes at him, reflecting on how God makes all the wrong people handsome.

Danny said, "C'mon, don't look at me like that. All I'm asking is that you come to a soiree my investors are holding this weekend. Not as my date, but as a satisfied user."

"I doubt *you* have many satisfied users." There, Maggie could do innuendo too.

Danny clarified, "A satisfied user of the MathPal."

"But I don't *use* the MathPal."

"No, of course *you* don't. But your school does. You can tell them you think the MathPal's wonderful."

Maggie thought no such thing. But saying so now seemed neither politic nor particularly Christian. She hedged. "I don't *know* how wonderful it is. I don't have the testing data. *You* do."

Danny said airily, "All right, so no testing results. But I'm sure you can sing the MathPal's praises in some other way. After all, the kids love working on it, don't they?"

Maggie couldn't deny it. "It's popular. But that doesn't mean . . ."

"Tell me, how many other math programs can you think of that kids'll work on every day without whining?"

Maggie sighed. "I see your point."

Danny rubbed his hands together. "Right. So it's settled. I'll pick you up at seven sharp on Saturday."

"I didn't say I wanted to go."

"Of course, you want to go," said Danny.

Maggie laughed. "Give me one reason why I should."

"I'll give you three reasons." He ticked off his fingers as he went. "One, because you owe me a favor since I was such a good sport about this little incident. Two, because your school benefits if Edutek's stock goes up. And three, because you are simply dying to spend time with me." Danny fluttered his eyes at her with mock coquettishness.

Embarrassed and titillated at the same time, Maggie quipped, "You really are insufferable."

Danny leaned down toward her, and Maggie panicked. If he kissed her, she had no idea what she'd do. Instead, he asked, "Are you going to put that on my report card?" He wiggled his eyebrows. Was this man ever serious? Maggie frowned, and he said quickly, "Sorry, that was cheesy."

Maggie took a step back. "I don't have time for this. I have to get back to work."

"So that's a yes?" asked Danny.

Maggie said nothing. She turned and walked to the door. Then she turned back, saying, "All right, I'll go. But, like you said, it's strictly business. This is a professional courtesy, that's all."

"Yes, ma'am." Danny executed a surprisingly snappy salute.

Maggie rushed out of the stairwell. She hoped she might catch up with her dignity somewhere down the hall.

20

LIFESTYLES OF THE RICH AND BOOZY

Maggie realized her mistake as soon as she settled into Danny's pricey black Tesla ($140,000!—she'd googled it). As she swiveled to reach for her seat belt, her dress strained menacingly against her midriff. She felt a stab of bright panic as she pictured her side zipper parting like the Red Sea to reveal her Spanx-encased rump in all its glory.

This was Diane's fault! She'd goaded Maggie. "This is a swanky La Jolla party, not some lame PTA fund-raiser. It'll be packed with billionaires and rich-bitch trophy wives. You can't wear some bargain from Burlington Coat Factory. You got to bring your A game."

Then, with steely-eyed solemnity, Diane said, "Maggie, it's time . . . time for the red dress." When Maggie shook her head, Diane pressed, "You can't keep that dress hanging in plastic forever. And don't give me that 'I'll-be-daring-when-I-lose-five-pounds' crap. You've got to be daring *now*. Our bodies aren't getting any better. Someday, our tits'll be on the floor. So flaunt 'em while you got 'em."

Diane's carpe diem, *live!-live!-live!* speech wore Maggie down. Maggie stuffed herself into Spanx and a push-up bra that was a miracle of modern engineering. Then, for the first time in three years, she put on her red dress. It was a designer number with spaghetti straps, a close-fitting bodice, and a flaring skirt. Looking in the mirror, Maggie marveled at the glamorous stranger reflected back at her. She sucked in her cheeks, put her hands on her hips, and cocked her right leg as if she were on the red carpet. She spent the next ten minutes striking poses: aloof beauty looking off into the distance, vixen bending forward as if offering her boobs as an hors d'oeuvre, and—her favorite—sexy superspy brandishing her weapon ("The name's Bond, Jane Bond"). The one thing she forgot to do was sit down. If she'd done that, she'd have realized that the only movie character she'd be playing would be the Incredible Hulk—as she burst out of her dress with a crazy roar and carnage ensued.

Terrified now as she sat in Danny's car, Maggie held her black wrap protectively against her chest while he droned on amiably about who'd be at the party. Panic sirens roared in her head so she caught only snippets of what he said: "Walter Tilmore's place . . . major stakeholder in Edutek . . . high expectations."

She snapped out of her stupor when Danny asked, "Should I turn up the heat?"

"Uh, no. Why?" asked Maggie.

"'Cause you look like you're freezing. You're clutching at your shawl like a refugee."

Maggie laughed a bit too loudly. "Sorry, I guess I'm nervous."

Danny nodded. Tightening his grip on the steering wheel, he said, "Yeah, me too." And Maggie could see that he was nervous, but it had nothing to do with her. This Walter Tilmore must be one scary guy.

Maggie's mouth fell open when she caught sight of Tilmore's lair—a modernist behemoth of glass and steel looming high on a La Jolla hillside. Its huge plate-glass windows offered an unobstructed view of Tilmore's elegant guests milling about on all three floors. It was like looking at a gorgeously lit, life-size ant farm full of rich people.

As soon as Danny pulled up alongside the house, a valet yanked Maggie's door open and offered his hand—which she took gratefully.

She needed all the help she could get limboing her stiff, corseted body out of the Tesla. In a seamless chivalric handoff, Danny took Maggie's arm just as the valet let go of her. He led her up the steps and over the threshold.

Maggie quickly scanned the crowd, confirming what she'd suspected—that she'd swum way out of her financial kiddie pool and into the One Percent's deep end. Maggie knew little about clothes. To her, Prada was like Azerbaijan—she'd heard of both, but she wouldn't have known either one on sight. Still, she knew enough to recognize gob-smacking luxury when she saw it. The women at the party were all painfully thin and wore gorgeous dresses that hugged their gym-toned bodies. Their faces were carefully made up and had that bounce-a-quarter-off-it tightness born of surgical enhancement. In contrast, the men had allowed their faces to age and their bodies to thicken, within tasteful limits. The men's conservatively cut clothes revealed way less skin than the women's did, but their Rolexes and Italian shoes made it plain they'd spared no expense in tending to themselves. Maggie had to work hard to suppress a frown at the crowd's unabashed opulence. Obsessed as she was with her school's meager budget, she felt like a starving pauper walking past a bakery window stuffed with pricey cakes—she was both overawed and tempted to throw a rock.

But she forgot her envy as soon as she caught sight of the sunset through the living room's front window. The sun was melting into the sea in a riot of orange and purple hues, bookended on each side by La Jolla Cove's famous jagged cliffs. The vista showed pelicans soaring over the waves while sea lions frolicked on the rocks. Mesmerized, Maggie murmured, "It's beautiful."

"Not as beautiful as you," said Danny.

Maggie snapped out of her reverie. "Laying it on a bit thick, aren't you?"

Danny laughed good-naturedly. "I don't believe in stingy compliments."

"Or accuracy?"

"Accuracy is overrated," said Danny.

"Is that your personal slogan?"

Danny smiled. "It's on my family crest—over a painting of a magic eight ball. I—"

Danny was cut short by a loud, booming voice from across the room. "Danny boy—how the hell are you?!"

Danny turned and broke into a wide grin that did not reach his eyes. "Walter!"

As Walter Tilmore strode across the floor, his guests parted for him, murmuring unreturned greetings. Tilmore cut an impressive figure. A tall, silver-haired man in his early sixties, he had an impeccable tan and a whipcord-firm physique. He wore slacks, handmade Italian loafers, and an open-throated blue button-down shirt that accentuated his piercing blue eyes. He would have been handsome, but his eyes were set too close together and his mouth had a cruel cast to it.

As soon as Tilmore got close enough, he clapped Danny hard on the back. "How's my Danny boy?!" Danny smiled, and Tilmore's gaze floated down to Maggie. He leered. "And who's your little friend?" Maggie tightened her already viselike grip on her shawl, preserving the mystery of her neckline.

Danny cleared his throat, signaling Maggie's nonbimbo status. "*This* is Maggie Mayfield. She's the principal over at Carmel Knolls Elementary, our beta-testing site."

"Ah, the principal. Tell me, how is it having a multimillion-dollar company operating out of your little schoolhouse?" Tilmore said this in a singsongy voice, as if talking to a toddler. Maggie'd gotten this dripping-with-condescension reception from businessmen before. Moneymen often confused educators with the children they taught.

She shot back in her best rapid-fire staccato, "Which company? We've had several multinationals beta test their products on our students. Of course, those companies had less access to our kids, and they were more transparent with their data."

Stiffening, Tilmore said only, "I see." Maggie pigeonholed him as the sort of man who preferred women be ogled, but not heard. Tilmore turned back to Danny. "And how is the testing going, Danny boy?" In less than a minute, Maggie counted three Tilmore references to the old Irish "Danny Boy" tune. Plainly, Tilmore thought the reference was a witty one and intended to flog Danny with it.

Danny said, "Great. The MathPal is—"

Tilmore went on, "Let's hope this one actually works." Maggie suddenly became aware that two younger toadies had materialized at Tilmore's side. They nodded as he spoke, like sound-activated bobble-heads. Tilmore continued, "Your other projects have been all fizzle, and no bang."

Danny countered cheerfully, "They say that whatever doesn't kill you only makes you stronger."

Tilmore smirked, "Try telling that to a burn victim."

Danny wisely chose not to concoct any can-do metaphors about burn victims. He began, "The early results for the MathPal are terrific. I'm optimistic—"

But Tilmore was playing to his little entourage now. "Ah yes, Danny's *always* optimistic. I remember when I started backing you. What was that? Ten years ago?"

Holding on to his smile, Danny managed, "Eight."

"So that makes you what? Forty-five now?"

Danny said mildly, "Forty-four."

Tilmore beamed. "Forty-four. Too old to play whiz kid anymore. Heh-heh." He elbowed Danny playfully, then went on, "I remember when you first hit the scene. Everyone said you'd be the Steve Jobs of the education world, going to revolutionize the whole shebang." Tilmore shook his head at the absurdity of the notion.

Then, stroking his chin theatrically as if trying to dredge up some hazy memory, Tilmore said, "So, first you had the Grammar Caddie. Remember that one? Ouf, that went over like a rump roast at a vegan convention." Tilmore laughed at his own joke. "Then you had that reading program for babies. Toddler Tomes, right?"

Danny nodded uneasily.

Tilmore continued, "That Toddler Tomes thing was a complete fiasco. It made babies even *less* articulate. Intellectually, these little buggers were trying to climb back *into* the womb."

Tilmore's lackeys laughed obediently at this. One of them snarked, "The tagline on the ads shoulda been 'Toddler Tomes—just think of all the money you'll save on college!'" More laughter.

Maggie felt her gorge rise. She spent half her day disciplining bullies. But she wasn't wearing her principal hat here. She felt like Superman being forced to stand impotently still as he watched a bank robbery in process.

When Tilmore finally stopped cackling, he sighed contentedly. He placed his hand on Danny's shoulder. "And now, you've got the MathPal. Let's hope this isn't strike three."

Maggie said, "It won't be."

Tilmore raised an eyebrow at her. "Really? And what makes you so sure?"

Maggie blustered convincingly, "Like I said before, my students have beta tested dozens of programs over the years. But I've never seen them respond to anything as positively as the MathPal. They love it."

Tilmore raised an eyebrow. "That doesn't mean the program is actually teaching them anything."

Maggie agreed with this assessment, but Tilmore's cruelty irritated her. Channeling Danny's words like an ersatz medium, she bluffed. "Name me any other rigorous math program on the market that kids'll work on every day without complaint."

Tilmore shrugged.

Maggie was relentless. "That's right. You can't. No one can. There isn't another program out there that assesses student aptitude, designs individually tailored lesson plans, and entertains kids *all at the same time*." Maggie held Tilmore's gaze, radiating a level of certitude that a fundamentalist would have pegged as "a bit much."

Tilmore asked, "What do the teachers think of it?"

Maggie shot back, "They think it's one of the most valuable tools in their arsenal." None of Maggie's teachers had said this to her. But they had not yet taken the opposite stance, so Maggie figured she could pass the Pinocchio test.

Tilmore pursed his lips, clearly impressed. "Really? What's so great about the MathPal?"

Maggie flailed. "It reinforces things, many things."

"Like what?"

Shit-shit-shit. Maggie stalled. "That's a good question. A fine question." Tilmore looked at her expectantly. She sputtered, "The MathPal reinforces, um . . . number sense. Counting. Uh, cardinality. Algebraic thinking. Pattern recognition." Now Maggie couldn't stop herself. She felt like she had math nerd Tourette syndrome. "Measurement and classification. Um . . ."

Danny gently laid a hand on her arm, a physical "down, girl." Maggie said, "Well, uh . . . you get the idea."

Tilmore nodded. "Very impressive." He looked at Danny with new respect. "Looks like you've got a winner on your hands."

Danny did not miss a beat. "That's what I've been telling you."

Tilmore grinned triumphantly. "Sounds like I'm *finally* going to get a return on my investment in you, Daniel." Tilmore's minions mimicked his gratified grin and mumbled appreciatively. Maggie had never witnessed smugness in stereo.

Suddenly, Tilmore leaned down toward Maggie, and she forced herself not to recoil. "Mind if I steal Daniel for a moment? I promise, I'll get him back to you soon."

Maggie nodded eagerly, desperate to get Tilmore out of her personal space. Tilmore took Danny by the arm. Before the two men glided away, Danny looked over his shoulder and mouthed "thank you" to her.

Maggie smiled back, then realized that she was suddenly and completely marooned in Rich World. She had no idea what to do with herself. She tried to look purposeful as she milled around the room, like a society dame searching for her coterie of oh-so-intimate affluent friends. And then she saw it: a gigantic chocolate fountain surrounded by piles of luscious strawberries. Maggie felt a pang of desire in her empty stomach. She hadn't eaten all day. She'd been too nervous. She lurched toward the dessert table as casually as she could.

But then, she saw something else that stopped her in her tracks— her boss, Arlene Horvath. Arlene wore a slightly dressier version of her usual garb, a snazzy powder-blue pantsuit with an expensive-looking scarf. Maggie's mind reeled. What was Arlene doing here? Had Danny invited her? Maggie thought *she* was the only school rep here tonight— the satisfied-customer-in-chief. How many testimonials did Danny need? Maybe this really wasn't a date; maybe it was just business.

Maggie shrank against a pillar, praying Arlene wouldn't see her. Her last conversation with Arlene had been about as pleasant as a hysterectomy. Maggie'd laid out new strategies for STEAM fund-raising, and Arlene had bristled, construing Maggie's attempts to raise money as a sign that Maggie lacked faith in the MathPal and the huge uptick it would bring in Edutek's stock price. Maggie'd had trouble defending herself against this charge because it happened to be true. The conversation devolved quickly because Arlene identified so strongly with the MathPal that—in her mind—doubting the MathPal was tantamount to doubting her, which Maggie secretly did. Arlene struck back at this perceived slight by voicing perverse pleasure at the paltry sum Maggie had raised thus far.

Now Maggie watched surreptitiously as Arlene yammered away to a small group of women. Even Arlene had found friends at this shindig.

Maggie felt bereft for a moment, like one of the outcasts who ate alone in the lunchroom.

But Maggie's loneliness didn't last. Suddenly, she felt a hand on her forearm. The hand belonged to a middle-aged blonde in a shimmery, silver-toned dress. Leaning clumsily in toward Maggie, the blonde said in a loud stage whisper, "Who're you hiding from?" The woman's breath reeked of wine. Listening to her at close range was like having an entire barroom try to blow out a birthday cake at once.

Maggie hesitated for a moment. The blonde egged her on. "C'mon, you can tell Winnie. I'll tell you my secret. I'm hiding from *him*." The blonde—Winnie—gestured sloppily toward an impeccably fit, fifty-something man with a spray tan and a full head of hair that had been shellacked back against his skull. He looked vaguely familiar to Maggie, but she couldn't place him. Winnie slurred, "Thass my new boss. We used to be coanchors, but then he blabbed upstairs. Said I drink too much." Maggie's eyebrows shot up, and Winnie explained, "I *do* drink too much, but it's only because of him."

Maggie said lamely, "Maybe it'll all work out for the best."

Winnie narrowed her eyes. "Nope. He's evil, that one. A human canker sore. Channel 5's Kyle McKellen. We slept together for two years. Then, when he was through with me, he crept upstairs and told them I'm a souse. They busted me down to field reporter. I covered a knitting circle last week. You know how far down in journalism hell you've sunk when you're stuck holding some old lady's yarn? You're in the gutter, that's where. Nothing but turds floating by."

Maggie said, "I, uh . . ." She didn't watch Fox 5. Netflix had wrecked her ability to tolerate commercials.

Winnie continued, "He's gonna get me canned. He'll say it's all about journalistic integrity. But that's crap. I'm the real reporter around here, not him. I won two local Emmys, and him? Nothin'. But I'll get back in the anchor's chair, you'll see."

"I look forward to it."

Winnie looked gratified. "So do I." She looked off into the distance for a moment, as if suddenly unsure where she was. Then she refocused her gaze on Maggie. Her eyes suddenly grew large. "Where's the baff-room?"

"I, uh, I don't know. I . . ."

Winnie said matter-of-factly, "'Cause if I can't *find* a baff-room, I'm gonna *make* a baff-room. Know what I mean?"

Maggie nodded. She craned her neck and surveyed the room. She couldn't see any bathrooms or hallways, just wall-to-wall guests. Beside her, Winnie said ominously, "Oh boy, here it comes."

Maggie spun round and caught sight of a pair of French doors. She grabbed Winnie's hand and dragged her out onto a mercifully empty veranda toward a clump of bushes. They made it just in time. Winnie retched into the bushes while Maggie held the woman's hair out of her face.

When it was over, Winnie stood up, wiping at her mouth. Then, smiling at Maggie with genuine warmth, she said, "Whew. That was a close one. But we made it. Winnie lives to fight another day. I'll . . ."

Maggie bit down on her lower lip. She gestured to the vomit-soaked front of Winnie's dress. Winnie looked down too. Head down, she said, "Oh boy." Then, looking back up at Maggie with a sloppy smile, she said, "That's a lot of forensic evidence, isn't it?"

Maggie did what she always did—she took charge. "Wait here." She ran inside and grabbed a stack of napkins from one of the food tables. Then she ran back out. While Winnie stood uselessly still, Maggie used the napkins to scrape the vomit off the front of her dress. Maggie tossed them in a small chrome trash can, and then ran inside to fetch some water. She returned to dab at Winnie's dress with another pile of wet napkins.

By the time she was done, after a full twenty minutes of Maggie pawing at the dress, Winnie looked almost presentable. Almost, but not quite. She still had a big wet stain across her chest.

As Maggie stared at it, Winnie followed her gaze. Winnie giggled. "Houston, we have a problem."

But Maggie was in fix-it mode. She yanked off her black shawl and draped it over Winnie's slim shoulders. Then she tied the shawl's ends together so as to hide the offending stain. All business, Maggie said, "There. That should do it."

Winnie studied the effect for a long moment and then beamed at Maggie. "You are a genius lady. *Genius!*"

Maggie put her hands on Winnie's shoulders and fixed her with her best "listen-to-me-now-if-you-want-to-live" gaze. "You're not out of this yet, Winnie. Here's what you're going to do. You're going to take out your cell phone and call an Uber. Then you are going to go home and take a long shower. Then you get straight into bed. Got that?"

Winnie smiled, then managed a sloppy salute. She loyally took out her phone and pawed at the Uber app. Minutes later, Maggie put her in a car.

As Winnie settled back, she grabbed Maggie's wrist. "Whassyername?"

"Maggie Mayfield."

"Maggie Mayfield, I owe you big-time."

Maggie exhaled loudly. "Yes, you do."

Winnie patted Maggie's hand. "I will always remember you, Maggie Mayfield."

Maggie smiled. "I sincerely doubt that."

With the earnestness of the truly drunk, Winnie vowed, "No, Maggie. I mean it. I owe you one. If you ever need anything, you call me. You got that?"

Maggie nodded.

Winnie winked and motioned for the Uber to take her home. Maggie turned and made her way back into the party, confident that she had earned her chocolate strawberries.

She was headed for the chocolate fountain when Danny caught up with her. "Maggie, where . . ." He drifted off for a millisecond, just long enough for Maggie to realize that her cleavage was bared in all its jaw-dropping, red-dress glory.

Danny recovered nicely, "Uh, your wrap. It's gone."

Battle weary from the Winnie fiasco, Maggie was too tired to be embarrassed. "Yeah, I gave it to a friend. She needed it more than I did."

Danny said, "Sounds like you're in a generous mood tonight."

Maggie met his gaze and—for once—managed not to blush furiously. "Want to find out?"

Danny looked stunned for a second, then nodded eagerly. He took her hand and led her back out to the valet. He drove dangerously fast back to her house—then, once settled in, he shifted gears and took his very sweet time.

21

DR. SEUSS WEPT

Diane was worried. Maggie hadn't responded to calls or texts since Saturday afternoon. Thanks to the long Veterans Day weekend, it'd been a full two-day media blackout between the friends, an eternity on the Maggie-Diane timescale. The La Jolla party must have been a complete disaster. Maybe Maggie had tripped in her stilt-like high heels and taken a header down some fancy staircase—her big sexy moment morphing cruelly into an *I Love Lucy* episode. Maybe she'd cozied up to Danny Z only to find out that he was already taken or gay or—even worse— unattached and hetero, but totally disinterested in her. Or worst of all, maybe Maggie had chickened out entirely. Diane had plenty of stock footage in her memory banks of Maggie hiding out at home—swaddled in blankets on her couch and eating ice cream as she heckled whatever rom-com was playing on the Lifetime network ("Check his browser, ladies!").

But no matter how bad things'd gotten as Maggie mourned her turd-blossom ex-husband, Maggie'd never missed a day of work. She'd never even been late. That gal was as regular as Tax Day. But here it was, twenty minutes past the first bell on Tuesday morning, and no Maggie. And there were people waiting! Maggie's tiny conference room was packed with half a dozen busybodies from the PTA Art Committee. They wanted to talk about that national art contest the school did every year. Diane couldn't remember the contest's name— Aspirations? Asphyxiation? Something like that. Diane wasn't much for art. Museums made her sleepy. But the contest was a big deal for the artsy kids—so Maggie always encouraged it.

Diane had plied the PTA women with coffee, but if Maggie didn't get in soon, she'd have to send them packing. Diane dreaded it. PTA women always got real huffy whenever things fell through, especially Rachel's mom—Andrea "do-you-know-who-I-am" Klemper.

So, when Maggie breezed in at 8:35, Diane murmured a prayer of thanks to the God she pictured as a cross between a throbbing ball of light and Gal Gadot's Wonder Woman. Sitting down at the table, Maggie said, "Sorry to be late, ladies. Car trouble." Then, perhaps sensing that this was not contrite enough, Maggie added, "It *won't* happen again."

The PTA hens nodded sympathetically, all but Andrea Klemper. For the gazillionth time, Diane wondered how that hyperaerobicized, uptight creature had managed to birth the fantastic, and fantastically awkward, Rachel Klemper.

Andrea cleared her throat, calling the meeting to order. "So, Maggie, we wanted to bring you up to speed on the Aspirations contest. The competition will be really exciting this year."

Another mom, a husky brunette with a distracting beauty mark, said, "Yes, Spaxxon is sponsoring it, and they're promoting it like crazy."

Diane shook her head. Spaxxon's oil pipelines had sprung leaks on three continents, giving the world its first nasty glimpse of a tar-black polar bear. Many of the doomsday prepper websites were screaming about Spaxxon bringing on the end of days. So now the company was trying to rehab its name by sponsoring kiddie art contests? Diane didn't want to be jaded, but sometimes, the world only made sense through shit-colored glasses.

Maggie poured herself a cup of coffee, murmuring, "Great, great." Then, blowing on her coffee, she said, "I think we're really going to knock this out of the park this year. Our art teacher—Miss Pearl—has already collected a ton of entry forms. And the theme . . . Wait, what's the theme?"

A few of the ladies looked uncertainly at each other. Alpha Andrea answered, "Ideas Take Flight."

Diane blurted, "Sounds like what happens when you get a lobotomy." Andrea raised an eyebrow at her, and Diane shot back her best haughty look. Diane took most scolding as incitement.

Diane got ready to tune up on Andrea, but then Maggie made a strange noise—a cross between a giggle and a sneeze. Rubbing at her nose, Maggie said, "Sorry, some coffee ran up my nose. So, uh, tell me, how can I support the Art Committee with this?"

Another PTA hen started droning on. They'd need the auditorium for the big exhibition in two weeks. And the contest should go into the morning announcements. And then . . . Maggie made another weird noise and put a napkin over her mouth. Standing, she said, "Sorry, ladies. Something's caught in my throat. I'll be back in a minute." Maggie strode out of the conference room, and Diane went after her, mumbling excuses.

Diane caught up with Maggie in the ladies' room. Maggie was splashing cold water on her face. Propping her hands on her hips, Diane said, "You want to tell me what the hell is going on?"

Maggie dried her face and hands, studiously avoiding Diane's gaze. Pursing her lips, she made another one of those weird, strangled noises. Diane said, "Maggie . . ."

Then Maggie broke into a fit of giggles. Diane checked the stalls to make sure they were alone, then asked, "What's gotten into you?"

Maggie grinned naughtily. "Technically, Daniel did."

Diane gaped. "Did you sleep with Danny Z?"

Maggie bit down on her lower lip, then nodded wordlessly.

Diane brightened. "Oh, sweetie, good for you." She hugged Maggie, then said, "Give me details. Did you do it at your place or his?"

Maggie grinned. "Yes."

"Wait, which was it?" After the Richard debacle, Maggie'd sworn up and down that she'd never be able to bring another man into her bedroom. Too many painful memories.

"Both." Maggie started giggling again.

Diane flailed. "So, wait, in one weekend, you had sex at his place *and* at your place? Is that right?"

Maggie's huge grin widened.

Diane sputtered, "Did you guys mark any other territory?"

Maggie pressed her hands to the sides of her cheeks as if willing them to cool. "Uh, let's see, in his car, in my car, on the kitchen table . . ."

Diane laughed. "Jesus, you sound like Dr. Seuss. 'I would do him in a box. I would do him with a fox. I would do him here or there.'"

Maggie finished giddily, "I would do him *anywhere*."

The two women giggled. Then Maggie stiffened. "Oh shit, we gotta get back in there. We have to be *serious*." Maggie straightened her shirt and flared her nostrils, girding for battle.

Diane forced back her grin. She followed Maggie to the conference room, and the two women avoided each other's gaze for the rest of the meeting. Meanwhile, deliciously dirty Dr. Seuss rhymes floated through their heads.

22

An Unlikely Friendship

Lucy had decided that art class was a waste of time. She understood why people needed art in the olden days. Back then, portraits were the only way for rich people to remember what their kings and fancy ladies looked like. But now, everybody had cell phones with superstrong cameras on them. Why spend an hour making some goofy drawing of a pile of fruit when you could take a perfect photo of it in two seconds? It didn't make any sense. What would be next, classes on whittling? Candlestick making?!

Aside from its pointlessness, Lucy hated art class because she sucked at it. She did not know how to suck at something. She had no frame of reference, no experience with sucking. Okay, that wasn't true. Lucy sucked at making friends. But making friends was not "doing" something. Making friends was just supposed to "happen" to you, like being born with blond hair. When it came to *doing* things, Lucy was tops.

But art was different. Smart people were supposed to like art, to *care* about it. And much as Lucy hated making art, she knew there was something there. Miss Pearl always brought in big, glossy posters of famous paintings: blurry Monets, vibrant van Goghs, and wacky Picassos. Miss Pearl said these guys had changed how people saw the world, how they understood it. And much as Lucy didn't want to believe that, she sort of did. She did not understand everything that Miss Pearl said, but Miss Pearl's passion—her fascination—made her hard to dismiss. Every time Miss Pearl brought in a new artwork or taught them a new technique, Lucy felt something shift inside her. She didn't have a word for this feeling. It was a mix of wonder, weariness, and envy—like how she felt when her little brother started playing with one of her long-abandoned toys, like maybe he'd discovered something she'd overlooked.

Today, Miss Pearl had handed out markers and smudgy pastels. She did not order the kids to draw any particular thing. She said they should "express" themselves. Miss Pearl said "express" as if every kid had something waiting to seep out of her, like farts or breast milk. But Lucy didn't think she had anything trying to get out of her. And if she did, it wouldn't come out in a drawing. It'd use a trapdoor or something.

Now Lucy sat marooned at the art room's back table with the only third grader even less popular than she was: "Big Rachel" Klemper. Rachel seemed resigned to her outcast status. When they'd taken their seats together, she had not even bothered to nod hello to Lucy. Instead, the bushy-haired girl—Rachel kept her huge mass of thick black hair tied back in a low ponytail—hunched over her paper and began drawing. Restless, Lucy raised her hand. Miss Pearl rushed over, saying, "Yes, sweet Lucy, how may I be of service?" Miss Pearl had a stagy way of talking that made most of the kids laugh. Lucy recognized this as a trick designed to "put her at ease." But Lucy did not want to be *at* ease. She did not belong there.

Lucy explained, "I don't know what to draw."

Miss Pearl nodded sympathetically. "Some days, inspiration sleeps in." Lucy frowned at her paper, not sure what to do with this "insight." After an awkward silence, Miss Pearl offered, "Maybe you could try a landscape. It's hard to do detail work with pastels, but they're terrific for landscapes."

Lucy nodded and smiled. She knew she had to reassure teachers like Miss Pearl. They were very needy.

Miss Pearl added, "You don't have to get this one perfect, Lucy."

Lucy stiffened. Her mother had warned her that anybody who tells you not to be perfect has a secret agenda. Either they pity you or they want you to let your guard down so they can get you. Lucy didn't think Miss Pearl wanted to "get" her. But pity was worse. Lucy hunched over her paper and got to work. Out of the corner of her eye, she saw Miss Pearl touch Rachel's shoulder before heading back to the front of the classroom. Big Rachel probably got that whole "don't be hard on your-self" speech from teachers all the time.

Lucy huddled over her paper and began to draw a blue waterfall. She worked on getting the lines perfect so the water would look like it was actually flowing. It went well until it went horribly wrong. Lucy got that sinking feeling like when she tried to pour milk out of a full gallon jug. At first, it lands in the glass like it's supposed to, but then it's suddenly all over the counter. Lucy sat back and frowned, her face reddening in frustration.

Beside her, Rachel whispered, "Waterfall, right?" Rachel didn't make eye contact with Lucy. Still working on her own paper, Rachel spoke out of the corner of her mouth as if they were in a spy movie.

Lucy nodded. Then realizing Rachel could not hear a nod, she said, "Yes."

Still keeping her eyes on her own work, Rachel said, "Didn't come out right, did it?"

Lucy rubbed the sides of her temples like the lady in the headache commercial. "No."

"Try turning it into a girl's hair."

Lucy spat back in a whisper, "But it's blue. Hair can't be blue."

"It can for the right girl." Still no eye contact from Rachel, but Lucy saw a smile flicker on her face.

Lucy studied the botched waterfall for a moment. It *would* make good hair for the left side of some edgy girl's head. Lucy quickly drew a matching waterfall for the right side, then a face, then the eyes. The first eye came out fine, but the pastel color on the second eye got all runny. Lucy's sweaty hand had smeared it. She started fuming again.

Rachel glanced at Lucy's paper, whispering, "You can fix that."

"How? People don't have runny eyes."

"People with allergies do," said Rachel.

"So I'm drawing a Claritin commercial?"

Rachel smiled, then shook her head. Putting her hand to her mouth as if she were about to cough, she whispered, "Change the blotchy eye into an eye patch, like she's a pirate."

Lucy did as Rachel suggested, and it worked. Then Lucy filled in the rest of the girl's face. As she worked on the mouth, Rachel told her, "Don't do a smile. She's not a Girl Scout."

"What do I do?"

"Make a sneer. She's got to be fierce." Rachel turned and modeled her best sneer. Lucy mirrored her, and the two girls giggled, then turned back to their work.

Miss Pearl announced, "Five minutes!"

Lucy rushed to fill in the pirate girl's neck and torso. She drew a skirt so she wouldn't have to draw the legs. Lucy was terrible at drawing legs, hands too. The hands she drew always came out tiny or like giant oven mitts. She started to work on the hands when she heard Rachel again. "Do hooks. Hands take too much time."

Lucy nodded. She drew a gratifyingly sharp hook. It was perfect. Lucy started on the second hook, then paused. As if reading Lucy's mind, Rachel said, "Maybe do something else for the other hand. Something funny. Like a hook holding a sign—a 'STOP' sign or 'NO DOGS ALLOWED.'"

Lucy grinned. "How about 'NO TALKING IN THE LIBRARY'?"

Rachel giggled and gave her two thumbs-up. So Lucy drew the 'NO TALKING IN THE LIBRARY' sign. Then she sat back and studied her work. She loved it. The pirate girl's mean expression and menacing hook worked beautifully with the library sign.

Beside her, Rachel said, "That *is* awesome. What's her backstory?"

Lucy said, "She used to be a librarian in a small town. But she got mad 'cause the kids in the library wouldn't be quiet."

"They pushed her too far," said Rachel.

Lucy nodded. "Yes, so she turned to crime on the high seas. Yarrr!"

"I love it."

"I know, right?" Lucy glowed with accomplishment. As she studied her handiwork, she decided maybe she wasn't so terrible at art after all. Maybe she was brilliant at it. Maybe her art talents had been roiling under the surface for years, just waiting to spew out. Maybe . . .

But then she saw Rachel's paper. It showed an orangutan crouching on the jungle floor next to a little girl. Lucy recognized the ape as an orangutan because of its reddish hair, long arms, and those puffy cheek pads that make orangutan faces look like catcher's mitts. The little girl beside it was sitting with her eyes closed, her face jutting forward expectantly. She was smiling, as though waiting for the go-ahead to open her eyes and unwrap a present. Only there was no present. Instead, the orangutan was reaching out and touching the girl's closed eyelid. The gentleness of the ape's expression and the girl's obvious delight made it plain that this touch was welcome. Miss Pearl's pastels made all the colors pop—the green of the jungle, the orange brown of the orangutan's hair, the pink of the girl's cheeks. And Rachel had used markers to draw in the finer details—the orangutan's dark, soulful eyes, the lines of its extended hand, the girl's eyelashes.

Lucy studied the drawing. "Why's the orangutan touching her eye?"

"It's how orangutans say hello to friends. It's how they show they trust each other."

Lucy could feel Rachel watching her, waiting for her reaction. Lucy said—in a hushed voice—"It's the most beautiful drawing in human history." Then Lucy frowned, not because she wasn't happy for Rachel. She *was* happy for Rachel, but she was also unhappy because she knew she could never make a drawing like that.

Rachel muttered an embarrassed thanks.

Lucy said, "I won't let you touch my eye. Because that's gross. But can we sit together at lunch?"

Rachel grinned. "Yeah. Let's do that."

Now Lucy grinned too. Her mother had always told her that she was lonely 'cause she was "best" at everything. But Mrs. Wong had also promised that—someday—Lucy would be friends with "other best people." Rachel looked like "best people" to Lucy.

23

KEEPING UP APPEARANCES—JUST BARELY

Maggie sang along with Beyoncé as she parked in her usual spot, the one marked "RESERVED FOR PRINCIPAL." As she emerged from her car, Starbucks cup in hand, Danny called out from across the empty lot, "Good morning, Principal Mayfield!" He shout-sang this, as if he were one of a giant crowd of children greeting her.

Maggie called back, "Morning!"

Danny rushed across the lot, slowed down only by his matching coffee cup. As soon as he got within striking distance, he kissed her on the lips. Maggie drew back quickly, scolding through clenched teeth, "Daniel . . ."

He laughed. "There's nobody here yet."

She looked around nervously. "Still, we've talked about this."

Danny pretended to look pained. Like an affronted soap opera character, he said, "I know, I'm just not used to being"—he pivoted here to look straight into camera no. 2—"someone's dirty secret."

Working hard to hold on to her indignation, Maggie asked, "Don't make jokes. How do you think the PTA moms would react if they found out I'm seeing you?"

Danny flicked up his collar like a smarmy 1980s star. "They'd be crazy jealous."

"Really?"

Danny smirked. "No woman can resist Danny Z."

Maggie raised an eyebrow. "So Danny Z likes to talk about himself in the third person now?"

"Yes, Danny Z does." Then he smiled at her, falling out of character. He leaned in for another kiss.

Maggie forced herself to step back. "The PTA moms would *not* be jealous. They'd be livid . . . and okay, some of them might get a little jealous. But 'livid' would be the headline."

"Not livid!" Danny put his hands to his face in mock horror.

Maggie's shoulders sank. "You don't take my job very seriously, do you?"

"I *do* take it seriously. I take everything about this situation seriously." Suddenly, his big brown eyes were full of earnestness, and Maggie felt a hitch in her chest. She wanted to dance from foot to foot and squeal, "You mean *us*, right? You're serious about *us*!" But she controlled herself. She looked at him evenly and said, "Good. That's, um, very . . ." She flailed, wishing for the gazillionth time that God would use cue cards. "You know, I'm not the only one who should care about appearances. It should be a real worry for you too."

Danny frowned. "I'm not sure I follow."

Maggie pressed, "What would your investors think if they find out we're, um, together?"

Danny wiggled his eyebrows. "They'd think I'm a lucky bastard."

"No, really, what would they think?" Maggie's voice cracked slightly. She knew Danny's investors' opinions governed his psyche more than those of any parent.

He eyed her shrewdly, as if sizing her up, then said, "They'd approve. You gotta remember, Maggie. I work in Silicon Valley, not down here.

Now, in San Diego, dating a bimbo is a prestige move, but not in Silicon Valley. Tech CEOs like to partner up with women of substance."

"They do?" asked Maggie.

"Yes, ma'am. Mark Zuckerberg married a doctor. Bill Gates's wife was a project manager at Microsoft, and now she practically runs the Gates Foundation. Steve Jobs's wife went to Wharton. All of them, heavy hitters."

"Whoa, are you telling me I'm not qualified to date you?"

"Are you kidding? You graduated from Columbia University, and you run a school on your own. Résumé-wise, you kick ass."

Maggie drew back. "Wait, how'd you know I went to Columbia?"

Danny shrugged. "I googled you."

Maggie frowned, feeling both flattered and obscurely spied on. "I'm not sure I like being googled."

"Why not?"

Maggie wrinkled her nose. "I dunno. The stuff on the web is all résumé stuff. I want to make sure you like me for the right reasons."

Danny grinned. "Trust me, I like you for all the wrong reasons." She was about to object, but he disarmed her by reaching out and pushing a stray lock of hair behind her ear. Then he let his hand linger on her face.

Maggie felt something lurch inside her again. "You're going to get me in big trouble, mister." She leaned in to kiss him, but then jumped back at the sound of a car pulling into the lot.

It was Jeannie Pacer's car—a battered blue Subaru with a bumper sticker that read: "FEELING CAT-TASTIC!" Jeannie parked in one of the designated teacher spots, less than a hundred yards from where Maggie stood. As Jeannie got out of her car, Maggie said loudly to Danny, "I'm not sure the district will go along with you on that. I'll have to check with Arlene."

Danny grinned wolfishly down at Maggie, and—for a millisecond—she worried he wouldn't play along. But then he said in his best, overloud businessman-doing-business voice, "Thank you, I would appreciate that." At the sound of Jeannie's approaching footsteps, he pivoted, saying, "Why, hello there. Beautiful morning, isn't it?"

Jeannie said primly, "It'll do." Jeannie was one of the few teachers Danny had not managed to win over.

She stopped just a few feet away from the noncouple couple. And Maggie said, "Morning, Jeannie. Is there something I can do for you?"

Jeannie said to Maggie, "I was hoping we could talk—alone." She eyed Danny as she said this.

"Certainly," said Maggie. "Mr. Zelinsky and I were just wrapping things up."

Danny nodded. "Good day, ladies." He turned and started walking toward Edutek HQ.

Jeannie said, "We need to talk about Connor. Mr. Baran's great, but I don't think we can Jazzercise our way out of this one. It's been two weeks, and the boy still can't . . ." Maggie watched over Jeannie's shoulder as Danny strode away. Her fear of getting caught had evaporated only to be replaced with a dreamy, distracted horniness.

As if sensing Maggie's eyes on him, Danny suddenly stopped and turned. He was a good two hundred yards away. He gave Maggie one of his devilish looks, and Maggie shook her head, her mind screaming, *"Don't do it!"*

Back on Earth, Jeannie droned on, "I try to stay centered, but yoga can only do so much . . ."

With Jeannie's back to him, Danny put one hand over his heart and used the other to reach out toward her melodramatically.

Maggie sucked in her cheeks and closed her eyes for a moment to keep from laughing. Jeannie continued, "Maggie, I know it's not pleasant, but we've got to face this . . ." Maggie forced her eyes back open.

Now Danny was blowing kisses, pantomiming as hugely as he could. Maggie flared her nostrils and bit at her cheek, willing herself to stay serious. A small squeak escaped her lips. Jeannie touched her arm. "Are you all right?"

Maggie put her hand to her temples for a moment until she regained control of herself. Then, when she felt safe enough, she said, "Sorry. I've been fighting a cold. I didn't want to sneeze on you. It's a nasty bug. I was up all night with it." She noted that—mercifully—Danny had finally disappeared from view.

Her monologue interrupted, Jeannie leaned back and studied Maggie. "I wasn't going to say anything. But you *do* look worn-out."

Maggie repressed a smile as the source of her fatigue pranced through her brain. "So, Connor's sessions with Mr. Baran haven't helped at all?"

"No, it's been a complete bust." Jeannie did not need to add "I told you so." Her barely repressed smirk shouted that for her.

Maggie's mind raced. Connor was scheduled to have his first therapy appointment in a few weeks. With Jeannie pushing for meds and Connor's highly suggestible mom on board, Connor would be whisked away on the Ritalin dragon. Maggie didn't think the boy belonged on meds, but what could she do?

It was all up to Mr. Baran now.

24

UNLOCKING CONNOR

Muscly, graying Joe Baran believed fervently in two things: the transformative power of sports and the wisdom of his wife, the Right Honorable Ella T. Baran of California's Superior Court. At home, she was Ella. But when Mr. Baran quoted her to others—as he often did—she was always "the Judge."

One chilly evening in late November, after Joe Baran's usual seven-mile run, he'd paced across his living room rug, venting to the Judge about little Connor Bellman. The Judge—a prim, small-boned woman with large, owlish eyes—ignored the stack of legal briefs on her lap and listened intently to her husband. This was not hard for her to do. Joe Baran was an inveterate optimist. Seeing him in despair did not qualify as a treat, but it was a compelling break from his usual, scheduled programming of relentless positivity.

This was a crisis. Connor Bellman was testing Joe Baran's faith. Joe Baran was one of sports' high priests. He had borne witness to its many miracles. He'd seen sports teach spoiled little me-monkeys teamwork, reshape doughy kids' bodies, and give semidelinquents legitimate goals. He'd even seen it make workaholic dads set down their iPhones and actually watch their children at play.

Mr. Baran thought sports could save anyone. Depressed? Do some laps and boost your happy-chemical endorphins. Lonely? Join a team and make instant friends. Restless like Connor? Wear that antsy-ness right out of the boy, and he'll focus like a sumo wrestler at a buffet. The hard part—the part that required Mr. Baran's unique expertise—was matching a kid to his or her particular sport. Not just any sport would do. Kids were like old-timey windup toys. They'd hum and come to life, but only if you used the right key.

But after weeks of one-on-one sessions every morning before school, Mr. Baran still hadn't managed to find Connor's key. Knowing the boy's attention flickered like a strobe light, Mr. Baran had started Connor off on racket sports: tennis and Ping-Pong. Hitting the ball to and fro required relentless movement and concentration. No lulls—lulls invite daydreaming. But Connor didn't need lulls to pull away his attention. Anything could do that: a brightly colored car, a low-flying bird, a silly sound he'd heard. Mr. Baran had lost two days to arm farts. Arm farts! Connor hadn't made the arm farts himself. No, it was just the thought of arm farts that threw the boy into bouts of helpless giggling. Then giggling made Connor think of the Joker, then on to Batman, and then that episode where . . .

From there, Mr. Baran moved on to basketball, soccer, karate, hockey, and then T-ball. Every sport reminded Connor of something else, and that something else led to another detour until Connor ended up standing stock-still, babbling whatever free-form, superhero-laden story lines came into his addled brain. Mr. Baran could never siphon off Connor's boundless physical energy because he could never get the boy to concentrate on chasing a ball or running or anything else for that matter.

Exasperated, Mr. Baran told the Judge, "That kid's brain is like confetti. It's all over the place. I can't get him to focus."

The Judge cleared her throat and pushed her glasses up the bridge of her nose—her signal that she'd heard all she needed and was ready to render a decision. Joe Baran stopped pacing and looked expectantly at his wife. "It sounds like the boy *does* have a focus, a very intense focus." The Judge's voice was as mellifluous as her husband's was gravelly.

Mr. Baran frowned. "I just told you, he can't concentrate on any game for more than—"

The Judge smiled. "I didn't say he focuses on *your* sports, only that he has a clear, consistent focus."

Mr. Baran took a deep breath and blew it out hard, making his lips flutter. The Judge was doing her cryptic Yoda thing again. "Ella, I don't know where you're going with this, but that boy—"

The Judge interrupted, with a slight edge to her tone, "Permission to treat the witness as hostile?"

Mr. Baran snapped his shorts' elastic waistband against his washboard abs and grumbled, "Permission granted."

The Judge perked up, straightening in her seat. "You say that when you tried to teach Connor tennis, he ended up spending half the lesson talking about Batman and the Joker, is that correct?"

Mr. Baran nodded, then—realizing the imaginary stenographer could not hear a nod—he said, "Correct."

"And when you tried to teach him basketball, he said the smack of the ball against the pavement reminded him of the sounds that Spider-Man makes when he hits bad guys, is that right?"

"Yes," answered Mr. Baran.

"And your swing-dance lesson made the boy think of Captain America's dance with Agent Carter, is that also right?" asked the Judge.

"Yes."

"So virtually every lesson you've had with Connor has been derailed by talk of superheroes, correct?"

Mr. Baran said hesitantly, "Yyy-yes."

"So, would it be fair to say, based on weeks of lessons, that Connor is in fact very focused on the subject of superheroes?"

"Yeah, but how does that help me get him moving?" Mr. Baran's impatience mounted.

The Judge grinned. "Darling, if you want the boy to concentrate, don't make the lesson about sports. Make it about superheroes."

Mr. Baran nodded, mentally sprinting—as he often did—from skepticism to total acceptance of his wife's advice. A lesser man might have been intimidated by such a brilliant wife. But Mr. Baran was smart enough to be grateful for her. He spent the rest of the evening on the internet, studying superheroes and their backstories.

◆ ◆ ◆

The next morning, Mr. Baran did not turn around immediately when Connor greeted him on the soccer field. Instead, he stood looking off into the distance, his hands planted on hips in the classic superhero stance. Connor asked, "What's the game today, Mr. Baran?"

Mr. Baran looked down at the boy, deadpanning, "This is no game. This is life and death. Today, you're not first grader Connor Bellman. Today, you . . . are . . . Spider-Man." Mr. Baran unfurled the Spider-Man T-shirt he'd had balled up in his fist, and Connor's face lit up. Mr. Baran put the shirt on over Connor's head, and the suddenly serious Connor gazed out across the field, mimicking Mr. Baran's pompous stance.

Connor asked, "What's my mission?"

"The Green Goblin has captured someone. He's holding her hostage somewhere. And you're the only one who can find her. Are you up to the challenge?"

Connor flared his nostrils, his blue eyes full of determination. "I was born for challenges like this."

"But wait, Spidey. This isn't just any ordinary citizen. The Goblin has taken your aunt May."

"Aunt May?!" asked Connor.

Mr. Baran nodded gravely.

Connor steeled himself. "I'll do whatever it takes."

"You see those cones out there on the field?" Mr. Baran gestured to the three cones he'd positioned at the far corners of the soccer field. "The Green Goblin has left a message under one of them. If you want to save your aunt, you'll have to get that message quick." Mr. Baran remembered to work in more pregnant pauses. "Before . . . time . . . runs out. Go now!"

Connor ran across the field with surprising speed. He upended the first cone, found nothing, then sprinted to the other end of the field. Still nothing. Then he ran across the field again to the last cone, reached under it, and retrieved a piece of paper. He peered at it, then ran back to Mr. Baran.

Connor thrust the paper at Mr. Baran, saying, "It—doesn't—make—any—sense." The boy's pauses were not theatrics. He was out of breath from running.

Mr. Baran peered at the paper, giving Connor just enough time to get his wind back. The paper said, *"How high can you climb, web crawler?"* Mr. Baran asked Connor, "What's the highest place on the playground?"

Connor whirled and pointed to the jungle gym.

Mr. Baran said, "Quick, Spidey. There may not be much time left."

Connor ran back across the field and over to the jungle gym. Mr. Baran ran alongside him, egging him on all the way. Connor climbed the jungle gym and began searching for someone—anyone—to rescue. Connor said, "Nobody's here."

But then, they heard it, as if on cue. And of course, it was on cue. A whimper came from the back part of the jungle gym, the long yellow plastic tube that joined the lower platform to the monkey bar platform. Diane called out feebly, "Is that you, Peter? Please come save me! I'm soooooo frightened!"

Mr. Baran smiled down at his sneakers, trying not to laugh.

Connor answered, "I'll save you, Aunt May!" He ran back to help "feeble" Aunt May out of the yellow tunnel. Meanwhile, Mr. Baran ran over to a bubble machine on the side of the blacktop and switched it on.

Diane emerged wearing a shawl that she'd tied loosely around her wrists. "Oh, thank you, Spider-Man. You've saaaaaaved me. I—" Diane stopped short when she caught sight of the bubbles now floating over the blacktop.

Connor said, "Bubbles! Cool!"

Diane looked at them doubtfully. "Those don't look like innocent bubbles to me."

From the sidelines, Mr. Baran said, "You're right, Aunt May. They're evil bubbles. Harmless to superheroes, but deadly to their beloved old aunties."

Diane squealed, "Oh my!"

Mr. Baran told Diane, "The only way you'll make it through is if Spider-Man cuts a path for you. But he'll have to kick and punch as many of the bubbles as he can . . . or you'll never make it."

Connor stepped forward, jutting out his chin. "Time to burst some bubbles."

For the next ten minutes, Diane cowered behind Connor as he flailed at bubbles. Connor kicked, punched, and high-jumped to destroy as many as he could, accompanying his moves with cries of "Take that!" and "You want some too?"

Whenever the action slowed down, Diane would squeal, "There's another one!" or "Oh, my heart!"

By the time the pair made it across the blacktop, Connor was covered in sweat, and the first bell had rung. Diane thanked Spider-Man profusely, abandoned her hunched old lady stance, and jogged over to the front office.

Mr. Baran pulled the now-damp Spider-Man T-shirt off Connor and told the boy to run to class. Connor ran, but then stopped and turned back. "Thanks, Mr. Baran. That was the most awesomest gym class ever. Can we do it again tomorrow?"

Mr. Baran shook his head. "No, tomorrow, we do the Flash."

Connor's eyes widened and he said in hushed tones, "I love the Flash."

"But only if you behave for Mrs. Pacer. You got that?"

Connor nodded eagerly, then turned and ran, yelling over his shoulder, "I can't be late!"

25

Stragglers' Thanksgiving

Maggie hacked away at the cucumbers on her counter as if the vegetables had offended her personally. She hissed, "I can't believe you invited Jeannie. You've ruined everything."

Maddeningly unrepentant, Diane swirled her wineglass, sending a red droplet down onto her Pilgrim costume's formerly pristine white collar. "I told you—I didn't know Danny was gonna be here. You said he works all the time, jetting off to San Fran and whatnot."

Maggie whispered back, "I've been sleeping with him for weeks. Of course he's here for Thanksgiving."

"Don't 'of course' me. There's nothing logical about your rules with this guy. You won't drive to school together, won't eat at the same lunch table, won't even shake hands in public. You act like you've got a restraining order."

Maggie shot a meaningful glance at the kitchen door. She whisper-scolded, "Please keep your voice down." Diane rolled her eyes. Maggie went on, "Look, just because I don't make out with Daniel against a locker doesn't mean we're not serious. I *have* to be discreet at school so the Jeannies of the world won't blab about us. But my home is a different story. This was supposed to be a quiet dinner—just you and me and . . ."

"And twenty neighbors," smirked Diane.

Maggie threw up her hands. "Yeah, fine. And twenty neighbors, neighbors who have *zero* connection to the school. Most of the people out there are over seventy. They don't care about my love life. They're too busy trying to remember where they left their car keys." This was true. The Eldridge Court "Stragglers' Thanksgiving" had started years ago as a mixer for all the cul-de-sac's residents, young and old, but the event's demographics had shifted. Now the yearly dinner on the black-top looked like a cookout at a nursing home. It was *the* highlight of the social season for lonely seniors whose children lived too far away. And Maggie—as a good-hearted busybody—had taken on the task of organizing the whole shebang, with Diane's assistance. The two women wore Pilgrim costumes to make the event more festive and mark themselves as the people in charge / waitresses. Though theoretically a potluck, Maggie did most of the cooking, so guests marched in and out of her house all afternoon, fetching side dishes and whatnot—hence, Maggie's frantic whispering.

Diane opened her mouth to answer Maggie, but her eloquence was cut short by her father's entrance. Lars walked jauntily—or as jauntily as a seventy-four-year-old could while wheeling an oxygen tank behind him—into the kitchen. Eschewing his usual uniform of bathrobe and pajamas, Lars was dapper in khakis and a blue button-down shirt that set off his gray eyes. His silver hair was combed neatly so that he looked like a grandfather from an L.L.Bean catalog. Maggie was glad to see him. Diane had been fretting about Lars's increasingly hermit-like behavior. Now Lars said, "Hello, beauty queens. Maggie, can I trouble you for another glass of wine? Your Mrs. Pacer is one thirsty gal."

Lars held out Jeannie's empty glass, and Maggie refilled it. Smiling, she asked, "Are you trying to get Jeannie drunk?"

"Lord, no! I'm trying to get her quiet. That woman has loads of opinions, and she's giving 'em out for free. Why'd you invite her?"

Maggie said pointedly, "Ask your daughter."

"Oh, c'mon," said Diane. "Jeannie's not *that* bad. Besides, I figured this little hoedown would clear the air between her and Maggie."

Lars frowned. "Pacer's been fighting with our Maggie?" Lars had grown overly protective of Maggie since her divorce from Richard. Despite his decrepitude, he'd offered loudly and repeatedly to "smack the snot" out of him.

Diane said, "No, they're not fighting. They're just not quite getting along. Like you said, Jeannie's opinionated."

Lars squared his thin shoulders. "Listen, Maggie, if you need any help deflating that windbag, you let me know. Deal?"

Maggie nodded, oddly touched. "Deal."

Lars exited, and as soon as the kitchen door swung shut behind him, Diane gave a delighted little squeal. "Oooooooh. He likes her. I knew he'd like her."

Maggie raised an eyebrow. "He called her a windbag."

"I know." Diane sighed wistfully. "He used to call my mom a windbag all the time. So sweet."

Maggie shook her head. Diane's matchmaking efforts always failed, and this latest attempt was wrecking Maggie's holiday. Maggie would have to spend the night acting stiff and formal around Danny so Jeannie wouldn't run back to school and blab to the other teachers. Maggie pursed her lips, plainly irritated.

Diane said, "Okay, I'm sorry I invited her. There."

Maggie frowned, dissatisfied by Diane's meager show of contrition. If a person says she's sorry, she should put her back into it. But there was no time to argue the point. The bell rang, and Maggie ran out to greet—and warn—Danny. He hadn't responded to any of her frantic texts about Jeannie's unexpected arrival. Maggie opened the front door, stepped outside, and pulled it shut behind her. All business, she told Danny, "I have to talk to you before you come in."

Danny leaned down to kiss her cheek, but she shook her head and put a warning hand on his chest. He asked, "Is this part of the Puritan thing?" He gestured at her black-and-white Pilgrim's costume.

Maggie felt the heat rise to her cheeks. She'd forgotten about her costume. "I know, I look ridiculous, but . . ."

Danny leered. "No, I think it's sexy. Want to earn a scarlet letter?"

"Keep your Hawthorne in your pants. Jeannie Pacer is here."

"Who?"

Maggie was stunned that he did not recognize the name. "Uh—Jeannie Pacer—first-grade teacher." The word "duh" was not stated, but implied.

Danny shrugged, his face a blank.

Maggie pressed on, "Jeannie is that older teacher, the one who gives you those sour looks. She . . ."

Danny shrugged again. "I don't remember her."

"How can you *not* remember someone who glares at you all the time?"

Danny smiled. "Dunno. I guess I tend not to focus on people who don't like me." This was the inverse of how Maggie's brain worked. When Maggie discovered someone didn't like her, that person got way more airtime in her thoughts. Perplexed, she stood frowning in her bonnet. Danny said, "You look like a pissed-off extra from *The Handmaid's Tale*."

Maggie's frown dissolved. As with everything she learned about Daniel, she decided almost immediately that this latest insight into his thinking was positive. Daniel's looks and charm were heavy thumbs on the scale of her smitten judgment. They kissed, and as the kiss deepened, she pulled away. Shaking her head to cow her own hormones, Maggie said, "No. Until Jeannie goes home, you are Mr. Zelinsky."

Danny objected, "So, we have a purely professional relationship, but you invited me to Thanksgiving? That doesn't make much sense."

An advocate for recycling, Maggie practiced what she preached—reusing Diane's bogus excuse for inviting Mrs. Pacer in the first place. "No, it makes perfect sense. Things are frosty between us—so I invited you to Thanksgiving to clear the air."

Danny started to quibble with this, but Maggie was soon ushering him into the house, calling out, "Mr. Zelinsky is here!" Introductions were made, along with promises of dinner in just a few minutes. Maggie scurried back into the kitchen, and soon she and Diane began carrying side dishes and rolls out to the cul-de-sac. Elderly neighbors milled toward their seats at folding tables covered in white linen, and Danny chatted them up like a solicitous host. Maggie noticed this, and her inner schoolgirl swooned, "That's soooo handsome of him!"

Goofily happy, she retreated to her kitchen to pull the turkey out of the oven. The great bird had roasted to golden-brown perfection. She set it on the stove top to cool. While admiring it, Maggie felt like the star of her own cooking show. One of her neighbors had cooked another turkey, so there'd be plenty for all. Thoroughly pleased with herself, she floated back outside. All the guests had seated themselves—all but her ex-husband, Richard.

Richard stood next to the center table, an oversize, holiday-themed bouquet of orange roses and yellow daisies in his hands. An ancient neighbor, near-deaf Gus Filby, was shoutily greeting him. Richard answered politely but kept his eyes fixed on Maggie. Gus called out, "Hey, Maggie, your boy's back! Bought flowers! Looks like he's sorry!"

Gus's long-suffering wife hissed, "Gus. You are *so* insensitive."

The party fell silent as everyone stared. Maggie stood paralyzed, mute with panic. Richard came forward, handed her the bouquet, and kissed her numb cheek. He murmured in her ear, "Maggie, can I have a minute?"

Diane lurched to the rescue, telling everyone, "Nothing to see here! Just a conscious uncoupling between two exes!" Diane strode over to Maggie. In one fluid motion, she blocked Richard and linked arms with semicatatonic Maggie. "Now, who's ready for some turkey?!" The crowd made enthusiastic noises, and Diane led Maggie back into the house, Richard on their heels.

Closing the door, Diane took Maggie by the shoulders: "Breathe, Maggie."

Maggie sputtered, "W-what is he doing here?!" She asked Diane, "Did you invite him too?"

"Lord, no! I'm gorgeous, not stupid," said Diane.

Maggie turned toward Richard. "What are you doing here?"

"Gus invited me." Richard said this complacently, like a kid flashing his hall pass.

Maggie's jaw dropped again, and Diane told Richard, "Oh hell no. You didn't just come for Gus. You came to stir up some shit."

Richard held up his hands defensively. "No, I'm not here to cause any trouble. I just, I miss the old neighborhood sometimes. And I wanted to talk to Maggie alone for a minute. Just a minute, I swear."

Diane glared down at Richard like an angry bouncer. To Maggie's eye, Richard was as handsome and achingly fit as ever. But Diane had a good six inches on him, and—thanks to all her extensive fight training for the apocalypse—she might have been able to take him. She growled, "Say the word, Maggie."

Maggie pictured Diane throwing Richard out onto the curb. The image had some appeal, but it didn't seem very festive. She put a hand on Diane's arm. "It's okay, Diane. Just give us a minute." Diane unfolded her arms, but did not retreat. Maggie clarified, "*Alone*, Diane." Diane shot her a hurt look, then shuffled outside.

As soon as the front door shut, Maggie told Richard, "You have exactly *one* minute."

Richard smiled. "Thanks, Maggie. I, um, I didn't mean to wreck your Thanksgiving. Just the opposite. I was hoping . . ." He stepped closer to her, and she took a matching step back. "You see, I've been working with a sponsor, and . . ."

"A sponsor? You mean like in AA?"

"Yes, and no. It's not AA. It's a twelve-step group . . . for porn addicts. We're trying to recover from porn addiction by relying on a Higher Power. Something greater than ourselves."

Maggie's brain snarked, *You don't need a Higher Power. You need oven mitts.* But that sentiment didn't seem very Christian. Maggie had an absurd urge to live up to her Puritan costume. Instead, she said uncertainly, "Oooh-kay."

Richard cleared his throat nervously. "So, um, I've been working on my ninth step—the one where I make amends to all the people I harmed with my addiction. And uh . . . you're at the top of the list. In fact, you *are* the list."

Maggie repeated, "Okay?"

"Thanksgiving seemed like the right time to make amends. So, I wanted you to know: I. Am. Deeply. Sorry."

Maggie waited in silence for a long moment, long enough to allow the sounds of her guests outside to filter back into her consciousness. Despite his solemnity, Richard's apology seemed somehow inadequate, underproduced. An emotional popgun in a CGI world. Years of suffering and the loss of a marriage required something more than a single "I'm sorry." Maggie managed, "Is that it?"

Sensing her letdown, Richard said, "No, I want to make it up to you." He stepped closer again, "I want . . ."

He reached out to touch her arm, and Maggie stepped back, shaking her head. "Oh no. No touching. This isn't *Pat the Bunny.*"

Richard exhaled, cooling his own jets. "Right. I understand. If you change your mind, I want you to know, I still . . ." But that was the problem. Richard didn't "still" want her. "Still" implied that he'd never stopped wanting her, but he had. And that had broken her heart. Maggie shook her head emphatically. Richard pulled back. "Yeah, got it. But look, even if we never get back together, I know that I owe you real amends. If I can ever do anything to make things up to you, please let me know. Okay?"

Maggie nodded. "Okay."

"Do you want me to leave? I can go home if you like."

"No," said Maggie. "I don't want you to be alone on Thanksgiving. You can eat with us, but then you go home, all right?"

Richard nodded. He opened the front door to find Diane standing just outside it, looming. He walked quickly past her out to the tables. As the two women watched Richard take a seat—just a few spaces down from Danny—Diane asked, "How much did you tell Danny about Richard?"

Maggie gulped. "*Too* much."

Diane eyed Maggie shrewdly. "You overshared during pillow talk, didn't you?" Maggie nodded. Diane said, "C'mon, let's go hack that turkey apart. You can pretend it's your ex."

The two friends carved the bird, then brought it out to the tables. Maggie took her time handing out platters of turkey. Then, like a child forced to go to her room at bedtime, she shuffled over to her seat between Danny and Diane. Lars, Jeannie, and Richard were there too.

Looking round the table, Maggie said with false brightness, "So have you all introduced yourselves?" Everyone nodded. Maggie said, "Good. Let's eat."

For the next few minutes, everyone at Maggie's table said nothing as they methodically shoved turkey into their maws. Laughter and snippets of chatter wafted to them from all directions, making the conversation blackout at their table ever more awkward. Once again, Diane came to the rescue, saying cheerfully, "So I was reading an article on all the stuff you're not supposed to discuss at Thanksgiving dinner: who prays to what god, who screwed who, who's pulling down the most cash. Sure was a looooong list, of course you can't talk health problems either 'cause nobody wants the nitty-gritty on how Uncle Merle's colostomy bag works." Diane laughed too heartily at this, and Maggie felt a pang of love for her friend.

Jeannie chipped in, "And politics is out. These days, talking politics is too scary. It makes me feel like a kid with one of those old jack-in-the-boxes. Turn the crank over and feel your stomach flip because you just don't know when the freaky clown'll *pop* at you. Only this time, the clown's your old friend spouting off about guns or gays." Jeannie shuddered.

Danny said gamely, "Anybody seen any good movies lately?"

Everyone shook their heads. Lars snorted. "Don't tell me *you* haven't seen any, Richard. I thought watching movies was your favorite hobby." Danny sucked in his cheeks and breathed deeply—stifling a laugh. Under the table, he gave Maggie's thigh a friendly pinch.

Lars's jab landed, but Richard answered good-naturedly enough, "That *used* to be my hobby, but not anymore. I've moved on to other things."

"What? They got sexy holograms now?" quipped Lars.

Seemingly oblivious, Jeannie said, "What? You mean like a hologram of Mae West?"

Danny said, "I saw a hologram on an award show once. It was Michael Jackson, I think."

Still glowering at Richard, Lars mumbled, "Another pervert."

Maggie shot Lars a pleading look, and Lars frowned and squirmed a bit, like a kid who'd been caught out. Silence fell, and Jeannie marched into the breach. "I saw a documentary on the Pilgrims last night."

"Did you?" said Diane.

Jeannie nodded. "Yes. It was one of those cheesy ones where they use reenactors. Ohmigawd, I love the way they light reenactments—all soft and gauzy. I wish they'd light me like that in real life. So anyways, it turns out the Pilgrims were a gloomy bunch. I guess predestination has a way of doing that to people."

Diane said, "Predestination? Sounds like airport talk."

Launching into teacher mode, Jeannie explained, "Predestination is the belief that even before you are born, Gawd has already decided whether you are going to heaven or to hell. It's like he's preaddressed your spiritual envelope."

Diane objected, "But if God's done that, why bother to be good?"

Jeannie answered, "To show everyone—yourself included—that you are going to be saved. The more virtuous you are, the less anyone can doubt you're headed for the pearly gates. The most virtuous Pilgrims were called 'visible saints.'"

Diane smiled. "Visible saints, like those alpha moms on the PTA."

Danny said, "Or Gwyneth Paltrow."

"*Not* like Gwyneth," said Jeannie. She frowned at Danny as if he were a student who'd burped loudly during story time. "The Puritans weren't smug. They thought if they made even a single misstep, they'd spend all eternity burning in hell. Terror kept them vigilant to their shortcomings. *They* were humble people." Jeannie focused on Danny as she said this. She had obviously concluded that he was not big on humility.

Danny said, "Hmm. I don't think I believe in hell."

"I do," said Lars. He glared at Richard again.

Danny went on, "It's just, if there is a God, I can't imagine him deep-frying people."

Diane lurched off subject. "I love deep-fried food. Those fried Oreos at the fair were . . ." Diane smacked her lips together.

Suddenly, Maggie leaped to her feet. "Oh God, the pies." She'd left two pies in her lower oven. She rushed over to her house.

One of her elderly neighbors, Fern, was in her kitchen. "I brought back one of your platters, sweetie." She patted Maggie on the shoulder, evidently oblivious to the smell of overbaked pies. As Fern exited,

Maggie mitted up and fetched the pies, setting them out to cool. The pumpkin pie looked fine, but the apple pie's edge had burnt slightly, so Maggie went to work trimming off the burnt bits of crust. Then she felt a pair of arms circle her waist from behind.

Danny whispered in her ear, "Hey, beautiful."

Maggie leaned back into his chest for a moment. He started to kiss her neck, and her arms went limp. She let her knife fall onto the counter. She closed her eyes and felt a minor riot in her groin. His kisses deepening, Danny cupped her breast, and Maggie roused herself from her horny stupor. "Not now, Daniel."

He gently turned her round to face him. He kissed her deeply, then set back to work on her neck, murmuring, "Yes, now."

Swimming upstream, Maggie said lazily, "Nnnno. We can't. Jeannie could come in. And what about the old people outside?"

Leaning into her so as to physically trumpet his erection, Danny said, "We're not old people."

Maggie bit down on her lower lip. She reached for a counterargument, but her rational mind had flipped its "WE'RE CLOSED" sign. "I've got guests coming in and out of here. We can't . . ."

Danny kissed her again. "Not in the bedroom."

"Yes, there too. Fern is gonna be back in here any minute to fetch those dopey party favors she stowed there."

"Well, that *is* a problem." He caressed her arm, then took her hand and led her down the hallway.

Maggie couldn't imagine Danny throwing open the front door to show off the enormous khaki tent his penis was making. She asked foggily, "Where are we going?"

"On safari." Just off the foyer, he turned and threw open the side door into the garage. He shut the door behind him and made a great show of flicking the lock. Then he took her in his arms.

What happened next literally came in a blur. His hands were up her black Pilgrim dress, easing down her non-Pilgrim panties. They kissed, feeling their way around each other and the garage's cluttered space. She leaned against the passenger side of her car, unzipped his pants, and yanked down his briefs, freeing his good-to-go penis. Still kissing her, he moved her round to the front of the car, and tilted her back onto the hood. Then he entered her personal parking space.

Soon, Maggie was lying spread-eagled, black boots dangling off opposite sides of the car as if she were the star of some erotic Pilgrim yoga video. Daniel moved inside her slowly at first, then quickly and with greater force as the car bounced on its tires. Maggie moaned and threw out an arm, hitting a tall stack of boxes. An old, long-forgotten basketball rolled off the top of the stack, bounced off the floor, and then smacked against the garage door opener's button.

Maggie registered confused panic on Danny's face as the door began to loudly roll back up on its hinges. Stuck on sexual autopilot, his hips continued to thrust forward, and he climaxed seconds later in full view of the twenty elderly guests out in the cul-de-sac.

He and Maggie froze, trapped in a spotlight of stunned silence. Then she heard Jeannie say, "Well, I guess we know what *she's* thankful for."

26

THE SCARLET LETTER

When the curtain rose on Maggie and Danny, Diane was too shocked to move. Jeannie's quip—which Diane would giggle at later—roused Diane from her stupor. Diane ran over to smack the gray garage control panel on the side of the house. As the door rolled noisily back down, Diane called out, "All right, show's over, folks! Back to our G-rated dinner!" A few people guffawed at that, and Diane hoped Maggie wouldn't take it too hard. These people needed a few giggles after seeing their sainted neighbor getting her turkey basted. Besides, it could have been worse. Three of the guests had heart conditions. Maggie was lucky the geezers' personal second hands didn't freeze forever when her and her boy toy's bodies yelled "Surprise!"

As the guests finished the last of their turkey, Diane recruited Jeannie to help fetch the desserts. Jeannie plated pie slices, and Diane handed them out, smiling her best "no-crazy-shit-to-see-here" smile—the smile a flight attendant gives you after your seatmate has thrown up all over your tray table. Diane had always liked flight attendants. If "visible saints" really did exist, Diane figured flight attendants would be God's first draft pick.

Eventually, Maggie's guests shuffled off to their houses. Jeannie threw out the paper plates and ran the rest of the food back into Maggie's kitchen while Diane bagged the now-dirty tablecloths. And a Thanksgiving miracle occurred as Lars worked cheerfully alongside Richard to fold and stack the chairs and tables for their trip back to the rental place. Watching them work, Diane grew wistful, reflecting on how it takes a village to clean up after an impromptu porn show. She loved her dad and hated Richard a little less for working together to help Maggie in her bizarre moment of need.

When the four finished clearing the cul-de-sac, they stood awkwardly together on Maggie's lawn. Suddenly, Maggie's house seemed intimidating, almost scary, as if the place were haunted by the ghosts of porn past, and in a way, it was—first by Richard's oeuvre and now by Maggie's unsavory debut.

Brushing his hands against his pants, Richard said, "I better be going. Tell Maggie I said thanks for . . . Um, tell her, uh . . ."

Diane supplied, "Dinner?"

Richard gulped. "Yeah, that." He walked a few steps away, then turned. "Diane?"

"Yes?" asked Diane.

"Take care of her, okay?" He looked at her pleadingly, and Diane remembered that she'd once liked this man.

Diane nodded, and Richard drove off—leaving three little Indians behind.

Lars jutted his chin and shot a look at Danny's black Tesla on the curb. It had a "DANNYZ" license plate, and Diane knew her father was thinking Danny must've gotten it from some *Assholes' Accessories* catalog. "Is that Zelinsky fella in the house?"

Diane said, "Nah. Danny slipped out the back and took an Uber back to his hotel."

Lars frowned. "Real chivalrous."

"Don't look like that, Dad. Maggie *asked* him to go. He has a big conference tomorrow morning. Besides, she'd rather hide in her bedroom by herself."

Jeannie said, "Cowering is not a group activity."

Diane added, "Plus, she probably didn't want us to think she was in her bedroom fooling around with him."

Lars frowned. "After what we've seen, who cares? In for a penny, in for a pound."

"So anyway, Dad, let me look in on her, and then I'll drive you back home."

Jeannie stepped forward, telling Diane, "No, you should stay. I'll drive Lars home."

Diane asked, "You got time for that? We live all the way up in Vista."

Jeannie said darkly, "I'm a sixty-five-year-old divorcée and it's Thanksgiving. Trust me, I've got time."

Diane thanked her and watched as Jeannie led Lars over to her car. Lars made a business of looking sour about the travel arrangements, but Diane saw him smooth his shirt and check his reflection in the car mirror. For Lars, that counted as primping.

Diane waved them off and then went inside the house. She knocked on Maggie's bedroom door. "It's Diane."

A groggy voice said, "Come in."

Diane entered to find Maggie under the covers, a box of tissues in her hand. Maggie's Pilgrim bonnet was knocked akimbo, and her eyes were puffy. Not meeting Diane's gaze at first, she said weakly, "How bad was it?"

Diane lied, "Not that bad."

Maggie looked at Diane searchingly, and Diane flashed her best flight attendant smile. Suddenly, Maggie collapsed into tears again. "Ohmigod! It was a fucking catastrophe!"

Diane sat down on the bed and took Maggie in her arms. Rocking Maggie gently, Diane said, "Oh. It's not that bad. Look on the bright side, at least there were no kids out there, just geezers." This prompted even louder sobs from Maggie. Diane flailed. "Who knows, they might forget all about this. They're old. Like you said before, half of 'em can't remember where they left their car keys."

Maggie drew back. Rubbing her nose with a tissue, she said, "This is not car keys. People forget car keys. Nobody forgets a Pilgrim lady getting humped on the hood of her car."

"It was quite a picture. I'll give you that."

Maggie sniffed. "I can't imagine what those people must be thinking."

"I *know* what they're thinking. They're shocked, titillated, and feeling superior—it's an emotional trifecta. This is probably the most exciting thing that's happened to them in a long time."

Maggie put her face in her hands again. "And Richard, poor Richard!"

"Oh, give me a break. Poor Richard's seen wayyy worse than that. Your sideshow was pure Merchant Ivory compared to the stuff on his computer. And I should know, I'm the one who found that stuff." Diane shuddered. Maggie pulled out a fresh wad of tissues and blew her nose loudly. Diane pointed to a box of Godiva chocolates on the nightstand. "Want a chocolate?"

Maggie shook her head and said huffily, "No, I don't want a chocolate."

Diane shrugged. She grabbed the box of chocolates and propped it open on her lap. She popped a chocolate into her mouth. Her mouth full, Diane said, "You sure you don't want one?"

Maggie frowned. "No. What about Jeannie? Do you think she'll talk about this to the other teachers?"

Diane winced. "Hard to tell. Jeannie's kind. My dad's right about her being a windbag, but she's a caring windbag. And she likes you."

"She does not," said Maggie.

"No, she does. Just because she doesn't sit the first time you yank the leash doesn't mean she's not a fan. She may not like Danny, but . . ."

"Why doesn't she like him?"

Diane shrugged. "Dunno. He's too slippery for her, I guess. But she likes you. And I don't think she'll want to see you squirm. On the other hand . . ." Diane trailed off.

"What other hand?"

Diane sighed. "Even if you like your boss, it's pretty danged hard to resist gossiping to coworkers when you catch her gussied up in a Pilgrim suit and getting rammed by the only fuckable dude on campus."

Deflated, Maggie fell back against her pillows, sigh-saying, "Shhhhhhhhhit." After a long silence, she asked in a small voice, "Can I have a chocolate, please?" Diane handed her two, and Maggie scarfed them down. Fortified, Maggie said, "At least I won't have to worry anymore about Richard. I mean, about how to tell him about me and Daniel."

"Yup. Richard has been briefed."

Maggie grabbed another chocolate, then winced again. "And Lars. I can't believe Lars saw me like that."

"Oh, don't worry. He didn't see much, just your black boots sticking out. Danny was the real star."

Maggie gave a rueful chuckle. Then she looked at Diane. "And you? Do you think less of me?"

"Hell no. The only thing I thought when I saw you up there was: 'Damn, I got to get out more.'"

27

The Reckoning

After Thanksgiving, Maggie avoided Jeannie for days. But now Maggie was cornered. The veteran teacher had snuck up on her. They'd have to have "the talk" about Daniel.

Maggie was alone in the cafeteria, inspecting Diane's decorations for Winterfest—the school's Christmas/Hanukkah/all-things-December celebration. She felt a tap on her shoulder—Jeannie. "Maggie, we need to talk."

Maggie stalled. "That's right. We *do* need to talk. I've been meaning to track you down. But Diane's going to kill me if I don't get back to her on these decorations."

Jeannie began, "I know we've had our differences, but . . ."

Maggie reached for a distraction. "Too true. And I have to say, I appreciate how much room you gave me with Connor."

"Connor?"

"Uh-huh. A lot of teachers would have been impatient with that situation, but not you. You gave Mr. Baran the time he needed to figure out Connor's needs, and now things are . . . Things are good, right?" Maggie spoke too fast, like an overcaffeinated auctioneer.

Jeannie conceded, "Uh, yeah. I got to hand it to you. Now that Connor's doing those superhero workouts, he's a delight to have in class."

Maggie arched an eyebrow at this last line. "A 'delight'? You've been writing report cards, haven't you?"

Jeannie shrugged. "Professional hazard. Write twenty report cards in a row, and it creeps into your language. You can get in trouble. One time, my ex-husband asked me how he was doing in bed, and I blurted out, 'Needs improvement.'" Jeannie and Maggie grinned at the anecdote, then fell silent. Jeannie's mention of sex had summoned the specter of the Great Garage Door Incident. Jeannie tried again. "So, anyways, I was hoping we could—"

Maggie interrupted, "These decorations are really something, aren't they? Diane spent all day making them."

"Wonderful, yes. But . . ."

Maggie tap-danced. "I told her to make sure we represented all the religious traditions. Christianity tends to hog the spotlight this time of year, doesn't it?"

"True."

Maggie hastened to add, "People from other faiths get so mad if you don't say anything about them."

Jeannie nodded. "Yes, saying nothing is almost as bad as actually saying something."

Maggie blundered on, "Yes, but we have to try. It's our job to educate." Maggie said this emphatically, as if daring Jeannie to contradict her. "We're trying to be ecumenical. So, we've got the usual candy canes, Christmas trees, snowflakes. Plus, menorahs and dreidels for the Hanukkah crowd." Maggie pointed to the decorations as she ticked them off. "But then I thought, *What about the Buddhists? Where's their namaste?*"

Jeannie frowned. "Do we have any Buddhist students?"

"I'm not sure. But we *do* have lots of Asians. Some of them might be Buddhist. I've been curious, but it feels racist to presume anything."

"Listen, Maggie, I wanted to . . ."

Maggie continued her verbal diarrhea. "We don't really have anything for Islam. I feel bad about that. Diane wanted to do cutouts of Muhammad, but they came out all wrong—like swarthy versions of Santa, and . . ."

"Don't Muslims think it's sacrilege to put up pictures of Muhammad?"

Maggie winced. "Yes, there's that, too."

"Uh-huh."

"I feel bad about leaving Muslims out. I want them to feel welcome at the school." Maggie jutted out her chin, proclaiming, "We're not building any walls at Carmel Knolls Elementary. I mean, we *do* have walls, but not ones to filter out any religious groups." Maggie shot an apologetic look at Jeannie. "Sorry, I don't mean to be political. I—"

Jeannie blurted, "I don't care about you shtupping Danny Z."

Maggie goggled, then stammered, "Well, uh, thank you."

"And I want you to know I haven't told anyone about you two."

Maggie's breath hitched. "I appreciate your discretion, Jeannie."

"But I worry that your relationship might be blinding you to certain problems here at the school."

"Problems?"

"With the MathPal," said Jeannie.

This caught Maggie off guard. Maggie had not shared her negative assessment of the MathPal with her staff. At first, she hadn't wanted to sink morale by kvetching about the MathPal since—no matter what she said—her school was stuck with it for a year. Then, once she tumbled into bed with Danny, whining about the MathPal seemed disloyal, even cruel. She didn't need to tell Danny the MathPal was a flop. Life would tell him that. Feigning innocence, Maggie said evasively, "I was not aware of any problems with the MathPal. The kids seem to love it."

Jeannie bristled. "Sure, they do. It's a video game."

"So what's wrong?"

"To start with, it's not teaching them anything."

Maggie blustered, "Is that so? Well, I, uh, Edutek's still refining it. So . . ."

"And the advertising is outrageous. We are talking beyond." Again, Jeannie stretched this last word out to four syllables—"bee-yaw-un-da." Jeannie's Brooklyn accent got more pronounced when she was indignant.

"What advertising?" asked Maggie. "I didn't know about any advertising."

"Are you kidding? The ads started after Halloween. Designer labels on the character's shirts, name-brand candy 'rewards,' and—of course—the latest high-end toys. They even slipped in an ad for Birachi's Toy Store, with the logo and everything."

Maggie stammered, "But, uh, we never agreed to . . . I don't think they can do that, can they?"

"But they *are* doing it."

Maggie felt her cheeks redden. "I didn't know. Are they doing actual commercials?"

"They don't need to! They shill products by working them into the games. So, when a boy avatar needs energy, he downs a Zammo! soda and gets superspeed. When a girl completes a mission, she celebrates by putting on some Sassy Smile lipstick or going"—now, Jeannie lapsed into a singsong—"sha-sha-sha-shopping."

"Sha-sha-sha-shopping?" echoed Maggie.

"It's a jingle—stupid, but catchy."

Jeannie was right. Maggie'd heard some third graders singing the jingle as they sashayed past. She'd noticed them because girls usually save hip swishing for middle school. Maggie hadn't noticed any of the kids wearing lipstick, but it was easy to miss that sort of thing, especially since she'd started stumbling around in a dopey, sex-sated daze. She asked, "Are the girls' avatars heavily made up?"

Jeannie sneered, "Like Bratz dolls."

Maggie winced. She shut her eyes and said, as calmly as she could, "Thank you for letting me know. I will talk to Daniel about this right away."

Jeannie pressed, "You think he'll get rid of the ads?"

"I don't know." Maggie didn't know what Danny thought was appropriate for children. And she wasn't sure he cared. When he lapsed into tech-speak, he called her students "users." But wasn't he the real user here?

Jeannie crossed her arms. "Look, I know we're stuck with the MathPal this year. But what about next year?"

"I . . . uh . . . well." The truth was that Maggie hadn't thought that far ahead. Giddy happiness had robbed her of her usual zest for long-term planning. "I suppose that depends on the program's test results. If they're strong, we might continue. And if not . . ."

"Then, we'll stop?"

Maggie hesitated a moment. She sensed a trap, but she didn't see any alternative answer. "Of course."

Jeannie exhaled as if the conversation had cost her great energy. "Good. I . . . uh . . . I don't mean to be difficult. It's just, I worry. You know?" Jeannie held Maggie's eyes for a long moment, and Maggie sensed the woman was trying to forge some telepathic agreement. If so, her Jedi skills were for shit.

Maggie said neutrally, "I understand."

"Good. I know you, uh, care for that man. But his program is garbage."

Maggie hedged. "I'll take a look at it again. But I might not be the best judge. I taught Spanish, not math."

Jeannie smiled ruefully. "Yes, but I'll bet you can *hablo* bullshit when you hear it, can't you?"

"*Sí.*"

28

MY PRETTY PROSTITUTE

Maggie stormed into her office and powered up the MathPal. She loaded the system's new "updates" and found that Jeannie had exaggerated nothing. It was all there and more—the plugs for flashy toys, sugary soda, and makeup. She texted Danny, asking him to come to her office as soon as he could. Then, because outrage is a dish best shared, she called Diane in and showed the program to her. Even Diane was shocked. She snarked, "*This* is why the terrorists hate us. Look at all that face paint. Forget Bratz dolls. That avatar looks like My Pretty Prostitute."

When Danny arrived, Maggie said haughtily, "Would you please excuse us, Diane? I need a moment alone with Mr. Zelinsky." Diane nodded and marched past Danny without a glance.

As soon as the door shut, Danny asked, "What's this about?"

Maggie began, "I've just been informed that you're using the MathPal to shill merchandise to my students."

Danny grinned, then said with mock innocence, "You mean you don't like my ads?"

Maggie didn't like his tone. She was looking for embarrassed contrition, not pert amusement. "I loathe them."

"Why?" asked Danny.

"We do *not* advertise products to our students."

He repeated, "Why?"

"Because it's wrong."

"Why?"

Maggie snapped, "Stop it with the whys. What are you, a toddler?"

His smile shrank, but did not vanish. "I'm not a toddler, and I'm not being facetious. I'm being intellectually rigorous here. I'm asking you to lay out your assumptions. So tell me, why—in this time when your school is starving for cash—why is it wrong to advertise to students?"

Maggie answered, "It's wrong because we are supposed to be educating them, telling them the truth about the way the world works. We need those kids to believe us when we tell them the world is round and Australia's a continent and it doesn't get windy just because God's blowing out birthday candles. We can't wreck our credibility by making ham-fisted sales pitches for sugar soda and kiddie lipstick."

Danny didn't flinch. "Point taken. And in a better world, you could hold to that stance. But this isn't a better world. Education costs money. State funds are drying up. The money will have to come from somewhere. So why not advertising?"

"Because this is a school, not a store."

Danny nodded. "Right. But let's not get too lofty. It's not like this place is above commerce. I mean, you spend huge chunks of time begging parents for cash for . . ."

"For things their children need. Supplies, teacher salaries, the—"

Danny cut in, "Yes, it's all very noble. I got that. But it's not really working, is it?"

Maggie blustered, "We're having some cash flow issues, but . . ." The school's STEAM fund-raising drive was still foundering. Old fund-raising standbys weren't working as well as they used to, and all her and

Diane's newer ideas were either outlandish or too expensive to execute. Diane's latest and most ludicrous proposal was to have Maggie participate in a new reality show where she would "battle" other school principal contestants for fund-raising. Much as Maggie loved her school, she would not go on TV to run obstacle courses, model swimwear, or be doused in brown "Principal Poo" foam.

As if reading Maggie's thoughts, Danny said, "Wouldn't it be great if you could just stop all that begging? If you could just focus on teaching kids?"

"Yes, but . . ."

"Advertising lets you do that. Take an example. Mr. Baran's hugely popular, right?"

"Yes."

"So, why not monetize that?" asked Danny.

"What?"

"Why not cash in on Mr. Baran's goodwill? Approach a corporate sponsor, tell them how beloved the guy is, and get them to pay his salary for a year in exchange for having him wear a T-shirt with their logo on it every day." Danny splayed his hands as if framing a marquee. "This class, brought to you by Coca-Cola. 'Have a Coke and a gym teacher.'" In case Maggie had never heard of Coca-Cola, Danny explained, "It's a play on the old Coke slogan. You know, 'Have a Coke and a smile.' Oh, c'mon, don't look at me like that."

"Like what?" asked Maggie.

"Like I'm something nasty you found stuck to the bottom of your shoe. It hurts my feelings."

Maggie repeated her incantation: "We don't advertise to our students. Don't you get that? Aren't there any limits for you?"

Danny shrugged. "I said no to the vaping people." Maggie glared at him. He raised his hands in surrender. "I'm kidding. What's the . . ."

"This is serious, Daniel. Get rid of the ads."

"Fine. I'll tone down the ads. We were only going to run the soda and makeup spots for a month or two, just to gauge how well they worked."

Maggie pressed, "And what about the toy ads?"

Danny caved. "Fine, we'll get rid of those too, for now."

"For now?"

Danny smiled his winning smile. "Look, I can't promise the MathPal's final version won't have any ads. The MathPal isn't set in stone. It's a moving target. We're trying loads of things—slicker graphics, advertising, sales of user data . . ."

"Sales of what?"

"User data," said Danny.

Maggie was incredulous. "Why would anyone want to buy intel on how our kids are doing with their math facts?"

Danny smiled at Maggie's quaint naïveté—as if she were a five-year-old who'd just asked whether butter comes from butterflies. He simpered, "No, babe. They don't care about that stuff. What they're after is consumer preferences—where the kids go on vacation, what movies they like, what products they want to buy, and all that. It's a marketing bonanza if you target it right."

Maggie balked. "You can't sell that stuff."

Danny said serenely, "I'm afraid I can. It's part of our deal with the district."

Maggie gaped. For a moment, she looked like she was trying to catch snowflakes in her mouth. Then it came back to her—the barrage of questions the MathPal had made her answer before she could log on to the program. Instinctively resenting the program's invasiveness, she'd concocted a phony identity—as a third grader named "Smelly Donut"—and had given bogus answers. But real third graders wouldn't do that—no, they'd gleefully hand over genuine, personal information, not realizing that doing so might subject them to years of commercialized online stalking. Maggie sneered, "You *sold* my students' information?"

Danny raised his hands defensively. "Whoa there. We didn't sell it, not yet. But sure, we analyzed it. You can't put a price point on data if you don't analyze it. Look, selling the MathPal to end users is just one way to monetize the program. We have to look at everything: advertising, sales of user data, whatever works. I can't take anything off the table yet. But I can agree to strip out ads from the version your kids are using. Good enough?"

Maggie said nothing.

Danny added in his best "but-wait-there's-more" voice: "And I will promise not to sell your students' user data. Eh, how's that work for you?"

Maggie nodded. She stopped glaring at him, but remained silent.

Danny persisted, "You're still not happy, are you?"

"No, I'm not happy." Maggie spat out the *h* in "happy."

"Why not?" Churlishness crept into Danny's voice. And Maggie was relieved to hear it. She detested his slick, reptilian everything-is-just-business patter. That patter wasn't just unattractive. It was somehow menacing, a threat to her way of life. Maggie respected capitalism, but she wished it would stay in its own yard.

Danny looked expectantly at her. She explained, "It's not just me who'll be uncomfortable with ads and selling kids' personal information, Daniel. Most public schools won't . . ."

Danny brightened. "Public schools aren't our target audience."

"We're not? Then who is?"

"People who can afford it. Public schools are strapped. The real money is in the private sector—homeschooling, swanky private schools, for-profit colleges. I mean, the reason we created the program in the first place was to . . ." Danny trailed off.

"What?" asked Maggie.

Danny eyed Maggie for a long moment, a mischievous smile playing on his lips. "I'll show you. I'll take you to Walter's place."

"I've *been* to Walter's place."

Danny walked over to Maggie's side of the desk and leaned against it. "I don't mean La Jolla. I mean Walter's *other* place . . . the one in Wyoming."

"Wyoming? You mean like Yellowstone and *Brokeback Mountain*?"

"No, like shotguns and canned goods."

"Huh?"

Danny leaned down so that his face was just inches from hers. He said, lowering his voice as if someone might be listening, "Walter thinks society is about to collapse. And he doesn't want to be around when the mobs come. So, he's built himself an escape hatch, a luxury bunker so his family can ride out the apocalypse in style."

"Are you serious?" asked Maggie.

Danny nodded. "Yup. It's a multimillion-dollar structure. He put the finishing touches on it last month, and he wants to fly me out next week to show it off."

"And what's this got to do with the MathPal?"

Danny grinned. "Come along and find out."

29

Travels with Walter

As Walter Tilmore's private jet glided through the clouds, Maggie leaned back in her deep leather seat and nursed her mimosa. She needed vodka to fortify her so she could make it through a full day of listening to Walter. Like the few other superrich men Maggie had met while groveling for school funding, Walter took his immense wealth as a sign that he was anointed, that he'd been chosen by the Almighty Market to rule or—at the very least—to philosophize.

Sipping a Perrier, Walter wore khakis, a tailored white shirt, pristine hiking boots, and an impossibly-expensive-looking fur-lined suede field jacket. With his silver hair and gleaming white teeth, he looked like Ralph Lauren's version of a "rugged" grandpa. Having already treated Danny to his views on the impending apocalypse, Walter had spent most of the flight lecturing Maggie. Though he'd told her to please use his first name, he insisted on calling her "Miss Mayfield." The formality seemed to amuse him, like calling a cat "Mr. Whiskers." "Listen, Miss Mayfield, the world's going in the crapper. Every time I watch the news, it's bursting with crazy."

"Amen to that," said Diane. She was perched on a couch toward the front of the plane, nibbling on a pastry taken from an enormous silver platter on the coffee table beside her. When Danny had invited

Maggie on this field trip, she'd insisted on bringing Diane along. For a survivalist blogger, seeing Walter's luxury bunker would be better than a trip to Disneyland. And when Walter heard about Diane's *Doomsday on a Budget* blog, he'd assented, tickled to show off his digs to a bona fide expert. Walter had required Diane to sign a confidentiality agreement, of course. He didn't want "the hordes" descending on his hidey-hole.

Walter repeated, "Every time I watch the news, it's crazy. One week, it's that Korean haircut lobbing missiles over Japan. The next week, it's SARS or that monkey virus that makes you crap out your intestines. What's it called?"

"Ebola," said Diane.

"Right, Ebola. Plus, there's global warming, race riots, opioids . . ."

"Terrorism!" said Diane. She'd become Tilmore's backup singer.

Walter nodded. "Yeah, those ISIS people aren't playing around. And let's not forget cyberterrorists."

"The grid could go down any minute," said Diane.

Walter continued, "The world's turning into a *Choose Your Own Adventure* book loaded with nothing but terrible endings. I can't take any chances. If society's going to throw itself off a cliff, I have to be ready. I have to protect my kids." He leaned forward in his seat, his tone suddenly full of fierce determination. "I'd do anything to protect my kids. If anybody—I don't care if it's Mother Teresa—if *anybody* pulls a knife on them or something, I'd slap the shit out of 'em."

"Mother Teresa's dead," said Maggie. She didn't point out that Mother Teresa hadn't exactly been famous for pulling knives on anyone.

Walter shrugged. "I mean, like, hypothetically speaking."

"Ah," said Maggie.

Walter eyed Maggie speculatively. "You don't have any kids, do you, Miss Mayfield?"

"Uh, no," said Maggie. She wanted to add, "But thanks for bringing up that painful subject." But she held her tongue, for Danny's sake. He'd invited her along as his "plus one." So she had to behave. She squeezed

Danny's hand now, and he squeezed back. He'd convinced her that there was no point hiding their relationship from Walter. Billionaires don't gossip in the teachers' lounge.

Walter smirked at the couple. "You two lovebirds may think you've found the real thing. But let me tell you, until you have kids, you have no idea what it means to love someone. I mean *really* love someone. I *thought* I knew what love was. I mean, Valerie and I lasted twenty-two years. Not too shabby, eh?" Walter looked to Danny for the expected compliment.

And it came. "You beat the odds on that one, Walter," said Danny.

Maggie forced a smile. Danny had told her about Valerie. Maggie didn't realize that men could claim bragging rights for how long they'd waited to abandon their starter wives. *Nice.*

Walter went on, "And later, when that marriage tanked, I moved on to Crystal, and I thought that was it, the end all and be all—me and Crystal against the world." Crystal was Walter's trophy wife—a curvaceous twentysomething with huge boobs and tiny brains. "I told Crystal I had no interest in having children. Zero. And we were careful, but I guess my swimmers were too strong." Walter shook his head good-naturedly, genuflecting at the thought of his own virility.

"Then, when Wally Junior came into the world, I just . . . well, I'd never felt anything like it. I'd stare at him in his crib for hours. He's a gorgeous kid, looks just like me." Maggie had to fight back a giggle. Tilmore was the master of the ricocheting compliment—every bit of praise he uttered bounced back to him.

Walter continued, "And once I realized what a great thing parenthood was, I *had* to have another one. Right away. Crystal kicked up a fuss, said we should put it off a while, but she came round. Trust me, I can be very persuasive." Walter winked suggestively at Maggie, and she had to suppress the urge to say "Ewww."

He finished, "So a year after Wally was born, presto, we had Matilda."

Maggie perked up at the name. "Matilda? Are you a Roald Dahl fan?"

Walter frowned. "Road who?"

Maggie said, "Nothing. He wrote a book called *Matilda*. He was British."

"Yeah, well, my Tilly won't be some pasty-faced Brit. She's gonna be a knockout, just like her mother. Only Tilly's smart. She takes after me in the brains department." Walter tapped his finger against his temple, in case anyone had forgotten where he kept his brain.

Maggie asked, "So why didn't they come along today?"

"Who?"

"Your kids," said Maggie.

Walter batted at the air. "Oh Christ. They're the last thing you'd want on a three-hour flight. Tilly'd be crying, and Wally'd be running all over the place. I mean, who needs the headache, am I right? I love my kids, but . . . small doses, you know?"

Maggie said, "Ah, right. So Crystal had to stay back to watch them?"

"Nah. We've got nannies for that. Crystal just didn't want to come. She hates the bunker, says she's claustrophobic." Walter put air quotes around the word "claustrophobic," plainly skeptical of anything that might inconvenience him. "She says the bunker makes her feel like she's being buried alive. Whatever. I figure she'll get over that phobia nonsense when the bombs start falling. Great chance for personal growth, am I right?"

Danny nodded. "Sure."

A static noise came from the loudspeaker. Then the pilot announced, "Mr. Tilmore and guests, please buckle your seat belts. We're going to begin our descent into Rabbaclaw."

Maggie checked her already buckled seat belt while Diane grabbed another pastry and headed back to her own armchair next to Walter. Maggie looked down from her window. She saw nothing below but vast snow-covered fields, broken up by only a few clumps of trees. Diane tapped Maggie's knee and leaned across to whisper, "Holy shit. It looks like White Witch Narnia out there."

30

Apocalyptic Chic

Rabbaclaw, Wyoming, did not look like a pleasant spot to wait out the apocalypse. Its vast snow-covered expanses were broken up by just a few trees and a single stretch of road. Maggie couldn't help thinking that when God started to fill in his test paper for Rabbaclaw, he left most of it blank.

As soon as Walter's jet came to a stop on the runway, the flight attendant handed out matching red parkas with "TILMORE TOWER" stitched on them. The pilot had warned that it was below zero outside—so everyone suited up and pulled on their fur-lined hoods while, somewhere, PETA wept. Even with the parka on, Maggie felt the wind cut through her as she climbed down the stairs to the runway. A hooded lone figure in a TILMORE TOWER parka hustled them over to an idling black minivan.

Walter sat up front in the passenger seat, and his hired hand maneuvered the van off the runway and up an empty road. Walter pushed down his hood and ran a hand through his thinning silver mane. Maggie could see his combed-over bald spot from the back seat, and she felt a twinge of unworthy glee. Walter patted the driver's shoulder. "So, Hank, how're the hydroponics coming?"

Hank grumbled, "Fine, Mr. Tilmore." Hank's voice was low and gruff, a manly man's voice.

Walter nodded. "Good." He turned and told his guests, "Hank here is the genius behind Tilmore Tower. That right, Hank?"

Hank said, "It was a team effort, sir."

"Ah, he's being modest. Hank's the best survivalist engineer in the country. I wanted the best, and I got the best. Right, Hank?"

Hank grunted, the macho-man version of fluttering a fan.

After a few minutes, the minivan approached a tall fence lined with barbed wire. Two guards in TILMORE TOWER parkas and not-so-welcoming black ski masks stood sentry in the gloom. They had automatic weapons slung over their shoulders so they could stop any-one from crashing Walter's postapocalyptic party. Maggie whispered to Danny, "A gated community? How California."

Danny whispered back, "Behave, and I'll give you a candy bar later."

The guards waved them through, and Hank drove them on to more snowy nothingness. Maggie frowned, asking, "Shouldn't Tilmore Tower have a tower somewhere?"

Walter laughed. "We *do* have a tower, my dear. But it's under-ground. Tell her, Hank."

Hank said, "Ma'am, the facility's inside a missile silo the govern-ment built back in the '60s. It goes fourteen stories down."

Diane said, "Whoa. It's like *Journey to the Center of the Earth*. I loved that show." Diane was enjoying herself mightily.

Soon, Hank pulled the van up alongside a massive metal doorway carved into the side of a low hill. It looked like the entrance to a hob-bit hole—if Bilbo Baggins had been a rich paranoid. Switching off the engine, Hank turned to say, "All right, folks. It's just a short walk over to the elevator."

As soon as Maggie got outside, the icy wind smacked her in the face again. She walk-ran as fast as she could, but Walter insisted on stopping the group so he could point out rows of solar panels mounted alongside the entrance. He shouted over the wind, "These beauties can store energy for eighteen months! They'll power the facility year-round!" The group nodded and made impressed noises—anything to get out of the cold.

Once they got inside the facility's large outer door, the wind died. As the group approached the elevator, Danny asked, "Will solar panels work out there?"

Walter smirked, "Yes, indeedy. I know today's chilly, but Rabbaclaw gets two hundred days of sunshine per year. We'll be just fine, Danny boy."

Diane piped up, "I wouldn't count on that."

"What do you mean?" asked Walter.

"Nobody's gonna be getting any sunshine when the bomb comes. Nuclear winter's gonna turn the lights off."

Walter waved this off. "Yes, but not for long."

Diane continued cheerfully, "Depends how many nukes get shot off and what kind. Right now, India and Pakistan are the odds-on favorites to get the party started. Course they'll use small nukes, like the ones we dropped on Japan. But that'll pump five megatons of black carbon into the atmosphere. Carbon rain'll clear up some of that, but the Colorado boys say we'll still be looking at twenty years of winter, easy. And if we drop the bigger stuff, then—"

Walter interrupted, "The Colorado boys?"

Hank explained, "The researchers at the University of Colorado, Mr. Tilmore. We talked about them." Hank looked at the floor as he said this, his square jaw clenched—the pose of a man straining mightily against the urge to say, "I told you so."

Walter absorbed this tidbit and quickly repackaged it to his liking. "So we've already taken their research into account? Good, that's good." He turned back toward the approaching elevator.

Behind him, Maggie shot Diane a questioning look. Diane responded by shaking her head. Then she splayed her hands and mouthed the word "BOOM." Maggie looked away, trying not to laugh. The elevator arrived, and everyone loaded onto it. As it descended, Tilmore bragged, "This isn't just any elevator—it's a Tindler."

Diane whistled. "Whew, a Tindler. These are the gold standard in prepper elevators. They say the ayatollah's got one, Richard Branson too."

Walter glowed. "This baby can get us all the way down to the bottom in fifty seconds flat. That's got to be some kind of record."

Diane said, "Nah. They got a Tindler over in Kansas that gets you down fifteen stories in thirty seconds flat." Walter scowled at her. Diane said apologetically, "I saw it on *Nightline*."

Danny offered, "Well, this is the fastest elevator I've ever been on. I'm not going to get the bends on this thing, am I, Walter?" Danny infused this question with all the "golly-gee" enthusiasm he could.

Walter simpered, "You get the bends by going *up* to the surface, not down, Danny boy. And don't worry: the pressure in this facility is kept consistent at all times. We have pressure systems, filtration systems, the works. Like I said, Hank's the brains behind the whole operation."

Hank mumbled something about it being a "team effort" again, and Walter repeated the bit about false modesty. But Maggie sensed Hank's reaction didn't stem from faux-humility—it was a disclaimer. Walter was too domineering to allow anyone full reign over his pet project. From the bit about the solar panels, Maggie guessed that Walter had overridden Hank's advice on key points. Walter was like a toddler throwing eggshells into batter, screaming that they'd make the cake "yummy crunchy." Only this toddler had paid for the batter, so he could wreck whatever he pleased.

When they got down to the bottom floor, the tour began, and Maggie *was* impressed. The lower seven floors were cut into luxury apartments—each equipped with sumptuously decorated bedrooms, a living room, a fully stocked kitchen, and an ultramodern bathroom (complete with bidets!). Every room had at least one false window: a flat-screen TV showing a continuous feed of a sun-drenched landscape to foster the illusion that you were up on the surface.

Looking at one such "window," Danny asked, "Is that a YALOS Diamond?"

"A what?" asked Maggie.

"A YALOS Diamond TV," said Danny. "It's got diamonds embedded in the screen. They go for $150 grand!"

Walter nodded. "More, Danny boy. And we've got ten different landscapes to choose from, each timed to show sunlight during the day and darkness at night. They keep your circadian rhythms from going haywire." Walter grabbed a remote and flicked to a feed showing the Eiffel Tower on a sunny day. "My favorite is Morning in Paris."

Diane said, "Ooh, can we see the other ones?"

Walter channel surfed while Danny and Diane excitedly chose their favorites. Danny loved "Caribbean Isles" while Diane preferred "Winter Wonderland." They sounded like teenage girls shopping for lotions at Bath & Body Works. Maggie smiled but said nothing.

After visiting the lower seven floors of luxury apartments, the tour moved up to two floors of jarringly ascetic "staff quarters." Diane quipped, "It's like that *Upstairs Downstairs* show, but in reverse."

Walter explained, "Obviously, the potential for exposure to radiation lessens the further *down* you go. So the prime real estate is below in the owners' quarters. But still . . . these floors should be pretty safe. And they'll be like Shangri-la compared to what's up on the surface."

Maggie asked, "So who's on staff?"

"Well, there's Hank of course." Walter gestured to Hank in case Maggie needed a visual aid. "Plus, there'll be the chef, medical staff, maintenance, security guards, and a masseuse."

Maggie nodded, careful to sound neutral. "A masseuse? I guess that makes sense. I imagine people will carry a lot of stress in their shoulders after doomsday."

"Oh yes," said Walter.

Maggie asked, "There's not much room for their families, is there?"
Walter beamed. "I specifically chose men without families."

"Really?"

Walter laughed. "I'm not running a day-care center."

Maggie nodded. "Of course not." Her brain flashed to the pharaohs. They'd had their pyramids stocked with everything they'd need for the afterlife, including their favorite slaves. Labor relations hadn't advanced much.

Given the bleakness of the staff quarters, the group did not linger there. Instead, they headed to the upper "common areas." The five floors of "common areas" included a fully equipped gym, auxiliary generator rooms, supply rooms, an elaborate greenhouse (complete with hydroponics!), weapons lockers (to keep out the riffraff!), a dog park with fake grass, and a swimming pool surrounded by murals of beach scenes. Walter pointed out the brand names of various features, and Daniel made impressed noises.

Maggie noticed that the common areas—unlike the residences—had loads of antibacterial gel dispensers. Gesturing to one, she told Walter, "You guys are big on hygiene."

Walter grinned. "There's going to be a lot of us down here—sixty people. It'll be crucial to keep the germs at bay." He took a squirt of gel and rubbed his hands together. Maggie suddenly remembered Danny mentioning that Walter had a touch of obsessive-compulsive disorder. She wondered if she'd want to spend end times trapped with Howard Hughes.

As Walter moved ahead with Danny, Maggie saw Diane shake her head again, glaring at a gel dispenser. Apparently having finally realized that Walter did not savor her criticisms, Diane whispered to Maggie: "These are a big mistake."

Cutting in on the women's conversation, Hank asked, "Why'd you say that?" He didn't sound offended, just interested.

Diane answered coolly, "Because—and I don't mean any disrespect here—if you've got sixty people living this close together, people are gonna get sick a lot no matter what you do. And if they're slathering this gel crap on their hands all the time, their bodies'll get resistant to antibiotics. Meds won't work when you need 'em."

Hank squinted at Diane. "Who *are* you?"

Diane squared her shoulders, evidently expecting some sort of fight over credentials. "I write a blog for preppers. It's called *Doomsday on a Budget*."

Hank's stern expression dissolved as he broke into a radiant grin. The smile transformed his features, suddenly making Maggie realize just how handsome he was. "You're Doomsday Di?"

Diane colored prettily. "I am. You read my blog?"

"Never miss it. You and *SGW* are my favorites." Hank's voice went up a bit toward the end of this sentence. He was a doomsday fan, and *this* was his Comic-Con.

Maggie asked, "What's *SGW*?"

Diane and Hank chorused, "*Shit's Getting Weird.*"

Diane asked Hank, "Do you ever comment?"

Hank nodded. "Course. I'm Builder29."

Diane's face lit up. "You're Builder29? Well, this *is* a treat."

Maggie edged away from the chatting preppers and headed down the hallway to catch up with her man. As she came around a corner, Walter and Danny turned. Walter said, "Ah, there you are. I've been looking forward to showing you this." He pushed open a side door and switched on a light. "*This* is our classroom." He said it with the same intonation of a British tycoon announcing: "Welcome to Jurassic Park."

Maggie walked in and looked around. It was the most opulent classroom she'd ever seen. Blond wood tables, Persian carpets, and pitch-perfect lighting made the room seem warm but not drowsy. Workstations featured ergonomic chairs, the latest Mac laptops, and high-end art supplies. Bookcases lined the lower walls, sporting complete collections of pristine Caldecott and Newbery prizewinners along with basic readers. And on the walls were *four* top-of-the-line electronic whiteboards—retailing at $10,000 apiece. Maggie knew the price too well. She'd ogled the whiteboards online, fantasizing about how they'd transform her school. And here were four of them—hoarded for a miser's rainy day. Maggie asked, "This is your fallback?"

Walter nodded. "Not bad, eh?"

Maggie managed to squeak out, "How much did all this cost?"

Walter grinned—obviously welcoming this question. "Not much. About a hundred grand, way cheaper than twelve years of private school."

Maggie's mouth had gone dry. "I see." The other parts of Tilmore Tower hadn't offended her, hadn't even touched her. Walter's gilded underground palace was no worse than the Kardashians' golden toilets or Beyoncé's diamond-encrusted Barbie dolls. Those things hadn't hurt Maggie because she'd never longed for them. But this classroom was different. It was chock-full of things she'd yearned for, not to hoard or to lord over—but to use. And unlike Walter, she knew *how* to use these things. To him, they were just shiny toys. To her, they were the tools of her profession, and they were being wasted.

She looked at Danny now. "How does the MathPal fit into all this?"

Walter said, "Let me field that one. The driving force behind the MathPal, behind all of Edutek's products, is to get rid of the most expensive, tedious part of the education system: the teachers."

"Excuse me?" said Maggie.

Walter went on, "It's mechanization, Miss Mayfield. It's the way the world is going. Supermarket cashiers give way to self-checkout machines. Autoworkers give way to robots. Soon, truckers will give way to self-driving trucks. As technology advances, it takes over ever more complex tasks. You can't stop it."

Maggie was incredulous. "So you think the MathPal is going to replace actual teachers?"

"I *know* it will. Maybe not in five years, maybe not even in ten. But it *will* happen. Why bother paying for teachers when you can have a much cheaper, more effective system like the MathPal? A system that delivers lessons based on the individual student's ever-changing skill set—without boring him for a second." As he'd spoken, Walter's voice had taken on the "but-wait-there's-more" tone of a used car salesman.

Maggie said, "I see." She felt Samuel L. Jackson levels of rage building up inside her. She had an almost physical need to tell Walter how lousy the MathPal was, how it could never replace her teachers. She wanted to tell him how destructive it was for children to have every lesson—every experience—tailor-made for their specific tastes, how disastrous it was to build children who could not tolerate a millisecond of boredom or discomfort. How selfish—how Walter-like!—those little monsters could be. She wanted to shake him by the shoulders and scream that he was wrong about inevitability. It was *not* inevitable that hardworking, dedicated professionals would step aside so that the Walters of the world could "monetize" and "optimize" everything. What was inevitable—what was *right*—was that there would be a comeuppance for all this hubristic, technological bullying.

She wanted to tell him this, but he was her boyfriend's boss. So instead, she did something she'd never done in front of two male witnesses. She fumbled in her purse, yanked out a chocolate bar, and wolfed it down Cookie Monster–style. The men's eyebrows shot up in unison as they watched her. When she was done, she wiped the edges of her mouth, telling them sheepishly, "I'm hypoglycemic."

Walter said, "Ah, well then . . ." He looked puzzled for a moment, as if unsure whether to be concerned or disgusted.

Danny, however, sensed an unmistakable disturbance in the Force. He said, "Obviously, the MathPal is nowhere near replacing teachers at this point. We're decades from doing anything like that, if ever. Right now, the goal is only to supplement what teachers are doing. And—"

Walter cut in, "We disagree about timing, Danny boy. But you're right. For now, the MathPal is a backup tool. But I take comfort—and so do my friends—from knowing it's there. If the bombs fall, our kids will need it. I've already sold prototypes of the MathPal to all of my friends. Word is spreading. Demand is skyrocketing." Buoyed by his own words, Walter headed out of the classroom, saying cheerily, "On with the tour!"

Maggie asked Danny, "Was this your plan—to market the MathPal to survivalist tycoons as a teacher replacement?"

Danny shrugged. "Among other things."

"Yeah, but that can't be a big market. I mean . . ."

Danny stepped in closer to her. "It doesn't *have* to be a big market. You don't need a gazillion sales . . . so long as you hit the right price point. If guys like Walter can blow $150K on a window TV, they can fork out a lot more for a decent math system for their kids. After all, the children are our future and all that."

"But how many guys like Walter can there be?"

Danny smiled. "There are *a lot* of Walters out there. The survival fad's caught on big with the jet set. Everybody who's anybody has a bunker somewhere. There are underground luxury condos springing up—or I guess, springing down—all over the world: here, Europe, China, and don't get me started on South Korea."

Maggie said sourly, "I assume there aren't many in Africa."

Danny balked. "Are you kidding?! What else do you give the dictator who has it all?"

Maggie sighed. Her eyes fell on one of the electronic whiteboards. Would the MathPal be like that? Paid for and never used? Was it just a tech version of Walter's subterranean swimming pool? His version of a gold-plated toilet? What a waste!

But then, a new thought dawned. If the MathPal didn't work—this might be the perfect place for it, at the bottom of a rich man's over-stuffed toy box. For the first time since she'd tested the program and gotten a sense of just how lousy it was, Maggie saw a way out. Maybe Danny could have all the success he needed in selling meticulously branded, overpriced snake oil to rich preppers. The MathPal could be like Tindler elevators or YALOS Diamond TVs. Maybe Danny could prosper, and no one would really get hurt.

He took her hand. "Come on, Maggie, they're waiting for us."

31

INSPECTING RACHEL

Lucy's mother did not believe in playdates. Playdates were a waste of time, an excuse for "lazy white kids" to play video games. So instead of a "playdate," Lucy asked for a "team meeting." Lucy and Rachel were working on a project for the school science fair. She explained science fairs to her mother, saying that student teams compete and only one team from each grade wins. Mrs. Wong asked if any kids lose, and Lucy said no. The "not winners" get a ribbon for participating. Mrs. Wong shook her head in disgust. "Sometime, a kid need to lose big in front everyone. It push him work hard next time." Mrs. Wong jabbed at the air with her index finger to show how shame could prod kids forward. The science fair wasn't until spring, still months away. Another parent—maybe one with lazy white kids—might have questioned the need to get such a big head start, but not Mrs. Wong.

Rachel arrived on the Wongs' doorstep on the first Saturday of winter break. Her heavily made-up, blond mother, Andrea Klemper, did not bother to get out of her expensive cream-colored car. Instead, Andrea talk-shouted from the driver's seat, explaining that she was rushing to take her son to an indoor soccer clinic. Mrs. Wong smiled and bobbed her head, saying loudly, "No trouble, no trouble." But as she turned and ushered Rachel into the house, Mrs. Wong muttered something in Chinese about white people having terrible manners. Strike one.

Still smiling, Mrs. Wong asked Rachel for her jacket. As she hung it on a pegboard, she said to Lucy in Chinese, "Sweet face, but how come so fat?"

Betraying nothing, Lucy answered casually in Chinese, "I'm not dating her, Mom." Lucy was used to her mother's parallel conversations. They were like watching a movie with painfully polite English-spoken dialogue and rude, brutally honest Chinese subtitles.

Mrs. Wong asked in Chinese, "Her mother works?"

Lucy said no, and Mrs. Wong shook her head. Mrs. Wong—a junior project manager for a giant pharmaceutical company—disapproved of women who didn't work. She prodded Lucy in Chinese, "What about her father?"

Lucy glanced at Rachel, who wore the look of a person trapped in an elevator, pretending not to have smelled a stranger's fart. She might not know Mandarin, but she sensed that the Wongs were discussing her—she smelled it. Switching to English, Lucy said, "Rachel's dad is a big-time lawyer. He travels all over the country, arguing cases."

Mrs. Wong asked Rachel—in English, "So you don't see your daddy much?"

Rachel said, "No, ma'am."

Mrs. Wong nodded. "Good." She approved of workaholics. She led the girls to the kitchen. Lucy had left a few nature books on the table in there—proof of the team meeting's seriousness. While the girls opened their books, Mrs. Wong fetched unasked-for snacks and drinks: SunChips, glasses of water, and sliced lychee nuts.

The girls argued over whether to do their project on butterflies or clown fish while Mrs. Wong chopped vegetables for dinner. Unable to remain silent for long, Mrs. Wong drifted over, asking, "Why do project on clown fish? Fish are for pan, not project."

Rachel said, "Most of the time, yes—but not clown fish. They're awesome. Did you know all clown fish are born male?"

Mrs. Wong said quickly, "I know, I know. So what?" Lucy knew her mother was bluffing. Mrs. Wong said you should never admit ignorance to a white person "because then they get you."

Rachel went on, "So, when the last female clown fish dies, the toughest, most dominant male fish *becomes* a female. Isn't that cool?"

Mrs. Wong nodded, saying, "That's 'cause women stronger and smarter than men. Only best man can become a woman. Like Bruce Jenner!"

Rachel said, "Yeah. He wasn't ready to become a woman till *after* he won a bazillion medals."

Mrs. Wong smirked, and Lucy felt giddy—proud and relieved that her two "best people" were getting along so well. Mrs. Wong drifted out of the kitchen, leaving the girls to their "work." And the girls spent the next two hours whispering and doodling on their drawing pads. Rachel drew a few clown fish, and Lucy ruffled the pages of her books to pantomime productivity.

Lucy said, "You were already good, but your drawings are getting so much better."

Rachel beamed. "That's because of Miss Pearl."

Lucy singsonged, "Yes, you're Miss Pearl's pearl."

Rachel simpered, "Sounds like someone's jealous."

"Not about Miss Pearl. I'm just jealous because you don't have to work on the MathPal. It's a moron game. Same stuff over and over, and then all that dopey dancing and fake rewards. And makeup, blech." Lucy gagged theatrically.

Rachel ventured, "The other kids like it."

Lucy frowned. "Other kids are zombies, just happy to play a video game. They don't have brains." As if on cue, both girls extended their arms and lolled their heads, growling, "Brains, must eat brains."

Mrs. Wong returned, saw them, and pursed her lips in disgust. "You supposed to be working on clown fish."

"We are," said Lucy. "Just look at Rachel's drawing."

Mrs. Wong bent to look at Rachel's art pad. Then she squinted at Rachel. "You trace this?"

"No, Mrs. Wong. I drew it freehand," said Rachel.

Mrs. Wong tapped the art pad. "Show me."

Rachel quickly drew a gorgeous clown fish as only Rachel could, and Mrs. Wong nodded, impressed. Without asking, she seized Rachel's art pad and began flicking through it. Lucy squirmed in her seat, delighted by her mother's interest, but her glee fizzled when she saw the panic on Rachel's face.

Mrs. Wong's smile dissolved. She put the pad down with a thud. The page she'd stopped on showed a pencil drawing of Mrs. Wong, her hands on her hips and her chin jutting out as if daring someone to punch her. Staring at the drawing, Mrs. Wong said sternly, "Tell truth, this picture of me?"

Rachel nodded wordlessly, and Lucy felt her hopes shrivel. Her mother would throw Rachel out and give Lucy one of her patented tongue-lashings.

But instead, Mrs. Wong grinned—a real grin, not her fake, tooth-bearing one. "So beautiful. So fierce. But my feet are smaller than that." She tapped the paper, commanding, "You fix it." Rachel bent to correct the drawing while Mrs. Wong leaned in, watching her. Lucy grabbed a lychee nut. Her friend had passed her entrance exam.

32

The Very Principled Maggie Mayfield

After her trip to Walter's bunker, Maggie decided to decide the MathPal was harmless. Once unleashed on the market, it would either flop or be relegated to the rarefied universe of "luxury goods." It would be a technological bauble for rich people—an overpriced program designed to educate wealthy preppers' children if and when society crumbled. Who cared if it didn't teach much math? Or if it was loaded with more ads than a *SkyMall* magazine? Maggie didn't have time to worry about how the One Percent might teach their progeny in some dystopian future.

No, what mattered were Maggie's students, here and now. They were locked into working with the MathPal, but only for a year. Danny had promised to strip out the ads and forgo selling her students' user data. Maggie would hold him to both promises. For the moment, her main goal would be to raise money so she could pay for STEAM programs here on out without mortgaging her school's soul.

And in the meanwhile, she would enjoy Danny. She deserved to enjoy something in this life, something fleshy and fun. A woman could not abide by Netflix and chocolate alone. She and Danny might have their differences, but he was a good man. She was sure of it, sort of.

She spent the second half of winter break camping out in his swanky San Francisco apartment. During the day, while Danny put in much-needed face time at Edutek's main offices, Maggie played tourist. She ate dumplings in Chinatown, took selfies on Fisherman's Wharf, and spent a whole day at Alcatraz touring the prison where Al Capone had writhed in syphilitic agony.

Nights belonged to Danny. Even though he worked long hours, he made time to treat her to late-night dinners out at San Francisco's priciest eateries. Maggie had feared that—after the thrill of sneaking around for weeks—their romance might wither in public. Instead, like countless gays before her, she found being "out" in San Francisco delightful. She loved strolling down the street, holding hands with Danny, and he enjoyed "showing her off."

Best of all was the sex. Maggie yelled "Oh God" so many times that Danny's neighbors must have wondered if he'd suddenly gotten religion.

Drugged with happiness, Maggie made the mistake of calling Diane one afternoon. Diane made appreciative noises as Maggie described her glorious vacation. But it was a half-hearted performance, and Maggie knew it. Like a petulant teenager, she snapped, "Why aren't you happy for me?"

"I am happy for you. It's just . . ."

"Just what?" asked Maggie.

"Don't get me wrong. I think it's great that you tore the dust cover off your snatch. I really do. And I wholeheartedly support fooling around with Big Red." Diane was fickle with nicknames—so Danny had morphed from "Homeland" into "Big Red." "But are you sure you want to get serious with him?"

Maggie blustered, "I don't see why not."

Diane sucked air in through her teeth, and Maggie could picture her wincing on the other end of the line. "I think you *do* see why not, Magpie. I mean, you've always been moralistic—a very principled principal. Whoever you're with has to square with that."

"So I can only date saints?"

"No," said Diane. "Your man doesn't have to be perfect. But he can't graffiti your church."

Maggie sighed. "You lost me."

"Look, I don't know many people who have a true calling, but you're one of 'em. Your whole life is about teaching kids. That means the three *R*s, but it also means character. Moral shit. And this guy is messing with kids on both levels."

Maggie snorted. "Daniel isn't corrupting children."

"No, he's not training them to be killers or congressmen. But he's messing with their heads. That MathPal nudges kids in the wrong direction. It makes 'em less smart and more materialistic, probably less focused too."

Maggie fumed, "Daniel is *not* the MathPal."

"Yeah, but he's the one pushing it."

Like a ventriloquist's dummy, Maggie channeled Danny's words. "Besides, it's unfair to judge the MathPal at this point. The program is not set in stone. Edutek is constantly changing it. It's a moving target. It's . . ."

"Slippery?" asked Diane.

Maggie bristled. "That's not what I meant, and you know it."

Diane answered, "Calm down. I'm on your side. If you're fine with Danny, I'm fine too. It's just . . ."

"What?"

Diane said softly, "I don't think you're fine, Maggie."

Later that night, as Danny slept, Maggie lay beside him, arguing inside her head with Diane. Danny was *not* sleazy. He couldn't be. The movies had taught Maggie how to spot sleazy men. Sleazy men could be handsome, but they had certain tells: slicked-back hair, an oily complexion, or a vulpine smile. Sleazy men didn't listen beautifully, lip-sync Elvis songs, or fuss over puppies on the street. No, sleazes cut off your sentences, listened to vaguely sinister classical music, and hated animals—except for puffy white cats that they stroked while sitting in oversize leather chairs. When a sleaze wanted a woman, he'd say something creepy like "You are my most exquisite possession." And Danny had never said that. So there!

Besides, Danny worked too hard to be a sleaze. Maggie was born and raised in Protestant New England, and conflated toil with virtue. She herself was a workaholic in good standing, and she was slightly in awe of Danny's industriousness.

Even when Danny was relaxing, he was still "at work." Case in point, he got up every morning at five thirty to work out. His living room was tricked out with an exercise bike, free weights, and an elaborate full-body Nautilus machine. When Maggie had teased him about "trying to look good for the ladies," he'd laughed, saying he needed to stay fit "for work."

Maggie asked, "Since when does a CEO have to look good in a bathing suit?"

"It's not about looking good. It's about looking young. Tech is a young man's game," said Danny.

"You're young," said Maggie.

"Are you kidding?"

"You're what? Forty-two?" asked Maggie.

He shook his head. "No, I'm forty-four." He said this if as delivering a cancer diagnosis.

"Forty-four is old?"

"Yes, ma'am."

"But Mark Zuckerberg is in his forties." Maggie had studied up on the Facebook mogul after Danny'd first invoked him as part of his holy trinity.

"Yes, he's in his forties *now*, but he was in his twenties when he founded Facebook. Forty-four is young for a titan of industry, but it's old for a person who's never had a hit." Danny smiled as he said this, but he couldn't hide the anxiety in his eyes.

Maggie consoled him, "Well, Methuselah, you look pretty spry to me." It made her feel vaguely unsafe to be with a man who felt so unsafe—the emotional equivalent of sitting on a rickety chair.

But Maggie soon twisted his insecurity into a virtue. It meant he was one of the good guys. Like Dorothy assuming all witches are old and ugly, Maggie assumed all "sleazes" were smug and lazy.

33

And the Winner Is . . .

January was a slow month at Carmel Knolls Elementary. Students and teachers moved groggily about, emotionally hungover from the holidays. But there were a few glimmers of liveliness. Mr. Baran opened his morning superhero workouts to all comers, and they became wildly popular, thanks to the elaborate scenarios "superassistant" Connor helped devise. Mr. Carlsen tricked students into learning chemistry by starting a Slime Club, and Lucy quickly established herself as the campus "slime queen," gaining much-needed cool points.

But for Lucy, Slime Club was not January's headline. Instead, she focused on the school's art contest, pretentiously dubbed "Aspirations." The theme was the equally pretentious "Ideas Take Flight." Lucy mulled it over, but all her ideas plummeted to the ground. A Tinker Bell wearing brainiac glasses? The Wright brothers having a stilted eureka moment?

Whoever won the school round would move on to the district level, then county, then state, and so on until achieving world domination. And Lucy wanted first prize for Rachel.

On the night of the contest, parents and students trudged into the auditorium, girding themselves to be uplifted by culture. Miss Pearl greeted people as they filed in, and she gave Rachel and Lucy an especially huge smile.

The contest entries hung in neat rows on the walls. Lucy and Rachel shuffled past them slowly, shepherded by Mrs. Wong. Rachel's father was out of town on business, but her mother was there all right. Andrea Klemper was on the PTA committee hosting the contest. She was working the refreshments table, resplendent in a tight, shimmery silver dress. She gave them a distracted wave, and Mrs. Wong reciprocated with her best obsequious-cute-Chinese-lady smile, telling Lucy in Mandarin, "She looks like Tinfoil Barbie."

Lucy pressed forward, studying the competition. She was gratified to see that most of the kids had skipped the "ideas" part of the "Ideas in Flight" theme and focused exclusively on "flight." The walls were crammed with clumsily made paintings of flying birds, planes, and rockets. Lucy whispered to Rachel, "You are soooo going to win."

Rachel didn't answer. Her eyebrows were knit together with worry. She looked like she expected a monster to jump out at her. And that's sort of what happened. Rachel's monster was a painting in the fifth-grader section. It showed a perfectly rendered pterodactyl flying over a Jurassic jungle. Then there was a wave of small white parentheses, the kind they use in cartoons to show something being broadcast from one tower to another. And on the other side of those marks was a pelican flying above the ocean. Attached to the pelican's foot was a red banner flowing out across the bottom of the painting. The banner said "EVOLUTION."

Lucy scowled at the painting. "It stinks."

Rachel answered, "It doesn't stink. It's beautiful."

"That's *why* it stinks," said Lucy.

Mrs. Wong said too loudly, "It's not gonna win. People hate birds. So dirty."

Lucy turned on her mother. "People don't *hate* birds, Ma."

Mrs. Wong folded her arms across her chest. "You'll see. I know things."

Rachel told Lucy, "I can't see my painting. Do you see it anywhere?"

Lucy shrugged. "Not yet. Don't worry. It's got to be around here."

They continued walking, looking at more birds and planes until a PTA lady took the stage with a microphone. The PTA lady was blond and painfully thin like Rachel's mom. They looked like they'd been bought at the same store. She said, "Isn't it a wonderful night out? I'd like to thank the contestants, and Sadie Pearl, our fabulous art teacher." The PTA blonde bubbled, "Don't forget to donate to the STEAM fund so we can keep Miss Pearl. She's the best. Isn't she the best?"

The PTA blonde went on, "And now, the moment of truth. The judges—I'd tell you who they are, but then I'd have to kill you, just kidding!—the judges came by earlier today, and they picked three winners. Now, obviously, all you kids are winners. But only three of you are actual winners. I mean, only three will go on to the next level.

"In third place, we have Ryan Samperson from the fifth grade for his terrific poem about the Wright brothers. Come on up, Ryan." A short gap-toothed boy ran to the front while the crowd applauded.

Mrs. Wong wrinkled her nose in distaste, telling Lucy in Chinese, "You can win with a poem? That's so lazy, like wearing sweatpants to a wedding."

The emcee went on, "And in second place, we have Lisa Mullens—also from the fifth grade—for her wonderful painting on evolution. Get up here, Lisa." A tall, lanky girl with frizzy red hair walked to the stage, beaming.

Lucy reached for Rachel's sweaty hand, and the two girls murmured a prayer toward the floor.

"And in first place, we have a surprise. As you may know, first place usually goes to a fifth or sixth grader. And we do have several honorable mentions from those classes. But today, for the first time in years, first

place goes to a third grader—Rachel Klemper. Come on up, Rachel."
Rachel ran up, and the PTA lady handed her a trophy, then gestured to
a large easel with a black cloth over it. Another PTA minion removed
the cloth to reveal Rachel's painting beneath. The microphone lady said,
"Here it is—the winner of this year's Aspirations contest."

The crowd made impressed noises as they stared at the painting.
And Lucy chided herself for ever doubting her friend would win.
Rachel's "Ideas in Flight" showed a little girl looking out her window
as books flew through the sunlit sky. Each book had wings, and was different from its fellows. In vibrant colors, Rachel captured the delighted
wonder on the girl's face and the sense of movement as the books flew.

Lucy beamed at her friend, and Rachel beamed back.

Mrs. Wong gave Lucy a playful slap on the arm, saying in Chinese,
"I told you, she's a winner."

The reception wound down quickly after that, the younger kids
loudly complaining about needing to go home so they would not miss
TV. Art was quaint, but TV was essential. It being a Friday night,
Rachel had arranged to sleep over at the Wongs'.

As the people filtered out, Rachel ran over to her mom at the
refreshment table. Lucy and her mother lingered close by, listening.
Rachel jumped from foot to foot, like a puppy begging for attention.
She spoke in a great rush. "It was awesome. Wasn't it so awesome?"

Mrs. Klemper straightened her tight dress. She agreed it "was quite
something." She smiled down at Rachel, but Lucy saw that the smile
did not reach her eyes. There was no warmth there.

Mrs. Wong stepped forward, telling Mrs. Klemper, "You must be
so proud. I tell my Lucy, 'How come you can't draw like that?' Such big
prize. Maybe get scholarship for best college, eh?"

Mrs. Klemper said blandly, "Well, let's not count our chickens."
Then she turned back to Rachel. "You're off with the Wongs tonight,
right, sweetie?"

Rachel nodded, unsure how to process her mother's lack of enthusiasm. She said numbly, "We're going for ice cream."

Mrs. Klemper took out her purse and pulled out some cash. "Well, let's make sure you treat the Wongs. And remember, honey, just one scoop. Those pounds aren't going to come off by themselves." She poked Rachel's substantial belly, and Rachel's cheeks reddened.

Mrs. Klemper told Rachel and Mrs. Wong, "I'm going to be stuck here, cleaning up. Then your brother's got that early morning soccer clinic. Oh well, no rest for the weary." She air-kissed Rachel's cheek, and Mrs. Wong steered the girls out of the building.

As they walked outside, Lucy sensed Rachel's disappointment, but Lucy didn't know what to do with it. So she babbled happily about what would come next. Rachel would win district, then citywide, then who knows! Rachel nodded, but said nothing. And neither did Lucy's mom.

Mrs. Wong opened the car doors and got the girls settled in, then she fumbled with the radio, still saying nothing. She turned on a pop station, too loud. And then Mrs. Klemper passed by, her high heels clacking noisily against the blacktop as she carried two trays to her cream-colored SUV. Mrs. Wong whipped her door open, telling the girls that she should help with the trays.

She slammed the door shut, and—inside—Rachel started to sway to the blasting pop music. Lucy pretended to get caught up in the music too. But over Rachel's shoulder, Lucy saw her mother walk stiffly over to Mrs. Klemper's SUV. She could not hear what her mother said to Mrs. Klemper, but—from her mother's fighting stance and the shocked look on Mrs. Klemper's face—Lucy knew it was not good.

34

GUERRILLA VALENTINES

Diane and Maggie stood in a tiny puddle of light beneath a street lamp, both of them clad in black. Maggie tugged on the bill of her black baseball cap to hide her face. Diane told her, "You don't have to do this."

"I want to do this," said Maggie. Both of them spoke in low, husky whispers, like female versions of Batman.

"This isn't your fight anymore. For Chrissake, it's Valentine's Day. You should be home with Danny."

"Daniel's in San Francisco."

"Again?"

"The man's company is up there, Diane."

Diane frowned. "Yeah, but he should be spending Valentine's Day with you, not holed up in some office. You aren't some old married couple. You're in the throes."

"The throes?"

Diane said, "The throes of passion—those early days of a romance where you bump into walls 'cause you're so stupid in love. I don't care how big a deal his job is. It's your first Valentine's Day. Danny should get his tail down here."

Maggie shrugged, as if this mutinous thought hadn't kept her up at night. She told herself it was silly to be sentimental about Valentine's Day, but the committee in her head wasn't buying it. They insisted *he should be here.* But since Christmas, Danny's already-long hours had gotten even longer. His investors were clamoring for results, and his staff was racing to analyze the MathPal's beta-testing data and prepare for the product's launch.

Maggie missed Danny, but she didn't complain. Complaints would make her seem unsupportive or, even worse, needy. Nothing bulldozes desire like neediness. Eager to change the subject, she told Diane, "Well, *you* should be in Wyoming with Hank."

Diane bristled. "Don't start on that. I told you, Hank's just a friend."

"A friend who's sent you enough flowers to open a funeral home."

Diane hip-checked Maggie. "Stop it."

Maggie singsonged quietly, "K-I-S-S-I-N-G, first comes love, then comes . . ."

"Are we going to do this thing or not?" Diane's voice had an edge to it now.

Maggie nodded, chastened. Diane pointed to the far side of the hotel parking lot. "You take the left section. I'll take the right."

Maggie grabbed Diane by the forearm. "You're sure about this setup?"

Diane said defensively, "Yes, I'm sure. I showed you the brochure, didn't I? Those Beta Nutritionals people will have those ladies in there for two nights. Tonight's all about *the problem.* They tell those poor suckers they're alone on Valentine's Day 'cause they *deserve* to be alone. They're too fat to love. The only way they'll get male attention is when they die and their hot gay neighbor smells the corpse. Then, tomorrow night's *the solution.* They're gonna sell them a fortune in bullshit diet supplements—some miracle crap they found in Asia or the Amazon or some other exotic A-place."

Maggie said solemnly, "Let's do this."

The two women split up, putting pink notes on each windshield. Every note was the same, each written out in Diane's loopy, feminine cursive (Maggie's handwriting was a bit too spiky—somehow vaguely threatening). The notes said: *"Save your money, sweetie. You're already beautiful."*

Maggie and Diane had begun their guerrilla Valentine campaigns the February after Maggie's divorce. They mostly targeted weight-loss seminars and a few of the meaner "what's-wrong-with-you-lady" how-to dating conferences. Every Valentine's Day, hotels in suburban Carmel Valley made a double killing: renting regular rooms out to beleaguered parents desperate for a night of nonfurtive sex and renting conference halls out to money-grabbing self-help gurus preying on women who hadn't had sex—furtive or otherwise—in eons.

Maggie and Diane had only screwed up one guerrilla Valentine mission. Diane had heard that there was an especially odious "nobody-will-ever-love-you" seminar selling subliminal CDs, but she got the address wrong. They ended up leaving *"Somebody loves you"* notes on windshields outside a women's shelter. They realized their mistake when some of the women came out for a cigarette break, found their notes, and started screaming, "Oh no! He found me!" Maggie and Diane apologized *a lot* that night. Maggie later soothed Diane, telling her, "That's the thing about helping people. Sometimes you screw up."

After Maggie and Diane papered this latest parking lot, they returned to Diane's car and huddled down to wait—like parents watching for their kids' reactions on Christmas morning. Maggie prodded Diane, "You should use the ticket." After months of nightly Skype sessions, Hank had surprised Diane with a first-class, round-trip ticket to visit him in Wyoming for Valentine's Day weekend.

Diane huffed, "I know I sound like Effie in *Dreamgirls*. But I am telling you: I'm not going. The whole thing seems fishy to me. A suspiciously good-looking loner sends me a plane ticket to Wyoming? Sounds like a setup for a Lifetime movie. He could be a psycho planning to kill me and harvest my organs or something." She shook her head ruefully. "Preppers are weird."

"You're a prepper."

Diane balked. "I am *not* a prepper. I write a blog for preppers. There's a big difference. For me, it's all talk, an intellectual exercise— how to survive the big one. It's like planning for some fantasy trip. But for Hank, it's different. He's down with some serious shit."

Maggie frowned. "You think he'll join Walter in the bunker?"

"Hell no. Don't get me wrong, Hank was happy to get paid for building it. I mean, the man's got to eat. Plus, it was big fun working out all those engineering problems. But no, Hank says there's no way he's living down there." Diane added darkly, "And all that that entails."

"What do you mean?"

"What do you think all those guns are for? *To keep people out.* Hank's playing along for now, but if the bomb drops and women and babies are begging to be let in, there's no way he's gonna shoot 'em down just so King Asshole doesn't have to share his hidey-hole. Hank says he's not built for that."

"So what's his doomsday plan? He has to have one."

"He's gonna bug outta harm's way. I don't know all the details, but near as I can figure, he's connected to some shady characters. If things get dodgy, they've promised to fly him to some compound he's got tucked away somewhere in South America."

"Sounds like a very solid individual."

Diane smiled. "Yeah, he is."

Maggie pressed, "Then why not go see him?" Having found salvation in a romantic relationship, Maggie was eager for Diane to find her personal Jesus.

Diane sighed. "There's no point. Hank's under contract. Tilmore's got him locked down in Rabbaclaw for the next three years. I can't see doing the long-distance thing, and there's no way I'm moving out there. I got too much here: my job, you, and Dad. I don't know how long Dad's got, but I'm not gonna bail on him."

Maggie frowned. It had never occurred to her that a Hank-Diane relationship might make her lose Diane. But she plunged forward, "It's not like Lars is all alone. I mean, your sister drops in sometimes, right? Plus, he and Jeannie are seeing each other now."

Diane rolled her eyes. "They play Scrabble once a week. That's hardly a grand love affair. And my sister . . ."

Just then, Diane's phone rang. It was the hospital calling to report that Lars had just been admitted to the ER. They needed her there right away.

Diane peeled out of the parking lot.

She never got to see the dozens of "broken" women trudge out of the Marriott to find pink notes on their windshields. Their expressions weren't discernible under the street lamps. But most of them skipped Day Two.

35

SOME ENCHANTED EVENING

Maggie parked the car while Diane ran into the hospital to see her father. When Diane burst into Lars's hospital room, he wheezed. "I'm fine."

Diane kissed his forehead. "You're a bullshitter." She studied him carefully. "You don't look so bad, no worse than usual." Lars had been tap-dancing on the precipice of death for years, so the bar for his appearance was set low.

Jeannie sat by his bedside, and her eyes were puffy from crying. Diane said, not unkindly, "Damn, Jeannie. You look like a wreck. Should I tell Daddy to scoot over and make room for you?"

Jeannie shook her head and smiled weakly.

Diane asked, "What happened, Daddy? Did you try rock climbing or was it ski jumping this time?"

Jeannie answered, "He had some kind of attack. One minute he was fine—he really was—but then he got overexcited, and—"

Lars cut in, "Jeannie's the one who got overexcited. She called the ambulance over nothing."

Diane put her hand on his arm. "You hush now. Jeannie's talking."

Jeannie's lower lip trembled. "His breathing got erratic, and his heart was racing. We were . . ."

Lars said, "We were playing Scrabble."

Jeannie went on, "I didn't know he was getting worked up. He . . . I didn't mean to . . ." She cried some more.

Lars reached out and touched Jeannie's bent head, murmuring, "It wasn't your fault, Jeannie." But Jeannie kept on crying. So then Lars gave Diane one of those "don't-just-stand-there-say-something" looks.

Diane told Jeannie, "It's not your fault. If Daddy here could just lose at Scrabble like a gentleman . . ."

Jeannie started sobbing even harder. Just then, Maggie came in. She looked at Lars and asked, "You alive?"

"And I vote," said Lars. He winked at Maggie, and she gave him a prim smile.

Jeannie was still blubbering, so Diane asked, "Maggie, can you take Jeannie outta here for a second? I think she needs some air."

Maggie nodded and quickly guided Jeannie out of the room. Then Diane sat on the edge of her father's bed. "How bad was it, Dad?"

"Not bad at all, gorgeous. Scout's honor."

Diane said, "It musta been pretty scary for Jeannie to jump up from a Scrabble game and call an ambulance."

"We weren't playing Scrabble," said Lars. He was looking at the wall behind Diane as he said this.

"What were you . . ." Diane faltered. Then she leaned forward, whispering, "You and Jeannie did it?"

Lars nodded sheepishly.

Diane blundered on, "I can't believe you'd take a risk like that. What were you thinking? You know what the doctor says. You take it easy, and you can expect another good five, maybe ten, years. But you go tomcatting around, and . . ."

Lars finally looked his daughter in the eye. "I wasn't tomcatting around. I was with Jeannie. I wanted to . . ."

"To what? To literally go out with a bang? Daddy, you can barely walk up a flight of stairs. What makes you think you can survive sex with Jeannie?"

"I've survived it plenty."

Diane balked. "You've done this before? Since when?"

Lars answered grumpily, "Since Christmas, when you went to Wyoming."

"Christmas?! You two didn't waste any time, did you?"

Lars shot back, "I'm seventy-four and carry an oxygen tank. I'm on a tight schedule."

"Why didn't you tell me?" asked Diane.

"You're my daughter. I don't talk about stuff like that with my daughter." Lars said this with the prissy indignity of a matron from a Jane Austen novel.

Diane replied, "Yes, I'm your daughter. I'm the one who'll have to rush out to the hospital to claim your body some awful day. And I want to brace myself if that day is coming up soon." She got worked up as she said this, and her face reddened. "I don't want you to die on me."

Lars took her hand, and the two of them sat in silence for a while. Then Lars said, more calmly, "I don't want to die on you, sweetie. But Jeannie's the best thing to come along in my life in a long while. I'm going to spend as much time with her as I can . . . and all that that entails."

Diane nodded. "Yeah, well, don't die *on* Jeannie either, Dad. Did you see how freaked out she was?"

Lars blushed a little. "She'll be all right. Jeannie's tough."

"You sure you didn't scare her off?"

Lars laughed. "One minute you want to break us up. Next minute, you're terrified we won't stay together. Pick a lane, sweetie."

Diane shrugged. "Consistency's never been my strong suit."

"Don't worry. Jeannie won't scare off." Lars grinned. "That woman can't resist me."

36

TRAPS EVERYWHERE

Miffed that her seventysomething father had been getting more action than she did, Diane reversed her decision and used Hank's plane ticket after all. Evidently, the trip went well because when Maggie asked, "How was Wyoming?," Diane had simpered, "How would I know? I barely stepped outta bed."

As spring rolled around, Diane was still in "the throes." And her grand affair made her more expansive and pushy than ever. Her new *live!-live!-live!* ethos could be grating at times, but Maggie played along with it as much as she could.

But not now. Now Maggie shook her head, telling Diane, "This is going too far."

Diane was relentless. "Oh, c'mon. It'll be fun. I asked around, and most of the teachers are on board. Even Jeannie was up for it."

"Of course Jeannie's up for it. She'd flash the pope if *you* suggested it." Since Lars's close call at the ER, the formerly contrarian Jeannie had morphed into Diane's toady. Maggie couldn't suss out all Jeannie's motivations, but they appeared to be a bouillabaisse of affection, gratitude (for having brought Jeannie and Lars together in the first place), and genuine contrition for having almost literally loved Lars to death.

Diane shrugged. "Look, the point is the kids'll love it."

Maggie held firm. "It's overkill. We're already doing the leprechaun traps. That's half a day wasted."

Diane bristled. "Those traps are *not* a waste. The kids'll learn about physics, engineering, strategy. Hank's got it all lined up. He's gonna dazzle 'em." Diane flushed prettily as she talked about Hank. She'd recruited him to teach an hour-long workshop on building leprechaun traps during his upcoming visit to San Diego.

Maggie hedged. "You're right. The kids'll get a lot out of making the traps. But still, the toilet thing—it's too much." Diane wanted to put green food coloring into the school's toilet bowls on the morning of Saint Paddy's Day. She figured the kids would get a huge kick out of finding hard evidence of leprechauns' existence: emerald leprechaun pee.

But Maggie was ambivalent about tricking kids like that. She wanted children to experience wonder, but not if it meant lying to them. Allowing kids to believe in leprechauns, even going so far as to help them build traps—that was one thing. But confirming magical creatures' existence by leaving bogus evidence was too much. It was the educational equivalent of fixing a crime scene.

Maggie and Diane continued bickering until Danny interrupted them. "Hello, ladies." With mock formality, he said to Diane, "Mrs. Porter, may I please have a moment with Mrs. Mayfield?"

Perhaps grateful for an exit strategy, Diane played along, "Yes, Mr. Zelinsky, you may." She strode out of the room, carefully closing the door behind her.

Danny clicked the lock shut and drew the blinds. Maggie objected, "Daniel, I told you. You can't do that. You might as well hang a sign up saying—"

He interrupted her with a long kiss, and Maggie supposed that was one way to settle an argument. Drawing back, she said, "What's gotten into you?" She sat down in her desk chair, hoping to signal—to him and to her own libido—that she meant business. This was a school, after all.

Danny didn't answer right away. Instead, he perched on the side of her desk like a sexy male secretary and looked down at her. Happiness and excitement mingled on his face, and he bobbed his head slightly, as if agreeing with the universe that "yes, this was good, this was very good." Finally, he told her, "*This. Is. Big.* You're going to love this."

Maggie feigned astonishment. "Ohmigod, you're pregnant?!"

"No, better. Well, sorta better." He paused again.

"Tell me."

"The financial press got hold of our testing data, and they're going berserk."

Maggie frowned. "Wait, how'd the press get . . ."

Danny brushed this off. "I dunno. Somebody must've leaked it."

"But how did . . ."

Danny plunged on, "Anyway, the stock shot up this morning. Fifteen bucks in three hours! Do you know how huge that is?"

Maggie fumbled to keep up. What she knew about the stock market could fit onto the tab of a tea bag. "Wow, that's . . . that's great."

He grinned at her. "It *is* great. If this price holds, we'll be able to pay out a fat dividend by the end of next quarter. Even better, CNBC says Telectronics might want to acquire us. And you know what that means."

Maggie gave a noncommittal "ah." Financial jargon was a foreign language to her. She understood nothing but the speaker's mood.

Danny prattled on, "Of course, a lot will depend on how the launch goes. Right now, we're set to distribute specialized hardware and software. But there could be an apportunity here."

"A what?"

"An apportunity. It's what you call it when an app—you know, like on your iPhone—can improve the user's experience. An apportunity."

"I see." Maggie tried to sound suitably impressed.

Danny continued, "Walter wants to hold back on the app. He's afraid people won't buy the software package if they've got it. But I told him the app will make us sticky."

Maggie wrinkled her nose. "Being sticky is a good thing?"

"Yes. A program is sticky if users come back to it a lot. It's about retention."

"Ah, well then." Maggie decided she wouldn't ask any more questions. She did not want to ruin the flow of Danny's story. So she just leaned back and nodded, making appropriate "uh-huhs" and "well thens" as needed.

She jolted awake, however, when he said, "We're already getting calls from school systems on the East Coast."

"Wait, what?" asked Maggie.

"Look, if the MathPal becomes the gold standard, everyone wants to be an early adopter."

Maggie stammered, "B-but, uh, I thought you were just going to market it to, you know, the rich bunker guys. Remember? That whole thing about niche markets and how you don't need to sell a lot if you have the right point price . . ."

He corrected her. "Price point."

"Yeah, that. What happened to that?"

"That was always just one of our sales avenues. And anyway, that was way back."

"Way back? Just two months ago, you said . . ."

Danny nodded but waved her off. "I know, I know. But that was before we got back our first batch of test results."

"They were good?" Maggie strained to keep the incredulity out of her voice. The past months of gossip in the teachers' lounge had done nothing to dispel her opinion that the MathPal was a dud.

Danny glowed. "The results were phenomenal—for the lower grades, K to third."

"What about grades four to six?"

Danny shrugged. "No difference there. At least, the standardized test scores didn't show one." He seemed almost cheerful about the fact that his program did nothing for the older half of the school's population. Evidently, Edutek could make plenty by targeting younger students.

"But how can you tell the younger kids improved at all? I mean, we don't start doing standardized tests on them until third grade. So you have no baseline."

He grinned. "We *made* a baseline. We used progress rates from previous years—years where the kids *only* had teachers, no MathPal. We used those years as our baseline, then extrapolated from there."

"But how?"

His smile widened, then he boasted, "Okay, this part was my idea. We went back through the younger kids' files. We looked at old homework papers and tests so we could quantify normal progress rates for K through third, and *that* became our baseline. Good, eh?"

"You did all that?"

"Yes, ma'am, and it was *a lot* of work. Why do you think I needed staff down here?"

"But I don't remember authorizing . . ."

"You didn't authorize it. The parents did. Remember that waiver I had them sign back in September? It gave me access to all of their kids' old academic records and papers."

Maggie nodded. She couldn't imagine Edutek wading through years' worth of homework and performance tests. But they must have been doing *something* in their offices.

Danny bragged, "Our data proves the MathPal had a huge positive impact on younger kids' skills. With results this good, we couldn't just limit ourselves to the high-end market. We had to pivot to the mass market. You understand?"

"I guess I can see that." Maggie's brain reeled. None of her K–3 teachers had reported an uptick in math skills, an uptick beyond that normally produced by the school's own curriculum. But maybe they'd underestimated their students. That was possible, right?

Danny leaned in toward her, asking, "So can we celebrate tonight?"

"Tonight?" echoed Maggie.

"Well, I'd celebrate with you right now, but you told me not to." Danny wiggled his eyebrows.

Maggie laughed. The man she loved was elated and eager to share his big moment with her. "Tonight then, it's a date."

She watched him go, then sat stock-still at her desk for a few minutes. She felt vaguely disoriented, undermined somehow—as if someone had broken into her house just to rearrange the furniture. Nothing looked right, but the news was good, wasn't it? The MathPal worked. Daniel's testing data proved it.

The data also proved that she, Maggie Mayfield, had been—wait for it—wrong. She should be happy to find herself in error. Danny deserved to succeed. And if the MathPal worked, it'd benefit the school. Edutek's stock grant to the district would be worth something. It might fund STEAM programs for years to come. Everyone would live happily ever after.

Maggie should be exhilarated. So why did it feel like she'd just been caught in one of Hank's leprechaun traps?

37

Survey Says . . .

In the days after Edutek announced the MathPal's stellar test results, Maggie saw her own bemused astonishment mirrored on the faces of her teachers. She asked, but none of them had noticed a huge uptick in their students' skills, just the usual slog to grade-level competence. None of the kids had *Good Will Hunt*ed her way up to the board to write out complicated math proofs. But Edutek's "data" said otherwise. So maybe the teachers weren't looking hard enough? Or perhaps they were measuring their students' skills the wrong way? Edutek's announcements shook the K–3 teachers' confidence. When discussing the MathPal, they sounded like insecure fourteen-year-old girls—lots of singsongy sentences ending in question marks.

With studied casualness, Maggie trolled the lower school playground for intel but learned little. The kids had plenty of thoughts all right, just none about the MathPal's efficacy as a teaching tool. So while gap-toothed Audrey from second grade hung upside down from the jungle gym, she told Maggie she "loves, just loves" the MathPal's dance team game because she wants to be a dancer when she grows up, and her mom's going to get her an agent, only it's hard to make it "in the business," so maybe she'll become a senator instead. First-grader Noah—a red-haired boy in a "SCHOOL DROOLS" T-shirt—said the MathPal's Summer Camp program was better than real summer camp because it didn't make him sing "dopey songs." And kindergartner Seth Wardlow said the MathPal's Wild West program was "broken" because it didn't make bullet noises, and it was "unfair a-cause Miss Cariddi shushed" him for yelling "pew-pew" when he played it.

The only useful feedback Maggie got came from Lucy Wong. Maggie approached the pigtailed third grader as she stood on a bench, studying the playground through bright-pink plastic binoculars. Rachel sat beside her, hunched over a drawing pad. Maggie began, "Hello, girls."

They chorused, "Hello, Mrs. Mayfield."

Lucy sheepishly asked Maggie, "Am I in trouble?" Kids were not supposed to stand on the benches.

Maggie glanced around the playground to ensure they were not being watched. Like an old-timey cop pretending she hadn't just seen someone come out of a speakeasy, Maggie said, "Nah, you're not in trouble. You were just getting down from that bench right now, weren't you?"

"Yes, ma'am." Lucy scrambled down, then stood next to the bench with her hands folded and a too-wide grin on her face—innocence personified.

Maggie winked at Rachel, then told Lucy, "I wanted to ask you about something."

Lucy cocked an eyebrow. "Are you doing a survey?"

This threw Maggie. "Why do you ask?"

Lucy breathed on the lenses of her binoculars and rubbed them against her shirt. "I saw you talking to the kids on the monkey bars." Lucy squinted meaningfully, "It looked . . . suspicious."

Maggie bit her lip in amusement. "It wasn't. What's with the binoculars anyway?"

Lucy and Rachel exchanged a look. Then Rachel nodded for Lucy to spill whatever kid secret they had brewing. Lucy said, "We're planning war games."

"Against who?" asked Maggie.

"Different enemies. Boys, zombies, zombie boys. There are lots of risks. We need to be ready." Lucy said this with perfect seriousness, but Rachel was stifling a giggle.

Maggie said "ah" as if this made sense, then tried again. "Lucy, I wanted to ask you about the MathPal. What do you think of it?"

Lucy frowned in contemplation, then said neutrally, "The animation is all right—but not as good as Rachel can do." The girls high-fived without making eye contact, their deadpan expressions intact.

Maggie pressed, "Okay, did the program teach you much?"

Lucy squinted again. "Is this off the records?"

Maggie nodded, suppressing a smile at the mangled idiom.

Lucy said, "I didn't learn anything from it."

"Nothing? Are you sure?"

Lucy nodded. "No, it does some math stuff, but all *really* easy. And—"

Maggie cut in, "But doesn't it get harder as you go along?"

"You mean like asking you to add small numbers and then moving on to big numbers?"

Maggie nodded eagerly. "Yes, like that."

"No, it doesn't get harder. There's just more of it. It's like you start on a hike, and the ground is flat at first, and then it turns into a big hill, and that's the hard part. Only, there is no hill on the MathPal. It's all flat. All easy." Seeing Maggie's face fall, Lucy added hastily, "But there are colors. It's like walking on a flat path through . . ."

"Through foliage," said Rachel.

Lucy nodded. "Yeah, it's a stupid walk, but it's pretty."

Rachel said diplomatically, "Don't feel bad, Mrs. Mayfield. Lots of people love stupid pretty."

Maggie frowned. "Yeah, but not me."

38

APRIL IN PARIS

Over the next few weeks, reality became like a Monet for Maggie—it only made sense if she didn't look too close. She still had her doubts about the MathPal. But thanks to its leaked test results, Edutek's stock price soared to giddy heights. A *20/20* piece on the dire state of America's "ossified" education system touted the MathPal as a high-tech cure-all. Other news outlets followed up on the story, often interviewing Danny. And why not? Photogenic, charming, and "on the verge of revolutionizing education," Danny made a ridiculously yummy interviewee. One Fox News reporter had flirted so outrageously with him that Maggie could have sworn he'd made her ovulate.

Not that Maggie was jealous. Oh no. She had plenty of character flaws: (1) a controlling nature, (2) a weakness for chocolate, and (3) a tendency to enumerate her own deficiencies. But she was not a jealous woman. She trusted Danny, for the most part. Though he was away a lot—off publicizing the MathPal—he seemed more into her than ever. During their brief nightly chats on the phone, he told her he loved her, and he began dropping hints about her moving to San Francisco. Wouldn't she love to work for a charter school? Or maybe start a new one? Or what about going into curriculum development?

But Maggie couldn't see leaving Carmel Knolls Elementary. This was where she fit—most of the time. Tonight was an exception. She felt painfully awkward parading about at the school's gala. The gala and its all-important auction were about extracting the parents' money. With Edutek's cash petering out, its stock was the only "asset" left in the district's STEAM cupboard. True, the stock price was soaring, but so had the *Hindenburg* right before it exploded. Now more than ever, Maggie was determined to extricate her school's destiny from the MathPal. So, heigh-ho, a begging she would go.

This year, the gala's theme was "April in Paris." Accordion music wafted through the auditorium while elegantly dressed parents milled about, giddy at the prospect of a childless evening. Diane had subtracted a decade from the partyers' faces by switching off the room's harsh overhead fluorescents and relying instead on more forgiving string lights and table candles. A ten-foot model of the Eiffel Tower—festooned in more string lights—glowed in the corner of the room, and waiters walked about in berets, plying guests with appetizers, wine, and champagne. Maggie had objected to the sheer volume of booze on hand until Diane pointed out "the substantial research" indicating that donors are more generous when tipsy. Diane never actually substantiated this "substantial research," but Maggie did not feel like nitpicking.

Danny was at Edutek's Silicon Valley office yet again, so Maggie flew solo for the third year in a row. She told herself it was best for him not to be there. After all, they still weren't "out" as a couple at Carmel Knolls. But she felt somehow bereft, and—looking at the French pastries on the buffet table—she also felt hungry. She could afford to splurge because she'd lost weight. Her once-tight black cocktail dress hung too loosely against her frame. Her appetite for sweets had exited stage right as soon as Danny entered on stage left in her life. But over the past few weeks, her sugar cravings had returned—not meekly, but in grand style. So now, the pastries were calling to her—chocolate opera cake, crème brûlée, and éclairs. She was tempted to gobble them Hungry Hippo–style.

She tried to look nonchalant as she fetched an éclair—it was important to look like you want the thing you're eating, but not that you want it. Just as she was about to bite into the pastry, she felt a tap on her shoulder. She turned to find Arlene beaming at her. The district superintendent wore one of her signature pastel pantsuits—a pink one this time—but she'd nodded to the gala's Paris theme by pinning a French flag to her bosom. Arlene simpered, "Hello there, Maggie."

Feeling caught out, Maggie waved her éclair around awkwardly, stammering, "Buh, hello. So, um, to what do we owe this pleasure? I thought you didn't do school galas."

Arlene flicked her wrist, making her clunky bracelets jangle. "I usually don't. But I couldn't resist. The education world has caught MathPal fever, and Carmel Knolls is patient zero."

"What a nice way of putting it."

Arlene bubbled, "Isn't it?" Beside her, a small, wiry man with thick glasses nibbled on a pastry. His dainty, quick motions reminded Maggie of a mouse. Following Maggie's gaze, Arlene said, "Where are my manners? Maggie, this is the district's new comptroller, Simon Petal. And, Sy, this is Maggie, she's the principal here at Carmel Knolls."

Simon offered Maggie his hand. "Ah, Maggie. Arlene's told me so much about you."

"All good I hope," said Maggie too brightly.

Simon smiled, but said nothing to this.

Arlene cut in, "No worries, Maggie. I couldn't resist a little gloating when I told Sy the whole MathPal saga. Back in September, you were miserable about having the MathPal beta tested here. I practically had to talk you down from the ledge, am I right? I'm right."

Maggie laughed dutifully. She hated being Arlene's studio audience.

Arlene winked. "Oh well, no one's clairvoyant. Even I had no idea how big the MathPal was going to be. This is going to be quite a feather in my cap." A naked careerist, Arlene was blissfully unaware that most ambitions look better with their clothes on. She gave Maggie's arm a squeeze. "You must be over the moon."

"Must I?"

"Oh yes. If the price holds, the stock Edutek gave to the district back in September is going to be worth . . ." Arlene turned to her moneyman.

"Worth millions," Simon answered.

"And Sy knows this stuff cold," said Arlene. Leaning in toward the little man, Arlene cooed, "And we've all got to do what Simon says." The two administrators laughed at their private joke, and Maggie wondered idly whether they were sleeping with each other. The thought made her feel vaguely nauseated. Arlene continued, "But think of it, Maggie. *Millions*. Enough to fund STEAM programs for the next ten years, maybe twenty."

Maggie nodded, inhaling deeply. "Save the STEAM programs" had been her mantra all year. It steadied her now. She flailed to make conversation. "So, uh, how about . . ."

Suddenly, Diane materialized at Maggie's side. Diane had an uncanny knack for knowing when to rescue Maggie—like Lassie sensing that little Timmy had fallen down the well. For the Paris theme, Diane wore an oversize beret and a classic painter's smock with bright paint splotches all over it. She held a palette in her hand and had drawn an old-timey, finicky mustache over her lip. "Hello, Arlene. I am *so sorry* to interrupt. But I need Maggie's help with the silent auction. Can I steal her for just a moment?"

Arlene waved her hand magnanimously. The MathPal's success had led her to assume an almost regal manner.

Grateful for an escape, Maggie excused herself and followed Diane toward the auction tables. "What's the problem?"

Diane mimicked Arlene's throaty drawl. "'I didn't mean to startle you, Maggie dear.' But you looked desperate to get away from that hag."

"And Sy," added Maggie.

"Sy?"

Maggie explained, "The new district comptroller, Simon Petal. I think they may be an item. Arlene kept calling him Sy."

"Ewwwww. Bureaucrats breeding." Diane shuddered.

For the next two hours, Maggie and Diane mingled with the parents, congratulating the moms on their faux-Parisian outfits and egging on the dads to outbid each other on the auction. Maggie was grateful to see that the teachers were working the crowd as hard as she was. Sadie Pearl discussed a new art exhibit in La Jolla. Mr. Carlsen listened patiently to a wannabe inventor's design plans, and Jeannie feigned interest in some mom's blather about the healing power of pottery. Only Mr. Baran—usually the life of the party—took a much-needed break, spending most of the night dancing with his wife, the Judge.

Thanks to Diane and the PTA, the gala was turning out to be a hit. Mightily pleased, Maggie headed out to the ladies' room. She peed, washed her hands, and was about to leave when she heard a muffled sob coming from one of the stalls. She called out tentatively, "Everything all right in there?"

A stall door flung open, and a bleary-eyed Andrea Klemper emerged. The PTA denizen wobbled precariously on her stilettos, and Maggie stepped forward to steady her. "Maybe you should sit down, Andrea." She maneuvered the obviously soused woman down onto the linoleum floor just under the paper towel dispenser.

Andrea slurred, "S-sorry. I'm not supposed to have wine."

"AA?"

"No, juice cleanse." Andrea hiccupped loudly. "It's supposed to get the toxins out."

"Well, you look pretty healthy to me." Maggie wasn't lying. Andrea was thin and toned with shiny blond hair and a perfect complexion.

Her image was the one other moms used as a cudgel to beat themselves with whenever they reached for a forbidden cupcake.

"Trust me, I'm chock-full o' poison," said Andrea.

Maggie gave an obligatory, "Now, that's not true."

Andrea shot back, "It *is* true. I'm a terrible mother."

Maggie said nothing now. She didn't want to cockblock Andrea's insights—booze fueled or not.

Andrea went on, "I've never known how to act around that kid—Rachel, I mean." Maggie nodded sympathetically, but her sympathies were with poor, young Rachel, not the inebriated figure before her. Andrea said, "I wanted to save her, but I couldn't."

"Save her?"

Andrea sniffed and rubbed her nose. "She's fat. There, I said it. She's always been fat. It was so surreal when she and Alec were born—a thin, blue-eyed golden boy and a fat, olive-skinned girl. It looked like Alec came into the world with his own Mexican nanny. I . . . Oh shit, is that racist?"

Maggie nodded. "Breathtakingly so. But go on."

Andrea continued, "I tried to help her. I started her on a diet as soon as the doctor said it was safe. She'd ask for a cookie, and I'd give her a carrot. I trotted her to every mommy-and-me exercise class I could find. I read her children's books touting good nutrition. I even started locking the pantry at night. But nothing stopped her. You know, one time, I actually caught her going through our garbage like a raccoon, looking for cookies." Andrea sniffed again, then huffed, "Don't look at me like that!"

"Like what?"

"Like I'm some kind of monster, Cinderella's mean stepmother. I love Rachel. I *want* her to go to the ball someday, but boys don't ask fat girls to dance." Maggie opened her mouth to object. But Andrea held up a hand. "Don't give me that Dove-campaign-love-your-body crap.

I don't care how much a girl loves herself, if she's a fat blob, her life is gonna be hell. Trust me, I know."

"Were you chubby when you were little?" asked Maggie.

Andrea nodded. "It was awful. Girls wouldn't play with me. Boys called me 'Double-Wide.' They'd make truck horn sounds when I passed. I couldn't fit into regular stuff, so I had to get all my clothes from Big Sally's."

Maggie winced. "Sounds hard, but—"

Andrea cut in, "And you know what my mother did? *Nothing!* I'd come home in tears, and that woman would feed me Twinkies. Twinkies! She said I was just as God made me. It never occurred to her that God has some off days."

Maggie sighed. She'd seen this too many times. Moms and dads reacted against their parents' blunders only to make equally devastating, fresh mistakes of their own. Like generals, parents were always fighting the last war.

Andrea was searching Maggie's face now, waiting for advice or absolution. Maggie said, "Look, I get why you want a thin kid. But a thin kid is not what you have. You have to love the child you've got, even if she's not the child you thought you wanted for yourself."

Andrea bristled. "I love Rachel. I just want her to . . ."

"To be thin. And until then, you will withhold your approval? But what if Rachel never gets thin? What then?"

Andrea struggled to keep up, asking, "You mean, like if she's got a gland problem or something?"

Maggie's patience waned. "No, I mean what if she never goes on a diet, what if she stays this size? What if she *wants* to be this size? Do you really want to spend her entire childhood focused on the size of her butt?"

"I don't . . . ," Andrea sputtered.

Maggie went on, "Rachel is a magnificent kid. She's smart and kind. And she's a fighter. She beat dyslexia. She was two years behind her class last year, and now she's reading above grade level. She won the school art contest, for Chrissake." Now it was Andrea's turn to wince. Maggie prodded, "Oh, c'mon, you had to be proud of that one."

Fresh tears rolled down Andrea's face. "Ohmigod, I was so ashamed."

"What?!"

Andrea explained, "I was shocked. I mean, with Alec, every time he scores a goal, I'm so proud because I know I helped him get there. I took him to the soccer clinics. I practiced with him in the yard. But with that art show, I did nothing. Rachel did it all on her own. I gave her no help, no encouragement. I knew she could draw. You'd have to be blind not to see that, but I had no idea just how talented she was. So, that night, when she won, it was like . . . It was like I was watching her graduate from college—only I didn't even know she was enrolled. Afterward, Rachel came over and was begging for my attention. She was so needy, like a puppy. But I was too shocked to respond. She was looking for a standing ovation, and I gave her polite applause. And that Wong lady, she caught up with me in the parking lot and . . ."

Maggie bit back a smile. She knew how forceful Mrs. Wong could be. "She made a meal of you?"

"There was nothing left but bones." Andrea closed her eyes and leaned her head back against the bathroom wall. "I've screwed up so much. What do I do now?"

"Practice loving Rachel the way she is . . . And drink a lot of water when you get home."

39

ANDREA'S ATTEMPT

A week later, Andrea Klemper accompanied Rachel and Lucy to the district-level art contest—much to Lucy's annoyance.

Mrs. Klemper was so irritating. She hovered behind Lucy and Rachel all evening. Whenever they passed a strong contestant's work, Mrs. Klemper would fumble all over herself to reassure Rachel ("It's okay, baby. It's an honor just to make it this far."). Even worse, she laughed too hard when Lucy made wisecracks about the competition, saying "Oh, Luce!" and "You're too much!" Lucy had never had an adult suck up to her before. She found it unpalatable.

But Rachel didn't seem to mind. She wasn't chummy with her mother. That would have been gross. But Lucy could tell Rachel was happy to have Mrs. Klemper there, all to herself. Awful Alec had stayed home with a sitter, and Mr. Klemper was out of town on a case.

Lucy wasn't sure what had prompted Mrs. Klemper's sudden interest in Rachel. Maybe it was Rachel's triumph at the school contest. Lucy had read somewhere that success has many fathers, but failure is an orphan. When Lucy told her mother this, Mrs. Wong said the opposite would be true for Lucy. If Lucy failed, Mrs. Wong would never leave her alone ("I nag you from beyond the grave. Whoooo!"). Lucy suspected it was her mother's tirade that had driven Mrs. Klemper to Rachel's side. Mrs. Wong was the Michael Jordan of shaming people.

Today, Mrs. Wong had to root for Rachel from afar. Lucy's brother had a big piano recital that required every available ounce of the Wongs' adulation. But Mrs. Wong had given Rachel a bracelet with a number eight charm. Mrs. Wong said, "The number eight is powerful good luck."

Eventually, "the moment you've all been waiting for" came, and an uncharismatic emcee started to announce the winners. It would have been dramatic, but the list was too long, one winner per grade plus way too many honorable mentions. When they got to the third-grade category, Lucy squeezed Rachel's hand, and she heard Mrs. Klemper whisper, "No matter what, baby, I'm so proud of you."

Then the emcee said it—"First place for third-grade competition goes to Rachel Klemper." Rachel and Lucy jumped up and down, hugging each other. And Mrs. Klemper pumped her fist in the air, crying, "Bull's-eye!" She'd said it too loud, and it was completely out of place at this staid competition. But Lucy liked her for it. It was a start.

40

CRAZY HAIR AND SOCK DAY

Time moves strangely as the school year winds down. For adults, it's a mad rush. Teachers shepherd students through final projects and plan sentimentally charged end-of-year events (so meaningful!). Meanwhile, parents scramble to attend said meaningful events and sign their kids up for stimulating summer camps. But for kids, the spring crawls. Every new test, each new project, is one more obstacle between them and their hard-earned freedom. You can almost hear Morgan Freeman's narration as they burrow their way out of academic prison to sweet, sun-drenched leisure.

The academic year culminates in "Spirit Week." Each day offers some new event or costume: Pajama Day, the Teacher-Student Softball Game, Superhero Day, et cetera. The last Thursday is—drum roll, please—"Crazy Hair and Sock Day." Connor and Mr. Baran marked it by arranging a superhero-themed sock scavenger hunt for the entire school. Meanwhile, Lucy and Rachel wore "BFF wigs"—mimicking each other's hairstyles.

Spirit Week was so absorbing, such a total experience, that it tended to block out the real world. Maggie and Jeannie were so enmeshed in it that they had no idea how absurd they looked as they stood watching movers take away the remnants of Edutek's headquarters. The movers chuckled at the tableau the women presented—two mature women— one, Maggie, with seven ponytails tied back with small toddler socks, and the other, Jeannie, with little red balloons threaded through her gray hair and rainbow-striped socks pulled up to her kneecaps.

Watching the movers work, Jeannie said, "Oy, I sure got that one wrong."

"What?" asked Maggie.

Jeannie said, "I didn't see that the MathPal was actually teaching my kids. To be honest, I still don't see it. This class doesn't *seem* any further ahead than my old classes. But I must be wrong. You can't argue with hard data."

"No, I guess not." Maggie fiddled with a Hershey's Kiss in her pocket, comforted by its presence.

Jeannie went on, "Maybe I'm too old for this game. If I can't gauge where my students are, then—"

Maggie interjected. "Don't be silly. You're one of the best teachers I've ever met. We've just never had anyone go back through all the homework and tests for the early grades. We couldn't afford the man-hours. We had no benchmarks."

Jeannie smiled ruefully. "It's all numbers these days. Everything has to be quantified, measured. Once kids hit third grade, we pummel them with standardized tests. And those test scores are all that matter."

"It's like a Fitbit for education," groused Maggie.

"So much data, and so little actual knowledge," said Jeannie. "Listen to me. I sound like an old fart. Next, I'll start whining that we should give up email and go back to the Pony Express."

"Yee-haw," said Maggie.

Jeannie said, "I guess, deep down, I'm a technophobe. But do they have to mechanize everything?"

Maggie sighed. "I don't like it, but I guess it's inevitable. The new pushes out the old. It's like that General Sherman quote." Maggie fell silent.

After a pause, Jeannie said, "So are you going to tell me what Sherman said or what? I'm old, but it's not like I knew the guy."

Maggie flushed. "Sorry, I didn't want to be pedantic."

"We're teachers. Pedantic is our job," answered Jeannie.

"Right. So back in the 1800s, General Sherman—I think it was him—he said something like it was too bad for the Native Americans, but the US would *have* to take their lands. He said they couldn't stop westward expansion any more than they could 'stop the sun or the moon.'"

Jeannie shot back, "So there's nothing anyone can do? Mechanized teaching is inevitable?"

Maggie shrugged.

Jeannie said, "Calling something 'inevitable' is a great way to dodge responsibility, isn't it?"

Maggie nodded. Just then, Danny came from behind a corner. He smiled at the women, and quickened his pace. Jeannie said quietly—so only Maggie could hear—"Look, it's Mr. Manifest Destiny." Then she scrambled off.

Danny watched Jeannie bustle away. "She still hates me."

Maggie shrugged, perversely pleased that someone had remained immune to Danny's charms. "The truck's almost loaded."

Danny smiled. "Yep. We've got all the electronics, the minifridge, the tables."

A mover walked by, rolling a dozen bankers' boxes full of documents on a cart. He asked Danny, "Back of the truck, right?"

"Right," said Danny.

"What're those? I thought Edutek was paperless." Being green was part of Edutek's do-gooder, modernist mystique.

"Edutek is. But your school's not. Those are boxes of the younger kids' homework and quizzes. You know, just in case our investors want the backup for our analysis." Maggie nodded. Danny called out to the mover, "Put the docs in front of the pinball machine. Okay?"

"The pinball machine?! Ohmigod, you really are leaving," said Maggie in mock, real despair.

"I told you. You're welcome to come with me."

Maggie sighed. "And I told you. My life is here. Edutek is your baby. This school is mine." She gestured round at the playground, trying to sound more certain than she felt.

He took her hand. "You could start a new school in San Fran. I know a bunch of people who'd love to invest."

Maggie gulped. "And you could move in with me down here. Maybe commute up to Edutek for a while?"

He stepped in even closer to her. "I'm not sure I could swing that."

She tried to keep her tone light. "Sure, you could. I'll help you. I've got an in with Edutek's CEO."

"You do?"

She blustered, "The guy's wrapped around my finger."

"Yeah, he is." Danny was suddenly sincere. He leaned down and whispered in her ear, "Come to San Francisco, Maggie."

Maggie pulled away, struggling to hold on to her composure. "Daniel, we've been through this. I'm not leaving my job—my school—just to follow my boyfriend around." She said "my boyfriend" in her best California Valley girl voice.

Danny leaned down and kissed her, and for the first time ever on campus, she did not stop him. Then, he asked, "Would you move for your husband?"

Maggie drew back, searching his eyes. "Are you serious?"

"Yes, ma'am."

A voice came over the loudspeaker. It was Diane. "All right, kids, everyone on the blacktop in five minutes for the school cheer. And don't hold back. I want you to yell loud enough to scare off the birds."

Danny pulled back. He said, "Look, I know you've got a lot going on here, but think about it, all right?"

Maggie nodded dumbly. She suddenly understood the stupor that could lead a female lemming to jump off a cliff after its mate.

Danny went on, "I'll be gone through the end of the week, but come by the apartment this Sunday, and we'll talk. Okay?" Danny had an apartment in Carmel Valley, an apartment he'd be leaving all too soon.

Maggie nodded again—still at a loss for words. It was like she'd pulled a reverse *Little Mermaid*—losing her voice *after* nabbing her man. She watched Daniel get into his Tesla and drive away.

When he disappeared out of sight around the bend, Maggie suddenly snapped out of her trance. She squealed, *"Diane!"*—startling two birds.

41

An Inconvenient Truth

The following Sunday, Maggie felt like she was floating as she drove to Danny's place—floating in a happy way, not as part of some sad dissociative episode. She and Diane had dissected *the proposal*.

Okay, it wasn't a full-on proposal. There'd been no ring, no getting down on one knee, no "Will you make me the happiest man in the world, my dearest Margaret?" It was vaguer than that, more like Danny announcing the formation of an "exploratory committee" for his potential candidacy as a husband. A promise of the potential for a promise. Not great, but the word "husband" had been bandied about. It had been bandied!

Maggie pinballed between possible futures. She told herself she couldn't move to San Francisco. No, everything she loved—except for Danny—was here: her school, her friends, her Diane, her neighbors, her staff. She didn't know a soul up in San Francisco, except for Danny. And it wasn't like he could carry her around in a baby sling all day.

But how could she turn down the chance to be Mrs. Danny Zelinsky? He was perfect—sweet, sexy, considerate, smart, funny, and soon-to-be-rich. Maybe she could start a whole new life up there. She could find work at one of Silicon Valley's upscale private schools (so swank!) or at one of the publicly funded charter schools (so earnestly dedicated!). Or maybe she could turn around some terrible public school in one of San Fran's seedier areas. Did they have seedier areas up there or had Google paved the streets with gold?

But wait. The plane ride from San Fran to San Diego was just an hour. An hour! Couldn't Danny commute up to San Fran? If he became a rich jet-setter, wouldn't jetting be one of the perks? He could work up there five days a week and then fly down to Maggie on the weekends. Sure, their lives would be compartmentalized—like on those TV Land sitcoms where people share a room by drawing a line down the middle. But it could work, theoretically.

Maggie kept giddily planning her alternative futures as she pulled into Danny's driveway. She used a key to open his apartment door. Six months in and she still savored the intimacy of having a key to his apartment. He loved her, he wanted to marry her, and they could make it work. All the materials were there; they just had to shape it into something. She arrived an hour before Danny was scheduled to arrive. She wanted to tidy up the place before he got there. She didn't want to plan her happy future next to piles of laundry.

She worked her way through his living room, stopping to admire the magazines strewn about the coffee table—all with headlines touting the MathPal. Now that Danny was her fiancé, sort of, she savored his accomplishments even more, imagining herself at parties—a glass of merlot in her hand—saying things like, "Oh yes, my Daniel came up with the MathPal. But you already know that, don't you?"

The magazines fawned over the MathPal. The *Economist* said it might close the proficiency gap between the US and other countries. *Woman's Day* promised it would "get rid of sourpusses" and "make math fun!" *Time* said it would revolutionize early math education, doing for math what the Rosetta Stone had done for foreign language learning. This last tidbit nettled Maggie. She remembered only too well how California and other states had used the availability of Rosetta Stone and other such programs to justify cutting foreign language instruction from the elementary school curriculum. The Arlene Horvaths of the world had reasoned there was no need for living, breathing Spanish teachers (like Maggie) when computer programs could teach the kids. Arlene said it was a "win-win," but Maggie had her doubts.

Putting such doubts aside, she fanned the magazines neatly out across the coffee table, then headed for the bedroom. She made the bed and then turned to the desk, and that's when she found it: a single pink sheet of paper. It was an invoice from Birox Document Disposal, charging Edutek for the shredding of twelve boxes of documents just days ago.

It was the invoice's bright-pink color that drew her eye. She'd have never noticed it if it had been plain white. But once she saw it, she couldn't unsee it.

Her mind flashed to the workmen rolling document boxes out of the school on a cart—the boxes of homework and quizzes that Edutek had supposedly used to come up with its baseline for the K–3 kids, the proof that those kids had reaped some huge benefit from the MathPal. Danny had told her he was taking those boxes in case his investors wanted "backup" for Edutek's analysis. But what if he'd secretly had the boxes destroyed, their contents shredded? There was only one reason to do such a thing, right?

Maggie groaned. Then she grabbed the invoice and ran out of the apartment.

42

THE BIGGEST LOSER

Diane listened as only she could. Then she said, "Maggie, you have *got* to stop cleaning men's rooms."

Maggie laughed through her tears. It was true. She'd discovered Richard's porn habit during a wifely cleanup of his study. And now, her Mrs. Clean instincts had screwed up her life all over again. Maggie sniffed back some snot. She had cried all the way to Diane's place. "I'm right, though. Aren't I?"

Diane sighed. "Yeah, he's covering his tracks. It all makes sense now."

"What do you mean?"

Diane pursed her lips, as if she'd tasted something sour. "I thought it was weird that Edutek shrugged it off so easily when it didn't see results for the upper grades. I mean, if the MathPal was that good, why wouldn't it work for the older kids?"

"Huh?" Maggie felt sluggish.

"Maggie, baby, he couldn't shill the MathPal for the older kids 'cause we *have* a baseline for them. Thanks to state standardized tests, we *know* exactly how much kids improve from fourth grade on. You can't lie about how much the MathPal is helping them."

"I see," said Maggie.

"It's like on *The Biggest Loser*," said Diane.

Maggie bridled. "You're saying I'm the biggest loser?"

"The TV show, Maggie. It's a show where obese people lose weight at a ranch."

Maggie said, "Why on a ranch?"

"That's not my point. Anyways, the show can't lie about how much weight the contestants lose because—*bam!*—as soon as those fatties show up at the ranch, the show weighs them. Then at the end of every week, the contestants get half-naked and step up onto a giant-ass scale. And—in front of God and the viewing public—a big, noisy digital readout shows their weight down to the pound."

"What does that have to do with the MathPal?" asked Maggie.

Diane gave her best "elementary, my dear Watson" smirk. "*The Biggest Loser* can't lie about how much the contestants are losing because of those scale numbers every week. And Edutek can't lie about grades four to six because we've got years of standardized test results on those guys. But Danny could lie about K through third because we don't have any tests for those years. We don't get any test results at all till the end of third grade, so—up till then—Edutek can make up whatever it wants. It'd be like if they sent a real fat kindergartner to *The Biggest Loser*, said she was losing all kinds of weight, but they don't actually weigh her till the end of third grade. She coulda lost nothing, coulda lost a ton. Nobody knows."

"But wouldn't you have an idea how much she lost by watching her slim out?"

Diane suddenly looked cranky. "Don't poke holes in my analogy, Mag."

"Sorry." Maggie's phone buzzed again. It was Danny texting to ask where she was. "What do I do now?"

"Only one thing you can do—confront him," said Diane.

"What do I say?"

"You know what to say. Tell him the jig is up. You found the invoice. Tell him he shouldn't lie, that public schools are strapped. They don't need to be wasting piles of dough on some math program that doesn't even work. And if that fails . . ." Diane trailed off.

"If that fails, what?"

"Tell him he shouldn't lie because he's lousy at it. He's not as smart as he thinks he is. I mean, what kind of idiot destroys twelve boxes of damaging documents, but keeps the damn receipt?"

Maggie felt her lower lip tremble as she teared up again. She'd fallen for a con artist, and not a very clever one.

43

Opportunity Costs

Law & Order had lied. It had conditioned Maggie to believe that when you confront an evildoer with his crimes, he will deny it. The erstwhile cop always has to peel away the layers of denial so that the perp's "I have no idea what you're talking about" becomes "yes, I knew about it, but I had nothing to do with it," which then morphs into "I just helped a teensy bit," until finally you get "*Yes! Yes! It was me,* and I'd do it again if I could!" Cue sinister, slightly deranged cackle. *Chunk-chunk.*

But Danny did not follow that script. When Maggie confronted him in his apartment with the receipt and demanded to know whether he'd had the kids' old quizzes destroyed, he hadn't denied it. He had the good grace to wince, but that was all the remorse he could summon.

He studied the receipt, then shook his head. "I should have destroyed this."

"Why didn't you?"

He shrugged. "Reflex. I always keep my receipts so the company will reimburse me. Pretty stupid, eh?"

Maggie nodded. "Diane says you're lousy at being a con artist."

"So Diane knows too? What am I saying? Of course, Diane knows. She's your diary."

Maggie felt a tear well up in her eye. She blinked it away. "So that's it? You're not going to deny any of it?"

He reached out and tucked a strand of hair behind her ear. "Not unless you want me to."

Maggie plopped down onto his couch, emotionally winded. Without saying a word, Danny walked over to the coffee table, slid open a drawer, and pulled out a Hershey's Kiss. He handed it to her. "Here, eat this, it'll calm you down."

Maggie unwrapped the candy slowly, as if she wanted to keep the wrapper for later use. She popped the chocolate into her mouth, and— dammit—it did calm her down. She looked up at Danny. "What made you give me that?"

He grinned down at her, the white of his shirt contrasting gorgeously with his brown eyes and fiery red hair. Oh, how she'd miss running her fingers through that hair! Danny said, "Maggie, I've been with you since November, long enough to know about your chocolate habit. I kept a pack here in case of emergency. And this looks like an emergency to me."

Maggie nodded. She studied the carpet, her cheeks reddening. Her chocolate habit—her fixation on sweets—embarrassed her. She'd taken heroic measures to hide it from Richard, knowing how disgusted he was by weakness, specifically her weakness. She'd tried to conceal it from Danny too, but he'd figured it out. Her voice suddenly small, she asked, "You're not turned off by this?"

"No. It's cute. It's not like you're mainlining heroin."

Sniffling (crying always made her congested), Maggie said, "I can't believe you did this. You lied to the whole world about the MathPal."

"I didn't exactly lie. Haven't you ever heard of puffery?"

"Puffery?" asked Maggie.

"Yeah, people do it all the time to sell their products. You know— some instant crap calls itself 'The World's Best Coffee.' Bleach toothpaste promises 'Whiter Teeth in a Flash.' Or my favorite—'I Can't Believe It's Not Butter!' Now that one took balls the size of Montana."

Maggie considered this, then shook her head. "No, those are just slogans. People know to block that stuff out, like background noise. What you did was different. You didn't hook people with a jingle or a slogan. You gave them a bigger lie, a more specific one."

Danny sighed. "Oh, c'mon. You're making too big a thing out of this. It's not like I'm peddling poison. I mean the MathPal didn't slow your kids down, did it?"

"No, but . . . that's only because I have great teachers on my staff. They were able to blow ten minutes a day on the MathPal and still cover our math curriculum. Other schools might not be so lucky. They might . . ."

Danny brightened. "Or maybe—and this *could* happen—maybe kids at other schools will find the MathPal way more helpful than your students did. Maybe the MathPal's slow pace and fun graphics will make all the difference for kids with lousy teachers. You can't rule that out. Neither can I."

Maggie felt rage well up inside her. "Is that how you think we build curriculum? Do you think we just throw random shit at kids and hope some larnin' will stick?"

"Uh, no. I . . ."

"Every piece of my students' day has been thought through in advance. You know why?"

"Why?" Danny asked this with all the zest of a man opening the lid on a garbage bin.

"Because—for a good teacher, a good school—building curriculum is painful. For everything we choose to show our students, we have to choose against something else. Doing the poetry slam means there's not as much time for writing prose. Spending more time on dioramas means less time with maps. Time is limited, so everything costs something. You tell teachers nationwide that they *have* to make room for the

MathPal—that it's the gold standard for K through third, and teachers are going to have to cut something—something essential—to fit your program in."

Danny exhaled loudly. "Look, you don't need to tell me about opportunity costs because I know all about 'em."

"What?"

"Sorry, sometimes I forget you didn't go to business school. Opportunity costs are what you were talking about. If you choose to do X, then it costs you the opportunity to do Y."

Maggie echoed, "Opportunity costs." She pulled a tissue out of a box on the coffee table. "Great, I learn something new every day."

Danny put an arm around her. "Maggie, c'mon, I'm not asking for a giant chunk of the day. It's a few minutes, that's all. The MathPal's harmless, like a placebo. If I stood on the corner handing out sugar pills, I wouldn't be doing any harm. A lot of people would take them and go away happy, feeling like they'd done something to take care of themselves."

"But you're not *giving away* anything, are you?"

"No, I'm charging money, but not an outrageous amount. Just fifty bucks per user. That's way less than a lot of ed software."

"But your program *doesn't* do anything. Every dollar schools spend on it will be wasted. And schools can't afford to waste money. We're strapped already. I can't afford science for Chrissake. Science! I can't even give my kids a snake-proof fence."

"You can now," said Danny with a smile.

"What are you saying?"

"We gave you guys a huge chunk of stock. So long as our stock price goes up, your district will have plenty of cash. Your kids'll get all the STEAM programs you want, and then some. It'll be snake-proof fences all around."

Maggie squirmed in her seat, discomfited. She had been so busy pointing out Danny's conflicted state that she hadn't noticed her own.

Her kids versus everyone else's. Maggie believed in justice in the abstract, but her kids—their faces—were so tangible.

Danny leaned in, saying, "Sweetie, you just don't understand the software business."

"I do too," said Maggie petulantly. Even she knew how absurd this sounded.

Danny said patiently, "If I wait to develop my ideal product, a product that can teach kids math in minutes a day without them experiencing a millisecond of boredom, I'll never get it launched. It's like the iPhone."

Maggie frowned. "But my iPhone *works*."

Danny waved this off. "Yes. *This version* works. But do you remember the first iPhone? How it froze up constantly? How the touch screen kept glitching? How slow it was?"

Maggie huffed, "I couldn't afford the first iPhone."

Danny bowed slightly. "I genuflect at your noble poverty. But I bought it. So did a lot of people. It had problems, but Apple released it because it couldn't wait to develop a perfect product. So it went with its MVP."

"Most valuable player?"

"No, minimum viable product. It's the product you put out when you don't have anything better. It's passable, not perfect. You sell it so you can stay in business long enough to release the next version, the better version that you wanted to release all along."

Maggie frowned. Danny went on, "That's why Apple keeps releasing new iPhones. It's why every piece of software you ever buy will nag you with constant upgrades. In Silicon Valley, you don't wait for perfect. You do the best you can, sell it, then move on. In Silicon Valley . . ." Maggie tuned out for a moment here, repulsed by the reverent way Danny invoked Silicon Valley. If people in Silicon Valley did a thing, it must be the smart—the right—thing to do. As he babbled on, Maggie felt as if a heavy weight had been laid on her chest. Danny was a good man, but nowhere near as good as she'd thought he was. And finding that out wasn't just disappointing. It hurt.

Perhaps sensing Maggie's distance, Danny launched his final attack. "If you won't let this one go for your school, will you at least let it go for me?"

"What?"

"I need a win, Maggie. You heard Walter, I've already had two strikes. I get a third, and I'm out."

"Is that so terrible?" asked Maggie.

"For me, it is. Yeah. I've spent my entire professional life in Silicon Valley, and it's been one failed launch after another. I can't have another dud, okay?"

"That's just Walter talking. Don't let him in your head. You're young. You're talented. There'll be other . . ."

Danny shook his head. "Young? Maggie, I told you, by Silicon Valley standards, I'm a dinosaur. Forty-four years old without a single hit. If I blow this one, nobody's gonna invest in me again. I doubt anyone would even hire me."

"That's ludicrous. Someone would give you a shot. I mean . . ." Maggie petered out, aware of how naïve she must sound.

"Silicon Valley doesn't work that way, Maggie. Trust me, I've busted my ass there for two decades, and it's been nothing but flubbed projects and bad timing. I *need* this. *We* need this."

Maggie frowned. "We?"

"Yeah, we. If Edutek hits it big, everybody wins. Your school gets all the money it needs. Edutek finally gets on solid footing. We get married. It's happily-ever-afters all around."

Maggie recoiled. "*This* is how you propose?"

Danny smiled sheepishly. "I didn't plan it this way. You kind of forced my hand. I was hoping to make some kind of grand gesture. Light up the jumbotron at Gallcomm stadium. Or maybe, have one of those ad planes fly over the school with a 'WILL YOU MARRY ME, MAGGIE?' banner."

Maggie wiped her nose again. "A banner in the sky would have been lovely."

"I can still do it, Maggie. Mr. and Mrs. Zelinsky—it's got a nice ring to it, right?"

Maggie nodded. "It does, but . . ."

"But what?"

"I can't . . . We can't build a marriage on a lie."

"What? There's no lie. We love each other. The MathPal's a side issue."

"If it's a side issue, then why tie the proposal together with me keeping silent on the MathPal?"

Danny pulled at his shirttail, exasperated. "Because I can't see marrying you if you force me to tank my company because of some prissy moral standard."

Maggie pressed, "So there's no way you'll go public about the MathPal being a dud?"

"No, I can't do that."

Maggie nodded, finally understanding. "But what if I don't go along? What if I can't go along?"

"You mean . . ."

"What if I go to the press about the MathPal?" Maggie said this in a great rush, scared she'd lose her nerve.

Danny sighed. "Well, that'd be the end of everything, wouldn't it?" He balled up the shredder invoice and tossed it in the wastebasket. Then he looked into her eyes. "But I don't think you'll do that."

He leaned forward and kissed her. Maggie kissed him back, as salty tears ran down her face. Soon they were making love. And Maggie had to admit—it was the best closing argument she'd ever heard.

The white Xerox copy of the receipt lay forgotten at the bottom of Danny's wastebasket, but the pink original was tucked away safe inside her purse.

44

HOSTAGES

Maggie told Diane all about her conversation with Danny, omitting only the sex at the end as irrelevant and unseemly. Diane heard her out, then said, "Sounds awful. Did you at least get to sleep with him? You know, one for the road?"

Maggie pursed her lips primly.

Diane said, "I'll take that as a yes."

"Can we move on, please?" asked Maggie.

"Sorry. This *is* a conundrum. If we stay quiet, our kids can pig out on science, PE, and whatnot, and other schools'll cough up a ton of money for a dud program. But if we tattle, our kids go without. We've got ourselves a *Sophie's Choice*: our kids versus all the other kids in the world."

Maggie shook her head. "Sophie wasn't choosing between her kids and someone else's. She was choosing between her own two kids."

"Now, *that* was a shit deal."

"True. But it's not just Carmel Knolls versus everybody else. It's Carmel Knolls *and Daniel* versus everybody else."

Diane squinted at Maggie. "You love him, don't you?" Maggie nodded wordlessly. If she talked about Danny, she'd start crying again.

Diane shrugged. "Way I see it, if you want to go on loving him, you've got to take him out of the equation."

"Huh?"

Diane said gravely, "I know what runs you, Maggie."

"Chocolate?"

Diane grinned. "No. Helping kids. You're gonna do whatever you think will help the biggest number of kids the most."

"So we tell the world about MathPal, then?"

"Not necessarily. If you think the MathPal is not so bad, if you think the system can bear one more piece of crap curriculum, then maybe you let the whole thing go. Maybe, the 'greater good' here is to keep Edutek stock high and make sure your kids have STEAM programs for the next twenty years."

Maggie sighed. "I can't do the us-versus-them thing. Every time I think about it, I vomit in my mouth a little."

Diane made a blech face, then leaned forward. "Wait, what if we make it so there's no conflict?"

"Come again."

"At the gala, Arlene told you that if the Edutek stock price holds steady, we could fund STEAM for the whole district for the next ten, maybe twenty, years. Right?"

"Yeah, but . . ."

Diane went on, "Well, what if we sell the stock now, while the price is high? The district'll have all the money it needs for our kids. We won't have to worry about what happens to the stock price later."

Maggie struggled to keep up. "Yeah, but that doesn't fix everything. I mean, we still have to decide whether or not to expose Edutek."

Diane frowned. "I know. Dumping the stock doesn't solve *everything*. But it solves *something*. Way I see it, Danny's holding our kids hostage. He's saying, 'Either you let me lie about the MathPal or your kids won't get their STEAM teachers.'"

Maggie bristled. "He didn't say that. He . . ."

"No, but that's what he was implying."

"No, he was just warning me that one thing—us losing the teachers—would follow another, exposing the MathPal. He was pointing something out to me."

Diane snorted, "Yes, he was being real helpful."

"Can you please get to your point?" asked Maggie.

"My point is this. We've got three things at play: whether we let a bunch of other schools get suckered into buying the MathPal, whether we let Daniel lie to everybody, *and* whether our kids get their STEAM teachers. I say we take care of our kids first, take them out of the equation. And *then* we can figure out what to do about your boyfriend."

Maggie nodded. "But how do we get the district to dump the stock?"

Diane smirked. She mimicked Arlene's throaty voice, "My dear, we call our new district comptroller, Sy. He's a friend of mine, a close friend."

45

Tricking Simon

On Monday morning, the first weekday of summer, Maggie and Diane drove to their empty school. They had to make the call from there. The district phone system's antiquated caller ID could not differentiate between calls from the district office—Arlene's office—and calls from district schools. So mousy Simon Petal sitting in his district comptroller office would not be able to tell who was calling him—Arlene or Diane.

Maggie and Diane went over their script once more. Maggie hissed, "Remember to call him 'Sy.'"

Diane put the call through. Mimicking Arlene, she said, "Hello, Sy. It's Arlene."

Simon Petal chirped, "Hello, Arlene."

"Sy, I was wondering if you could get something done for me quickly."

Simon cooed, "Anything for you, dear. I live to serve."

Diane made a gagging gesture, but kept her voice Arlene-throaty. "Oh, Sy. You are too much."

Maggie frowned, unsure whether Diane was overplaying her role. But evidently not, because Simon simpered, "I know." Diane scribbled out a note: *"If this turns into phone sex, I'm outta here."*

Diane continued, "I'm calling because I want you to sell off our Edutek stock, right away."

"Are you sure that's wise? The stock is hot. It's been going up-up-up."

"I agree with you, Sy. But the powers that be have decided we should sell it now, in case the MathPal's launch doesn't go well. There are some rumors out there that the MathPal's all hype."

"And you've run this by the school board?"

Diane plunged on, "They're the ones who told me to call you."

"I see. All right, well, I'll put the sale through right away."

"How right away?"

"End of the hour," said Simon.

Diane sighed. "That'll have to do. Thanks, Sy. Toodles."

Simon echoed, "Toodles." And just like that, Diane and Maggie became white-collar criminals without even knowing it.

46

Maggie Makes Her Move

Maggie spent the rest of the afternoon wrestling with herself. Her love for Danny was so intense, so achingly immediate. The needs of other kids, other schools, were comparatively nebulous. Coming down on their side felt prudish, borderline officious—like pulling a bride out of her limousine to hector her for allowing guests to throw rice, instead of birdseed. Yes, Maggie knew tattling was the right thing to do, the "correct" thing. But did she have to? Danny was so charming, so handsome, so hers. Should she give up a lifetime with him just so she could have a joyless moment of consumer activism? On the other hand, could she spend a lifetime with someone she didn't fully trust? And how could she respect herself? Wouldn't she be complicit?

By nighttime, she decided to cash in a favor and call Winnie Lawlor. Maggie didn't normally trust journalists, but she hoped the boozy blonde would have a soft spot for her. Maggie'd given the woman her shawl. That had to count for something!

The next morning, just after dawn, Maggie stood waiting for the reporter under the nurse's skirt. The twenty-five-foot-tall nurse was part of San Diego's brightly colored "Kissing Statue." The statue commemorated Japan's surrender—ending World War II—by reenacting a classic photo of a jubilant sailor kissing a nurse. Maggie had no idea whether the nurse was jubilant about being grabbed and kissed, but she tried not to think about it. The statue stood on the waterfront next to the dour gray USS Midway Museum. For adults, the statue was a bit of kitschy nostalgia. For Maggie's younger students, especially the kindergartners, it was scandalously erotic.

But for Maggie, the statue was—above all—convenient. Though the area would overflow with tourists in just a few hours, it was deserted at six in the morning. And Maggie doubted that any passing jogger or homeless person would notice her meeting with a reporter at the nurse's feet. The Kissing Statue was such a spectacle that anyone milling about it became virtually invisible.

Still, Maggie had taken precautions against being recognized. She wore a drab brown trench coat, a broad-brimmed hat, and sunglasses. And at 6:10, Winnie Lawlor approached. The reporter looked freshly scrubbed and wholesome—nothing like the soused, loudmouthed creature Maggie had sent away from Walter Tilmore's house in an Uber months earlier. Trim and fit in a body-hugging lululemon tracksuit, Winnie had pulled her blond hair up in a high ponytail, and her fresh face seemed devoid of makeup—like Post-Rehab Barbie.

Winnie dispelled any mirage of wholesomeness as soon as she opened her mouth. "This better be good, Maggie. I left a very handsome stranger passed out in my bed."

"Does that happen to you a lot?" Maggie didn't sound prudish, just interested.

Winnie answered, "Sure, it's like Christmas every morning. I never know who Santa's left under the tree."

"You're positive you don't have a drinking problem?" asked Maggie.

Winnie sipped from a coffee cup. "I'm fine with my drinking. It's other people who have a problem with it." Suddenly all business, Winnie said, "So are we going to do this or not?"

"Yes, but nobody can know this came from me. My name must never come up. Understood?"

Winnie nodded. "You shall remain an anonymous source."

And so, standing underneath the giant nurse's skirt, Maggie told Winnie about the MathPal: the doctored test results, the bogus claims of greatness, the media stories touting it as the next great thing. As Maggie spoke, Winnie scribbled frantically on a notepad. She'd asked to record Maggie, but Maggie'd refused.

At the end of Maggie's sordid tale, Winnie asked, "Do you have any proof of this?"

Maggie reached into her purse and pulled out the pink receipt she'd taken from Danny's apartment. It showed that Edutek had shredded documents to cover its tracks. Winnie asked, "Can I keep this?"

Maggie nodded. "Yeah, I don't want it."

Winnie studied the receipt, initialed by Danny. "Whew. So this Zelinsky guy, was he the only one in on the cover-up?"

"I don't know. I don't know how Edutek works. But you should know Daniel is a good man. A really fine man. I think he was just under a lot of pressure."

"Sure, yeah, whatever."

Maggie felt her heart sink. "This is going to be terrible for him, isn't it?"

Winnie took a deep breath, then exhaled. She said, not unkindly, "He's not really my concern. But you are. You're a source now. And I need to explain what that means. I won't tell anyone you brought this to me, but I can't guarantee people won't figure it out on their own. When you leak a story, you can't control where it goes. Understand?"

Maggie hesitated. "I, um . . ."

"A story is like a tiger," said Winnie. "When you leak it, you control the tiger's first bite. But after that, the tiger will go after the juiciest flesh, wherever that is. Got it?"

Maggie flinched. She'd said nothing of her personal relationship with Danny, of Edutek's stock grant to the district. She had no idea what the tiger would do with any of that, but she was about to find out.

47

You Always Hurt the One You Love

Maggie tried to warn Danny. She left messages asking, then pleading, with him to call her back. By noon, she couldn't wait anymore, so she blurted it out in a voice mail, "Maggie here. Daniel, I . . . We need to talk. I told a reporter about the MathPal, the shredded documents, all of it. I'm so sorry, sweetie. Not for what I did. I had to do it. But I'm sorry for all the pain it'll cause you. Please call when you can."

But Danny didn't call back. And Winnie Lawlor did not waste any time. She had the MathPal story ready for the five o'clock news, and she'd done a bang-up job.

The story's lead-in made Maggie nauseated—an ominous basso profundo saying, "Next up at five, a Fox exclusive: How the Makers of the MathPal Fudged the Numbers and Tricked the Entire Education System."

Winnie showed clips from Danny's *20/20* interview—handsome, charming Danny shilling his handsome, slick product. Then she established the local connection by explaining that Edutek had beta tested the MathPal at San Diego's own Carmel Knolls Elementary. In case viewers didn't know what a school looked like, Winnie showed stock footage of students filing into Carmel Knolls Elementary. Maggie's breath hitched. It could have been worse. If the story had broken while school was in session, there would have been reporters sticking microphones in her little students' faces. Next, the camera showed talking heads from the education world climbing over each other to praise the MathPal and its "fantastic potential."

And finally, the camera returned to Winnie, saying: "Sounds too good to be true? Well, it *is*. Fox 5 has obtained evidence from an anonymous source indicating that Edutek fabricated the MathPal's supposedly wondrous beta-testing results. And just days ago, Edutek chief executive officer Daniel Zelinsky tried to cover up that fraud by shredding thousands of documents." The camera showed a blowup of the pink Birox receipt. "Fox 5 will keep you updated on this story as it develops."

Two days later, after still not hearing back from Danny, Maggie banged on the front door of his Carmel Valley apartment, begging him to let her in.

She'd almost given up when she heard a soft click and the door swung open. He looked exhausted. His eyes were bloodshot, his face covered in stubble. He gave her a bleary-eyed smile, saying, "Hey, Mag. Come in."

Maggie walked in, and he shut the door carefully behind her. He told her, "You're lucky. The camera crews are gone, for now."

Maggie said meekly, "I tried to warn you. I . . ."

He waved this off. "Yeah, I know. I got your messages after the story broke. But hey, it was thoughtful of you. Thanks." He said this perfunctorily, as if thanking her for a fruit basket.

He led her into the living room and gestured for her to sit on the couch. She asked, "You understand why I did it, why I had to do it, don't you?"

Danny sighed. "Yeah, I can see your side." He sounded detached, almost bored. "It was stupid of me to expect you to keep a secret like that. You can't cheat with the principal."

Maggie smiled feebly. "So what happens now?"

"What do you think?"

Maggie ventured, "I think there'll be more bad press, and schools will probably rescind their preorders for the MathPal."

"Probably?" There was an edge to Danny's voice now.

Maggie gulped. "Definitely."

"What else, Maggie?"

"Excuse me?"

"What else do you see in your crystal ball for me and my company?"

She hesitated. "I, um, I think you won't be able to launch the MathPal, and that'll hurt."

"Go on." His eyes, normally so expressive, were dead now. He looked at her as a stranger might.

"Um, I guess maybe Edutek might go under?"

"That's right. Very good. I'd reward you with a chocolate, but I threw them out."

"You did?"

"Yes, ma'am. Crushed them down in the bin with my foot, sorta like what you did to my career." He said this jokingly, but the joke fell flat.

Maggie felt a tear glide down her cheek. She wiped it away. She didn't want to look like she was playing for sympathy. Her pain wasn't the point now. Danny's was. "I'm sorry, Daniel."

"Oh, you're sorry, well, I guess that makes everything all better, doesn't it?" The edge had gone from his voice now, as if he was too exhausted to bother hating her. "Lemme ask you, Maggie. What do you think is going to happen to me now? Hmm?"

Her hands were folded in her lap. She kept her eyes on them, not daring to meet his gaze. "Um, you'll maybe get a slap on the wrist? Or you'll have to step down as CEO? Something like that. I don't know how these things work, Daniel."

"That's right. You don't." His anger flared.

Maggie wiped a tear away, then turned to say what she'd come to say. "Daniel, I know you probably think that if the MathPal goes down, that's it. Your career is over. But I know that's not true. That *can't* be true. You're so smart and charming and talented. There'll be other products, other companies even. You're going to make it past this, Daniel. I know it. I believe in you."

Danny answered, "Let me get this straight. You admit that you have no idea how my world works. But somehow, in that Holly Hobbie brain of yours, you're sure I'm going to come out okay because . . . what? Because you believe in me? What does your believing in me have to do with anything? I'm not Tinker Bell. You can't raise me from the dead by just 'believing.'" Danny fluttered his eyelashes, mocking Maggie's naïveté.

Maggie winced. "So what happens now? What's the process?"

Danny rubbed his face for a moment, took a deep breath, and blew it out. "I don't have a process, Maggie. My world doesn't work like your world."

"What do you mean?"

He smiled bitterly. "In your world, a kid comes forward and tattles on another kid. Then the tattler goes off on her merry way, and the kid she's ratted on gets a good talking-to. Then you pat him on the head and send him back to class. Maybe, if it's serious, you'll call his parents and tell them about what he did. Maybe they'll take away his iPad for a few days; maybe they'll just threaten to do that. Everybody gets to go back to their own life. The end."

"And in your world?"

"In my world, well, let's see. I'm . . ." He closed his eyes for a moment, visibly willing himself not to lose his temper. "Maggie, do you know why I didn't call you back when you told me you'd gone to that reporter?"

"Because you were mad at me?"

"No, that's not why. I mean, yes, I was mad at you. I was fucking furious at you. But no, that's not why I didn't call you. I didn't call because as soon as Winnie what's-her-face hit the airwaves, I got myself a lawyer. And my lawyer told me that I should cut off all contact with you."

"But why? I don't . . ."

"Because I'm under investigation, Maggie."

Maggie drew back. "What? By whom?"

"Oh, there's the Securities and Exchange Commission, for starters. Edutek is a public company, remember? And we lied to the world . . . I lied . . . about what our product could do, and our stock went through the roof. That's securities fraud, Maggie. Look it up. It's a big no-no.

"And then, there's my investors. They're pretty ticked off about this whole brouhaha. And as you might imagine, the Walter Tilmores of the world are not an especially forgiving bunch. And after that, who knows? If things get salty enough, the Department of Justice might join the fun. So many possibilities for your viewing pleasure."

Maggie studied the floor for a moment. "I'm so sorry, Daniel. I didn't think . . ."

"That's right. You *didn't* think. You saw me doing a bad thing. So you told on me, figuring everybody would be nice and reasonable about punishing me. But it doesn't work that way, Maggie. By the time they're through with me—"

Maggie cut in, "No, we'll figure this out. I'll stand by you. I'll do whatever it takes. Whatever you . . ." She faltered then, dismayed by the look on his face. It was the look of a man listening to a stranger spout nonsense—a detached, bemused expression.

"Maggie, you don't get it. The time to stand by me is over. *We're* over."

"But I love you. I . . ."

"And I loved you too. But it's done."

48

RICHARD'S AMENDS

Maggie spent the next few days hunkered down in her house with Diane—crying, eating chocolate, and watching the MathPal scandal spin out on television. Danny's looks and charm—so useful in shilling the MathPal—made his downfall media catnip. The Securities and Exchange Commission was investigating him and everyone else on staff at Edutek. And Edutek's stock price had plummeted.

Diane assured her, "Maggie, you did what you had to. I know he's dreamy and all, but that man was going to take serious chunks of change out of schools across America."

"He said he wasn't going to charge that much."

"Oh, bullshit. Those tech companies don't go by some 'take a penny, leave a penny' system. There was a reason those investors were drooling all over themselves. They thought Edutek was going to make a killing."

"So?"

"So nobody gets to make a killing unless somebody gets killed."

As talking heads on TV threw around alien phrases like "securities fraud" and "insider trading," Diane and Maggie started to grow nervous. The media hadn't noticed Maggie's involvement yet, but it was just a matter of time. Wasn't it? Maybe she and Diane needed lawyers too. There were so many hidden rules underfoot, rules that could snap shut like bear traps. Diane proposed going to Richard. "He's in corporate compliance, right? This is his jam."

Maggie colored. "The last time he saw me, I was lying spread-eagled on the hood of a car while Daniel was humping my brains out."

"Don't forget the Pilgrim dress. That Pilgrim dress sorta completes the picture."

"Thanks for reminding me. I like my traumas to be as specific as possible."

Diane smiled. "Honey, don't be that way. I bet Richard would jump at the chance to help you. Remember all that twelve-step stuff he said about making amends and whatnot. That sounded like some real sincere crap."

And it was. As soon as Maggie called, Richard eagerly agreed to meet with her and Diane. He came to Maggie's house, sat on the couch, and listened as the two women explained what had happened. While Winnie Lawlor had focused exclusively on Edutek's lies about the MathPal, Richard probed further. He got it all—including Diane's bogus call to Simon Petal.

After listening, Richard sighed and leaned back on the couch, plainly exhausted. His methodical questioning had cost him. "Okay, ladies, I'm glad you called me. I really am. Now, here's my advice: you need to lawyer up, and you need to do it right *now*."

Maggie balked. "But we haven't done anything wrong."

Diane echoed, "Yeah. Going to Winnie Lawlor was a public service. Maggie didn't have to squeal on Danny Z. But she did it anyways because it was the right thing to do."

Richard responded, "Yes, and if that's all you'd done, you'd be in the clear. But it's *not* all you've done. You tricked the district into dumping the stock *before* you went public on the MathPal."

Diane shot back, "Of course we did! We needed that money for STEAM projects—PE and science and tech and art and music and—"

Richard cut in, "It doesn't matter what you needed it for. You're not allowed to sell off your stock if you have insider information telling you the price is about to drop."

Diane bristled. "But we're not insiders. We don't know anything about stocks and whatnot. I don't understand half the stuff you're talking about."

Richard went on, "*Yes*, you're not insiders when it comes to securities law. I get that. But you *were* insiders when it came to Edutek."

Diane answered, "Nah-uh. We . . ."

Richard was losing his patience. "You were insiders. You had information that Edutek was keeping private information with the potential to tank the stock price. And you used that information in deciding when to time your trade."

Diane answered, "But it wasn't *our* trade. It was the district's trade. We're not gonna see a penny of that money. We just wanted to make sure the kids would be covered. That's all."

Richard replied, "Again, it doesn't matter *why* you tipped off the district."

"We didn't tip them off. We tricked them. I made the call myself," Diane boasted.

Richard snapped at Diane, "Has anyone ever told you that you're proud of all the wrong things?"

This put Diane back on her heels. "Um, no."

Maggie asked Richard, "So we're not off the hook just because we won't see any money out of this?"

Richard sighed. "That's right. When Diane told that Simon guy to dump the stock, you both committed insider trading. The fact that you tricked him doesn't change that. It just means they can come after you for fraud too."

Maggie asked, "And will they? Come after us, I mean?"

Richard nodded. "Yeah, they'll come. The government may not have gotten around to it yet, but eventually, they're going to notice that the district made a big trade the day before the story broke. And they're going to want to know why."

Diane broke in, "But that'll take them a long . . ."

Richard shook his head. "No, it *won't* take them long at all. You two left a paper trail. They'll check the trading records. Then they'll go to Simon Petal, and he'll say Arlene told him to make the trade. Next, they'll go to Arlene, and . . ."

"Oh God, no," said Maggie.

"Oh God, yes," answered Richard. "Arlene will say she didn't know about the trade, she never made that call. And then—in no time—they'll figure out that you and Diane called him. The beta testing was at *your* school. Once they learn you were involved with Zelinsky, it'll be easy to piece out."

"And then?" asked Maggie.

Richard reached out and put his hand over hers. "Then they'll have you. You and Diane. On the criminal side, you'll be looking at charges for insider trading and fraud, at the very least. They might want to throw in some public corruption charges too, what with you both being public servants."

Diane murmured, "Oh my God. It'll be awful. We'll be a movie of the week."

Maggie asked, "Will they let us keep our jobs?" As soon as she asked, she knew the answer.

Richard shook his head. "No, you're out the door, Mags. It'll be a miracle if they don't claw back your pensions."

Diane objected feebly, "But we're the good guys here."

Richard said—not unkindly—"Good guys don't commit securities fraud."

49

THELMA & LOUISE

Maggie thanked Richard and saw him out. Then she and Diane huddled at the kitchen table.

Diane blustered, "I'm not going to jail. I say we *Thelma & Louise* our way outta here."

Maggie was incredulous. "Don't you remember what happened to them at the end of that movie? They drive off a cliff. They commit suicide."

"Oh," said Diane, flattened.

Maggie said, "We don't both have to go down for this. I'll tell them I was the one who called Simon, that I dumped the stock. You knew nothing about it."

Diane frowned. "They're not going to buy that. You can't even do a decent Arlene."

"I don't *need* to do a decent Arlene. I just have to convince the police I could do one good enough to fool Simon Petal."

Diane bristled. "No. You're always taking credit for everything. I want them to know I'm the one who tricked Simon."

"Credit? There's no credit here, just jail time!"

Diane rolled her eyes. "Oh right. You think I'm just gonna stand aside and let you rot in jail by yourself? No way. If anyone's taking the fall, it's gonna be me."

It was late, and Maggie's blood sugar was sinking from the pint of ice cream—okay, two pints—that she'd plowed through earlier. "You *can't* take the fall. I'm the one who was close to Daniel. There are twenty traumatized senior citizens on my block who can testify to that. And I'm the one who blabbed to Winnie."

"You said Winnie protects her sources."

Maggie snarked, "Winnie gets plastered every night. We're not talking Woodward and Bernstein."

"You're not taking the fall for me," said Diane.

"Yeah, well, you couldn't take the fall for me if you wanted to." Maggie softened. "But it's kind of you to offer."

Diane bowed her head in acknowledgment. "Same to you."

Maggie mumbled, "So what do we do?"

Diane was firm. "We lam it. We get out while we still can, and we go someplace they'll never find us."

"We can't just leave."

"Sure we can."

Maggie sputtered, "But the school, we can't leave the . . ."

"You heard what Richard said. If they find out about that trade, there's no way we're keeping our jobs."

"No, we could fight this. We could . . ."

Diane shook her head. "Maggie, even if we fight it, and let's say we win somehow, you think it's gonna be good for the kids to have us around after a stink like this, after we've been—what's the word—compromised?"

Maggie winced. She couldn't do that to her school. If she became tainted, she'd have to go. She said softly, "That school is my whole life—everything, everyone I care about is there. My kids, my . . ."

Diane took Maggie's hand. "I know this is going to hurt. I know what that school means to you, what the people there mean to you. But trust me, with your personality, you'll make new enemies wherever you go."

Maggie swatted Diane's shoulder. "That's not funny."

Diane smiled. "It's a little funny."

Maggie popped a chocolate in her mouth. She knew leaving Carmel Knolls would be as painful for Diane as it was for her. Then she remembered. "What about Lars?"

This stumped Diane for a moment, but she rebounded quickly. "Daddy's got my sister. And more important, he's got Jeannie now."

"You think you could handle leaving him?"

"It's hard, but eventually you have to let your parents leave the nest." Diane was half joking. Maggie knew she'd miss her father terribly.

"And what about Hank? Aren't you going to miss him?"

Diane broke into a radiant grin. "Hank's gonna be our ride."

50

ARRANGEMENTS

The friends did not have much time. Over the next few days, the news broke about Danny's romance with Maggie. The press had no proof of her involvement with his "scam," but that didn't stop them from speculating. Local news anchors made a meal of her "Thanksgiving Sex Show" with Danny. Most of Maggie's neighbors had no comment, but ancient Gus Filby talked enough for everybody, wheezing: "When I saw them in that there garage, I almost had an infarction."

The authorities had not yet noticed the school's conveniently timed trade. But they would close in soon. The feds had already called to schedule "an interview" with Maggie. When she asked if she needed a lawyer, the agent told her: "Oh, I don't think you need to waste your money on that, so long as you've got nothing to hide."

That night, Maggie finished packing her things and headed over to Diane's house. They were all there: Lars, Diane, Hank, Richard, even Jeannie. For once, Maggie was not in charge. Diane was.

Diane had started the ball rolling by enlisting Hank. Calling him on Skype, she'd explained the MathPal saga—the falsified data, her bogus call to Simon Petal, all of it. Then she relayed Richard's thoughts, how he'd told her and Maggie to lawyer up because the feds would be onto them in no time. Diane said, "I'm not waiting round for that. I want to bug out." "Bug out" was prepper-speak for "leave the country."

Hank asked, "So what do you need from me on this, Di?"

"I was hoping you could use your connections to help me and Maggie get outta here. I know you've got that place down south. Can we maybe use it?"

Hank hesitated, "You mean, like, uh, go there on your own? Without me?"

"Well, me and Maggie could go alone if we *have* to. But I was kinda hoping you'd come with us . . . if you've got the time, and, um, the inclination."

Hank nodded, and Diane saw the ghost of a smile surface under his beard. "Well, that's all right, then."

"What's all right?"

"I'm in." His smile broadened. "But I've got terms."

Diane straightened in her seat. "What terms?"

"I handle our documents, disguises too. Okay?"

Diane nodded. "Fine, I was always crap at doing makeup anyway. That it?"

Hank said, "I don't trust strangers. So if we go, we use my plane, my people to get down there. Not yours."

Diane shot back, "Well, that's easy. I haven't got any 'people.'"

"Yes, you do. You got me."

Diane smiled. "I guess I do."

Hank had a "go plan" all set within the hour. Maggie balked. "How can he put this together so fast?"

Diane smirked. "He's been prepping for Armageddon for ten years. We're talking some serious groundwork."

Lars proved to be a harder sell than Hank. Diane told him, "I can't do time, Dad. If I go in with hardened criminals, who knows? There'll be loads of peer pressure. They could turn me to the dark side. I'm a people pleaser, and you know it."

Lars was skeptical, so it was Hank who persuaded him. Hank explained his plan in painstaking detail. Maggie wasn't sure how much Lars actually understood, but he nodded sagely—like a man pretending to understand an auto mechanic explain what went wrong with his carburetor. Maggie suspected that Hank himself—more specifically, Hank as Diane's lifetime mate—was what appealed to Lars. His little girl would finally settle down.

Maggie brought Richard on board to help with the plan's financing. He'd sell off their house and use his financial wizardry to get the proceeds to her—without being detected. It would be the first and only time Maggie would benefit from Richard's furtiveness. She told him to consider his amends complete. She asked him to do one last favor for her, and he immediately agreed.

The group met and chatted amiably as they wolfed down their last supper together. Only Jeannie sat silent. Lars had insisted on telling Jeannie everything, and Diane had seen the sense in that. Her father couldn't bear the secret alone, and Diane trusted Jeannie—she had no choice.

After they packed Hank's truck, Lars and Richard hugged "their girls." Diane huddled with her father, while Jeannie drifted over to Maggie's side. She asked Maggie, "Are you going to be all right without them?"

Maggie frowned in puzzlement. "Without . . ."

"Without the students, *your* students."

Maggie and Jeannie had had their differences, but they were both educators. School was their medium. It was the "what" in "what mattered." Maggie sniffed back a tear. "I'll be all right. And they'll be all right too. You'll see to that, won't you?"

Jeannie nodded, and the two women embraced. Jeannie's arms were surprisingly strong for such an old broad, and that comforted Maggie. Her students would need someone strong.

Then it was over. Hank and Diane sat up front while Maggie sat in the back. She peered out the back window until Lars, Jeannie, and Richard disappeared from view.

51

THE CHIPS FELL WHERE?

Winnie had warned Maggie that once she unleashed the press, she would not be able to control the MathPal story. And Winnie was right. The first wave of stories focused on Danny's lies, how he'd tricked everyone into believing that a gussied-up video game could revolutionize the way American schools taught math. Next, the press honed in on Danny's "tryst" with Maggie.

Then came the bomb that Maggie dreaded most—the government revealed the district's suspiciously timed stock trade. For one awful news cycle, the world was convinced that the district superintendent, Arlene Horvath, had used her feminine wiles to dupe Simon Petal into making that trade. But then Arlene produced an alibi, and the government quickly figured out that the call ordering the trade had come from Carmel Knolls Elementary.

And so the press returned to the Pilgrim "sex show" incident. Fascination grew as the tabloids fabricated a love triangle.

Low-resolution iPhone photos had caught Danny walking next to a particularly dishy blonde—PTA denizen Felicia Manis. Were the couple an item? Was Maggie a woman scorned? Felicia denied the affair, and so did Danny. But both benefited from the speculation. Felicia's husband, who had taken his wife for granted of late, began showering her with attention—reasoning that if other people thought his wife was a "siren," he should too.

As for Danny, his courtly protestations that he had never slept with Felicia only heightened his already obvious desirability. He developed a dedicated fan base. Ultimately, the Securities and Exchange Commission settled with him out of court, forcing Edutek to pay a stiff fine. Danny also had to promise to never again serve as an officer of a public company. Banished from the tech industry, he embarked on a lucrative career as a motivational speaker and life coach. His TED Talk on "Resiliency & Redemption" garnered millions of views.

Meanwhile, Richard managed to quietly sell Maggie's house and funnel most of the proceeds to her without detection. He saved a small sum to carry out his last errand on her behalf. Using a prepaid credit card, he arranged for a prop plane to fly over Carmel Knolls Elementary on the first day of school. At recess, hundreds of students looked up to see a bright banner being towed across the sky, saying: "HAVE A GREAT YEAR! —MRS. MAYFIELD & MRS. PORTER."

Richard still works in corporate compliance for a large San Diego company. It's a dull job, but he fills his ample spare time participating in triathlons. One day at a time, he has managed to abstain from pornography for more than a year now. He is very eager to date, and all that that entails.

◆ ◆ ◆

Life at Carmel Knolls Elementary went on, but not as smoothly as it had under Maggie's benevolent dictatorship. Jeannie Pacer took over as principal, but would only agree to serve on an interim basis. She insisted that she wanted to retire soon so she could spend more time with her life partner, Lars.

With the district's STEAM budget secured, Mr. Baran, Mr. Carlsen, and Miss Pearl stand to enjoy years of job security. Their only complaint—whispered among themselves—is that they cannot thank the two women who engineered their happiness.

Jeannie and Lars donated the remnants of Diane's menagerie to the school, and Mr. Carlsen keeps the animals' cages in a well-lit section of his room, marked as "PORTER'S CORNER." Murray the parrot has become a school mascot, and Mr. Carlsen has trained him to shout *"Eureka!"* on cue.

Connor Bellman has advanced to second grade, and—having formed an exercise habit that he'd keep for the rest of his life—he pays attention in class as much as possible without ever crossing into brown-nose territory. Lucy and Rachel have moved on to fourth grade, and are—in Lucy's words—"ready to dominate." Lucy continues spending as much time as she can in Mr. Carlsen's lab while Rachel lingers in the art room with Sadie Pearl. Both girls are excelling. They plan to create comic books about two female superheroes who run a school for misfits by day and fight crime by night. Lucy will write it, and Rachel will handle the illustrations. Mrs. Wong says an author credit will help Lucy get into college, and Mrs. Klemper has vowed to use her "connections" to get it published.

Arlene Horvath—initially embarrassed by the MathPal debacle—managed to turn it to her advantage. She took as much credit as possible for "uncovering" the MathPal's many deficiencies. And she has intensified her public relations efforts, speaking at dozens of education administration conferences. She dreams of someday rising to become the United States' Secretary of Education, but fears she may not be qualified for such a lofty position.

Walter Tilmore could easily afford to lose the millions he ultimately lost when Edutek's stock tanked. He made noises about suing Danny and Edutek, but got distracted by other business ventures. He still enjoys showing off his elaborate doomsday bunker, but he has had trouble retaining talented personnel.

Maggie and Diane remain at large, their whereabouts unknown.

52

Somewhere in Ecuador . . .

Schoolchildren frolic on a sunbaked playground. The noon bell rings out, and most of them trudge back to class. Two boys—dark-haired brothers with large almond-shaped eyes—linger behind on the playground. The older brother has found a black widow. He asks, "Only female black widows are dangerous, right? Or was it the males?" The little brother says he'll catch the spider and pull its pants down to find out. The boys bicker about how to check spider genitalia. And suddenly, a wolf whistle pierces the air. Only one person in the boys' lives whistles like that: Señora Marguerite, head of school.

She orders the brothers to back slowly away from the spider, telling them in perfect—albeit too formal—Spanish that they must never touch spiders. She says, "Don't you know what happened to that little girl in Portoviejo? The old lady in Machala?"

The boys' eyes widen to become saucers. "No, what happened?" one asks.

But the Señora just closes her eyes and shakes her head slowly. Some things are too grisly to be discussed. The boys run back to class.

The Señora grabs a piece of wood and dispatches the spider with a whack. From behind her, a tall gray-eyed blonde calls out: "That's not very neighborly. We need those spiders to kill off the damn bugs."

Maggie turns and smiles at Diane, who ambles awkwardly onto the playground, her belly swollen. She's seven months pregnant. Maggie asks, "How're you doing today?"

"I'm fat. My feet are swollen, and this alien spawn inside me won't stop kicking. My days on the catwalk are over."

Maggie says, "Oh, honey, don't say that. *You. Are. Glowing.*" Maggie means this, but she infuses the compliment with sarcasm so Diane will accept it. "Where's Hank?"

"Working on the nursery."

Maggie cooed, "See, he's excited about the baby."

"He just wants more company in that stupid bomb shelter. We have to be the only three-room schoolhouse in Ecuador with its own doomsday pit."

Hank had engineered Diane and Maggie's escape. He'd called in some shady favors and had them flown down to his postapocalyptic haven in Ecuador. He'd built a substantial house aboveground years earlier, and he added a sturdy schoolhouse in less than two months. Now he spends most of his time building and fortifying the family's bomb shelter. He is a happy prepper. He's ratholed enough from his stint with Tilmore to last him decades, and Ecuador has a thriving expat prepper community—his people. Most importantly, Hank has Diane, and a baby on the way.

Diane is adapting, but slowly. She still speaks only a few Spanish phrases so that most of her interactions with locals degenerate into impromptu games of charades. But Maggie will help Diane with that— she has to teach Spanish to someone.

Maggie, as always, is mad busy. She spends her days working with the children, haggling with vendors for textbooks, and helping her two teachers with their lesson plans. Maggie teaches classes too, English and basic math. The school is still in its infancy—growing, but fragile. To avoid discovery, she's grown out her hair and dyed it red, an unconscious homage to Danny. Whenever panic gnaws at her, she reminds herself how notoriously difficult it is to extradite anyone from Ecuador. Sovereignty forever!

Diane asks, "Are you coming to the festival tonight?"

"No, I've got too much to do around here."

Diane presses, "Eduardo is going to be there."

Maggie deadpans, "That must be very exciting for you."

"You gotta get out there sometime, Maggie."

"Thanks but no thanks. I'm not interested in meeting that guy. I don't care how much Hank likes him."

Diane is relentless. "He's tall."

"Yeah, well, I'm closed for business."

"He's rich. He owns a factory in the capital."

"I *said* I'm not . . ."

"It's a chocolate factory, Maggie."

"Well, it can't hurt to say hello."

Acknowledgments

Okay, here goes. Thanks to my beloved, challenging children—Jacob, Lily, Daisy, and Oliver. Your experiences and personalities inspired this book, so I dedicated it to you. So there! When you grow older and tell your future therapists how terrible I was, I'll point to the dedication in this book. The therapists will probably tell me it proves nothing and I'm being defensive, but still! Double thanks to Oliver for recommending a worm mascot and to Jacob for drawing the worm cartoons so brilliantly.

Thanks also to my brilliant, endlessly supportive husband, Johnny Chen.

Endless gratitude to my parents, Mort and Ingrid Cooperman. Yes, Dad, there is a bit of you in Lars. And no, Mom, you are not any of the flawed mothers in this book. You are wonderful.

Thanks to the educators in my life: my much-smarter-than-I-am sister, Jessica Choi (a phenomenally gifted teacher); my even smarter best friend, Deborah Cunningham (who develops curriculum for her nonprofit—Primary Source); and the hypercompetent teachers at my children's schools. Plus, I have to thank my own grade-school teachers, the ones who somehow jammed math and grammar into my candy-addled mind.

Thanks also to my friend—the mightily esteemed outgoing principal of my kids' elementary school—Wendy Wardlow for offering advice and encouragement. And no, Wendy is *not* Maggie. I've never seen Wendy in a Pilgrim outfit.

More thanks to my witty, eerily insightful editor, Jodi Warshaw, and the other kind folks at Lake Union Publishing (Amazon). And thanks to my agent, Amy Tipton (Signature Literary), for her endless support and to Jenna Free and Carrie Wicks for their editorial guidance.

Another round of thanks to the friends who helped me "birth" this book: Kate MacPhail, Anna D'Angelis, Nicole Smokler-Monsowitz, Kathleen Maugham, and Letitia Capriotti.

And finally, thanks to the readers of this book. I'm amazed you stuck it out to read the acknowledgments. *That* is hard-core.

BOOK CLUB DISCUSSION QUESTIONS

1. What do you think of the friendship between Maggie and Diane? Is it inherently unequal because of Maggie's position as Diane's boss? In what ways is Diane the dominant partner?

2. Do you think that Maggie and Diane should have been punished more?

3. What drew Maggie to Danny beyond his looks and their compatible body parts?

4. What did Lucy get out of art class—other than finding Rachel? What does a whiz kid learn from the experience of failing at something?

5. Do you think Danny's conscience was clear? Did he somehow delude himself into thinking the MathPal was harmless? Is it harmless?

6. What do you think of Rachel's mother, Andrea? Was she wrong to pressure Rachel to lose weight? Or was she just being honest about what society wants from girls?

7. What do you think of Lucy's mom, Mrs. Wong? How does she differ from the "Tiger Mom" stereotype?

8. What do you think of billionaires like Walter Tilmore building luxury bunkers? Why did Tilmore's classroom in the bunker make Maggie so angry?

9. Do you think Maggie should have reconciled with Richard?

10. How did you feel about the book's ending? Who wins out? Who loses? Should someone have gone to prison?

11. Does it matter whether public schools expose young kids to science, art, music, and PE? What about foreign language instruction? What if the school's students are barely competent at math and English? Which subjects are essential, and who should decide?

Kudos if you've waded through the above questions. By now, some of you might be exhausted, punchy, or tipsy. Below are less bookish, more gossipy (but still profound!) questions. Enjoy!

12. Have you ever had a ridiculously gorgeous friend like Felicia Manis? Did you resent her? [Note: If you have never had a friend who is prettier than you are, you are ridiculously gorgeous, and there is a strong chance that the women in your book club resent/hate you. Just sayin'.]

13. How do you feel about Facebook and other tech behemoths selling your personal information? Do you resent it? Are you indifferent? Is it sort of flattering?

14. Who was your least favorite elementary/middle/high school teacher? Why? What did he/she do to you? Go ahead and vent. You're safe among friends—unless that teacher is in the room.

15. How is Walter Tilmore's bunker similar to the setup in Downton Abbey? Would Lord and Lady Crawley force their servants to sleep upstairs in the spartan, less safe rooms? If doomsday comes, do you think Tilmore's servants will agree to this arrangement? [Note: The Pollyannaish author neither condones nor opposes class warfare—unless it turns out well for everyone, or almost everyone.]

ABOUT THE AUTHOR

Photo © 2016 Jamie Moore

Kathy Cooperman spent four years performing improvisational comedy, then decided to do something less fun with her life. After graduating from Yale Law School, she went into criminal law, defending "innocent" (rich) clients. These days, she lives in Del Mar, California, with her husband and four challenging young children. *Crimes Against a Book Club* was her first novel. Follow her on Twitter @Kathy_Cooperman or contact her on Facebook. She is happy to Skype with or attend book clubs. It gets her out of the house.